"Nom de Dieu, Lysette, Will You Rest Content at Last?"

How dare he! But for him, she might have been out there in the garden with André, and Marielle left to weep in her pillow this night! She shook his hand free.

"If I can take him away from her, I shall!" she said viciously. She pushed past him into her room but he followed, closing the door behind him and leaning up against the paneling. By the light of the candles his gray eyes glittered like cold steel, his patience stretched thin.

"Stop it!" he growled, shaking her by the shoulders. And then his arms were around her, his mouth on hers, crushing her lips in a fierce kiss. She struggled in his embrace, imprisoned as much by the unexpectedness of his attack as by his encircling arms, her hands pushing frantically against his chest. But his mouth, warm and insistent, seemed to drain her of all resistance.

Dear Reader,

We, the editors of Tapestry Romances, are committed to bringing you two outstanding original romantic historical novels each and every month.

From Kentucky in the 1850s to the court of Louis XIII, from the deck of a pirate ship within sight of Gibraltar to a mining camp high in the Sierra Nevadas, our heroines experience life and love, romance and adventure.

Our aim is to give you the kind of historical romances that you want to read. We would enjoy hearing your thoughts about this book and all future Tapestry Romances. Please write to us at the address below.

The Editors
Tapestry Romances
POCKET BOOKS
1230 Avenue of the Americas
Box TAP
New York, N.Y. 10020

LYSETTE

Ena Halliday

A TAPESTRY BOOK

PUBLISHED BY POCKET BOOKS NEW YORK

Books by Ena Halliday

Lysette
Marielle

Published by TAPESTRY BOOKS

An *Original* publication of TAPESTRY BOOKS

A Tapestry Book published by
POCKET BOOKS, a Simon & Schuster division of
GULF & WESTERN CORPORATION
1230 Avenue of the Americas, New York, N.Y. 10020

ISBN: 0-671-46165-6

First Tapestry Books printing February, 1983

10 9 8 7 6 5 4 3 2 1

POCKET and colophon are registered trademarks
of Simon & Schuster.

TAPESTRY is a trademark of Simon & Schuster.

Printed in the U.S.A.

Chapter One

SAVE FOR THE SMALL SPOT OF BLOOD ON HIS CHIN AND THE crimson line encircling his neck, dripping away into nothingness where his body should have been, Duvalier's face had never looked more natural. It was as though the indignities visited upon his person had failed to disarray his customary mask of hauteur, one eyebrow raised scornfully, the lips curved ever so delicately in permanent disdain. Or perhaps his aristocratic breeding had forbidden him to acknowledge the torment he had suffered until that merciful moment when his head had been severed from its body.

Crouched within the ruined carriage, her body hidden from view by the jumbled cushions and velvet draperies, Lysette could feel no horror at the sight of his face. He had looked just so—arrogant, bored, heavy-lidded eyes half closed—two summers ago when her husband, Guy, had introduced her to Duvalier at Fontainebleau. One of Cardinal Richelieu's most capable Royal commissioners, Guy had said, a skillful mediator in local disputes, dispensing the King's justice in whatever corner of the realm he was summoned to. Until now. Lysette closed her eyes and swallowed hard, feeling the nausea rise in her throat. Ah, *Dieu!* That was worse. With her eyes closed, the terrible sounds around her were intensified: the frenzied oaths and shouts of the rabble, their blood-lust not yet sated; the sickening thud of fists and heavy boots against Monsieur Gossault's flaccid body, though the unfortunate man had long

1

since ceased to cry out; the sobs and pleas of Madame Gossault, begging the mob to leave her husband in peace. Pitiful fools! Why had the Gossaults not stayed hidden in the overturned carriage with her? She was safe, covered by the velvets, in the midst of the madness that swirled around the market square. Safe. But, perhaps . . . a straggler . . . ? Her eyes flew open in sudden panic and she pressed her face close to the carriage's pierced fretwork; the carved and gilded swirls gave her a wide view of the marketplace, while screening her from discovery. Only Duvalier's sightless eyes were turned in her direction; the bloody pike upon which his head had been impaled had been thrust carelessly into the ground and forgotten in the fresh excitement the Gossaults had provided.

Lysette groaned inwardly. Were they madmen in Paris? She knew little of politics and cared less, but any fool could see that with the war against Spain and the heavy taxes that had followed the peasants had grown desperate. Their children died of starvation in the streets—eyes sunken, bellies bloated—and the King's men raised the price of the salt in the Royal warehouses. The wine producers saw their wholesale taxes raised again and yet again; their only recourse was to cut the wages of the peasants who worked for them. And then Paris had decided to tax the retail wine in the taverns and shops. It was all madness! The entire region was in ferment. Since April there had been reports from Angoulême and Limoges of armed uprisings, town halls burned to the ground, a poor surgeon from Bergerac murdered because he had been a stranger.

That was what had finally persuaded Lysette to go home to her brother in Chartres. Conditions in the north of France were far less unsettled than they were here in the south. Besides, her husband Guy, as a Royal notary, had sometimes dealt unscrupulously with the peasants while he was alive, overcharging them for the wills and deeds he drew up, or using their ignorance to cheat them of what little they owned. As Guy's widow, the Marquise de Ferrand, Lysette might be imperiled should the peasants of Soligne reach the breaking point. She had sold what little jewelry remained to her, and settled the last of Guy's debts, sending a letter ahead to her brother to notify him of her arrival. Was it only this morning that, impatient for the journey to begin, she had sat in this very coach, perched on these velvet cushions, and smiled across at Monsieur and Madame Gossault? M. Gossault was a wheat broker and, in spite of the heavy taxes, he had managed to grow rich and fat; it was whispered that he hid his inventories from the tax assessor. They had sat opposite Lysette in the carriage, smug and fat and satisfied, like two swollen dumplings, while Madame waved her pudgy fingers and shook her head, the better to make a show of the gaudy jewels on her hands and ears, and Monsieur bragged of the noble title he was going to buy at the Court.

It was market day in Soligne. The square in front of the church had been crowded with stalls and carts piled high with the produce of midsummer, broad beans and golden peaches, melons and cabbages. There were baskets of fresh daisies and crisp round loaves of bread stacked neatly in careful pyramids, and long strings of smoked sausages hanging like garlands from the tops of the stalls.

From her seat in the carriage at the edge of the square, Lysette had watched the scene with an odd sense that something was not quite right. The sky was overcast, gray, and murky, the air heavy and close, charged with a strange tension. The well-to-do bourgeoisie, the wives of merchants and artisans and town officials, shopped as usual, joined by the servants of the few aristocrats who lived in the vicinity of Soligne, but the peasants and the farmers' wives, their faces pinched, market baskets clutched tightly on their arms, stopped at carts, asked prices, clucked their tongues, and turned away empty-handed.

There were more men in the square than usual. Perhaps that was it. Tight knots of men, gathered near the steps of the church, grumbling little groups, milling about with sullen, angry eyes. With a start, Lysette had recognized several of the young men as farmers' sons who had volunteered for the Army in the spring. For a few crowns they had marched off to fight against Spain, reluctant to go during the growing season, aware that their going left the fields woefully short of laborers. Yet the coins they would bring back at their dismissal in the fall might keep their families from starvation in the cold and barren winter. But here it was barely August! What were they doing home in Soligne? Deserters? Lysette had frowned and stirred uneasily on the velvet cushions. As if to echo her thoughts, Monsieur Gossault had spoken up.

"I shall be glad to leave Soligne," he had said. "I think there will be trouble. I have heard that since the price of salt has gone up, no one has purchased any from the Royal warehouse."

Lysette shrugged in indifference. "Sooner or later, the people will need salt. Where else are they to get it, since it is forbidden elsewhere? In spite of the price, they will return to the King's storehouse!"

Monsieur Gossault lowered his voice and leaned forward. "They say that salt is being smuggled into Soligne under the very noses of the town council!" He leaned further forward and placed one puffy hand on Lysette's own two, folded demurely in her lap. "Gigot was arrested under strange circumstances only last week, and the town is buzzing with the rumor that the Mayor has sent for a Royal commissioner to hold the trial!"

Lysette tossed her dark curls, uncomfortable with the damp fingers that covered her own. "And so . . . ? If it is found that Gigot has been smuggling, he will be hanged or sent to prison, and there's an end to it!"

"But the Royal commissioner has the power to force every family in Soligne to buy its quota of salt. I tell you yet again there will be trouble!" Monsieur bobbed his head up and down, his pink jowls quivering, his expression benign and angelic, but his large enveloping hand did not move. Bored with the conversation, Madame Gossault had turned and was leaning out the window, waving a coin in her bejeweled fingers and motioning to a young girl who carried a tray of sweet pastries.

Lysette frowned, annoyed at Monsieur Gossault's continuing presumption. "Pooh! What care I? My brother's estates in Chartres are rich with wheat and barley! There will always be salt on his table . . . and gold in his coffers!"

"Ah, but the pity of it, my dear Madame la Marquise! That your late husband left you with so little! And to be at the mercy of a brother's generosity. . . . such a brave and noble woman!" And here Monsieur Gossault patted Lysette's hands in sympathy. Then, with a swift glance at his wife, munching on her pastry in happy oblivion, he allowed his sweaty hand to drop lightly onto Lysette's knee. "Be assured, Madame," he continued smoothly, "I stand ready to render you what service I may. Chartres is not so far from Paris, n'est-ce pas? If you should chance to come to Paris—alone—I should be happy to see that you are not at a loss for companionship!" He smiled a conspirator's smile, and gave her knee a squeeze.

Lysette's violet eyes flashed. The fat pig! How dare he! She had half a mind to wring his bulbous nose and listen to him squeal, but contented herself with brushing his hand disgustedly from her lap as though it were a piece of dung. The sudden movement caught Madame Gossault's eye, and she turned from the window. Lysette smiled disarmingly at them both. "How kind you are! How I shall miss the tender concern of all my friends in Soligne! But you are mistaken, Monsieur. I am not a destitute widow. My dear Guy left me rich in the memory of his love, custodian of his spotless name. I shall rest content in Chartres, living off my brother's crumbs, needing no one to ease my loneliness. No man can ever replace my heart's love, the very breath of my days, my own Guy!" Madame Gossault, profoundly moved by such tender sentiments, clutched her husband's arm tightly and smiled lovingly at him, her eyes filled with tears at her own good fortune. Her husband blushed to the roots of his thinning hair, embarrassed at his own crassness. How could he have thought for a minute that a grieving widow, and a young and pretty one at that, would be willing to be an old man's mistress, no matter how many titles his gold could buy!

Lysette lowered her eyes demurely. The fat fools, she thought. Had her charm ever failed her? Growing up in a motherless house, petted and pampered by two older brothers and a father who doted on her, had she not learned early how to let her violet eyes go all misty and tender, veiled behind her long black lashes, while her mouth drooped forlornly? What could they deny her then, the sweet child? How glad she had been, as she grew older, to realize that she would never be a tall or a large woman, but would remain dainty and petite even into adulthood. And here she was now, at twenty-two, a wife since the age of nineteen, a widow since last year, small-boned, elfin, with the sweet innocent face of a lass of sixteen. They had never stopped looking at her like a child, all those years of growing up, while she expanded her repertory to include coy smiles and wheedling and pink-lipped pouting. Not that she had not loved them dearly: it had simply become a habit to want her own way and to use those enchantments a woman had at her command.

And, truth to tell, the lines had become blurred long since: her artifice had become art, intrinsic to her nature, and the men in her life had clothed that art with love and had willingly acquiesced in her game.

When her father died, she was inconsolable. He had been her king, her prince, her paladin. She saw him still with the grieving eyes of a thirteen-year-old: he had been the tallest, the strongest, the handsomest of men. Her elder brother had inherited the title and the estates at Chartres, but he had trained as a soldier and spent, by choice, half the year in the field; her younger brother, studying for the Church, had received an appointment for a small village near Rouen. It was decided that the young Lysette would be happier in a more stable household, and she had been sent to live with her father's elder sister and her husband. She had not been unhappy with them, for they treated her kindly, making few onerous demands upon her. She could sew a little, and was taught to cook (although she despised both endeavors), but when her aunt attempted to instruct her in managing a large household, she had balked at the complexity of domestic purchases and menu planning and bookkeeping, stamping her dainty foot and insisting that these were chores for a servant and a housekeeper. Cowed by those flashing violet eyes darkened to the color of the midnight sky, her aunt discontinued her training. Lysette by now had learned that what could not be accomplished by charm and wheedling could be brought about by a flood of tears or a noisy tantrum. Not all her lessons displeased her, however. She learned to ride as skillfully as a man and discovered a talent for the lute, pleasing both her riding and music masters with her interest and enthusiasm. They praised her fulsomely to her uncle, scarcely aware that their approbation had as much to do with her charm as with her skills. For Lysette had discovered that men especially were susceptible to feminine guile.

Poor Monsieur Gossault, still crimson with shame! He had scarcely been a match for her! Still, she had not completely lied to him, she thought bitterly. She had indeed a legacy from Guy! A mountain of debts, the memory of a faithless marriage, the humiliation of her dependence on her brother. Oh, she had been ripe for Guy! Bored, stifled in her uncle's household, waiting impatiently until she should be twenty-one, that she might collect her inheritance and live her own life. It had become too easy: to manipulate the people around her, to have what she wanted. Yet she ached for something more, something that did not even have a name. When she discovered that her inheritance would revert at once to her, as a dowry, should she marry, she felt like a prisoner on the edge of freedom, searching for the key that would open the door. And then Guy had appeared. The Marquis de Ferrand. Ah, *Dieu*, it had sounded grand! He had known her father. He reminded her of her father, tall, broad-shouldered, incredibly handsome, with a certain air of maturity and her father's inclination to find her coquettishness charming. She had only to admire a comb or a brooch in a shop window and it appeared on her vanity table the following day, and when she pouted he scolded her lovingly, coaxing her into smiles again like a doting and indulgent father. Fearful of losing him, she devised elaborate schemes to force him into marriage, was afraid to put them into effect, agonized, suffered. And then, without any prompting, he asked her for her hand. Her brother had come from Rouen to perform the ceremony. She had been nineteen. Madame la Marquise de Ferrand.

Sitting in the carriage this morning, as the coachman whistled to his horses and swung himself, grunting, onto his box, she laughed ruefully to herself. What a little fool she had been! It was one thing to scheme and beguile to get your way; it was quite another to know the wisdom of those desires. For while she had charmed Guy into marriage, it soon became apparent that he had assuredly tricked her as well.

He had taken her to live in Soligne, near Limoges, a small town, an undistinguished little village in southwest France, where he held the post of Royal notary. They had moved into a small rented house with but one servant, and she soon discovered that his title of Marquis was all that remained to him, the family estate long since foreclosed for lack of money. No matter how much Guy swindled his clients, they seemed always to be struggling, teetering on the edge of ruin, and when he had died last year, she had found that the bulk of her dowry had vanished, gone to pay off his monumental debts. Until now, she had managed alone in Soligne, unwilling to be dependent on her brother (and on the sharp-tongued shrew he had married!), ashamed to admit to her bad judgment: that, for all her games, she had managed to outsmart herself.

Lysette had shifted uncomfortably in her seat, her eyes on the lowering sky. Would they never start? The heavy carriage had jerked forward for an instant and then stopped. From the edge of the town, where a small chapel marked the crossing of the dusty highroad, a bell began to toll. It was answered at once by the church in the market square, its sonorous bronze carillon echoing the call as though it were a signal. It had been so sudden that Lysette, her thoughts still on Guy, had shuddered involuntarily and looked with concern to the Gossaults. And surely it *had* been a signal of some sort. The groups of men no longer lolled in dim corners, but gathered together in ranks, to be joined by more and more of their fellows, men who seemed to crowd into the square from every quarter. Some carried pitchforks and stout cudgels, but Lysette was sure she had seen a musket or two. Alarmed, she had leaned her head out of the carriage, meaning to order the coachman to make haste, to head his team out of Soligne as quickly as possible.

But it was too late. Duvalier, the Royal commissioner, had already ridden into the square—proud, imperious, aristocratic. Alone. (Why, in the name of *le bon Dieu* had they not sent him with troops?) The mob, for such it had become, had fallen back, reformed, and then, like waves enveloping a drowning man, had surged forward, crowding around until horse and rider had gone down and been swallowed up. There was a moment of eerie silence, and then a roaring, shrieking, triumphant cry that seemed to come from a thousand throats. Lysette had clapped her hands over her ears, and Monsieur Gossault had wrung his fat fingers together in anguish. The coachman, fearful of the crowds that pressed ever closer, swelling to the edges of the marketplace, had abandoned his box and vanished down a narrow lane. The square had emptied of its patrons, who had disappeared behind closed doors into the safety of their comfortable houses, while the vendors had gathered such of their stores as could be quickly saved, and sought refuge in the church.

Half a score of armed men appeared, in blue and yellow uniforms that marked them as the town militia; their presence momentarily diverted the rabble from Duvalier. Lysette ducked her head down as the square filled with the crack of musket fire, sharp and loud even above the din of the screaming mob. The carriage had lurched violently as the unreined horses, terrified by the sounds, had reared up in panic. With a jolt that had sent Lysette flying across the seat into the arms of Monsieur Gossault, the carriage had careened into the marketplace, scattering carts and baskets and tables piled high with goods. It had ploughed into a mound of cabbages, rolled wildly and unevenly over a large sack of turnips, tipped precariously on two wheels and overturned with a splintering crash, where it lay in an upside down heap, its wheels spinning crazily, while the horses, released from their harness, had fled in every direction.

Dazed and winded, Lysette had found herself face down in the coach, her cheek pressed against what had been the inside roof of the carriage. Her arms were tangled in the velvet draperies, and a heavy weight on her back made it almost impossible to move. The weight stirred, groaned, whispered in a terrified croak that she scarce recognized as belonging to Monsieur Gossault.

"Mon Dieu! Wife! Are you there?"

From the mound of pillows beside Lysette there emerged a soft bleat. "Armand! Help me! Let us leave this terrible place!" Madame Gossault struggled to move and sit up, while her husband, shifting his weight to help her, pressed more heavily onto Lysette's back until she thought she would suffocate.

"No, No!" she hissed. "Stay where you are! We are safe here! Would you brave that mob? No one has seen us in here! Look!" Easing her shoulders partially from under Monsieur Gossault (and she had despised one single fat hand on her body!), she indicated the carved openwork that ran along the top and bottom of the windows. Pressed low against the roof, they had peered out onto the square. The militia had been dispersed: one or two brightly clad soldiers lay face up on the cobblestones, their cheerful blues and yellows now dabbled with great gouts of scarlet, the colors intensified by the somber sky. The rest of the militia was nowhere in sight. Occupied with something on the far side of the market, the throng was indifferent to the ruined carriage. Indeed, the drabness of the sky and the dark brown of the tumbled velvets virtually obscured the interior of the coach and its occupants.

"Yes, ladies," said Monsieur Gossault, beginning to recover his courage as well as his voice. "We would be well advised to remain here as long as we must. It will be soon enough to leave when the madness has passed. Let us be as comfortable as possible." Carefully they had shifted about, rearranging the pillows and draperies, until all three lay prone on the inside roof, side by side, well hidden from view.

There was a sudden shout of laughter from the mob. Having routed the last of the militia, they had turned their attention back to Duvalier. The crowd parted to make way for him, and Lysette caught her breath in dismay. He had been stripped naked, his hands lashed firmly in front of him with a stout length of rope, by which means he was being paraded about the square; his body, already discolored by bruises and scratches from the first onslaught, was now assaulted afresh. Blows rained on him from all directions as he passed—fists and clubs and rocks—and once the edge of a hoe caught him in the small of his back and drove him to his knees. He struggled to rise, but the brawny young farmer who held his tether jerked savagely on the rope and sent him sprawling, face in the dirt, arms stretched cruelly in front of him. Not a sound escaped his lips. Painfully he rose to his feet to continue his stumbling progress through the marketplace, the tugging rope leading him on. A peasant woman, her eyes burning with a hatred fired by years of desperation, flew at him, a feral cry on her lips. Her fingers clawed at his raw flesh, gouging bloody furrows, while she shrieked and cursed in a strangled voice.

Lysette had shuddered. It frightened her—the fury of the mob, the angry despair and bitterness that pulsated in the square, a living thing she could almost taste, feel, even here in her hiding place. Like a great boil it had festered and putrefied, needing only the appearance of Duvalier to lance its rawness and release its poisons.

Salt! The cry of salt on a hundred lips. Half a dozen sturdy peasants had appeared, trundling a large barrow piled high with sacks of salt, bragging of how they had fought off the guards at the Royal warehouse, that no one need ever pay for salt again. With a glad cry, the crowd had pressed forward, laughing, cheering, ripping open the sacks of salt, filling bowls and pans and pockets with the precious stuff. It was market day with a vengeance. The women retrieved their baskets and turned to the ruined stalls and carts, forgotten until now, and ransacked and pilfered freely as though Duvalier's presence had removed all moral constraints. The market took on a festive air, as people laughed and joked, scampering among the wagons, filling their arms and baskets with fruits and smoked joints and salt—the King's salt. Duvalier, forgotten in the hungry rush for the food, sagged with exhaustion, his face revealing for the first time the agony he had suffered.

Ah, *Dieu!* thought Lysette. Perhaps now they will be satisfied. Mayhap they will leave him in peace. But she had not reckoned on Duvalier's aristocratic pride: incapable of humility, he had marshaled his flagging spirits, drawing himself up to stand tall and dignified, scorning his pain and humiliation. Goaded thus into fresh fury, the mob had resumed its torments. With a ferocious shriek, an old hag had brandished fistfuls of salt in Duvalier's face, then had pelted his ravaged flesh with the stinging substance. Others took up the sport, coating the bloody gashes and open wounds with salt. Duvalier, his body rimed with the searing crystals, never flinched. Determined to wring a cry of pain from those soundless lips, a word, a response, anything, a husky young man, a deserter from the Army, planted himself before Duvalier, taunting him with coarse oaths while the crowd fell back, sensing a new and more dangerous game, a deadly challenge that went beyond mere physical torments. The man cursed Duvalier's ancestors, questioned his paternity and called his wife a whore, his jibes couched in the foulest language. Hauling on the rope that still bound Duvalier, he jerked up the poor man's arms, thus exposing his naked genitals. Look. See, he had said, pointing in mockery, while Lysette had wept for shame in her hiding place. The Royal commissioner was not a man, he had said, but a woman, fit only for other men's use. He would show them, he said, how a man treated this woman who hid in men's clothes. To the salacious pleasure of the mob, he advanced toward Duvalier, fumbling with his clothing, the front of his breeches already swollen in anticipation. Duvalier's haughty face, stiff with contempt, stopped him in his tracks, flustered, cowed, burning to regain his dominance. With a strangled curse he swung his ham-like fist into Duvalier's groin; the commissioner gasped and staggered backward, his face drained of color. The crowd was hushed, waiting.

And then, incredibly, Duvalier had smiled. The smile of a nobleman nearly out of patience with his vassals, but still tolerant. A patronizing smile. The young man, enraged, had whirled to a ruined butcher's stall, snatched up a large knife and, in one ferocious stroke, had parted Duvalier's head from his body.

Madame Gossault had gurgled weakly and Lysette had buried her face in her arms and wept. She could hardly bear to watch as the mob, cheering and singing, had marched around the square, banging on tin pots and brandishing the long pike which now held Duvalier's bloody head. Someone had found a dozen hogsheads of wine, abandoned by their owner, and the gaiety mounted to a delirious frenzy as the afternoon wore on.

And then Madame Gossault had begun to gag and choke. "Armand! *Nom de Dieu!*" she had croaked. "I cannot breathe! I shall be sick! Is there no escape from this horrible place?" And she had sobbed in terror.

Soothing his wife as best he could, Monsieur Gossault had raised himself up from his hiding place and scanned the market, assessing their chances of escape. To be sure, the rabble was now at some distance from the carriage—their snake-like parade winding in among the stalls and carts, the head of Duvalier bobbing high above their ranks—and one side of the coach let out onto a portion of the square that was now empty. Lysette had urged them to stay, not to risk the back alleys where hostile and drunken peasants might yet lurk. But Madame Gossault had been adamant. They had pushed open the heavy door and crawled out, shutting it again on Lysette, and scurrying down a small dark street next to the square. With a sigh, Lysette had watched them go, then resettled herself in the carriage, half glad for their leaving because it gave her far more pillows and draperies within which she could burrow. Hearing the parade turning back once again toward the coach, she had pressed herself more firmly to the floor, her head comfortably placed so she could peer through the open carvings, and adjusted the heavy coverings. Odd. She had noticed at that very moment that the velvets smelled of the open road: dust and clover and sweet grasses.

There had been a sudden piercing shriek, and the Gossaults had come running into the middle of the square, pursued by the ravening horde. As Lysette had watched in horror, the women, their thin and hungry faces sharp in contrast to Madame Gossault's overfed bulk, had swarmed about her like locusts, pulling the rings from her fat fingers and ripping the jewels from her ears, while she screamed in pain and terror and clutched at her torn and bloody earlobes. Then they had turned upon Monsieur Gossault, beating and kicking and pummeling, as though he were some lump of clay to be molded and reshaped.

Now Lysette looked into Duvalier's dead eyes and prayed for an end to the madness. She felt suffocated and sick, her body stiff from the hours she had lain in the coach, fighting down the nausea and the panic that threatened to engulf her. She no longer cared about the Gossaults, or Duvalier, or the soldiers who lay dead in the square; terror had focused her thoughts on herself alone, and if the torment of others would help to keep her safe in her refuge, so be it. She did not care. Let them go on beating Gossault's lifeless body. Let his wife scream and cry. Let me be safe. Ah, *Dieu!* Let *me* be safe!

Chapter Two

THE THIN WHIP SNAKED THROUGH THE AIR, TRACING A WIDE ARC, and crackled sharply against the fine cambric shirt. The Baron d'Alons, his wrists bound firmly to the whipping post, twitched violently as the lash cut across his back, but made no sound. Ten times the whip snapped, while the drummer beat out the count and the troops watched in stony silence, with surly faces and mutinous eyes. At length the sergeant at arms ceased his labors, coiled up his whip, and saluted his commanding officer.

Seated stiffly on his horse, his steel casque resting in the crook of his arm, André, Comte du Crillon, nodded to the guards, who stepped forward and loosed the Baron's bonds. D'Alons, his fine shirt now criss-crossed with scarlet, turned painfully and bowed to André, a wry smile on his lips, his eyes filled with understanding and even sympathy. Frowning, André withdrew a scroll from under his breastplate, unrolled it and read aloud to his troops.

" 'From his Majesty, Louis XIII, by the grace of God King of France, to his officers in the field: It has come to our attention that certain of our troops, more especially certain of our officers, have seen fit to absent themselves without leave. Such disgraceful conduct must not go unpunished. Those noblemen who would bring disgrace to France and to themselves must be tracked down without mercy, stripped of their rank, privileges, and pensions, and subjected to whatever punishment may be deemed appropriate.' It is signed by Louis, King of France, in

14

this, the year of our Lord, 1636." André's blue eyes swept his troops, noting the sullen shuffling of feet, the worn cloaks and jerkins, the weary faces. He withdrew another piece of paper from his doublet. "I have here another letter from his Majesty," he said, allowing his frown to soften a bit. "It is a personal letter to me, but it concerns all of you. 'My dear André,' it begins, 'I send you my warmest greetings. Every letter that comes to me from the Prince of Condé is filled with praise for you and your brave men. Without their courage and fortitude, Condé could not have held the siege against the Spaniards at Dôle. I know that as loyal Frenchmen they will not hesitate to follow wherever duty leads them. I charge you, in my name, to distribute to each man a bounty of ten crowns when he is released from your service.' The rest of the letter is personal."

André tucked both letters quickly into his doublet and slipped his casque over his blond hair, tightening the leather strap under his chin. He smiled in satisfaction as his men pulled themselves up with a new sense of pride, and the cries of *"Vive le Roi!"* filled the air. Grasping the reins in his gauntleted hands, he wheeled his horse sharply about, nodding briskly to his lieutenants and signaling the march to begin. Buoyed by the prospect of extra pay, the foot soldiers shouldered their pikes and muskets, their steps almost jaunty on the dusty road. From a little knoll off to one side, André watched them pass: good men, brave men, nearly five hundred strong. They had fought well at Dôle, holding the siege against the Spanish cannon, against the monotony of waiting until starvation or disease should force the Spaniards to relinquish the city. And then to be told, incredibly, that they must raise the siege! That they must march to Angoumois to battle Frenchmen! To kill their own brothers who were rising up in protest, armies of peasants who must be kept from banding together, lest France be plunged into civil war. André sighed deeply, his head sunk on his chest.

"Liar!"

André looked up quickly. A laughing face. A wide grin. A head of flowing orange curls and fiery mustaches, strangely cooled by pale gray eyes. A friend's face.

"André, *mon ami!* You are not only a liar, you are most probably a fool as well!" said Jean-Auguste, Vicomte de Narbaux.

"What the devil do you mean, Jean-Auguste?" said André,

guiding his horse into step beside Narbaux's until the two friends rode side by side.

"Let me see the King's letter. No, no. Not the proclamation. I read that for myself. His . . . personal letter!"

André laughed ruefully. "Well, it *did* begin 'My dear André!'"

"From Marielle?"

"Of course."

"And the five thousand crowns?"

"I have a banker friend at Limoges who will be happy to loan me what I need—at an exorbitant rate, of course! And if the grape harvest at Vilmorin is good this year, I should be able to pay him back with no difficulty."

Narbaux laughed. "Ah, if your men but knew the softling who lurks behind your scowl!"

"What could I do? There are scores of my men who should have been released from service by now but for these uprisings. How else am I to keep them from open rebellion or desertion? And do not speak to me of softlings, *mon ami!* You yourself sent your own men home with a bounty. I'll wager that did not come from the King's coffers! And you have been in the field long past your obligation of three months! Why did you not return home with your men?"

Jean-Auguste shrugged. "Someone had to keep you company and out of mischief! Marielle would never forgive me if I allowed another woman to look at you!"

They fell silent for a minute. André sighed deeply. "I much regret Baron d'Alons!"

"It could not be helped."

"Yes, I know. He had to serve as an example. Still . . . such a promising career . . ." André sighed again. "Well, we are all anxious to be home."

"Your boys are well?"

"When last I saw them. Alain has just begun to talk, though I fear François will never allow him a word! And Marielle spoils them outrageously! Sometimes I think . . ." Crillon broke off abruptly as Jean-Auguste began to roar with laughter.

"Has it come to this, then? Where once we spoke of war, now we speak of children! What is it . . . seven years now since your marriage? And each year my good friend becomes less and less a companion at arms and more a docile husband, gossiping over domestic trifles like a toothless crone!"

"My dear Vicomte de Narbaux," said André waspishly. "You had best beware the trap yourself! When you were still a Baron—you with that milksop's face and bushy mustache—you were scarce a catch for any woman! Now that the King has made you a Vicomte and increased your landholdings at Chimère, some poor woman, starved for love, may be persuaded to overlook your faults and take you well in hand! Truly, my friend, you should find a wife," he added, more seriously.

Jean-Auguste turned toward André, a wry smile twisting his lips. "I found one . . . once. Alas! She was already married to you! No, do not disturb yourself, *mon ami,*" said Narbaux quickly, seeing the look of distress on André's face. "I have long since ceased to envy you for Marielle—she belongs to you. I envy you both for the happiness you have found!"

Du Crillon laughed ruefully. "Do you remember how jealous I was of her?"

Narbaux snorted. "I remember how often I saved you from murder, my hotheaded friend! Does jealousy still come between you?"

"I do not know! Not for my part, you understand, but lately . . . Marielle . . . *mon Dieu!* I did not think my mistresses would return to haunt my marriage!"

"But surely you are mistaken! Marielle? Jealous? It is hardly to be believed!"

"Not jealous then . . . fearful. I have been away too much—she has too many lonely hours to dwell on what has been. When we parted, there was a strange uneasiness between us . . . a foreboding . . ." He sighed deeply. *"Eh bien!* After this campaign in Angoumois, I shall have the whole of the fall and winter to assure her that she has nothing to fear from the past!"

"And if you fail," said Jean-Auguste wickedly, "I shall most assuredly steal her from you this year! It is time I had sons of my own!"

A terrified shriek split the air. Lysette, exhausted from terror, drained of strength by the horrible events in the marketplace, had begun to drift off to sleep; the scream jolted her awake and she shivered, half expecting to see a peasant face leering in at her. No one seemed to be noticing the carriage. The cry had come from Madame Gossault. The young deserter, the murderer of Duvalier, now quite drunk, was struggling fiercely with her, one hand clasped tightly about her ample waistline, the other tugging at the neckline of her gown. Hampered by his drunkenness and her large bulk, he soon realized that she was no match for him, and he began to roar with laughter, even while they battled, and cried out for someone to help him, to take pity on him. There was much joking and ribald laughter as the crowd gathered around; puffing with his exertions, the young soldier promised to share her with any man who would help him to subdue this fat cow. At length a red-faced farmer stepped forward, his face split by a toothless grin, and grabbed Madame Gossault from behind; his large hands on her shoulders, he dragged her backwards and pulled her across a large mound of turnip sacks, then held her down while she shrieked and kicked wildly. The young deserter had already dropped his breeches, to the shouting approval of the mob; those fat legs, savagely beating the air, gave him pause. But the rabble was not to be denied its satisfaction. With an ugly cry, their faces frozen into ferocious smiles, two robust women joined the fray, each to clutch a thrashing foot and part the fleshy thighs. Lysette watched in horrified fascination as the young man squatted before Madame Gossault and used her like a whore in some back alley. With each savage thrust of his loins she squealed piteously, and the crowd cried out in collective release, in climax to all the years of bitterness and frustration: "Ah! Ah! Ah!"

Paralyzed with fear, on the edge of hysteria, Lysette began to laugh softly, her mind incapable of absorbing any more horror. It was really quite funny, when you stopped to think of it. What a fool Madame Gossault was! One had only to remember Monsieur Gossault's flabby body and sweaty hands! That young soldier was robust and virile—Madame Gossault should welcome his attentions, not struggle against him! Yes. Robust and virile. And young. Not like Guy . . . Guy. . . .

Guy's slippered feet padded softly across the tile floor, making a gentle slapping sound that was muffled as he crossed the Savonnerie carpet that Lysette's aunt had given her for her last birthday. In the large bed, Lysette clamped her eyes shut tight and drew the coverlet up to her nose, filled suddenly with fear and regret. She was not unmindful, in a generalized way, of what was about to happen, for she had torment-ed her aunt often enough until the poor woman had ex-plained the strange things that occurred between men and women; still, until this moment, she had not ever thought about herself in such a situation. It was always other wom-en. Other women. Even in the months that Guy had courted her he had been so deferential, barely touching her, that she had never thought of this. Or did not wish to. He was so handsome, his dark hair curling about his wide shoul-ders, so much like her father—ah *Dieu!* She had only wanted to be pampered and petted, to be cared for, as she had always been cared for by her father and brothers and uncle. Not to have a man touch her and do terrible things to her body!

She bit her lip. How foolish. To be so upset! And all because of a doublet! They had sat at her uncle's table, eating their wedding supper, while everyone smiled and wished them well. Then Guy had led her gently away, guiding her up the stairs to their rooms, his hand beneath her elbow, his head bent attentively to hers. It had been such a lovely moment, filled with romance and dreams come true, she had not wanted it to end, but sat in an alcove in the corridor, looking out over the gardens and the peaceful evening. Guy had smiled tolerantly at first, but as she lingered, he had begun to tap his foot in impatience and slowly to unbutton his doublet, suggesting that she too might be more comfortable out of her heavy velvets. And then he had removed his doublet—padded, quilted, brocaded, with loops and bows and ribbons, she had seen it a score of times—and oh! the thin and bony shoulders beneath that glorious exterior! She had been dazzled by the width of his doublet, never wondering what was beneath. She had looked at him, in the last fading light of the alcove window, and seen why he had reminded her of her father. He was nearly as old as her father. The shiny black hair curled unnaturally around his temples as though it did not belong there, and she had realized with a start that it was in all likelihood just a wig. She had fled to her room, while Guy, misunderstanding her haste, had preened himself and promised he would come to her room as quickly as he could.

"Lysette!"

She opened her eyes and lowered the coverlet to her neck, trying bravely to smile. Guy stood above her, his face lit by the small bedside candle, long dressing gown loose on his spare frame. It *had* been a wig. His hair was black, true enough, but it glinted with silver and hung sparse and stringy to his chin. *"Ma chérie!"* He slipped out of his dressing gown, and sat down, naked, on the edge of the bed; there was an arrogance to his bearing (she had not noticed *that* before, either) that suggested he considered himself irresistible to women. He leaned forward and kissed her on the mouth—his lips were dry and rough and faintly unpleasant; she had a sudden childhood vision of kissing her aging grandfather, and nearly giggled aloud. He prodded her gently until she made room for him in the bed, then slipped under the coverlet to lie beside her. He did not seem to mind the linen nightdress she wore—she had not had the courage to take it off before he entered the room—and for that at least she was grateful. Taking her by the shoulders, he pulled her on top of him, catching her mouth in another dry kiss. She was not uncomfortable—she was dainty and petite enough to rest easily on his relatively larger frame, but she found herself hard put to find a place to rest her hands, repelled by the dry raspiness of his naked shoulders and chest. His arms clasped her tightly, firm hands clutching and kneading her buttocks through the soft fabric, while he twitched and grunted beneath her. It was all so silly! Was this what love was all about? The desire to giggle rose strong within her—how she would laugh in the morning when she tried to tell her aunt what had happened!

And then, so suddenly that the smile was still on her face, Guy rolled over with her and pushed up her nightdress, rough hands forcing her knees apart; his weight, heavy on her body, brought with it a sharp pain that subsided to a dull ache as he labored above her, face contorted with the effort. She fought back her tears, wishing she were dead, closing her eyes against the sight of him. Of his old face! Satisfied at last, he stood up, slipping on his dressing gown and patting her cavalierly on the top of her head. Then he was gone. As though she were a dog! As if she were his horse, back from a successful ride! She stumbled out of bed and vomited into the chamber pot.

Madame Gossault began to whimper and sob. The toothless farmer had taken his turn with her, and a gawky lad of fourteen, so excited by his good fortune that he had barely had time to take his place between those fat legs before his passion was spent, squandered by the frenzy of youth. Most of the rabble had found fresh amusements on the far side of the square. Madame Gossault moaned and tried weakly to rise, then gave a helpless little squeal as yet another bumpkin, a big oafish fellow, pushed her down again and groped at his breeches, while two of his companions gathered around, joking coarsely as they awaited their turn.

"No! Please. . . . *nom de Dieu!*" she gasped. "In the carriage . . . a young one . . . a pretty one . . . ah, *Dieu!*"

Lysette froze with fear as the three men turned to peer over at the coach. Perhaps they would not come looking for her! Perhaps they did not believe Madame Gossault! They hesitated, then turned their attention back to the corpulent form still sprawled across the turnip sacks. Lysette had just begun to breathe when one of the men glanced again at the carriage, shrugged his shoulders, and approached quickly, pulling open the heavy door and pawing among the velvets, while she struggled to extricate herself from the draperies that had suddenly become entangled in her arms and legs. With a triumphant shout, he dragged her forth, kicking and squirming, and slung her under one brawny arm, where she hung writhing and helpless as his fellows ran to join him. He set her down roughly and the three men linked arms, imprisoning her in the circle thus created; they laughed uproariously as she whirled about, seeking an escape, throwing herself violently against one steely arm and then another. She felt sick with panic and dread. Where were the nice people of this town? The smug merchants, safe behind their shuttered windows! Was there no one to care, to save her?

"But it is Madame la Marquise de Ferrand, *n'est-ce pas?*" One of the men, a hairy fellow with a bushy black beard, was peering at her closely.

She caught her breath and stared at him. Surely she must know him! "Yes, I am the Marquise de Ferrand." A client of

Guy's. That was it! His name! Dear God, his name. . . . She hesitated, then smiled regally, painfully aware that the three of them towered over her, that her gown was rumpled and her hair in disarray. "I remember you quite well, my good man. . . ."

"Baptiste."

"Yes. Of course. Baptiste. I had not forgot!" She smiled her most dazzling smile, then fluttered her eyelashes shyly.

"How could you forget, Madame? Did I not come to your husband, Monsieur the notary, with twenty-five crowns and instructions to draw up a deed to a little piece of land beyond Soligne?" Lysette smiled uneasily, scouring her mind to remember if Guy had told her anything. Baptiste inclined his head to Lysette. "Can you read and write, Madame?" She nodded. "How fortunate you are, Madame, how privileged your life! If I could read . . . but alas! I must have someone to look at the papers and tell me why, after all this time, I have neither the land nor the twenty-five crowns!"

Lysette looked away in consternation. Damn Guy! Curse her own foolishness in never caring or questioning his dealings! She did not even have twenty-five crowns left to her name, and the look on Baptiste's face made it clear he meant to collect the debt in quite another way.

"But what happened to your gold and your land?" growled one of the other men.

"Can you not guess? Monsieur's pretty little wife needed a new petticoat!" Baptiste's large hands fumbled at Lysette's skirts; she pulled free and backed away from him, only to be stopped by another pair of hands that grabbed her from behind and clamped her wrists to her sides.

"When my wife needs a new petticoat, it does not cost me twenty-five *ecus!*"

"Ah, but a Marquise is different from other women!" Baptiste leered at Lysette and stepped forward, his face so close she could smell the wine on his breath. He smiled and licked his lips, but hatred glowed in his eyes. "A Marquise is soft and delicate! You see?" He clawed at her bodice, wrenching the fabric away from her neck, tearing, groping for her bosom while she cursed and struggled vainly against those pinioning hands. She kicked and screamed, little caring that her breasts were exposed, her shoulders bare; the ultimate terror would be to share Madame

Gossault's fate, and she fought against the rough hands that pawed at her skirt and tore at her petticoats.

Of a sudden, there was bedlam in the square—the crack of muskets, and screaming and the high-pitched whinny of horses; the market became a fearful storm of men and smoke and blood and death. There were soldiers with pikes, and mounted soldiers who swept through the mob like great scythes, harvesting destruction with their flailing swords. Women shrieked in terror, and gnarled farmers threw up their hands and pitched forward onto the ruined fruit stalls, their heads split open like so many melons.

Baptiste fled, and one of his companions, but the other still held tightly to Lysette, who stood, rooted to the spot, without the sense to break free of him or take cover. Out of the whirl of smoke a mounted rider appeared, tall and regal, with eyes that blazed blue fire. The sight of Lysette, her bodice bare, her arms still imprisoned, seemed to infuriate him. With a growl, he leapt from his horse, one heavy knotted fist crashing into the farmer's head and knocking him to the ground; the other hand, clutching a pistol, aimed straight for the man's chest. He thought better of it, took a deep breath, and tucked the pistol into his wide sash, contenting himself with raising up the farmer by his neckerchief and driving his fist once again into the man's face. Then he straightened up and turned to Lysette.

The tumult in the square had ceased almost as abruptly as it had begun. In the sudden silence, Lysette could hear the blood pounding in her temples. The man took her breath away. Not even Guy, seen through the romantic haze of her childhood fantasies, had seemed so wonderful. He was tall, and blond, to judge by the golden curls that spilled out from beneath his casque; his skin, bronzed from the sun, only made his eyes seem more remarkable. Blue. The color of the sea, the color of sapphires, warm and rich and glowing. He was not a callow youth; neither was he old, as Guy had been. In his prime. She judged him to be in his middle thirties, old enough to know what he wanted from a woman, young enough not to have to seek it in a hundred beds, as Guy had done.

She realized that he was staring at her naked bosom, and she blushed, though not without a certain sense of vanity. She had admired herself often enough in a mirror to know her breasts were beautiful, firm and rosy and tantalizing, and never more so than when her glossy black hair curled enticingly on her creamy flesh, as now it did. Did he notice, she wondered, how attractive she was?

And then she began to shake, the hours of terror at last taking their toll, a trembling that shook her slight frame beyond her powers to control. He hesitated, frowning in consternation at her sudden weakness, uncertain how best to ease her distress. She felt gentle hands on her shoulders, a soft mantle covering her nakedness, strong arms that turned her about and cradled her quivering form. With a grateful moan, she gave way to her pent-up emotions, sobbing out her fear and grief; at length, quieting, she felt her head begin to spin, a giddy slide in and out of consciousness, fragments and images whirling in her brain. She was aware that he had walked away, that there were cries in the square, and barked orders, and Madame Gossault's wailing; still the comforting arms held her, her only anchor in a sea of confusion. She felt herself being lifted, carried over a threshold and up a dim flight of stairs, then placed on a soft bed. Sighing, she curled up among the pillows, spent, exhausted, and let herself drift off into oblivion. For a fragment of a second, just as sleep overtook her, she opened her eyes to see the face that bent close, pale gray eyes filled with concern, a boyish face, an open, friendly face, crowned with a mass of bright orange curls.

Chapter Three

LYSETTE ADJUSTED THE SOFT LEATHER GAUNTLETS, STRETCHING them carefully over her fingers and past her wrists, taking pains lest she damage the fine embroidery and beading. They contrasted strangely with the rest of her outfit: the coarse peasant skirt and chemise, the clumsy leather shoes, the sleeveless chamois jerkin, somewhat oversized on her petite frame, that one of the young soldiers, blushing shyly, had presented to her. Searching the ruined coach several days after the riots, she had come across the gauntlets wedged in between the seats, the only possessions of hers overlooked in the casual looting that had gone on sporadically that first night, committed as much by the troops who had come to quell the disturbance as by the peasants and the bourgeoisie. The rest of her clothing were cast-offs, what she had managed to wheedle from acquaintances.

Order had at last been restored to Soligne; the Comte du Crillon, empowered to act as Magistrate by the Crown, had held the last of the trials this morning, condemning the leaders of the uprising to the galleys. The murderer of Duvalier had been hanged in the square; for the rest, Crillon had issued a general pardon, and the Governor of Angoumois, aware of the desperation that had driven his peasants to near rebellion, had petitioned Paris to rescind the tax on retail wine purchases. Madame Gossault, still in a state of shock, was being tended by the wife of the richest banker in town, whose solicitude was motivated at least as much by sympathy as by the knowledge that the bulk of Monsieur Gossault's fortune still remained in the vaults of Soligne.

Lysette smoothed her jerkin, wishing it clung more closely to her curves, and laid a gauntleted hand on André's sleeve, her lips curved in a helpless smile. He turned brusquely, brows knit in preoccupation, and she felt her heart leap in her throat. *Mon Dieu!* How could it be that one frown on that handsome face had the power to move her more than a score of smiles on any other? His blue eyes softened at sight of her and she smiled more deeply, until little dimples appeared on her downy cheeks.

"If you please, Monsieur le Comte"—she indicated the large mare—"would you be so kind . . . ?"

He put his hands about her tiny waist and lifted her into the saddle; she contrived to wobble precariously for a few seconds so that he clasped her more tightly, his firm hands steadying her. Violet eyes filled with consternation, she fidgeted in the saddle, as though she were not sure where to put her legs, until he was forced to take her knee in his hands and rest it in its proper niche on the sidesaddle. She smiled in gratitude, her eyes warmed by the fire his touch had set ablaze within her; he reddened and turned away, calling for his own horse and issuing last-minute commands to the column of men. Careful to see that he was not watching her, she adjusted herself comfortably in the saddle and picked up the reins with an easiness born of long years of familiarity. She was aware suddenly of eyes on her and turned about quickly. Monsieur le Vicomte de Narbaux, André's friend. She did not like him at all! He was regarding her now with eyes that were cool and amused, pale gray orbs that seemed to peer right through her, while his mustache twitched in a crooked smile.

How she hated him! If he had had his way, she would not be making this journey with Crillon and his men! André had paid off his troops and dismissed them, keeping only those three or four dozen who had been conscripted from his own estates in the Loire valley; now, his work at Soligne finished, he was preparing to lead them home. Half a score were mounted, the rest on foot. It seemed the perfect opportunity for Lysette. Without money, her welcome in Soligne wearing thin, she would be sorely pressed were she forced to remain until a message could be sent to her brother in Chartres and money forwarded back to her. She had proposed to André that she travel with him, only as far as Tours or Vouvray, so as not to take him out of his way; somehow, she would get a message to her brother from there. He had hesitated, and then Narbaux had interrupted: it would be too tiring for her, it would take weeks since the soldiers were on foot, it would be better for her to wait in Soligne and he himself would see that she had enough crowns to live on until relief came from her brother. She had begun to weep then, her violet eyes like two soft blossoms veiled by the gentle rain: she would be no trouble, she did not need more than a crumb or two of bread, and how could she stay any longer in Soligne after the terror and humiliation she had suffered? Gruffly André had relented, promising that he would have his own men escort her from Tours to Chartres; he would even buy her a sidesaddle and pay for it out of his own pocket. Through her tears, she had smiled triumphantly at the Vicomte, then softened her victory by assuring him how genuinely anxious she was to return home. She hoped he would believe that was her only reason, though her heart sang out the truth: André!

Now, laughing softly, Jean-Auguste swung his horse into place beside Lysette's. Why did he always look at her as though he could read her thoughts?

"You play a dangerous game, Madame la Marquise!" he chuckled, the seriousness of his eyes contradicting his laughter.

She tossed her black ringlets with contempt. "What need have I for games? Monsieur le Comte has been very kind to me! Would you condemn me for the sin of gratitude?"

"Take care that your gratitude goes not beyond the bounds of propriety!"

She smiled coquettishly. "And if it does? Would you be jealous?"

A light flickered for an instant behind his eyes, but he smiled. "Be warned for your own sake," he said gently.

Her eyes flashed. "For *my* sake? Pooh! You *are* jealous! He is handsomer than you, and braver, and kinder, and . . . and better in every way!"

He gazed at her steadily, the edge of exasperation in his voice. "And what if there should be a Comtesse du Crillon?"

Her face fell. "No! It is not so! It cannot be so! You are lying!" She bit her lip, her soft chin trembling. "At any rate, I care not a whit! He is my friend . . . and nothing more!" She prodded her horse skillfully with her knee, and made for the head of the column and André.

Laughing, he called after her. "Have a care that your 'friend' does not find out how well you ride! He might not enjoy being gulled!"

She contrived to avoid him for the whole of the day, hating him all the more because his frank and honest face attested to his inability to lie, and she knew it must be so, that André had a wife. Sullen, her jaw set in a stubborn line, she rode apart from the others, until a young junior officer, captivated by her pouting lips and smoldering eyes, took it upon himself to cheer her and coax a smile to that tempting mouth. By late afternoon, as the shadows lengthened in the forest glade, she had acquired two more admirers, and her silvery laugh trilled in the leafy gloom and was answered by a distant thrush. More than once André had turned, smiling, and she thought she saw a flicker of interest in those deep blue eyes. By the time they stopped for the evening at a small inn on the edge of the woods, she was confident that she could attract him—and even win him—wife or no wife! She had taken no lovers, nor even encouraged her admirers, since Guy had died, and had been a faithful wife while he was alive, despite his inclination to wander. But her aversion had had very little to do with scruples: she had simply not wished to be close to any man. André was different. She had but to look at him to know that she could be happy even as his mistress, comforting him when his fat and ugly wife played the shrew (for she had long since conjured up a most unflattering mental picture of the Comtesse du Crillon).

The evening was a pleasant one, the sky glowing with the luminosity of midsummer: though the sun had set hours ago, it was still light, as though the day were reluctant to give way to the darkness. The horses had been fed and bedded for the night in the small stable next to the inn; the men likewise, stuffed with bread and cheese and good ale, had found comfortable corners in the enclosed courtyard and lay snoring contentedly. Lysette had been given a tiny room in the eaves, but she lingered at the inn door, unwilling yet to go to bed.

There was a small bench around the side of the inn, facing

into the dark woods; after supper André and Jean-Auguste had taken a stroll in that direction. Lysette hesitated, then marched to the edge of the inn from where, leaning into the rough stone wall, she could see them. Narbaux, plumed hat held carelessly in his hand, lolled against a dark oak tree while André stood with one foot leaning on the bench; they seemed to be engaged in that kind of amiable conversation that is only possible between old friends. Lysette frowned. That hateful Narbaux! As though he were protecting André from her, never leaving his side for a moment! Well, she would show him!

She was glad she had taken off that shapeless jerkin; though coarse homespun, her chemise clung to her breasts in a most attractive manner, accenting each swell and curve, and the full long sleeves served to point up the daintiness of her hands. Reaching up, she pulled the pins from the back of her hair and shook out the tight chignon, letting the curls cascade down her back. She gloried in her hair—glossy and black as the wings of a raven, with that peculiar iridescence that seemed to glint with highlights of midnight blue and deep ruby and amber.

As though she had not a care in the world, she sauntered to the line of trees, then turned back to the two men, her face registering surprise at finding them there. She smiled demurely at them both, then perched on the edge of the bench and began to play with a soft curl beneath one ear.

"I begin to regret the journey already," she said with a sigh. "I fear me I shall never remove all the burrs from my hair!" Saying thus, she began to comb her tresses with slim fingers, stretching out her curls and sweeping them forward to lie alongside her breasts.

"With such lovely hair, Madame la Marquise need have no fear," said André gallantly. "There is not a burr in all this wide forest that would dare to despoil such beauty!"

"More especially if the briars do not reach above the horse's withers," said Jean-Auguste dryly.

Ignoring Narbaux, Lysette dimpled up at André, noticing with pleasure that he seemed unable to drag his eyes from her dainty white fingers stroking the jet-black curls. "How kind you are, Monsieur le Comte! How fortunate your wife must be, to have a husband who takes such an interest in a woman's looks. I fear me my late husband would not have noticed had he been married to a toothless hag!" And here she smiled dazzlingly, seemingly unaware that the even whiteness of her teeth made it clear what a blind fool her husband must have been. With deft hands she parted the hair at the back of her head, then frowned and ran one slim finger down the line of the part. She inclined her nape at André. "Monsieur, have I done it aright?" André harrumphed and shifted one uneven tress, while Lysette raised her eyes and beamed at Jean-Auguste, the violet depths glittering wickedly despite her innocent smile. Quickly she braided her hair into two thick ropes that hung down over her bosom, then jumped up and twirled about for their inspection. "Well, messieurs?"

André smiled indulgently. She looked like a sweet little child, her face framed in stray wisps and tendrils. "Enchanting!" he complimented. "What think you, Jean-Auguste?"

Narbaux looked skeptical. He made Lysette nervous—those gray eyes of his that saw too much—she was not sure she wanted his opinion.

"Pooh!" she said quickly. "How could Monsieur le Vicomte have the slightest idea of what is attractive—or even fashionable? With that great red monster growing on his face!" She pointed with contempt at Narbaux's flowing mustaches while André roared with laughter.

"You see, *mon ami?*" he gasped. "What have I been telling you? I have been minded more than once to shave off that growth of yours whilst you slept; now comes this charming creature to reaffirm what I have been saying all along! What say you? Will you finally let us see that bare face of yours? I vow it has been so many years, I have quite forgot what you look like!"

Narbaux flamed scarlet, his face as bright as his riotous curls, while André cackled and Lysette smiled maliciously, the victor of the battle, prepared to plant her flag on conquered territory.

Jean-Auguste fingered his thick mustaches and managed a laugh. "Very well," he said. "Agreed! But only on condition that you write that letter to Marielle you have been promising for weeks! And the one every second day after that!" He grinned as André looked shame-faced. "Well, my friend?"

"It is not necessary for you to lose your mustaches to remind me of my duty. I have been more than a little neglectful of Marielle. Keep your face's pride!"

Narbaux shook his head. "Nevertheless, I shall shave it off. I have given my word, and here's my hand on it!" The two shook hands warmly, and André bid them good night, striding jauntily off to the inn and his writing case. How like Narbaux, thought Lysette bitterly, to remind André of his wife, just when he had begun to notice her!

In the dimming light, Jean-Auguste turned to Lysette, his gray eyes serious. "It will soon cease to be a joke, you know, this pursuit of André."

Stung, her banners tattered from the final skirmish, Lysette jutted out her chin in stubborn defiance. She tossed her head angrily, and the two thick plaits swayed back and forth on her bosom. "I shall do as I please!"

He shrugged, then smiled crookedly. "I think, upon reflection, that that coiffure suits you. It strips away the pretense of womanhood and shows you for what you are—a selfish, wilful . . . child!"

Violet eyes widening in fury, she lashed out at him, her outstretched palm catching the side of his face with such force that he staggered back a step. She thought, for one fearful moment, that he would strike her back, but instead his eyebrows shot up quizzically in a look of such mild surprise—his face still glowing red from her fingers—that it was almost a condemnation. She fled to her room, burning with shame and humiliation, there to let the scalding tears flow and to untwist her braids with trembling hands.

The morning dawned gray and gloomy. Thick, ominous clouds roiled in the sky and scudded across the heavens, propelled by a strong wind. Pooh! thought Lysette, peering through the small dormer window. It will blow away in an hour or two. With determination she rolled up the ugly jerkin and tucked it away in the small packet that held her few belongings: a fresh pair of stockings, an extra petticoat, her comb and two or three spare hairpins. Not a woman indeed! She loosened the drawstring of her chemise and pulled it wide so it rested on the edge of her shoulders and bared the first voluptuous swell of her breasts. Let him call her a child now!

She skipped downstairs to the common room, pleased that the young officers around the table rose quickly to greet her, making a game of who should proffer her a mug of sweetened wine and some bread and cheese. André in particular smiled warmly, his blue eyes filled with frank admiration, setting butterflies to dancing deep within her. She dimpled prettily at them all, disappointed only that de Narbaux was not around to see her conquests. She glimpsed him at last through the open door; that bright orange hair was unmistakable. Quickly, but with seeming nonchalance, she finished off her breakfast and sauntered out into the courtyard. He was surrounded by the foot soldiers, the center of much joking and raucous laughter. At her appearance, the men fell back in deference and Narbaux turned about. Lysette almost gasped aloud, the change was so remarkable.

His face was now quite bare. Shorn of his large red mustaches, his appearance was astonishingly altered. The odd contrast of that bushy growth set against his open countenance had made him seem very young, boyish even, like a lad who wears his father's hat and appears all the more callow and tender. With the mustache gone, those thoughtful gray eyes dominated his face, diminishing the intrusiveness of the bright red hair that curled almost to his shoulders. With a start, Lysette realized he must be nearly André's age, a good ten years her senior. She had meant to show him that she was a woman; the mere application of his razor had defeated her, making her feel green and immature. He looked at her steadily, his eyes not once straying to her bosom.

"There is hardly an improvement!" she said caustically. "Perhaps if you could contrive to shave off your hair . . . !" And waited to see him flinch. Instead, he threw back his head and roared with laughter, while she stewed with embarrassment and anger. How dare he laugh at her! She aimed a ferocious kick at his leg, and smiled in triumph as her heavy shoe connected with a thud and he yelped in pain. Tossing her dark curls, she swept disdainfully from the courtyard, while he sat down on a bench and rubbed his shin, his body still shaking with merriment.

Glancing uneasily at the lowering sky, André gave the signal for them to mount up. Lysette was still so upset at Narbaux she hardly bothered to reward the gallant lieutenant who had helped her into the saddle; he contented himself with the thought that the touch of her dainty waistline beneath his hands was nearly as gratifying as one of her charming smiles. The innkeeper, his pocket fattened by the seigneur's gold, tugged at his cap respectfully as they rode out onto the road; his wife, her swollen body great with child, attempted to curtsy, swayed a little, thought better of it, and waved one work-roughened hand.

Lysette shuddered. How ugly she looked! How awful it must be to watch your body grow large and lumpish, to see disgust in a man's eyes, to know that all that could come of it was pain and suffering and a squalling creature who depended on you for everything! She had hated it, when Guy came to her bed, not only because his old and creaking body disgusted her, but because she lived in fear of conceiving a child. She had used all the tricks at her command—sulking, and tears, and vague ailments and malaise—to hold him at bay; surprisingly, he did not often seem to mind, bothering her only occasionally out of restless boredom. She submitted with indifference, but each time, when he had left her chamber, she would slip out of bed and fall to her knees, praying to le bon Dieu to keep her childless. She had almost been glad to discover that Guy was unfaithful, wishing only for her pride's sake that he was more discreet. If he seemed about to remind her of her wifely duty, she had but to pick a quarrel with him, chiding him for his latest indiscretion, then vanish into her room in a flood of angry tears. She had begun to suspect that he was barren—not one of his mistresses ever bore him a child; nevertheless she continued to use guile and tantrums to forestall his advances. It was a kind of revenge: if her lack of financial knowledge and control of the purse kept her a virtual prisoner in her own home, her difficult behavior guaranteed that she was mistress of that home, with Guy being forced to dance to her tune.

Lysette began to shiver. They had been riding for several hours now and the morning was well advanced; still the clouds had not broken and the cold wind blew with a cutting edge that seemed to bore into her. She fingered the top of her chemise and wished she had not pulled it quite so low; even the ugly jerkin seemed welcome now. But she had been so brazen about exposing her shoulders and breasts; how could she cover herself now without appearing more than a little foolish for her earlier immodesty?

Well, perhaps if she hung back a bit and let the column pass, as though she intended to retire a little way into the woods to relieve herself, she could tighten the drawstring on her chemise and raise the neckline a few unobtrusive inches, thereby gaining a modicum of warmth. She stopped her horse and dismounted, half minded to unpack the jerkin, ugly or no, then changed her mind and vanished into the woods. When she emerged, grateful for the small warmth the readjustment afforded her, she was surprised to see Jean-Auguste standing by her horse. She smiled regally at him, determined this time to have the upper hand, and took hold of the reins, waiting imperiously for him to help her into the saddle. His eyes flickered for a moment, taking in her now demure neckline, then came to rest again on her face with such an open blandness she was sure he was laughing at her. *Mon Dieu!* Why did he always make her blood boil? She nodded brusquely toward her horse, impatient for his assistance.

"Wait." He turned toward his own mount, searching in the saddlebag until he had withdrawn a heavy woolen cloak. "The day has turned chill. Wear this." He *was* laughing at her! She could see it behind those cool gray eyes.

Her own eyes flashed, sending out violet sparks, and she lifted her chin stubbornly, her full lips pouting in anger. "I hardly need your cloak, Monsieur! The day is quite pleasant!"

"Nonsense! Don't be such a vain little fool! Your shoulders can hardly be attractive if they are blue with the cold! Take the cloak."

Vain fool, was she? She would show him she did not need his interference! Fingers shaking in anger, she loosened the drawstring once again, this time dragging down the chemise below the curve of her shoulders until her back was half bare and her bosom exposed almost beyond the bounds of propriety.

He shrugged in disgust. "As you wish."

How he infuriated her! "Get out of my way!" she shrieked, and swept him away with elbow and forearm and tight-clenched fist, catching him just below the ribs so he gasped with surprise and exhaled quickly. Turning to her horse, she mounted with ease and galloped off to join the others, not daring to look back—lest his eyes should still be ridiculing her.

For the rest of the day she stayed close to André, laughing coquettishly as they shared the midday meal, smiling seductively at him when they rode side by side. *He* did not seem to mind her immodest chemise! At times during the day he would frown into the distance, his mind a thousand miles away: she had but to touch his arm with her soft fingers and the frown would melt, replaced by a friendly grin that did not hesitate to appraise her bosom as well. Her heart ached. How she longed to kiss that smiling mouth!

The sun had managed finally to struggle through the clouds, warming the day somewhat; nevertheless, by the time evening was approching Lysette was numb with the cold. They had not found an inn or farmyard nearby, and André decided that they would make camp in a small clearing near a flowing stream, trusting to providence to sweep the sky clean and forestall the rain.

While the men bustled about, rubbing down the horses and unwrapping packets of dried beef, Lysette huddled close to the large fire that they had built in the center of the glade. Would she ever be warm again? She really had been quite foolish, refusing the Vicomte's offer . . . he had only been trying to be kind. It was just that he made her uneasy, those cool gray eyes stripping her of pretense, making her feel guilty for every thought she had. She sighed deeply. *Mon Dieu!* She had never in her life felt so conscience-stricken, not even in church. She could smile at the priest, her eyes clear and untroubled, even while (if he chanced to be young and good-looking) her mind whirled with scandalous thoughts. She sighed again, hating herself. Wicked, wicked Lysette!

From the edge of the clearing, Jean-Auguste watched her elfin face, lit by the glowing fire. It was really quite remarkable, he thought. Lost as she was in reverie, she seemed almost placid and serene, a far cry from her usual coquettish smiles or stubborn petulance. A lovely face, delicate and fragile, a face of strange contrasts, deep violet eyes, black-fringed, smoldering against pale, creamy skin translucent as alabaster. And her mouth, unexpectedly full-lipped and sensuous, surprising counterpoint to the finely chiseled jaw and chin. She looked so soft and vulnerable and helpless. He laughed and fingered his bruises—well, perhaps not totally helpless! Still . . . he had not been particularly kind to her, baiting her into anger, and she was little more than a sweet—if spoiled—child. . . . He resolved to be more pleasant in the future.

Then André stepped into the circle of firelight and Lysette

smiled adoringly at him, her face glowing with a light that came from within. She stretched out her arms and he grasped her slim fingers and helped her to her feet, steadying her for a moment before releasing her hands. Cursing André's stupidity —and his own—Jean-Auguste stormed off into the woods in search of firewood.

Chapter Four

AT DAWN, THE HEAVENS OPENED UP, DRENCHING THEM WITH A cold rain; Lysette awoke chilled and sputtering, her small blanket scant protection against the driving storm. There was a flurry of men and horses as the column was hastily formed; there would be time later for food when they had found shelter. This time Lysette swallowed her pride and accepted the proffered cloak, murmuring her thanks to Narbaux and wrapping her head and shoulders in its dry warmth. She saw with a pang that he had only his casque and a short cape for protection, then shrugged her shoulders. After all, she had certainly not asked for his help, and one of the other men would have obliged her had Jean-Auguste not stepped forward. It was hardly her concern what he chose to do!

It rained all that day and into the night; when the men could walk no more through the blustering storm they found shelter in a half-ruined barn. In the morning it was still raining and the road had become a great mass of mud, thick and viscous, that sucked at the horses' hooves and made progress well-nigh impossible. To lighten the burden, André ordered them to dismount and lead their horses—even Lysette, whose slight weight was still too much for her mare.

By nightfall the rain had finally stopped and they found a farmer who was willing to let them use his stable and barn, and would sell them some hay for the horses. Madame la Marquise could spend the night in the house with the farmer's wife and two small daughters. Sighing with relief, Lysette stumbled into the farmhouse and plopped down before the fireplace. She had never walked so much in all her life! Tiredly she asked for a small basin of water, stripping off her muddy shoes and stockings and bathing her sore feet. Yes . . . see? There was a large blister beginning already to form on her left heel, and her toes were red from the clumsy shoes. She almost wept in self-pity, hating everybody and every thing that had conspired to reduce her to such misery. She pulled off her sopping garments, heedless of the giggles of the two little girls; wrapping a dry blanket about her naked body, she curled up on a small trundle bed in one corner of the room, instructing the farmer's wife to dry her clothes in front of the fire. In a moment, she was fast asleep.

The morning brought the welcome sun, warming the air and cheering spirits that had begun to flag. As they readied themselves for the journey, a young peasant appeared in the farmyard. The rain had flooded the road, he said; two or three leagues were well under water. If the King's general was heading northward, toward Paris, there was nothing to do but wait until the waters had receded.

André muttered an oath. "Is there no other way? A small path, perhaps. Some spot of high ground through the forest?" He swept his arm impatiently toward the north, where the land rose sharply and unexpectedly, and the deep green of the woodland trees stood out in high relief against the clear blue sky.

"There is only a goat trail, Monsieur, where the farmers drive their animals up to the flatland!"

"Wide enough for a horse?" The young man nodded. "Good! Will you lead us?" A moment's hesitation. André produced a coin and the peasant grinned and nodded his head enthusiastically.

Comfortably settled on her horse, Lysette smiled unaffectedly at Jean-Auguste. It was a genuine smile, springing from her sense of well-being, and a good breakfast, and the golden day. Narbaux raised one eyebrow quizzically, then thought better of his cynicism and returned the smile with warmth. He really was quite good-looking, she thought, especially with the mustache gone; not startlingly handsome like André who was, without a doubt, the most attractive man she had ever seen, but pleasant-looking, a nice face, strong and serious. Except, of course, when he grinned and the corners of his eyes crinkled up and he seemed ten years younger. He was fairer than André, with that coloration peculiar to redheads; whereas the sun had turned André's face to bronze, Jean-Auguste seemed barely touched by the elements, his skin a warm golden glow that served to point up the clarity of his gray eyes. She smiled again at him, grateful that his eyes seemed less penetrating this morning, and guided her horse past him to where André had just mounted up. Perhaps today, in the seclusion of the woods, there might be a moment that she could steal with Crillon alone.

The narrow path led up into the trees, dark and cool and still damp from the storms. With the young farmer leading the way, the foot soldiers clambered up the steep incline, followed by the men on horseback, then Lysette and André. Much to Lysette's chagrin, Narbaux had dropped back at the last minute to exchange a few pleasantries with his friend, and now followed close at their heels, bringing up the rear of the column. As though he were a chaperon, she thought with annoyance.

Almost at once it became apparent that they would have to dismount: the sharp slope had slick, damp patches here and there which made the ascent difficult even on foot, and extremely precarious if horse and rider should go down together. Lysette sighed peevishly, then turned helpless eyes to the young lieutenant who had just dismounted above her on the trail. He made his way quickly to her side; she slid from her saddle into his waiting arms, contriving to smile shyly as she did so. A few soft words, a melting plea from those violet eyes, and he found himself back on the path, leading her horse as well as his own, congratulating himself on his good fortune. For her part, Lysette was delighted to be so close to André, without a horse to intervene; after a few careful maneuvers on her part—a stumbling hesitation, a wobbly step on a mud-slicked rock—he was forced to hand his horse down to Narbaux, that he might be free to assist her.

Lysette picked her way carefully among the mossy stones and rotting logs, avoiding the oozing mud as best she could— she had had her fill of damp feet. Occasionally she paused and looked uncertainly about her, waiting for André's steadying hands about her waist, almost willing to risk the mud and filth if it would propel her into his arms. At length the woods began to clear, the trees giving way to thick shrubs and briars, dappled with sunlight and humming with a thousand insects. The path here was still narrow and quite steep, but dry, and well suited to her purposes. Deliberately, she stepped on a loose rock in her path; it yielded beneath her and slid out from under her foot, upsetting her balance and sending her toppling. She managed to twist about as she fell so that, as André caught her, she could throw her arms around his neck, her bosom pressed against his chest, eager mouth inches from his own. His blue eyes burned into her, deep and smoldering—surely he could feel her heart pounding against his breast! She was positive he was going to kiss her, his face filled with a longing that mirrored her own desire; unexpectedly he set her on her feet, loosing her twined arms and turning away in agitation. Aching with disappointment, she looked up to see Jean-Auguste's scowling face, lip curled with disgust. How she hated him! Tossing her curls angrily, she turned back to the path. There would be another opportunity on the journey!

The steep slope leveled off and they found themselves on a high plateau, thick with brambles and craggy rocks, the path so narrow that the briars caught at Lysette's skirts as she passed. The trail itself was strewn with sharp stones, and she stumbled along, noticing that her left shoe had begun to chafe distressingly again. She glanced back at André and Jean-Auguste, uncertain whether to speak up or not; after what had happened on the trail below, Narbaux at least would scarcely believe her. Better to manage as well as she could—this dreadful path could not go on forever! But after ten minutes she had begun to limp painfully, though she tried to hide it. She simply could not go on! She stopped and waited for André to reach her, her eyes avoiding Narbaux behind him.

"If you please, Monsieur le Comte," she said, her voice soft and timid. "I cannot walk another step. My shoe . . . the stocking . . . it is near worn through. If I could but ride a bit, or . . . or . . . be carried . . . or . . . ." Her words faltered and she crimsoned, feeling Jean-Auguste's mocking eyes on her, aware that she must sound like a fool.

Narbaux grinned sardonically. "Here, *mon ami*," he said, handing over the two horses' reins to Crillon. "It is time now for *me* to play nursemaid for a bit!" So saying, he bent to Lysette, grasping her firmly about the thighs and tossing her over one shoulder, like a farmer with a sack of onions. She shrieked furiously, demanding that he put her down, and wriggled against the strong arms that, vise-like, held her legs and prevented her from kicking. Her hands, however, were not hampered, and she pounded on his back with tight-clenched fists, and cursed him for a buffoon and a villain. Narbaux laughed as though it were a huge joke, and André joined in. She could hardly bear the shame of his laughter, but she was scarcely in a position to defend her pride; she ceased her struggles, praying that they would soon tire of the game.

One of the men called to André from the head of the column, and he left the horses and made his way forward, laughingly directing Narbaux to put the poor creature down; but Jean-Auguste readjusted Lysette on his shoulder and picked his way jauntily over the stony path, whistling like a schoolboy, the horses trailing behind.

"Please, Monsieur, let me go." A tiny voice, soft and wheedling.

The whistling continued, the pace never slackening.

"If you please, Monsieur le Vicomte . . . Jean-Auguste . . . please. I shall not complain of walking again . . . I swear it! Only let me go, I beg you!"

Narbaux stopped and set her on her feet, wary at her sudden change of mood. Her hair was in disarray, the thick coil tumbling down; slim fingers sought the errant hairpins tangled among the curls, and she deftly twisted and pinned the glossy mass until it was once again piled on top of her head. All the while she gazed at Narbaux with a look of such pain in her soft eyes that the grin faded from his face and he fidgeted nervously. Her pink mouth pouted adorably, almost too perfect to be genuine.

"Why are you so cruel to me?"

His face darkened, grew hard, and a small muscle twitched in his jaw. "I promised Madame la Comtesse I would take good care of her husband!"

She laughed airily. "Pooh! As though Monsieur le Comte needs an overseer!"

"You are scarcely unaware of your considerable charms! Even a man with a wife can hardly fail to notice, more especially as you seem bent on ensnaring him before this journey is done!"

"And would you have preferred to be the ensnared prey yourself?" she asked coyly. "Is that why you hate me so?"

He sighed in exasperation, like a stern parent with a stubborn child. "He has a wife! And two sons! He is devoted to them all!"

Her face fell and she turned from him, hurrying along the path to reach the column, now at some distance. Her foot burned like fire and she hobbled painfully, while great tears welled up in her eyes and spilled down her soft cheeks. She did not know if her tears were for the pain of her foot, or for herself, or for the image that seared itself into her brain—André, with his wife, with his family.

"Madame de Ferrand! Lysette!" His strong hand stopped her flight, catching at her arm and turning her about to face him. There was nothing artificial in the hurt he saw deep within her eyes. Their glances held for a long moment; at length he turned and whistled to his horse. Without a word, he lifted her with gentle hands and sat her sideways in the saddle. He held out his hand for the offending shoe, and when she had handed it to him, he turned away that she might lift her skirts and remove her garter and stocking. The blister on her heel was now quite raw and red, and she winced when his fingers touched it lightly. Scanning the thickets, he reached out and plucked a bit of thistledown; with Lysette's help, he placed it over the angry sore and anchored it by means of her stocking. While she refastened her garter, he ran his finger along the inside of her shoe, finding a rough spur of leather, the cause of all her misery. He took out his knife and pared it smooth, then slipped the heavy shoe back onto her foot as though it were a silken slipper. She was surprised at his gentleness, confused by his kindness, knowing she would hate him again in a moment because he was the only thing that stood between her and André.

The days passed uneventfully. The weather was fine, clear and warm, the air sweet with summer. They had traveled by now into the valleys watered by the Loire and its tributaries, and the sight of terrain that was so like home had sped their steps. By tacit consent, and without a word from André, the men pressed on quickly, marching farther and longer hours each day. They stayed often in open fields, or an occasional country inn, and once, near Poitiers, they enjoyed the hospitality of a doddering Baron, who welcomed them to his country manor house and kept André and Jean-Auguste up half the night recounting his exploits as a soldier under the old King Henry IV. Crillon avoided the towns as best he could; though there had been little rioting this far north, there was always the danger that the sight of troops, even so small a complement, might stir up the local populace.

Lysette was exhausted by the pace. It was enough just to eat and sleep and drag herself into the saddle day after weary day; she had not the energy to fence with Narbaux. As for André . . . though she convinced herself that the tiring journey drained her and robbed her of her looks, making her hardly worth his attentions, she avoided him not so much out of vanity, but because of the nagging thought that perhaps—with a wife, children—he truly took no interest in her. Her heart ached with the thought. How could *le bon Dieu* be so cruel? To send her such a man—strong and dominating, stern and just, yet capable of laughter and tenderness, a man whose every glance turned her knees to water and set a fierce flame to burning within her bosom—and make him blind to her! No! She refused to accept it, preferring to tell herself that it was only the tiring speed of their journey, not his anxiety to be home and with his wife, that prompted his casual indifference.

One evening, near sundown, with the sky glowing pink and orange on the horizon, they saw three horsemen approaching them from the east, their faces lit by the rays of the setting sun. It appeared to be a nobleman and his retinue.

André reined in sharply and motioned the column to halt. He and Narbaux exchanged surprised glances.

"Le Comte d'Ussé!"

"So it would seem! I thought he was with the army in Flanders!"

Ussé rode up and the men exchanged pleasantries and introduced Lysette. The Comte's glance swept her apprecia-tively, and when she held out her gauntleted hand he bent her wrist down and kissed the naked flesh between glove and sleeve. "Madame la Marquise de Ferrand! Is there not a parable somewhere of flowers blooming in the wilderness? And lo! this long and tiresome journey blossoms with a lovely rose, pale and delicate!" Lysette smiled demurely then glared at Jean-Auguste who, smirking, had begun to massage his ribs. One word, she thought. Let him dare to say one word! She dimpled again at d'Ussé, turning her back resolutely on Narbaux.

Ussé was a small man, compactly built, with a barrel chest and thick arms that ended in strong stubby hands. He was dark and swarthy, his hair crisply short, with a small peaked beard, well trimmed; by far his most striking feature was a large black patch that covered his right eye, a strange contrast to the cold blue of his left eye. He nodded to André. "I am on my way home to Trefontaine, but I had thought to stop here for the night. There is a pleasant grove yonder, just beyond the knoll, with a small stream. Maybe if you have had your fill of the road's dust today, you will join me. I should be pleased to take supper with such distinguished gentlemen . . . and their lovely lady!"

André frowned, annoyed at the insinuation, but Jean-Auguste interjected smoothly. "Madame la Marquise has been through a terrible experience at Soligne. She was nearly killed in the riots. We are escorting her home to her brother where, it is hoped, *le bon Dieu* will cleanse her mind of all the horrors she has known." He looked sympathetically at Lysette, content, for once, with her artifice; she did not disappoint him. Violet eyes cast down, she turned away with a deep sigh, while d'Ussé squirmed in the saddle and cursed himself for his unseemly innuendo.

In spite of Crillon's inquietude, it was decided to spend the night in the grove. There was an open meadow where the horses could graze, and the men had been many hours on the road; it seemed a sensible place to stop for the day. André concluded that his reservations about spending the night in the company of Ussé and his men were due to his antipathy toward the Comte. In truth, he had never particularly liked the man—angry, discontented, forever railing about the King's lack of gratitude and the meagerness of his royal pensions, all the while letting his estate at Trefontaine fall into ruin while he gambled away what money he had in the salons in Paris. He was not a gentleman when it came to women, either. André scowled as he watched Lysette encouraging his attentions. She wasn't exactly a child, and it was none of his concern, after all . . . but she was so young, so vulnerable. He laughed to himself. Marielle would tease him if she were here. She always said that he was born far too late, that he should have lived in the time of great knights and fair damsels, of chivalry and legends. Marielle. He ached to have her in his arms, to feel a woman's softness pressed close. It had been four long months, while his body tormented him, and he envied Jean-Auguste and the casual encounters of bachelorhood. Not that he would—or could—be unfaithful to Marielle; but the long separation had begun to weigh heavily upon him, disturbing his sleep and haunting his dreams.

The men set up camp, stacking logs for a fire to be built when darkness came, and clearing some of the dense underbrush. Lysette, with Ussé at her elbow, sat down on a large rock and began to fan herself with her glove, feeling hot and dry. Ussé beckoned to one of his men, who vanished into the trees and appeared a moment later with a fine linen handkerchief dripping from the stream.

"Madame." He wrung out the handkerchief and proffered it to Lysette, who took it gratefully and dabbed at her lips and temples and neck, holding its refreshing coolness against her bare cleavage, and smiling her thanks at him. His smoldering glance followed the movements of her hand, his one good eye traveling over her face and bodice with the softness of a caress. It was very nice to have him look at her in that fashion, and she shivered in pleasure. Besides, André seemed mildly annoyed, as though he were jealous. He *must* care for her!

They ate supper quickly, while Lysette swore to herself that she would never again look at dried beef and goat cheese and ale when this journey was over. As darkness fell and the fire was lit, the foot soldiers found patches of moss or soft boughs and were soon fast asleep; André and Jean-Auguste joined Lysette and Ussé and several of the junior officers around the fire. They began to discuss the riots at Angoumois while Ussé clucked his tongue in sympathy and Lysette sat, eyes downcast, looking for all the world as though every horror they recounted had happened to her personally. But when the topic turned from Soligne to the general political situation to the war and the siege at Dolê, Lysette yawned in boredom, and made as though to rise.

"Wait." Ussé nodded to his lieutenant. "I have some very agreeable wine that I found in Clermont. Perhaps you will join me." He passed round a large leather flask that his man had given him, first pouring out a bit into a cup that had appeared from nowhere and handing it to Lysette. The wine was good, the first they had had for more than a week. It eased the weariness of the long day, and they drank freely, released from the cares of the march. The conversation drifted and faltered, as questions were asked, hung in the silence, and then were forgotten. They will all soon be quite drunk, thought Lysette in annoyance.

André frowned and rubbed the back of his neck, trying to capture a thought that had nagged at him all evening. He turned to Ussé, his voice somewhat less crisp and clear than usual. "Were you not with the army in Flanders?"

"Aaah! Why should I stay?" Ussé's voice, too, had lost some of its steadiness. "Richelieu did not send me nearly enough money to pay my troops, and the Spaniards kept pouring in from the Netherlands! There was not a fortress that held! Why should I play the fool? I gave one eye for the King at La Rochelle in '28—I did not care to give another at Corbie!"

"Corbie?" Narbaux sat up in alarm and shot a sharp look at André. "What has happened at Corbie?"

Ussé shrugged. "Their commander surrendered to the Spaniards after barely a week."

André shook his head, trying to clear it of the wine. "But if Corbie is in enemy hands, Paris will be threatened!"

"No," said Ussé. "When I left Paris, Louis had already rallied the citizens and they were volunteering in droves to retake Corbie. And Richelieu managed to find the money to pay them!" he added bitterly. "Besides, when we left Corbie, we saw to it that there was not a bakery or a flour mill left standing on the road to Paris. The Spaniards will find it hard to advance if there is no bread for their troops!"

Du Crillon lifted the leather flask in disgust. "And did you also relieve some poor wine merchant in Clermont of his stock?"

Ussé laughed shortly. "The fortunes of war, *mon ami!*"

André growled a curse under his breath, his eyes like burning coals. The air crackled with tension as the two men glared at one another. Narbaux sent Crillon a warning glance.

With a silvery laugh, Lysette jumped up suddenly. "Messieurs," she chided, "I fear me you have all had too much to drink! Else why would you quarrel about something that has happened days ago and far away? Shall we do battle here in this wood . . . and in the middle of the night? Come, come!" She held out her hand to André, taking the flask from his grasp. "It would be better if this were filled with clear water! Monsieur le Comte," she said, smiling at Ussé, "will you accompany me to the stream?"

"Willingly, *ma belle!*" He tucked his hand under her elbow and guided her to the small path that led to the water, while, behind them, André uncurled his fists and Jean-Auguste exhaled in relief.

The path was narrow and dark, and several times Ussé swayed against Lysette, shoulder and hip brushing for a split second, whether from the confining trail or the amount of wine he had consumed, she could not tell. They reached the stream and she knelt to fill the flask; turning, she held up one hand for him to help her up. But when she was on her feet, he stood in the pathway, his solid bulk looming large before her, and would not let her pass. At first she misunderstood, thinking only that he was waiting for her, but as she tried to brush past him his thick arms went about her in a bear-like grip and his mouth pressed down upon hers. She struggled furiously, feeling suffocated against that massive chest, held so close to his body that however much she tried to move her head she could not escape his hungry lips. She was too angry to be afraid, and the evidence of his passion, his body hard against her, only enraged her further. But his masculine weakness was her strength. With all her might she drove her knee into that part of him that was most vulnerable, and watched in satisfaction as he doubled in agony before her. Then she ran for the safety of the firelight, quite forgetting the water pouch. With a snarl that was half a moan, Ussé pulled himself to his feet and pounded after her, his face contorted in pain.

André and Jean-Auguste looked up in surprise as Lysette broke into the clearing, her breath coming in hard gasps; they could hardly misunderstand when Ussé limped into the firelight a moment later, his eye glaring balefully. André reached for his sword, but one of the young lieutenants stepped quickly in front of him and Narbaux put a restraining hand on his shoulder.

"Madame de Ferrand is right, *mon ami*. We have all drunk too much wine! I fear we shall all have aching heads by morning, and some, perhaps"—he nodded at the still suffering

Ussé—"will know pain more cruel!" Lysette giggled and Narbaux doffed an imaginary hat in her direction.

Crillon took a deep breath. "I think it wise," he said to Ussé, "that you and your men leave at dawn tomorrow. And you, Madame," he added, scowling at Lysette, "I want you near to me this night. I cannot guarantee your safety to your brother if you put your own virtue in jeopardy!"

Meekly, she hung her head, placing her blanket across the fire from him, as he directed, her eyes filled with contrition. But her heart sang within her as she settled down for the night. He did care! Had he not been ready to fight Ussé in her behalf? Was he not there, just beyond the smoldering logs, his strong face achingly handsome in the firelight? Smiling contentedly, she closed her eyes and slept.

In the morning, Ussé and his men were gone. The story of Lysette's defense had made its way through the camp, and the young officers gathered around her, full of admiration, exchanging ribald jests at Ussé's expense. Lysette positively glowed with all the attention, her triumph all the sweeter because Narbaux had just come into the clearing from the path that led to the stream. She could not resist the opportunity to flaunt her admirers, allowing them to kiss her hand and then dismissing them with an airy wave of her fingers. She flounced over to Narbaux and smiled sweetly at him.

"Good morning, Monsieur le Vicomte!"

He grinned crookedly, the corners of his mouth twitching. "Here!" he said. "I thought perhaps you would like to keep this." In his hand was Ussé's forgotten wine pouch.

Lysette wrinkled her nose in disgust. "Why should I want such an ugly thing?"

"As a token . . . to remember Monsieur le Comte d'Ussé!"

"Mon Dieu! Whatever for?"

His gray eyes studied her coolly, and there was seriousness behind the lighthearted words. "I once knew a man who loved to hunt. And every stag who gave up his life gave up his antlers as well, to be mounted and displayed. The man had one long gallery in his hunting lodge—filled from end to end with his trophies." His eyes took in the young officers busily saddling their horses, then swept back to bore into hers. "How many trophies have you a mind to collect on this journey?"

Stung by his sarcasm, she almost struck him across the face, then thought better of it, remembering that he always managed to best her when she lost her temper. Instead, she let her violet eyes go soft and hazy; reaching up a gentle finger she stroked him lightly on his upper lip.

"But then I think my trophy room already has . . . one red mustache!" And smiled victoriously as his face crimsoned and he fled.

Chapter Five

LYSETTE'S HAND PLUCKED SAVAGELY AT THE LARGE OAK LEAF SHE held, tearing shreds from its edges and rolling them into damp balls between her fingers. Corbie! They were talking of the fall of Corbie again, as they had since the night Ussé had spent with them. Always Corbie . . . until she thought she must scream with boredom!

André shook his head. "I cannot understand it. To capitulate within a week! It must have been a cowardly surrender!"

Narbaux hunched forward on the grass, his knees drawn up to his chest. "And the road to Paris . . . wide open! God knows what is happening . . . no matter what Ussé said about a mobilization!"

Crillon jumped up and paced the small clearing. From the lake far below the sounds of laughter and shouting drifted up to break the stillness. "To be here, unable to do aught . . . to know nothing . . ." He kicked at a small rock in frustration, sending it clattering against the trunk of a tree.

"Well," said Jean-Auguste philosophically, "we shall know soon enough when we reach Vilmorin. If the news is bad, Madame la Marquise can stay with Marielle, *n'est-ce pas?* I shall go home to Chimère to see how many men I can conscript for a new force. And you?"

"I do not see how Vilmorin can spare another man!" André waved his arm toward the sounds from the lake. "And how can

I ask them to serve for yet one more campaign?" He rubbed his chin thoughtfully. "The village of Vouvray . . . perhaps . . ."

"But it is nearly September! The grape harvest . . . every man in the Vouvray region will be in the vineyards . . ." Narbaux plucked morosely at a blade of grass.

Lysette smiled a tight smile, her fingers still worrying the leaf. How tiring it was, all this talk of war. For days they had thought of nothing else, both of them, and had ignored her to the point where she would almost have welcomed a fight with Narbaux rather than his indifference. And perhaps there was something more. She had not forgotten how he blushed when she jibed him about his mustache. She had meant it only as a cruel taunt, but . . . *had* he shaved it off to please her? Well, she would never find out as long as they continued to speak of the war and Spain! They had stopped at the lake to refresh themselves and the horses after a long hot day; André and Jean-Auguste had offered to keep her company in this sun-dappled clearing while the rest of the men bathed below. She might as well have the oak tree for company! Jumping to her feet, she plucked another large leaf and began to fan herself vigorously.

"Monsieur . . . André!"—she had days ago slid into the habit of calling him familiarly by his name—"it is so very warm here! I am minded to shed my clothes and join the men in the cool lake if I cannot find some relief from this heat!" Violet eyes gazed helplessly at André.

"Ah, Madame," he said, suddenly contrite. "I beg pardon of you. But . . ." his blue eyes danced merrily, ". . . do not join my men, else we shall never reach Vilmorin!"

She smiled archly, then allowed a small unhappy frown to crease her brow. "It looks so cool in that stand of pine. I would walk alone, but . . ." She sighed, sad eyes cast down. "Well, mayhap I will be safe enough. I cannot ask you both to walk with me. The men would return and wonder where we had gone! No matter!" She squared her shoulders bravely and turned her steps toward the small pine grove.

"You cannot go alone," said André gallantly. "Let us leave Narbaux here to stand guard. I weary of the cares of war. There will be no more talk of Corbie today! Come!" Without a backward glance at Jean-Auguste, Lysette skipped off through the trees behind André. It was indeed cooler here in the woods.

She breathed a sigh of pleasure and relief, and swept the curls back from her forehead. Though she wore her hair up in the back, twisted in a thick coil, her face was framed by small tendrils and ringlets, in the current fashion, and they had begun to cling damply to her skin. She pushed them back, patting and smoothing, fingers dancing lightly on the curls, while André watched intently, fascinated by the small feminine movements.

"We shall reach Vilmorin soon . . . André?"

"Three or four days at most, Madame de Ferrand."

"Lysette. You must call me Lysette! 'Madame de Ferrand' puts me in mind of an old harridan . . . and surely you do not think me old!"

He laughed indulgently. "Hardly old . . . Lysette."

"Nor yet too young?"

"No. Charming and lovely, and quite the right age." His eyes were warm and admiring; she felt her heart thump in her chest. "Will you be glad to get home to your brother?"

She shrugged, her face thoughtful. "I do not know. It was my home once, but with my brother's wife now mistress, I fear me I shall feel the intruder. Well, I shall be glad at least never again to eat goat cheese and dried meat!"

"It is a soldier's diet, but hardly suited to a fair maiden!"

She dimpled prettily. He was full of compliments today! She contrived to let her mouth droop, pink lips set in a pout that was far more captivating than woeful. "I have seen several orchards as we passed . . . a sweet pear would be most welcome."

"We have seen no villages or farmhouses, else I might be minded to give a few sous for a basket or two."

"Why must we pay? You are the King's soldier. Surely he will reimburse the people for his own army!"

André shook his head at her naivete. "The Royal Treasury can hardly be concerned with every farmer's claim! What is the poor man to do if no one pays him for his plundered orchard?"

"Pooh! Who cares? Comte d'Ussé took the wine he wanted, did he not? And your own men looted in Soligne! Why should I not have a pear if I want it?"

André frowned, and when he spoke his voice rumbled in his chest. "Had I caught a single man of mine looting, I would have had him flogged on the spot! You speak like a child! You have not seen what war can do to a village, stripped and ravaged—it is far uglier than what happened at Soligne! I vow I shall not willingly be a part of it!''

Stupid. Stupid Lysette. To have made him so angry . . . and for what? *Mon Dieu!* She could feel pity for the farmers too, but after all, what harm was there in taking a few pieces of fruit? When she was a child did not her brothers sometimes creep into a neighbor's tree to fetch her an apple or two? And no one ever seemed to mind! She bit her lip and turned away. Best to talk of something else. She sat down on a fragrant bed of pine needles, sniffed their heady scent appreciatively, then stretched out full length upon her back, cradling her head in her upraised arms. "I suppose you will be happy to see Vilmorin again."

His expression softened, a gentle smile replacing his scowl. He sat down beside her and rubbed his chin absently, lost in thought. "Always," he said, more to himself than to her. "It is a place of rolling hills and vineyards, very special!"

"We have vineyards in Angoumois!"

"Ah! But not like Vouvray! Because of the caves!"

"Caves?"

"Yes. All along the Loire, from Tours to Blois, but especially in Vouvray. Vilmorin is less than two leagues from Vouvray—our caves are near as numerous as theirs."

"But what on earth are the caves used for?"

"To keep the wine. To live in!"

"Surely Vilmorin is not a cave!"

He laughed aloud at that, his eyes smiling down on her where she lay. "No. Vilmorin is a very beautiful chateau. It was built by my great-grandfather, who entertained the Court on many occasions. There are far more rooms in it than Marielle and I shall ever fill. Though when the children are playing in the long gallery, Vilmorin does not seem large enough! I have been tempted more than once to seek refuge in the caves."

"But where are the caves? I do not understand."

"Look," he said, smoothing away a patch of pine needles. Lysette sat up and leaned close to him, while he traced a line in the soft earth with one outstretched finger. "Here is the river Loire. Here is Vilmorin, set on a slight rise above the river. Now here, behind Vilmorin, are the bluffs. They are quite steep in places, but the land above the cliffs is fairly level. That is where the vineyards are. In the cliffs themselves are the caves. Some of the *vignerons* live there, in the caves, although most of the men who work my vineyards have quarters at Vilmorin."

"How long your fingers are!"

"What?" André shot a surprised look at her.

"Your hand. Next to mine. Look." She held up her palm to his, her fingers seeming all the more delicate and fragile against his strong hand. "Such nice hands. Hardly a soldier's hands!" She turned his palm down and ran one soft finger along the bronzed knuckles, tracing the line of the bones down to his wrist, then traveling up again to his tapered fingers. "Guy's hands were ugly. He had a callus—just there—from all his cramped writing . . ." She rubbed the smooth edge of his finger, then looked up into his face. It was a face in torment, the eyes filled with pain and guilt . . . and desire. A small pulse throbbed on his temple in counterpoint to his heaving chest.

"André . . ."

He swallowed hard and jumped to his feet, his voice husky in his throat. "Jean-Auguste will be wondering what is keeping us. Come."

Hiding her disappointment, she held out her hands to him. Reluctant, fearful of the lure, he helped her quickly to her feet, then dropped her fingers as though her touch burned like fire. He turned in the direction of the lake.

"Wait," she said. "Please"—brushing the pine needles from her skirt and her hair—"I cannot . . ." she said softly, and presented her back to be groomed. His hands swept across her shoulders, dislodging the sprigs; of a sudden they gripped her arms so tightly that she thought she would swoon, feeling the pressure of his fingertips through her chemise. She looked back over her shoulder, trying to turn in his arms, to collect the kiss she had been aching for, scheming for, since the first moment she had seen him.

His eyes were dark with agony, panic lurking in their depths. With a strangled oath, he released her shoulders and groped for her hand. "Come! It grows late!" And pulled her, half running, out of the woods and into the safety of the clearing.

Jean-Auguste was still sitting where they had left him on the small patch of grass; at their precipitous appearance he looked up, startled.

"I must see to my horse," André growled, "his shoe . . . he

seemed to limp . . ." With an angry scowl to hide his agitation, he was gone.

Lysette took a deep breath and turned away, avoiding Narbaux's eyes. Her brain whirled with doubt and frustration. Why had André fled at the last moment? Was he blind to the love she felt for him? And then to be marooned here—alone—with Jean-Auguste! She stole a furtive glance in his direction and flinched at the look in his cool gray eyes. His unwavering gaze burned into her, filled with condemnation and disgust. She stirred uneasily, then jutted her chin out in defiance.

"He cares for me!"

"Indeed?" One eyebrow lifted sardonically. "Did he tell you so?"

Hateful man! "Was he not ready to duel with Ussé on my behalf?"

He laughed mirthlessly. "Must you always think like a child? André is an honorable man, very chivalrous toward women. It is his nature. He defended Marielle's honor more than once, and not only because she happens to be his wife. Perhaps because he was a bit of a rakehell himself in his single days . . ." He shrugged. "He does not like lechers. And more to the point, he does not like Ussé!"

Hands on hips, she planted herself in front of him, dainty mouth twisted in scorn. "And would you not have fought for my honor?"

He leaned back, his hands on the grass behind him, and sighed deeply, a man at the edge of his patience. "I would have forbidden you to do anything so foolish as to go off into the woods alone with Ussé!"

She smiled sarcastically. "I went off into the woods with André—perhaps you should have forbidden that!"

"I should certainly have warned him—judging by the look on his face!"

She beamed in smug triumph and hugged herself contentedly, her eyes straying to the pine grove. "If you but knew . . . !"

His face darkened, a small muscle working in his strong jaw. "I have no doubt you tried him sorely!"

"Pooh!"

"André is a man, after all . . . many months from home and the soft companionship of a woman . . . *any* woman!"

"Oh!" she shrieked in fury and swung her hand against his face, flesh striking flesh with a sharp snap, like the crack of a whip. He rocked sideways for a moment, only his steadying hands preventing him from toppling, his face registering merely mild surprise, though his cheek glowed as brightly as his hair. His coolness infuriated her still further and she aimed a kick at his chest; deftly he grabbed her ankle and pulled, upsetting her balance. She sat down hard in a flurry of petticoats, jolted for the moment into inactivity.

"Cease," he said mildly. "I have no wish to do battle with you!"

She glared at him, all her frustration with André, all her unsatisfied passion, all her doubts (was it only release from his hungers that André saw in her?) centered in hatred for Narbaux. He saw everything, he spoiled everything, his eyes stripping away her artifice until she felt naked, the very gentleness of his nature a kind of accusation. She longed to see him beaten, defeated, humbled; struggling to her knees she attacked him yet again, pummeling him about the shoulders, digging her nails into his neck, gouging and clawing, her anger fueled by her own feelings of helplessness. Like a man warding off a troublesome gnat, he raised his arms and tried to brush her away, grimacing in annoyance.

"Lysette! *Nom de Dieu!* Will you cease?"

For answer, she lunged once again, this time succeeding in bowling him onto his back; she was upon him at once, slim fingers tangled in his red hair. Viciously she tugged at his curls, glad to hear him yelp (no wig, this!); it was too much, for all his even-tempered tolerance. He rolled over with her, his weight pinning her to the grass, while she bucked and squealed and struggled, her hands slapping fiercely at his cheeks. He managed at length to grab one flailing hand and then the other, forcing her wrists down to the ground and holding them there while he caught his breath.

"You have prodigal hands, *ma petite,*" he gasped, his face red from her assault. "Take care lest I employ my own hand in such a way that you will walk—and gladly!—until we get to Vilmorin!" His voice was still mild, but the coldness in his gray eyes made her blood run to ice and she gulped, stilling her frenzied activity at last.

There was a shout of laughter from above them. Turning her head, Lysette saw André grinning down, his face radiating—what? (satisfaction? relief?) to see them thus. She was aware, suddenly, of Jean-Auguste's body pressing firmly upon hers, thighs, hips, breasts in intimate proximity.

André laughed. "Aha, my bachelor friend! I wondered when your natural inclination would assert itself! And perhaps, after all, that is where a woman belongs, especially one as charming and lovely as Lysette! But you might seek the privacy of the pine grove—I fear the men will be returning soon from their swim!" With a sly apology for having disturbed them, he vanished in the direction of the lake.

Lysette flamed bright crimson, embarrassed and humiliated by André's words, his easy assumption of a romantic encounter. Bitterly she began to weep, great tears of shame welling up in her violet eyes and coursing down her temples. Narbaux arose slowly, his face filled with compassion for her genuine distress; what had begun as a romp had ended by hurting her. She did not resist when he put his hands about her shoulders and helped her up; once on her feet, however, she brushed him aside and turned away, sobbing broken-heartedly, her forehead pressed against the trunk of a tree. He let her weep for a while, understanding the anger, and frustration, and shame that spilled out with her tears. At length he handed her a linen handkerchief that he pulled from his pocket.

"Lysette, listen to me," he said gently. "André is not for you! He and Marielle . . . they love one another! Leave them in peace!"

She sniffled and blew her nose, then turned to him, stubborn mouth set in a petulant line. "If they are so much in love, what harm can I do?"

He smiled indulgently and cupped her delicate chin in one strong hand. With his forefinger he wiped away the last of her tears. "André is a man of flesh—no stronger nor weaker than any other—he is not fashioned of stone! You are a lovely woman, warm and desirable—I'll wager you might tempt the devil himself! You can only make mischief if you persist in this folly, and hurt Marielle and André. And yourself in the bargain."

She shook her head impatiently, dislodging his gentle hand.

"Have you taken it upon yourself to protect André, like some doddering old duenna?" she asked, her voice heavy with sarcasm.

He sighed in exasperation. "They are my friends! They have been so for many years! Shall I stand by—and do nothing—while you amuse yourself? I know not why you married the Marquis de Ferrand—I can scarcely believe you had aught but the most selfish reasons—but André and Marielle married for love, and love is a precious and fragile blossom. I will not see it crushed by a willful child who knows nothing of the heart's ways, but fancies herself smitten by a pair of blue eyes!"

"Pah!" she said scornfully, stung by his words. "And to think that André imagines that I . . . that you . . ." She gestured with disgust toward the patch of grass upon which they had lain together. How she despised him and his hateful words!

His cool eyes raked her body, traveling from her toes to the top of her head, a slow, unhurried appraisal that peeled away petticoat and stockings, skirt and chemise, and came at last to rest upon her face. "I scarcely think you would be worth the effort," he said with indifference.

Furious, she raised her hand to strike him, then stopped, remembering his threat, and seeing the ominous way his gray eyes had suddenly narrowed. She scoured her brain for some spiteful words to hurl at him, but her own fury prevented her from thinking clearly; only the arrival of the men in the clearing saved her tattered pride.

She woke as the first rays of the sun came streaming through the pine boughs. She had been dreaming of André, of lying in his arms, his warm blue eyes adoring her, the sweetness of his mouth on hers. No! It was not fair—to lose the dream! She closed her eyes again, shutting out the intruding day, and tried to drift back again into sleep, into André's arms. It was no use. Sleep, and the dream, eluded her; she contented herself with conjuring up her own image of him, placing him in her mind's eye (just so) and herself at his side. She knew if she opened her eyes she would see him in reality, sleeping just within her line of vision where she lay (for since Ussé he had insisted she stay near to him at night), but she preferred her imagination. She could relive again and again the moment when he had held her in his arms, hands tight on her shoulders, desire smoldering in his eyes. How ridiculous Narbaux had been, to suggest that André's passion had sprung only from his basest needs; she had only to remember that moment to know how close André had come to declaring his love for her! It was just Jean-Auguste's way of being irksome!

Narbaux. How he plagued her! She had watched him uneasily all evening long, uncertain of his mood: would he have beaten her? She had no wish to be whipped like a child, nor ever had been. Her father had forbidden her nursemaids or tutors to touch her, though most children were raised by the rod as a matter of course, and Guy was not inclined to exercise his husbandly prerogative, avoiding as best he could anything that would turn her sullen or difficult. But Narbaux . . . ? Upon reflection, she decided that he was only trying to frighten her; he was really too gentle and easy tempered deliberately to hurt a woman. It was André who could sink into black moods, or lash out at his men when they disobeyed his commands, while his voice rumbled and thundered; but except for an occasional edge of impatience and a cutting word or two, Narbaux was calm and placid. With a start, Lysette realized that never had she seen him truly angry, though she had provoked him often enough. Surely his softness was a kind of weakness, and she was a fool not to turn it to her account. She had reacted to him badly at every turn, unable to deal with him, resorting to physical assaults to hide her frustration. Never before had she had to strike a man's face to hurt him; one baleful glance, one violet spark from her eyes, had been enough to bring pain to the strongest man.

Was it his eyes? Cool, detached, searing her soul. Mayhap she only imagined that they plumbed the depths of her being; if she were wise, she might avoid his glance and bend herself more diligently to captivating his heart. And why not? She did not care a fig for him, but her pride had been hurt by his insults. Not worth a man's effort, indeed! She might love André, want him, long for him and, yes, scheme for him; but she would bewitch Narbaux if she could, for the pleasure of humiliating him!

A soft noise disturbed her reverie. She opened her eyes in time to see André, in shirtsleeves, and bootless, disappear down the path that led to the lake. Cautiously, she looked about her; no one else seemed to be stirring. She rose slowly to her feet, slipping out of her own shoes and wrapping her skirts about her to keep them from catching on the bushes. She made her way slowly down the path, in no hurry to overtake him; she did not want to be discovered until they were well out of sight and sound of the clearing.

The lake was small and irregular, with thickets crowding to the shoreline, steep banks carpeted in moss and fragrant grasses. Just ahead of Lysette, the path veered to the left; directly in front of her a large weeping willow tree jutted out into the lake, forming a kind of dogleg that angled sharply away to the right. From where she stood, Lysette could just see André's upper body above the line of bushes near the shore; as she watched, he gathered up the fabric of his shirt and slipped it over his head. She felt her heart catch. His shoulders and back were as bronzed as his face, and his chest had a mat of fine gold, sun-bleached like the hair on his head, that glinted in the early morning light. His shoulders were extraordinarily broad, strong muscles firm beneath flesh whose smoothness was marred only by small hollows and indentations, the scars of old battles. Lysette felt her knees go weak, he was so beautiful. She craned her neck and stood on tiptoe, wishing she might see more of him, shameless in her voyeurism. He disappeared from view; there was a soft splash and he reappeared in the lake, strong arms cutting the glassy water with sure strokes. Heart pounding, she pushed through the underbrush to the right of the path, heedless of the branches that caught her clothing. Here the edge of the lake lapped up gently against large stones, creating a foamy backwater as it washed ceaselessly back and forth. She was hidden from André's view by the willow tree; he could not see her—nor her trembling—as she shed her clothes and waded out into the foam. She was a good swimmer, thanks to her brothers' teaching, but she had already determined to struggle in the water as she reached André; her eyes scanned the shoreline, seeking a small clearing where she might ask him to carry her. She had never felt more excited—nor more wicked—in all her life. Swimming slowly, she reached the willow tree, then swung wide around it into the spot where she knew André must be.

The first thing she saw was Narbaux's orange hair.

"Good morrow, Lysette!" he called cheerfully. "André, look! We are to have company!"

Lysette sputtered in shocked surprise, forgetting for the moment to keep herself afloat. Damn Jean-Auguste! He had not been here when first André came to the lake, she could swear to it! Had he followed her? Had he watched her with the same lascivious eyes as she had watched André? She felt herself burning with shame; in her agitation she swallowed a large mouthful of water and began to cough and choke violently. Instantly the two men began to swim toward her, their faces dark with concern. *Mon Dieu,* but this was intolerable! To be naked in the lake with one man was romantic, lovely; with two it was ludicrous!

"No, no! Please, Messieurs!" she gasped. "It is not seemly! Stay where you are. I am quite fine." She smiled brightly at them both, reminding herself of her morning's resolve: she would simply not allow Jean-Auguste to upset her. After all, his coming to the lake might be perfectly innocent—far more innocent than her reasons, she thought wryly.

"You must forgive me, gentlemen, for disturbing the privacy of your swim," she said demurely. "I had thought to swim alone so early in the day!"

"Why then, Madame, you shall have your wish! Come, Jean-Auguste!" Exchanging wicked grins, the two men swam for the shore and made as if to stand up in the shallows.

"Mon Dieu! For shame!" Lysette blushed scarlet and held up her hand before her eyes; the sudden roar of their laughter obliged her to look in their direction: they were still modestly enrobed by the waters of the lake. "Oh! Wicked, horrible men, to tease me so!" She pouted beguilingly and turned away, making small circles in the deep water to keep herself afloat.

"André, *mon ami,* we have been properly chastised! A true gentleman would escort the lady from the water first!" So saying, Narbaux began to swim rapidly in Lysette's direction, while André grinned and Lysette shrieked, warning them both to keep their distance. As Jean-Auguste approached, she slapped at the water with the heel of her hand, splashing his face and slowing his advance; still he did not stop. With a desperate squeal, she turned and fled, skimming through the water with all the strength she could muster. Once or twice his hand nearly caught a dainty foot threshing the water, which served to propel her forward in even greater haste; at length, laughing and gasping, she appealed to André for succor.

Reaching Narbaux's side, André lunged, and soon the two men were grunting and wrestling, each trying to submerge the other, while Lysette backed off to a more discreet distance. Jean-Auguste, already winded from chasing Lysette, was forced at last to yield; panting, his face split by a tired grin, he saluted André and made slowly for the shore.

"Wait!" André called, seeing the look of consternation on Lysette's face. "There must be a way to protect Madame's delicate sensibilities! Perhaps, Lysette, *ma petite,* you had better leave first! Your things . . . they are around the bend?"

She nodded, mute once again before the warmth of his smile, the clarity of his deep blue eyes. Reluctantly she turned about and paddled toward the willow tree; then she stopped, uncertain as to whether, in their lighthearted mood, she could trust them. "But you must not look—or watch me!" she warned, and flashed a winsome smile toward Jean-Auguste, resting in the shallows. *"Either* of you!" She was gratified to see his pleased response. Oho! she thought, my red-haired friend, I shall do you in with charm—just wait and see!

She dressed slowly near the tree, wringing out her curls and retwisting her chignon; by the time she returned to the clearing, André and Jean-Auguste were already there, saddling their horses and ignoring the good-natured jibes directed at their dripping locks. Lysette's appearance, wet hair freshly groomed, chemise clinging revealingly to her damp flesh, caused not a few murmurs and raised eyebrows. The young lieutenant who had taken such an interest in her sulked throughout breakfast, and when it was time to start the day's march he did not appear at her side, as was his custom, to help her into her saddle.

"May I?" It was a nonchalant Jean-Auguste, a crooked grin on his face. "Since I seem to be partly to blame for your abandonment this morning!"

She opened her mouth to speak, to pursue her campaign with some beguiling remark, and then thought better of it. He might appreciate frankness instead. More especially because sincerity in this instance was not difficult. "It is scarcely necessary," she said kindly. His eyebrows shot up in surprise. "I can hardly pretend to you, Jean-Auguste, that I am a stranger to a horse, though my young admirer yonder seems not to have noticed!"

He laughed shortly, still half skeptical at her open response. "Then let me assist you because I wish it."

She smiled her assent and then, not waiting for his hands about her waist, reached up and rested her own hands on his shoulders, her eyes radiating warmth and gratitude. For a moment he seemed almost reluctant to hold her, and when at length he swung her up into the saddle, his grip was less than steady, as though her yielding closeness had upset his usual composure. He handed her the reins, but when she would have turned her horse about he held the bridle, unwilling to let the moment pass.

"I . . . trust I did not spoil your morning," he said, genuine concern on his face. "It seemed wise to keep you from folly if you . . . *eh bien!* I could not be sure . . ."

She smiled brightly at him. Damn him! It *had* been deliberate! "How could you spoil aught? I enjoy swimming, and your company—both of you—was most welcome!"

"You swim well. It is rare to find a woman with such skill."

She dimpled prettily at him. "Ah, my fine gallant! But could you have caught me?"

He shrugged his shoulders and shuffled the dirt at his feet. "Well . . ."

Twirl the silken noose and let fly. "What would you have done had you caught me?"

His head snapped up, jolted by the unexpected question, the open seduction in those hazy violet eyes. He gaped, feeling foolish, aware of her game, captivated nonetheless.

Capture the prey and bind him fast. "Perhaps, the next time, I shall let you!" She did not stay to enjoy her triumph; prodding her mare with her knee, she moved to the head of the column and André, confident she had shaken Narbaux's peace of mind enough so that he would forget to play chaperon for a few hours.

Chapter Six

THE SILVER ORB OF THE MOON SHONE DOWN UPON THE CROSS-roads: two narrow threads of dust, pale gold earth of Touraine, that bisected one another and then went their separate ways—over the rise of the hill, through the dark and leafy woods, on to some distant town—never to meet again. Like André and me, thought Lysette, her heart aching within her breast. She wrung her hands, feeling helpless and desperate.

At the junction of the two roads there was a small shrine, with a statue of the Virgin, placed there to protect and cheer the travelers and wanderers who might pass. Lysette crossed toward the blue-robed icon, half tempted to sink to her knees and offer up her own prayers; guilt and shame made her turn away at the last moment. How could she pray to the Virgin to deliver another woman's husband to her eager embrace? And there was so little time left!

As she had hoped, her advances to Narbaux in the morning had unnerved him enough so that he had kept his distance all the day. She had ridden with André, smiled at him, flattered him shamelessly, longed for evening to fall, for the opportunity to be alone with him. At twilight they had come to the crossroads, and the men had shouted in happy exuberance. The sight of the altar, a landmark to many of them, meant that home was not far away. Their joy had been Lysette's dismay, a warning that her chances were fast escaping. And then, tonight, as soon as they had finished their meal, André had yawned and curled up at the mossy base of a large elm tree, falling asleep almost at once; sick at heart, Lysette had tossed restlessly nearby. At length, unable to sleep, she had left the dim woods and come to stand here at the crossroads, beneath the cold uncaring eye of the moon.

A sudden movement behind the shrine, a shadow darker than the nearby bushes, made her jump, aware of the isolation of the spot.

"Forgive me, Lysette. I did not mean to startle you." It was Narbaux's voice, strangely subdued. He stepped from beyond the bushes, and came to stand beside her, his bright hair pale and silvery in the moonlight. "I could not sleep."

"Nor I. Mayhap it is the night."

"Or the place." He turned and indicated the brambles. "There is a large rock beyond the thicket—not a velvet cushion, perhaps—but a pleasant enough spot to sit and watch the moon. . . ." He motioned with his hand and she followed him to a large flat boulder, tucking her skirts demurely around her as she sat. The moon shone full upon his face and she was surprised by the look she saw there. Distant, distracted, a small furrow carving a line between his brows. He did not at first seem inclined to speak; only when she stirred restlessly did he rouse himself and smile in sheepish apology for his silence.

"We are very near to home now. Less than a day's ride to Vilmorin and Chimère—though of course it will take us two days because the men are on foot." He lapsed again into silence, his eyes straying to the bright moon, the silvered shrine.

"Have you been here before?"

He laughed mirthlessly. "Many times. Many times . . ." His voice was heavy with remembrance. "It was our rendezvous . . . my brother and me . . . from the time I could ride alone. I would come here to meet him after he had been away—even when he came from Paris and it would have been easier to ride directly to Chimère. He would travel an extra half day—no matter how long the detour—knowing I was waiting here. And then we would ride home together. There might be pressing business at Chimère, or a charming wench from Vouvray to usurp his days, but here at the crossroads, and on that ride . . ." He smiled crookedly, his voice trailing off.

"And is he yet at Chimère?"

"He is dead."

"Oh."

"The smallpox."

Silence again. At length Lysette sighed, her face in the moonlight pensive and filled with regret. "They told me Guy had died because his heart burst within him. But how can that be so? How can something fail that was not there to begin with? *Mon Dieu,* do not pity me!" she exclaimed, as Jean-Auguste turned compassionate eyes to her. "I did not care! Have pity rather on the poor people of Soligne who were so often his victims. There was scarce a soul in all the village who would call him friend!"

"Why then, you must have been very lonely!"

His words were so unexpected, probing a wound she hardly knew existed, that she flinched and tears sprang to her eyes. She turned her head to the shadows so he would not see. Lonely. She had not allowed herself to think of it before. Lonely . . . there had never been a moment, in all the years since her father had died and she had gone to live with her aunt and uncle, that she had not been lonely, empty, waiting. She frowned. How dare Narbaux pry into her soul! "Lonely!" she sneered, tossing her head in contempt. "Only while Guy was alive!"

"Mon Dieu! Why did you marry him?"

She shrugged. "The years were passing. What was I to do?"

He laughed aloud at that. "And what are you now? Twenty? Twenty-one?"

She drew herself up. "Twenty-two!" she said haughtily.

"And with a face as sweet and fresh as a child's! Fear not, my lovely, you will be breaking hearts until you are in your dotage!"

His superior tone irked her. "Are you such an old man yourself that I must endure your condescension?"

"I have seen eleven more summers than you—for whatever it is worth in wisdom and experience."

"And André?"

"André is thirty-eight," he said sharply, "and sowing his oats almost before you were born!"

"Pooh!" she said, her temper rising. "Guy was near fifty!"

"Is it a husband you seek or a father?"

Furious, she jumped to her feet. "I seek a man," she said

scornfully, "though *le bon Dieu* knows where I shall find him!"
She turned to go, but his hand, firm on her arm, stopped her.

"I beg of you," he said earnestly, "do not seek for him at Vilmorin."

She wavered, minded to lash at him with sharp words, then changed her mind. It was really quite foolish to argue all the time over André. She was determined to have him, Jean-Auguste equally determined to prevent it, if he could. If she only remembered to hold her temper in check, all would be well. In many ways, Narbaux was a softling, surprisingly manageable, susceptible to her charms if she put her mind to charming him. And a pleasant man besides. Until André's name had entered their conversation, she had felt comfortable, at ease, sitting here with him in the moonlight. And though she had chafed at his intrusion this morning at the lake, she could not deny that his antics had made her laugh with a lightheartedness that was all too rare in her life.

"Must we quarrel?" she asked, eyes wide with dismay. "I should like to remember these last few days with pleasure, not the rancor of angry words!"

He ducked his head sheepishly. "Then let us be friends."

"Will you give me your hand on it?" she asked softly.

He clasped her fingers in a firm handshake, then turned her delicate hand this way and that, examining the slender fingers, the smooth skin that caught the light of the moon on its velvet surface. Surprised, she caught her breath, thinking for a moment that he would bring it to his lips; instead he chuckled, a rumbling laugh deep in his throat. "What a lethal weapon this is! By my faith, I have suffered less in some campaigns than I did from your dainty hand! Do you always attack your adversaries thus?"

"Never!" she giggled. "Most men are far more susceptible to smiles than to blows!" She stopped, surprised at her own frankness. It was odd. Though she hated his piercing eyes that saw through her games and deceptions, she felt comfortable, relaxed in his presence, as though his very awareness relieved her of the necessity of pretense.

He laughed. "Even I am susceptible to your charming smiles!"

"Though you mistrust me?" It was more a statement than a question.

"Though I mistrust you!"

She sighed in mock dismay and fluttered her eyes at him. "Alas! And here am I, a defenseless maiden, alone, in the dark of night. . . ."

"Beneath the full moon?"

She ignored his interruption. "In the dark of night, with a strange man who speaks to *me* of trust!"

"Fear not, fair maiden, I shall escort you to the safety of yon forest, where you may sleep peacefully in your leafy bower. . . ."

"And hard ground! *Mon Dieu*, but I shall welcome a soft bed!"

He grimaced. "In your leafy bower, where you may sleep in peace and dream of . . ."

"André!"

His face went hard, eyes narrowing to harsh lines. "You *are* a fool!" he spat, and turning, strode angrily into the woods.

They reached the river Loire by mid-afternoon of the next day, crossing a rickety wooden bridge just below Tours. Following the course of the river, they came at evening to a flat sandbar that jutted out into the placid waters; here they decided to make camp.

Lysette and Jean-Auguste had been coldly distant all the day; now, supper finished, they sat apart, Narbaux to puff thoughtfully on his pipe, Lysette to stare morosely into the fire and curse the bright moon, the open sandbar. Tomorrow. They would be in Vilmorin tomorrow. And not a patch of privacy in this whole cursed spot! It was enough to make her cry with frustration. Sighing deeply, she arose and sauntered to the edge of the river. Tucking her knees under her, she sat upon the sand and plucked idly at the leaves of a nearby shrub, tossing them into the gentle current. The sounds of the men slowly stilled behind her as, one by one, they settled in for the night and fell asleep. She had no wish to rest, to return to the campsite, to see André asleep in the moonlight, tantalizing, splendid, unattainable.

"Is it a water nymph, then, here by the shore, washed up by the river?"

She jumped at the sound of André's rich baritone and sprang to her feet, turning to greet him, her heart pounding wildly.

"More like a siren of the deep," said Jean-Auguste, his voice cool and amused, "waiting to trap the unwary!"

She wondered if he could see the look of contempt on her face, but she composed herself and smiled tightly. "Neither, Messieurs. Only a weary traveler, glad to see the end of this long journey."

André nodded in understanding. "I regret if it has caused you discomfort. I have been thinking of late that the sooner you are joined with your family at Chartres, the happier you might be. You are welcome, of course, to stay and rest at Vilmorin for as long as you wish, but whether or not I must mobilize a force and march to Corbie I will see to it that several of my men escort you to your brother at your convenience."

"You are very kind, Monsieur, and I shall be forever in your debt." She flashed a malicious glance at Narbaux, then smiled slyly to herself. This time she would best him! Let him try to interfere now! "But I have never thanked you properly for your goodness to me." Her soft voice caressed Crillon, the words meant for him alone. "Please . . . may I . . . André?" Aware that Narbaux watched helplessly, she put her arms about André's neck and stood on tiptoe, pulling his face down to hers. How tall he was! How handsome his strong face was in the moonlight! She made as though to kiss him on the cheek; at the last second she turned her face, the movement so natural it seemed an accident, and kissed him full upon the mouth, closing her eyes and swaying gently against him. He started, surprised, half convinced it had been his fault, and pushed her away, stumbling out an apology.

"Forgive me, Lysette . . . Madame . . . I had not meant . . ."

There was a note of mockery in Narbaux's voice, but his words were soothing, ever the mediator. "You scarce need to apologize, André! I have no doubt that Lysette appreciated the innocence of your kiss! You were not offended, *ma petite?*" He bent thoughtfully to Lysette.

Relieved, André turned back to the river, his mind already on other things. "Well then . . . let us enjoy the beauty of the night, and the prospect of home on the morrow. Look," he said suddenly, and pointed to a large leaf that glided gently on the placid river, swirling as it encountered small eddies, skimming across the glassy waters. "Do you suppose if Marielle were in the gardens of Vilmorin tonight, and cast a leaf into the Loire, it could reach us here?" He laughed softly at his own fancy, the sound barely hiding the aching loneliness in his voice.

Lysette heard only the pounding of her heart. He had not even noticed! He did not even care! She had trembled as she kissed him, and all he could speak about was an absurd leaf! And Narbaux knew. She could not even suffer her humiliation alone, but had only to turn her head to see his gloating grin. Murmuring a soft good night, she stumbled toward the campsite, hardly knowing whether to cry or scream, her hatred of Jean-Auguste as strong as her passion for André.

A strong hand gripped her arm and turned her about. Narbaux! She clenched her fists, tempted to strike him, but he held fast to her hands until her fury had abated. She could not even look at him.

"Perhaps it is for the best that André is blind," he said gently, his voice so filled with warmth and sympathy that she looked up in surprise, expecting to see mockery in his eyes. He smiled his crooked grin and brought her hands to his lips, uncurling her tense fingers and planting a tender kiss on the velvet skin. "For my part, *ma chère*, I think that any man who would spurn your kiss is a bit of a fool!"

Confused, unhappy, she choked back a sob of frustration and pulled her hands away, retreating to the safety of the campfire, and a night full of troubled dreams.

In the morning the young officers gathered around to bid them farewell. They were all men of Vouvray, merchants' sons, scions of the lesser nobility, moneyed enough to afford horses. Now that they were so close to home it seemed foolish to delay their arrival because of the slow pace of the foot soldiers. André paid them their due, advising them that he might again have need of their services, and watched them gallop off down the dusty road, his impatient heart filled with envy.

The path they followed took them along the edge of the river that flowed, wide and serene, to their right. On the left of the road, and at some distance, Lysette could see the line of the chalk cliffs, their pale yellow surface pocked with the hollows and natural caves that André had described. Here and there, a cave entrance had been covered with a wooden door, a small window. Sometimes a chimney poked incongruously above the line of the bluffs. They were indeed strange houses, tucked away into unexpected angles of the limestone, and Lysette smiled to see strings of laundry emerging from the very cliffs and geese perched precariously on rocky outcroppings.

Just after noon, Narbaux rode up beside Lysette and indicated a spot some distance ahead. Above the line of the trees she could see rounded turrets and a slate roof; she did not need to be told it was Vilmorin—the sudden joy that lit up André's face made it apparent. He quickened his horse's pace, while Lysette and Jean-Auguste followed suit, leaving the foot soldiers behind to straggle home in their own time.

Vilmorin was a large, golden-stoned chateau, its two wings perpendicular to the river and embracing a neat gravel courtyard into which they now rode. To their right, the land fell away into gardens and terraces until it reached the Loire, the wide expanses of lawn broken here and there by large old trees. Midway between the chateau and the river was a small building, a summerhouse, perhaps, that looked like a miniature castle with stone walls and tiny turrets, the whole bedecked with climbing roses.

Out of this building emerged a large and buxom woman, like a great ship in full sail, trailing in her wake two small boys. The elder one, as blond as André, began to jump up and down excitedly, and raced up the terrace toward them; the woman picked up the younger lad, a boy of two or so, with reddish brown curls, and hurried to them as fast as her large bulk would allow. André leapt from his horse and swept the elder boy into his arms; the younger one, suddenly shy and fearful, clung for a moment to the woman before letting himself be swung into the air in his turn.

Lysette watched the scene in agony, her heart filled with pain and jealousy, seeing André slip away from her. But there was more anguish to come. André by now had both boys in his arms and was chattering away to them, laughing and merry. Of a sudden he stopped, the smile frozen upon his face, his eyes drawn to the chateau. Lysette followed his glance. There in a doorway was a woman, the most beautiful woman she had ever seen. Dear God, she thought, let her not be Marielle! even as André slid the children slowly out of his arms and strode to her side, taking her hands and smiling down into her eyes.

She was tall and slender, with a regal bearing and elegance

that made Lysette painfully aware, for the first time, of her own short stature, her coarse clothes. Marielle's hair, a rich russet, was thick and curly, and she wore it loose and full about her face, rather than pinned up in the current fashion. She was clad in a taffeta gown of pale green that served to point up the smoky depths of her hazel eyes, the creamy opalescence of her skin. When she smiled up at André her face was lit by a radiance that made her glow. He kissed her gently and she blushed, suddenly shy in the presence of others.

Jean-Auguste dismounted and turned to Lysette, his hands raised in assistance; she shook him off, feeling isolated, preferring to keep her distance from a scene in which she was so obviously superfluous. There was a flurry of hugs and kisses as Marielle and Narbaux embraced like old friends, and the buxom woman clutched André in a hearty bear hug, receiving a resounding smack to her ample bottom as reward.

"Louise, you devil!" he laughed. "Have you been keeping that husband of yours out of mischief?"

"Aah! Grisaille can look after himself! It is enough to tend these twigs of yours!" She gestured with her chin at the two little boys, running happily among the adults, scarcely aware of the why of all this gladness, but enjoying it nonetheless. "Now go and kiss your wife like a rightful husband—none of your bird pecks—and leave the children to me! Mayhap your homecoming will end in more burdens for us all!" She snickered and jabbed André in the ribs, while Marielle flamed scarlet.

"André?"

Crillon turned at the soft plea in Lysette's voice, disconcerted at his own neglect. She smiled in forgiveness and held out her arms for his help; he swung her easily out of the saddle and led her to Marielle.

"Marielle . . . Lysette . . . Madame la Marquise de Ferrand. Lysette, my wife la Comtesse du Crillon. Lysette was caught up in the rioting at Soligne—we are escorting her to her brother at Chartres."

Marielle smiled warmly at Lysette. If she felt uneasy, her serene face did not betray it. "And will your husband, Monsieur le Marquis, join you in Chartres?"

"Alas! I have worn widow's weeds near to a year now—I am quite alone in the world! But for André's kindness . . ." she sighed and gazed worshipfully at him, letting the eloquence of her silence complete her words.

Was there a sharp edge to Marielle's voice? "Methinks my husband has long since found his metier as champion to unfortunate demoiselles! But you must all be weary. Louise! See to the travelers . . . hot water for baths . . . and send Dominique to attend Madame la Marquise . . . come, *mes petits.*" She picked up the younger boy and led the elder by the hand, sweeping past Crillon toward the chateau. "André, *mon chère,*" she said, as casually as though it had been only yesterday, rather than four months, since they had seen one another, "you will see to the horses, will you not?"

Chapter Seven

ANDRÉ FOUND MARIELLE AT LAST IN THE NURSERY WITH THE children, crouched down, exchanging secrets with the blond François. Eyes blazing blue fire, he strode into the room, oblivious to the look of alarm on the face of the young servant girl.

"You!" he barked at her. "Attend to the children!"

The poor girl nodded in fear and curtsied quickly, hardly daring to lift her head, trembling at the anger in his voice. So this is what it would be like, now that the master was home! She took François by the hand and led him to a corner where Alain was happily playing with small blocks of wood, piling them one atop the other and gurgling with joy as he demolished them in one sweep of his pudgy hand.

Without a word, André hauled Marielle to her feet, his hand firm about her slender wrist. Despite her squeaks of protest, he pulled her out of the nursery and down the wide corridor until he came to an open door that led to an airy sitting room, bright with the afternoon sun. Marching her inside, he slammed the door behind them and swung her around to face him, his arms circling her shoulders and waist.

"Now, Madame!" he growled, and crushed her in a fierce embrace, bending her backward over his arm, his mouth possessing hers in a hungry kiss. She responded ardently, her soft body yielding to him, slender arms twined about his neck.

74

When at last he released her, her breast was heaving and some of the anger had drained from his eyes.

"I vow, Madame, if ever you force me to seek you out again, I shall seek you with a switch from a willow tree," he said, his tone milder than his threat.

Her green eyes flashed dangerously. "Am I to sit about forever, then, until you choose to return home? Do you think that Vilmorin needs no overseer while you are away? There are tasks to be attended to, responsibilities to be borne—shall I abjure all this and wait, like some foolish sit-by-the-fire, for that moment when you deign to return and notice me?"

He smiled sheepishly and held out his hands in conciliation. "Marielle. Love. Only remember the months I dream of your welcoming kiss; vouchsafe me that, at least—no matter how pressing your duties."

She came in to his arms then, all supple compliance and tenderness, and when they kissed it was as equals, partners in love, each responding to the needs of the other. At length he lifted her in his arms, murmuring sweet endearments, and carried her to a little door cut into the paneling that led to his bedchamber. Pushing it open with his booted foot, he entered the room and then stopped, his handsome face twisted in annoyance. Within the room two young footmen were heatedly arguing about the placement of a large tub of steaming water. A gangly young servant, her face scarred by smallpox, was busily shaking out doublets and breeches from a large armoire. At the sight of the master, his lady in his arms, they gaped and shuffled about uncertainly. Wriggling out of André's grasp, Marielle stood up and smoothed her skirts, determined to salvage as much dignity as she could from the situation. She dismissed the servants with an imperious nod of the head, then thought better of it and called back the young girl.

"Suzanne. A moment." She rummaged through the armoire. "Monsieur le Vicomte de Narbaux will need fresh garments— see that he gets these." She handed the clothing to Suzanne, who curtsied quickly and vanished from the room. Pulling forth a fine linen doublet, Marielle laid it neatly on the bed and returned to fetch breeches and hose, shoes and a snowy cambric shirt, bustling about capably from armoire to bed to cabinet, once again the orderly mistress of her home. André sighed, looking in vain for his sweet beloved of but a minute before.

"Will you shave, André?" she asked. He nodded halfheartedly, then frowned and pulled her toward him, his mouth seeking hers. She answered his kisses with her own, but when he would have urged her down upon the bed she chided him gently. *"Nom de Dieu,* André. Not now! You are covered with dust and the bath is waiting and hot. Besides, we have guests and I must see to them. Please, *mon chér!"* She smiled seductively, her rosy lips pursed in invitation. "And in exchange I promise you I shall not leave your bed until cockcrow!"

"Hussy!" he laughed, slapping her bottom familiarly. "I shall hold you to that promise!"

While she set about filling a small basin of water and stirring up lather for his shave, he untied the long baldrick sash slung diagonally across one shoulder and stripped off his doublet. He removed his embroidered linen cuffs and untied the separate collar, rolling up his sleeves and turning back the collarless neckline of his shirt.

"It is not a very heavy growth," she said, stroking his raspy chin.

"No," he agreed, contemplating his face in the small mirror set into the shaving stand. "But then I shaved often on the journey."

"What a surprise it was to see Jean-Auguste with his mustache gone! I scarce recognized him! He has never been clean-shaven since first I met him!"

"No. It is perhaps twelve years that he has clothed his face thus."

"And then to shave it off?"

"I confess I was surprised. It was so sudden. And unexpected."

"Did he do it for her?"

Startled, André glanced at Marielle, mildly astonished at the question, wary of the sudden edge in her voice. "Mayhap," he said. "I had not thought of it before."

"And is that why you shaved so often?"

He put down his razor, minded to turn her about, to read the expression on the face she now kept hidden from him, but she stepped to the bathtub and busied herself with stirring the water. He shrugged and resumed shaving. Perhaps he had only imagined her sudden coolness.

She strolled about the room, fanning herself with dainty fingers. "It is so very warm! I can scarcely remember when September has troubled me so! But it has been good for the grapes—I think you will be pleased with the vineyards. Grisaille thinks the harvest can begin in a week or two." She sighed and contemplated her reflection in a large Venetian mirror, its etched and faceted edges casting sparkling rainbows on the chestnut hair that curled and flowed down her back. Putting her hands behind her neck, she piled the heavy tresses on top of her head, preening this way and that in the mirror. "Think you I should wear my hair up?"

He frowned. "I have always preferred it down! Why would you wish to change it?"

"It would be cooler on these warm days. *She* wears her hair up."

"What?"

"Your charming companion!"

"*Nom de Dieu,* Marielle! What foolishness is this?"

"She is very pretty!"

"I had not noticed."

Marielle turned to him, eyebrow raised skeptically, but fear lurked in the hazy depths of her green eyes. "When have you not noticed a pretty woman, more especially one you have traveled with? She is more than a little fond of you!"

He put down his razor and wiped the lather from his face. "Nonsense! Jean-Auguste, perhaps. They spent a great deal of time together. Come, come, Marielle, will you frighten yourself with false imaginings? Come and help me with my boots, and let us speak no more of Lysette." She winced at that, and he cursed himself for not using Lysette's title. In Marielle's present mood, even so slight a matter as names would feed her fears. Dutifully, she helped him off with his boots, and chattered idly about Vilmorin and the children as he stripped off his travel-stained clothes, but the coolness remained in her eyes. He was tempted to forget his promise and take her to bed forthwith, trusting in his lovemaking to provide the reassurance his words could not; but when he made as if to hold her, she pushed him away and reminded him of his bargain. Reluctantly he stepped into the tub, letting the soothing water ease his limbs, wishing it could as easily wash away his disquietude.

She smiled tightly at him, trying to keep her voice even, probing the wound that brought her pain, unable to leave it alone, though her heart ached within her. "And you and . . . Lysette . . . did you spend a great deal of time together . . . alone?"

Angry, he was about to retort, to refute such nonsense; then he remembered the kiss in the moonlight (*had* it been innocent?), the temptation of Lysette's femininity in the pine grove. He harrumphed and shook his head vigorously, but he found he could not meet Marielle's eyes.

"Well!" she said, her voice suddenly bright with forced gaiety. "I must attend to supper. I thought we might take a stroll in the long gallery before we dine; with the windows open to the garden and the river breezes, it is quite delightful on these warm evenings. Do hurry, *mon chér*. The children will want to see you again before they are put to bed for the night." She blew him a kiss and swept from the room, seeming as lighthearted as a country maiden.

Damn! he cursed to himself. Holding his breath, he let himself slide down into the tub until his head was submerged, fingers rubbing vigorously at his hair. Would that his troubled spirit could be cleansed as easily as his body!

Lysette lowered herself into the tub and breathed a sigh of contentment, luxuriating in the scented waters heavy with the fragrance of lilac. She closed her eyes and leaned back, enjoying the pleasure of being pampered and waited upon. She had almost forgotten how lovely it was when one had money; the rented house at Soligne had had but one servant, a surly old hag who grumbled at the smallest chores, and Guy's profligacy had put the luxury of perfume almost out of her grasp—she could never afford the extravagance of scented oils for the bath. She wondered how it would be in the chateau at Chartres, now that she was dependent on her brother and his wife.

"I trust, Madame, that the water is hot enough?"

Lysette opened her eyes. The maid Dominique was leaning over the tub, an obsequious smile on her thin face. "Thank you, Dominique," she said, "it is quite agreeable. I do not like it extremely hot."

Dominique giggled slyly. "Except sometimes, Madame?"

"Whatever do you mean?"

"You know, Madame!"

Lysette shook her head, mystified.

"Why should I wish it hot—even sometimes?"

Dark eyes flashing wickedly, the girl knelt beside the tub, her voice lowering as though it were a secret. "My grandmother used to say you could tell when a lady had been . . . indiscreet . . . with a man . . . if she feared he had left her with more than the memory of one night's pleasure . . . you understand . . ."—she rocked an imaginary child in her arms—". . . my grandmother said the lady would take her bath as hot as she could *bear* it . . . to keep herself from *bearing* the other, *n'est-ce pas?*" And here she snickered at her own cleverness.

"Mon Dieu!" Lysette's jaw dropped in surprise. "But are you sure?"

"Ah, Madame, everyone knows it is so!"

Lysette laughed ruefully. All those wasted prayers when she feared a child from Guy! Though her aunt had tried to teach her to be a proper wife and housekeeper, it was clear she had neglected an important part of her education. Well, it was soon remedied. "Tell me," she asked, "is that all?"

"I scarce know everything, Madame." She blushed. "I am still a maid myself . . . but my grandmother used to say that was why high-born ladies ride so much early in the morning!"

"Riding?"

"Look you, Madame. A farmer's wife . . . does she ride a horse? Nay! A wagon and team, mayhap, but not a horse! And have you never seen the numbers of children that hang about her skirts? But a fine lady of quality . . . I tell you, Madame, it must be so!" The two women nodded their heads in agreement. "When I am married," continued Dominique, "I shall not be such a fool as that farmer's wife! My father says my mother is his to do with as he wishes, and she has a duty to obey, but . . ." She shrugged her shoulders, her thin face sly as a ferret's.

"But if a husband knows naught of what his wife does, where is the disobedience if she does as she chooses?" They laughed together at that, maid and mistress, like two wayward schoolgirls.

There was a gentle knock on the door and a pale maidservant entered, an older woman with stooped shoulders and eyes that seemed frozen in a permanent squint.

"Louise sent me with clothing for Madame la Marquise, but I fear it will need a great deal of adjustment." She laid out petticoats and chemises, and a pale blue silk nightdress and peignoir. "These will be fine, I think. They were always too short for Madame la Comtesse, but alas!" She sighed and held up a dark blue taffeta skirt and bodice, obviously fashioned for the tall and willowy Marielle. She waited patiently while Lysette finished her bath and stepped out of the tub into the warm cloth that Dominique draped about her, indicating that Louise had also sent along fine silk stockings and a dainty pair of shoes that seemed small enough for Madame. Lysette nearly wept for joy at the softness of the slippers, after the agony of the heavy shoes she had been forced to wear on the journey. Sure enough, the chemise and petticoat were not too large; surprisingly, the bodice of the gown needed only a tightening of its back lacings for, while Marielle was a good deal taller than Lysette, she was also quite slender. The skirt was another matter. While the seamstress turned up a large hem, sitting close to a bright window and hunching over the work, her nose a few scant inches from her flying needle, Lysette allowed Dominique to comb out her hair.

"You have lovely hair, Madame," she said, her hands deftly twisting the glossy black tresses. "Prettier even than Madame la Comtesse."

"Do you tend Madame, Dominique?"

"No. Only Louise. She has been with Madame since she was a bride—she fusses over my lady like a mother hen with her chickens!"

"Do you like Madame la Comtesse?"

Dominique glanced uneasily at the seamstress at the window, then lowered her voice. "She is kind enough, I suppose, but she is very demanding. Always there are chores to be done!" She sulked unhappily. "I should have married long since—a fine carpenter in Vouvray—but I could not see him often enough! Just when I would try to steal away for a few hours, she would find new tasks for me!"

"And the carpenter?"

"There was another maiden in Vouvray who did not have chores at all! Well"—she shrugged—"mayhap it is for the best. Each time I see her now, she has a swollen belly!"

Lysette giggled. "And no horse to ride!"

At length the seamstress was finished with her work and Lysette slipped into the altered skirt. She smoothed the taffeta with her hands, then tugged at the low-cut bodice, snowy with fresh lace, until her bosom peeped forth beguilingly. There was a large vase of soft pink peonies in the room; she plucked several of the blossoms and laced them into her chignon, admiring their fresh color against the midnight of her curls. Dominique offered her a small rouge pot which she declined, preferring instead the air of helpless fragility that her own coloring suggested.

By the time she was shown into the gallery, André, Marielle, and Jean-Auguste were already deep into conversation. It was a long room, with black and white parquet tiling, sumptuous tapestries on the walls, and windows to the floor that had been thrown open to the pleasant evening. On one wall was a wide brocaded settee upon which Marielle, elegant in white silk, was seated. The two men, engrossed in their discussion, stood before her; at the sight of Lysette they bowed formally. Marielle smiled a warm greeting, but her uneasy eyes took in every detail of Lysette's costume. For her part, Lysette could hardly stop looking at André; if he was handsome in soldier's doublet and casque, he was positively splendid in a well-cut creamy linen.

"We are discussing Corbie," said Jean-Auguste. Lysette smiled brightly, but her heart sank. Corbie was the last thing she wished to talk of! "It seems that Louis and Richelieu and Monsieur, the King's brother, have already formed an army to retake Corbie. Marielle tells us that the King has left Paris in the hands of the Queen and the relief forces have marched out. Unless the King sends for us, I can hardly see that our help will be necessary after all."

"Nor can I," said André, smiling. Lysette did not need to feign pleasure; she was already thinking of how long she could reasonably linger at Vilmorin—in André's company. She laughed to herself. Never had she cared more about a military campaign than she did about the fate of Corbie!

"I, for one, shall be glad to be home at Chimère," said

Narbaux. "I have missed the grape harvest for the last two summers—it will be a pleasure to enjoy my lands this year!"

"Have you given any more thought to what we discussed?" asked André.

"What is that?" asked Marielle in mock alarm. "Some new deviltry that you two are planning?"

Jean-Auguste laughed. "Hardly that! You know that the wines of Chimère, though admirable in every way"—and here he bowed haughtily to André—"have never produced the revenue that your Vilmorin wines have. The land is perhaps not so well suited to vineyards—too uneven, too many caves." He shrugged. "Whatever the reasons, I have found it impossible to increase our returns. But the new holdings that his most gracious Majesty saw fit to bestow—"

"For the price of a musketball. A fair exchange!"

"Hush, André!" cried Marielle, making a face at him. "None of your gibes! You were as proud of Jean-Auguste as I was."

André grinned sheepishly, then turned to Narbaux. "You must pay me no mind. But tell Marielle your plans. . . ."

"Hardly plans, as yet—ideas merely. But the new lands comprise a large wood and a goodly number of tenant farmers. The Cardinal has spoken again and again of the need to make France self-reliant—I have no doubt I could obtain a loan to establish some sort of manufacturing. Glass making, perhaps, or even cloth. The silks of Tours have begun to enjoy a wide reputation—it might be possible to employ a master craftsman from there to instruct my tenants."

"Trade?" said Lysette with a sneer. "A nobleman in trade?"

André bristled. "There is no shame if the goods are derived from the gentleman's own domain!"

Narbaux laughed. "No need to defend my honor, mon ami! If I found enjoyment in forging Toledo steel, I should do so, though the Court buzzed with the scandal of it!"

"It is still trade to me," said Lysette, dismissing the subject with an airy toss of her head. She paced the gallery, hardly interested in their conversation, more concerned with how attractive she looked in the evening glow. Surely André must notice! A finely shaped lute hung on the wall, its wooden belly glistening, buffed by the hands of a loving craftsman. Looking to Marielle, who nodded her assent, Lysette lifted it down and began to pluck the strings, twisting the pegs and listening carefully to the sounds produced. She settled herself comfortably in a small armchair.

"Will you play a tune or two?" said André.

Lysette smiled, her deft fingers strumming soft chords; then with a wicked grin she began to play a raucous tune, a bawdy ballad she had heard on the streets of Soligne, piping out the words in a clear, sweet voice, the innocence of her face belying the rough verse. Jean-Auguste and André roared with laughter; Marielle's face was frozen in a polite smile, though it was clear from the flush that stained her cheek that the song was not to her liking. The song ended, André asked for another; this time Lysette chose a soldier's tune, an army ballad her brother had taught her—though the words were more harmless, the complex melody served to display her virtuosity, and she preened in the open admiration she saw in the eyes of both men.

"'There is yet another verse," said André, taking down a guitar and going to stand beside Lysette's chair. He played and sang it for her, repeating it again as she picked up the tune on the lute and tried to follow the words.

"You play so well," she said. "What shall we play together?"

He suggested a lively galliard, but she shook her head. "Do you know 'My Love is Fair'?" He nodded and strummed out the first chords; she picked up the melody and began to sing, a tender love song that came as much from her heart as her throat or her skillful fingers. His rich baritone joined her soprano, and the sweetness of the sound filled the gallery and vibrated in the silent air long after the song was finished.

Marielle sat quietly, her hand to her mouth, green eyes cloudy and troubled; at last she smiled faintly and rose. "That was charming. You are very gifted, Madame. You should perhaps go to Court. The King plays the lute himself; I have no doubt he would admire your playing greatly." She took Narbaux's arm and nodded to André, careful to avoid his eyes. "Shall we go in to supper?"

Though Marielle sat quietly at table, seeming to retreat more and more into herself, the men, freed from the burden of Corbie and the risk of a fresh campaign, ate and drank with abandon, their cares forgotten. Lysette, luxuriating in a well-cooked meal, a succulent joint, washed it down with more wine than was her wont, and soon the three were laughing and joking, filled with lighthearted gaiety, recounting for Marielle all their experiences on the journey.

"By my faith, Marielle," laughed André, "you should have seen Ussé's face!"

"Ah, my fine gentleman," said Lysette, pouting. "You may laugh now, but you scolded me most unkindly then—it was small comfort to know you were only concerned with my welfare!" She smiled a radiant smile to show him he was forgiven. Marielle bit her lip in dismay.

Jean-Auguste raised a cynical eyebrow. "I do believe, upon reflection, that Ussé was never a match for Lysette!"

She giggled. "But I thought I might be bested the day you caught me swimming alone!" She turned to Marielle, eyes wide. "Can you imagine? To think you are alone, secluded, and to come upon two such great oafs as these! They had passing sport at my expense, I can tell you!"

"It is of small matter," cut in Narbaux hurriedly.

Lysette's voice trilled gaily. "Small matter indeed! When I feared to leave the water lest my modesty be compromised?"

"It was a game only," said André, smiling uneasily at Marielle. "A few moments of foolishness, nothing more!"

"Yes, of course!" agreed Lysette in bright reassurance. And then, suddenly serious, "But I marked the number of scars you bore on your person, André. It must have been a fearful campaign!" And her soft eyes caressed him with tender concern.

"It was the campaign that won me my bride," he said softly, remembering, turning with fondness to his wife. But Marielle had heard only the intimacy in Lysette's voice, seen the ardor in those violet eyes; with a choking sound she fled the room, face as pale as her silk gown.

Jumping to his feet, André followed her, his forehead crumpled in a deep frown. For a moment, sounds drifted back into the salon—the angry rumble of André's voice in counterpoint to the shrill acrimony of Marielle's—then there was silence.

Lysette shifted uneasily in her seat, then rose and walked to the window as though nothing untoward had happened. Behind her she could hear the scrape of Narbaux's chair, and when he spoke she knew he was standing quite close to her.

"You are either a naive child or a heartless woman. If I were sure you had done that intentionally, I would break you over my knee like a wayward twig."

She turned to him, her eyes wide with pained surprise. "What do you mean? Can you suppose for a moment that I could be so cruel?" She collapsed into tears, burying her face in her hands. "I had not meant anything by it," she sobbed, her voice muffled. "It was foolish, I know. . . . The wine . . . I was feeling quite giddy. How shall I forgive myself if I have hurt them?" Helpless, she looked up at him.

His jaw was set in a hard line, but at the sight of her tearful face he wavered, his fierce glance softening, filled with sympathy for her, for her childlike thoughtlessness. He muttered under his breath and turned away.

With a heavy sigh she left the room, hurrying as quickly as she might to her bedchamber. Tears had always been her ultimate weapon, and she had had little doubt that he would melt under her onslaught; still, it would have been folly to remain in his presence and risk those piercing gray eyes. No matter how skillful her art, she could not sustain a protracted campaign under his withering stare. He would see through her and know that, in her heart, she was filled with triumph at the mischief her words had caused. Poor André! Who would comfort him, now that Marielle burned with jealousy?

Laughing to herself, she hurried to her room, careful to keep from skipping along the passageway, lest that hateful Narbaux be watching her.

Chapter Eight

LYSETTE TOSSED AND TURNED ON THE WIDE BED, UNABLE TO sleep. She had yearned for its softness for weeks, and now she could not find a comfortable spot, but lay wide-eyed and restless, watching the small candle sputter on the hearth. Perhaps it was the moon—on the wane, but still bright with autumn clarity—that flooded the room and forestalled sleep. It was a warm evening, with scarcely a breeze to disturb the soft window curtains; she felt suffocated on the big bed—the cloying closeness of the heavy velvet bed hangings, the pallet that engulfed her body. At last she rose, throwing on the blue silk peignoir, and padded barefoot about the room, jumpy and restless as a caged animal. She lit another candle and set it upon a small table next to a gilded armchair. Perhaps she might read for a bit. There were several books that had been left for her pleasure; she chose the least profound, a slim volume of verses, and tried to concentrate on the words. The sounds of the chateau, the night, the room, intruded on her thoughts. The ticking of the small clock on the mantel. The hoot of a distant owl. Soft footsteps that seemed to whisper in the corridor just beyond her door. It was no use. She put down the book and went to the door. Perhaps a stroll in the garden or the breezy gallery that looked out upon the terraces and the river.

The corridor was lit only by a candle or two, and the cool tiles were pleasant on her bare feet. She made her way down the polished marble staircase and searched out the long gallery. It was most agreeable here. Some of the floor-length windows had been left open to the night and the air was sweet. The black and white tiles of the floor were punctuated at regular intervals by strings of moonlight that poured from the evenly spaced casements; the shadows between soft and dark as velvet. She stepped to the nearest open window, meaning to go out into the garden, then stopped, her heart pounding in her breast.

Bathed in moonlight, his golden hair turned to silver, André paced the wide lawn, head down, hands behind his back, lost in thought. Once or twice he absently plucked a rose from the wall of the small summerhouse nearby, worrying it with his fingers until it was reduced to shreds.

Ah, *Dieu!* Her heart soared with longing and desire. Would there ever be a more opportune moment? She would go to him, tell him of her love, take what love he could give her, and be content. He could hardly be cold to her ardor—had he not shown his hunger, his need that day in the grove? And again when she had fallen into his arms? It was not foolish. He did love her! He did!

Trembling, she took one step toward the open window. Suddenly, from the shadows there emerged an arm—strong, sinewy, white-shirted—that blocked the doorway. She drew in her breath sharply and turned to face Jean-Auguste. No! she almost screamed aloud. Not this time! He would not stop her! He could not! She pushed with both hands against the rigid arm, implacable as the bars of a cage, that stood in her way. That kept her from Love, waiting in the soft night. They struggled silently, he with the calmness that was part of his nature, she with a fury born of desperation; when she would have slipped under his arm, he grabbed her from behind, strong hands on her shoulders, and held her fast. She sobbed in frustration and tried to turn about, to pummel him with her fists; unexpectedly he released one shoulder and pointed out into the garden.

Under the soft moonlight, Marielle's gown shimmered and billowed, the ribbons and laces fluttering in the night air in rhythm to her flying feet. André stopped and turned, and held out his arms to receive her in welcoming embrace. Two silvered bodies merged into one; lips, arms, twined and fused, a joining that seemed to deny there had ever been separation. Stricken, Lysette watched in tormented fascination, helpless to turn away, unable even to close her eyes against the sight that tore at her vitals. Even after André had picked up Marielle in tender arms and carried her into the small summerhouse, she could not move from the window, but stood staring out on the shining lawn as though its very emptiness belied the living beings who had so recently kissed in the moonlight.

At length, with a sob she fled, grief and shame speeding her on, to the safety of her bedchamber.

"Lysette!"

Narbaux caught at her arm as she reached the door, and swung her about, his face etched with concern. His very solicitude turned her misery to fury, drying up her tears with the heat of anger.

"*Nom de Dieu,* Lysette," he said gently, "will you rest content at last?"

How dare he! But for him, she might have been out there in the garden with André, and Marielle left to weep in her pillow this night! She shook his hand free, her jaw outthrust in stubborn determination. "If I can take him away from her, I shall!" she said viciously, "though a score of Jean-Augustes block the way!" She pushed past him into her room but he followed, closing the door behind him and leaning up against the paneling. By the light of the candles his gray eyes glittered like cold steel, his patience stretched thin.

"I warn you," he said, his voice deep and firm, "if you break Marielle's heart . . ."

"Marielle! Always Marielle! Do you think I am a fool? I have seen the way you look at her! Does André know, I wonder, how you look at his wife?" She smiled maliciously at his sudden discomfiture, noting with satisfaction that his iron glance had wavered, and a flush stained his cheek. "Lovely Marielle," she purred, her voice heavy with sarcasm. "Sweet Marielle. So good! So kind! The queen of Vilmorin—beloved by *all* her subjects!" She flounced about the room and drew herself up haughtily, holding out her hand to him in regal condescension. "How good of you to come, Jean-Auguste," she said, in cruel mockery of Marielle's voice. "When I tire of my husband, I shall be yours!"

"Stop it."

She tossed her curls at him. "Were you wounded in your last

campaign, *mon chère?* André and I were so proud of you! *I* was so proud of you!"

"Stop it, Lysette."

"You are both such brave soldiers—mayhap we could hold a tournament to see which one of you shall win my hand. The hand of the sweet, kind, good Marielle!" She danced in front of him, her face mocking Marielle's sweet serenity, her voice shrill with scorn.

"Stop it!" he growled, shaking her by the shoulders. And then his arms were around her, his mouth on hers, crushing her lips in a fierce kiss. She struggled in his embrace, imprisoned as much by the unexpectedness of his attack as by his encircling arms, her hands pushing frantically against his chest. But his mouth, warm and insistent, seemed to drain her of all resistance; his lips were firm, sweet, young. Young. It was a new and strange sensation, to be held, to be kissed thus, to be overwhelmed by youth. How could she ever have sold herself to Guy? Her heart caught, and a hungry sadness welled up within her breast; for the wasted years with an old man, for the sweetness of a kiss on the wrong lips. It should have been André. Ah, *Dieu,* it should have been André! Desperately she clung to Narbaux, her arms encircling his neck, and yielded to his ardent embrace, the strong arms that held her fast and made her forget for a moment her grief and disappointment. The tension drained from her body and she swayed against him, all soft willingness; as if in response to her surrender, his mouth was of a sudden gentle, no longer ravishing, but wooing. He kissed her chin, her cheeks, her soft earlobes; when she closed her eyes and dropped her head back, his lips explored the velvet hollows of her throat and neck. It was so comforting, so soothing. She felt warmed, calmed, like a child who clings to a favored toy to ward off the terrors of the night.

His hands had been around her waist; now he reached up and disengaged her twining arms from his neck, his fingers caressing their soft contours from wrist to elbow to curved shoulders. She trembled at the unexpected sensations his touch aroused, a strange tingling that seemed to start from deep within her, the sound of her own blood pounding in her temples, a warm tide coursing through her. He stroked her breasts through the silken peignoir and the tide became a flame that took her breath away. She did not resist when he slipped the peignoir from her shoulders; even when he loosed the drawstring of her nightdress and it fell about her ankles, she welcomed his gentle hands on her naked body. She had never known it could be like this; Guy, thinking of his own pleasure, had made scant effort to please her. She had come to believe a woman endured, tolerated, no more. She had been kissed a few times by her admirers, and had been pleased to discover a certain excitement that had been lacking with Guy, but nothing so extraordinary that she even gave it a second thought. Now, with Jean-Auguste's hands and mouth setting off rockets within her, she wanted it to go on forever.

Tenderly he lifted her and carried her to the bed, placing her gently down and sitting beside her. She lay passive, her eyes closed, every nerve and fiber concentrating on the waves of feeling that swept over her, unfamiliar and wonderful. His lips burned on her breast, his soft hands ranged her body, seeking out secret places that made her tremble and quiver in ecstasy. It was lovely. Lovely. She felt her senses reeling, slipping out of control—she alone existed in the void, she alone, and the fire that raged within her.

Suddenly, unexpectedly, she felt his weight leave the bed. Annoyed, feeling the excitement fade away, she opened her eyes and raised herself up on her elbows. His back was toward her; he had stooped to remove his boots and stockings. He straightened and pulled his shirt over his head; through half-closed eyes she admired the smooth sleekness of his back and shoulders, the strength of his muscular arms. She noted the scratches he still bore from their encounter that day near the lake, and she smiled indulgently and tenderly. Ah, *Dieu,* let him only caress her again and ignite the flames—she would never more raise her hands against him! He stepped out of his breeches and turned to her. Her eyes swept his body, seeing the fierceness of his passion, and she gasped, comprehending at last. As he lowered himself to the bed, panic began to rise within her. She did not want his body! His seed! His child!

She had only wanted the pleasure he gave to her. She felt somehow betrayed—by him, by her own passion, by stubborn reality. With a small cry, she clamped her knees together and tried to ward him off with her hands, sluing her hips away from his potent loins. Caught off guard, he sat back on his heels, watching her cringing form, scarcely believing his senses. Then, with a strangled oath, his eyes glowing like hot coals, he grabbed at her legs and pulled her under him. She struggled furiously, her fingernails raking his shoulders, but he parted her thighs with hands that were strong and determined, and entered her quickly, violently, so she cried out in shocked surprise. Even as she writhed and twisted, hating him, hating herself, she felt the cool smoothness of his chest upon her bosom, his mouth, so alive, so young, pressing on hers; despite her will, she felt herself yielding to him, responding to his passion, her hips rising to meet his every thrust.

It should have been André. André! She saw him suddenly before her—the handsome face, the warm blue eyes—as a wrenching thrill raced through her body, and Jean-Auguste shuddered and collapsed against her. It should have been André. Narbaux withdrew and sat up, half expecting a response; when none was forthcoming, he arose from the bed and began to gather his things. It should have been André! With a heartbroken cry she turned on her side and began to sob bitterly. Drawing on his clothing, Jean-Auguste watched in dismay, hardly knowing what to do. At length he leaned over her.

"Lysette." He touched her gently on one quivering shoulder, but she shook him off and wailed all the louder. In a moment he had left the room, closing the door softly behind him. She wept for a very long time, pouring out her disappointment and longing for André, wondering, even as she did so, how it was possible to feel so miserable, yet so strangely content, at the same time.

The horse raced into the wide meadow; its hooves, crushing the grass that shimmered under early morning dew, left a dark green trail through the pale haze. Wielding her riding crop, Lysette urged the mare ever faster—as though the devil rode at their heels—until the dew jetted upward in tiny sprays with each flying step.

And perhaps, after all, she was bedeviled. She had awakened early and sat up in a panic, remembering the night before. What was it Dominique had said? A hot bath. But it was too early.

There was no one stirring. And already she seemed to feel the dreaded seed growing within her! Damn Narbaux! She dressed quickly, putting on her old travel clothes. If she were lucky, she might find a stable boy astir who could saddle her horse. She discovered one curled up in the stall next to her mare; a couple of sharp kicks to his sleeping form brought him quickly to his feet, and ready—if not exactly pleased—to serve Madame la Marquise.

Now she rode fiercely, bobbing up and down in the saddle, her hair wild about her face. It must be so, what Dominique had said about riding. Could she not feel her insides jouncing with every stride of the horse, dislodging the enemy that would inhabit her womb? She thought again of Jean-Auguste and was filled with righteous anger; it was he alone who was responsible! After all, he had raped her, violated her person, gone against her will and her wishes. She did not care to dwell on her contribution to what had happened; she knew only that somehow she had let her guard down and Narbaux had taken control of the situation. In the future she must be more careful; now that she knew that a man's kiss could thrill her so she must be vigilant, lest another kiss, another man—André even!— reduce her to helpless victim. Still, she thought with a smile, slowing her horse to a walk, it had not been entirely unpleasant. There might come a time in her life when she would be willing to surrender totally to a man, let herself be swept away, though she could scarce envision it now, even with André. She liked having her way—she liked being the focus of a man's attention and concern, without having to reciprocate. Let the Marielles of this world subjugate themselves to a man's needs; if she could get what she wanted at the price of a smile or even a kiss or two, all the better.

She headed the horse back toward Vilmorin, letting the mare choose its own path, past orchards and carefully sculpted hedges. Just before the stables, she came upon a small, semicircular line of trees that turned away from the chateau and enclosed a patterned garden, centered with a splashing fountain and a small stone bench. She entered the garden, meaning to enjoy its seclusion for a few moments; too late she saw that Jean-Auguste was standing beneath one of the trees, deep in thought. He looked up in surprise, then strode toward her, his expression unreadable. She fidgeted uncomfortably in the saddle, half minded to bolt, feeling more awkward than angry. They stared at one another for long minutes, then, without a word, he lifted his hands to assist her down. She shrugged and dropped the reins, sliding into his outstretched arms; he set her on her feet and held her for a moment, strong hands about her waist. Perhaps it was the memory of the night before, his overpowering strength and masculinity, but she found herself for the first time conscious of how he towered above her; angrily she pushed his hands away, disliking the sudden feeling of helplessness, and sat down on the bench. She did not feel so small if she were not standing with him, and if he chose to sit beside her, his long legs stretched out before him, they would be nearly equal.

He slapped her horse's rump, sending the mare in the direction of the stables, then sat at the far end of the bench, staring morosely at the tip of one dew-stained boot. "I am surprised you rode out this morning," he said at last. "I should have thought you had had your fill of riding ere now."

She nearly laughed aloud at that, with the smugness of one who holds a secret, then remembered she should hate him for being the cause of her wild ride. "Can you blame me?" she said caustically. "My bedchamber scarce holds pleasant memories!" And smiled to see her barb had hit its mark.

He squirmed unhappily and kicked at a small pebble near his boot. "As to that . . . methinks I owe you a profound apology . . . and an honorable offer of marriage." He raised his head and looked at her intently, but the cool gray eyes, so expressive when they probed her soul, told her nothing.

"Do you offer marriage to every woman whose bed you invade?" Her violet eyes flashed maliciously, her voice heavy with sarcasm. "Or . . . could it be . . . am I the first? O callow youth! O more than fortunate Lysette! To be the vessel for Love's first thunderbolts!"

He flamed red at her cruel taunt, his jaw set in a hard line, but when he spoke his voice was low and controlled. "I am not usually given to raping a woman . . . nor even taking advantage of her unhappiness . . ." Lysette looked up sharply, feeling suddenly exposed, vulnerable. Jean-Auguste smiled wryly, his eyes full of regret. "I am aware that I was a poor substitute for André. Nevertheless, I dishonored you, and in recompense I offer you marriage if you wish it." He turned away again, once more preoccupied with his boot.

Lysette seethed. Oh, the effrontery of the man! To presume to read into her heart, to intrude on her feelings for André! And then to ease his conscience by offering her marriage, aware that she must surely refuse! She stood up, tempted to strike him across the face with her riding crop.

"Good morrow!"

It was a smiling André who greeted them, leaping from his horse and striding into the small garden. "I marked the trail in the damp grass and wondered who was riding before me!" Eyes twinkling merrily, he indicated Lysette's tousled hair. "It would seem, *ma petite,* that you rode with demons!"

She blushed, her hands flying to her tangled curls, embarrassed that he should find her so unkempt. Then her heart sank within her, remembering the figures in the moonlight, the reason for his gaiety this morning, and she pinned her chignon carelessly. After all, what did it matter? He might smile at her, look into her face—but those warm blue eyes were seeing only Marielle. He spread his arms wide, gulping in great draughts of air. *"Mon Dieu,* but it is good to be home! And you, Jean-Auguste—what do you propose? Will you stay a day or two at Vilmorin?"

Narbaux rose easily from the bench and shook his head. "Nay! I too have missed my home. I shall ride to Chimère after breakfast. It will allow me the better part of the day to see the vineyards."

Lysette looked up, surprised. "Is Chimère so near, then?"

"A good hour's ride, no more," answered André.

Jean-Auguste smiled. "Near enough for me to take my revenge! I have not forgot that you bested me when we hunted last autumn! I vow the red stag will be mine this year—more than a match for that roebuck you took last November!"

André clapped him on the back. "And if you do, I shall toast you in good Vilmorin wine!" It was a fresh challenge.

"When the harvest is in, *mon ami,* it will be the wines of Chimère of which the poets will sing!"

Lysette stood quietly, listening to the banter of old friends, feeling isolated, excluded from their warmth. She hated André. He had friendship. He had love. And not a crumb of kindness left over to see how her her heart ached for him. He smiled at her . . . impersonal, indifferent . . . she might have been a servant, an underling, a stone in the wall of his beloved Vilmorin. She longed to cry out: Look at *me! See me!* See how I love you!

"And you, Lysette," he said, "will you stay for a few days before you go to Chartres? Marielle would welcome female companionship, I have no doubt."

"I shall not go to Chartres," she said impulsively. "Jean-Auguste has asked for my hand in marriage. I . . . have . . . decided to accept his proposal."

André grinned in pleasure, while Jean-Auguste, struggling to hide his surprise, smiled tightly and crossed to Lysette's side, his eyes stormy and troubled as they searched her face. Dutifully he bent to kiss her, his hands gentle on her shoulders; she responded stiffly, torn with uncertainty, half minded to recall her words, feeling Andre's eyes upon her.

"I scarce can tell you how pleased I am!" exclaimed André, shaking Narbaux's hand warmly. "Chimère has long needed a woman's presence—and such a lovely and charming one as Lysette!" He turned to her, his blue eyes suddenly serious. "Jean-Auguste has been like a brother to me . . . how gladsome to welcome a sister!" He kissed her tenderly on one cheek, mistaking the sudden tears that sprang to her eyes as a surfeit of happiness, then turned again to Narbaux. "You will marry here, of course, in the chapel of Vilmorin. Marielle would not hear of anything else!" Jean-Auguste nodded in agreement, but said nothing. "And when is it to be?"

"I must see to Chimère—it should be made ready. . . ."

"Then Lysette must stay here, for propriety's sake. Will you wait until after the grapes are in?"

Narbaux looked thoughtful. "Perhaps it would be best . . . and it will give Lysette a chance to write to her brothers . . . a few weeks . . ."

A few weeks! To stay at Vilmorin—to see André happy—to imagine Marielle in his arms. "No!" she cried sharply. "I do not wish to wait so long! I scarce need my brothers' consent—there will be time enough to write to them after the ceremony . . ." She stumbled and stopped, aware that the two men eyed her strangely. She laughed demurely, and lowered her eyes, suddenly the shy maiden. "And we have had such a long courtship already—through Angoumois and Poitou—I could not bear to wait for weeks and weeks." Unable to manage a blush, she turned her back to them and hung her head.

"Very well. A week at most." Narbaux's voice was uncertain, and when she turned to meet his eyes she saw skepticism in their gray depths. She smiled tenderly to convince him of her sincerity, and was gratified to watch the doubt fade from his face. For his part, André was vastly amused by the whole exchange.

"Oho, my friend," he teased, "such impatience from your bride speaks well of you! I wonder if the women of the Court know how empty will be their days—and nights—when Lysette shall be at your side as Vicomtesse."

Jean-Auguste smiled crookedly. "And the men will envy me, will they not, *ma chère?*" His eyes, cool and searching, perused Lysette's face with such sharp scrutiny that she turned away, flustered, uneasy, wondering if he had truly accepted her reason for haste.

"Come!" said André. "Let us tell Marielle at once." He threw one arm about Jean-Auguste's shoulder and held out his other hand to Lysette, meaning to lead them both back to the chateau.

"Please." She shook her head. "I should like . . . just for a little . . . to be alone. You understand . . ." She bit her lip and fought back her tears, praying they would read modesty and sensitivity into her sudden emotion, rather than the unhappiness that now threatened to engulf her. André nodded understandingly and the two men circled the line of trees and headed back to the terrace. They made a strange contrast: André, looking for all the world as though it were he who had just been betrothed, laughed and joked animatedly; Narbaux plodded along beside him, hands behind his back, his face frozen in a lugubrious smile.

Lysette watched them out of sight, then slumped onto the bench and gave way to her misery. The reluctant bridegroom, she thought bitterly. He no more wanted to marry her than she did; he had felt honor bound to propose, that was all. But what had possessed her to accept? Was it the loneliness? Her envy of André and Marielle, that they should have each other, and a future together, while she had only the emptiness of Chartres and the meager gleanings from her brother's life?

And yet . . . why *not* marry Jean-Auguste? She sat up resolutely and wiped the tears from her eyes. Unlike Guy, he had money, estates, position. And he was kind and good, comfortable to be with. It was strange: Guy had been none of those things, though she had seen him through the eyes of youthful romance; yet not even her dislike of Jean-Auguste in their weeks together had served to blind her to his decency.

And he was perhaps more manageable than she had at first supposed, despite his piercing eyes. She was not sure that she had deceived him, yet he had been willing to advance the wedding, whatever her reasons, simply to please her. If he continued to be so agreeable as a husband, she might find this marriage very much to her liking. She frowned suddenly, remembering the night before. If only she did not have unpleasant obligations as a wife! It had been so lovely, indulging her senses, luxuriating in his kisses and caresses—if that were all he expected of her she would welcome him to her bed every night! But she had turned Guy aside often enough—she felt certain she could cool Jean-Auguste's ardor, more especially as he scarcely wanted the marriage in the first place.

She rose from the bench and smiled to herself. No, there was hardly a reason to be unhappy after all. All would be well. She would be Madame la Vicomtesse de Narbaux, with a fine husband and a good life. She made for the chateau, feeling pleased with herself, her rational decision.

Wicked Lysette. Save reasoning for the world. She paused on the grassy terrace, willing her heart to stop its wild beating, her brain from crying out the only reason that mattered, that had ever mattered: Chimère was a scant hour from Vilmorin—she had a lifetime now to be near to André, to love him, to win him.

Chapter Nine

"By my faith, Marielle, it is the most beautiful gown I have ever seen!"

Lysette swirled about the bedchamber, noting with pleasure how the taffeta folds of her skirts rustled silkenly, springing forth from the snug bodice. The gown, a soft purple, the color of wood violets, was trimmed at the waist with ribbons and rosettes. The sleeves, long and puffed, were slashed from shoulder to wrist—the slashes edged with more ribbons and silver lace—allowing the white satin undersleeves to peek through. The low-cut bodice, adorned with a lace-edged falling band, a kind of wide collar, accented the graceful curve of her bosom.

Marielle smiled. "I can scarce imagine what blandishments Jean-Auguste held forth to the merchants of Vouvray, to persuade them to work so diligently in your behalf!"

"Nor at what cost, *mon Dieu!*" Lysette shook her head in amazement. All week long Vilmorin had been filled with tradesmen, sent by Narbaux—silk merchants, seamstresses, bootmakers. She had started by ordering only what she might need; as the parade of shopkeepers had continued, she had indulged herself more and more, giving in to the smallest urges for this pair of embroidered stockings, those satin shoes balanced precariously on high cork heels. Marielle had suggested and advised, apprising her of the current fashions of the Court, the proper outfits for dancing at Fountainebleau, hunting at

Versailles. Lysette was dazzled. Though her father had held the title of Baron, he had not enjoyed life at Court and they had lived simply in the chateau near Chartres; the few times that Guy had taken her to Fountainebleau she had been self-consciously aware of the shabby plainness of her gowns, and had urged him to refuse as many invitations as possible, that she might not suffer in humiliation.

But Jean-Auguste was favored at Court; at his side, and dressed thus, what social heights might she not scale! She danced about the room, preening herself in the mirror, remarking how the color of the silk exactly matched her eyes. How thoughtful of Jean-Auguste! Though Lysette had had her choice of dozens of fabrics, Narbaux had personally selected the violet taffeta, and had sent it along to her with a note requesting she have it made into her wedding gown. It was a brief note, casual and noncommittal, the only word she had had from him all week. Still, it had been kind of him, and unexpected. As if in echo to her thoughts, Marielle spoke.

"How thoughtful of Jean-Auguste to have chosen that color for you! He must care for you greatly!"

Lysette smiled tightly. "It is only that he . . . notices much— the color of a woman's eyes . . . the secrets of a woman's heart." She tossed her curls airily. "I have no doubt he knew that I should have chosen the color myself, without his prompting! And as for caring—his heart was given long ago, I think!"

Marielle's head snapped up sharply at the tone in Lysette's voice. "Given, perhaps . . . but not taken," she said softly. "Never taken. And long since recalled." As Lysette squirmed uneasily at her words, Marielle stood up and placed a gentle hand on the violet sleeve. "I would be as a sister to you, as he has been like a brother to me—only a brother. What might have happened—and did not—was long ago, and of no importance anymore."

"Of course!" Lysette's voice trilled gaily. "How wise you are . . . sister!" And laughed at her own foolishness. What nonsense! To feel even a moment's pang of jealousy. Ridiculous! If Jean-Auguste had loved Marielle once—or loved her still!—what did it matter? It was André she wanted, and she did not feel jealousy toward Marielle for that—only hatred, and the nibblings of an uneasy conscience.

Marielle moved toward the door. "I shall leave you to dress for supper. There are things that need my attention." She paused, hand poised on the doorknob. "André is my whole life . . . as I am his." Then she was gone.

Lysette frowned at the closed door and tugged viciously at the lacings of her gown. The maid Dominique, who had been waiting quietly in a corner of the large bedchamber, rushed to her assistance. Lysette stood patiently as Dominique worked, but her brain seethed in turmoil. What had Marielle meant? She was gentle and sweet, and her soft green eyes smiled kindly, but Lysette had begun to suspect that they hid a discerning mind, an intuitive understanding every bit as sharp and piercing as Jean-Auguste's.

André had been busy in the vineyards all week, in preparation for the harvest; Marielle, ever the efficient chatelaine, had run the household, and cared for the children, and arranged for the wedding and the small party that would follow. Yet it seemed to Lysette, upon reflection, that there had not been a moment throughout all the days when she had been alone with André. Now she began to wonder: had Marielle intended it thus? Lysette had hoped to meet him on one of his early morning rides, but this week he had never been alone: Marielle was often with him, and once or twice he took along the young François, perched happily in front of his father's saddle. She had even climbed the bluffs to the vineyards, thinking to accost him in the fields; no sooner had she greeted him warmly than Louise puffed into view, carrying a jug of ale and a savory meat tart.

And now she was to be married upon the morrow. Narbaux would arrive in the morning for the noon wedding; there would be food and wine and dancing, and enough daylight left to see them safely home to Chimère before dark. If she did not declare her love to André this night, there might be scant opportunity in the months ahead. She smiled determinedly at her reflection as Dominique helped her on with a pale pink gown, one of her favorite choices because it made her look helpless and fragile. And André had not yet seen it. After supper, when they had all retired for the night, she would knock softly at his door, and play the soft bride, all blushing and fearful, a sister needing the strong comfort of her brother. She would cry on his shoulder and tell him of her doubts; with his arms around her, it was a small step from sister to lover.

André and Marielle were already seated at the ends of a long oak table, facing one another, when she entered the salon. André rose easily to greet Lysette and lead her to her place at the center of the table; as always, her heart caught in her throat at sight of him. She danced prettily away from the proffered chair and pirouetted about in a swirl of pink, carefully avoiding Marielle's eyes.

"Well, monsieur?"

His handsome face beamed approval, and she felt herself tingle down to her toes.

"Charming!" he said. "Jean-Auguste will quite spoil you before the marriage has yet begun! Marielle, *ma chère*, I wonder you do not often wear that shade of pink—it is most becoming!"

Marielle smiled tensely, but said nothing.

Lysette seated herself and sipped the wine that André poured, shrugging off his compliment as though she had not inveigled him into it in the first place.

"It would be so much more becoming had I one jewel to wear with it! I feel quite naked without a single pearl or locket!" Her slim fingers touched lightly at her bodice, the delicate movement catching André's eye and leading his glance— almost involuntarily—to the creamy perfection of her bosom.

"I have no doubt that Jean-Auguste will have thought of that. I am minded of the fine jewels his mother wore when we were yet lads." André grinned as Lysette's eyes sparkled. "Never fear! You shall be adorned as befits a Vicomtesse!"

Lysette smiled shyly. "I scarcely can believe my good fortune. To have found an amiable husband . . . and gracious friends"—her sweeping arm took in André and included Marielle at the last moment—"who would have thought, when I left Soligne, that the *bon Dieu* would smile so kindly upon me? And I have not thanked you yet for your gift!"

"I had thought to give Lysette the mare and saddle that brought her through the long journey," said André, as Marielle looked up in surprise. "She rides well, and the mare is a spirited mount."

"Yes, it is a fine gift," said Marielle. "I only wish I could have matched it. Lysette will need a personal maid at Chimère—I have agreed to let Dominique serve her."

"But Dominique will suit me well!"

"Nay! She is lazy and troublesome—perhaps it is her youth. She has just turned seventeen. At any event, you must ride her hard. I should have preferred to send Suzanne to you." Marielle shook her head, mystified. "But when I suggested it to Jean-Auguste before he left, he was adamant. He would have none of her!"

"Suzanne?" asked André. "The lass who is scarred by the smallpox?" Marielle nodded. "Mayhap it is because of Gabriel."

"His brother."

"Yes."

"But . . . he died of the smallpox!" exclaimed Lysette suddenly. "I remember that Jean-Auguste spoke of him once."

"Yes. They were very close," said André. "Gabriel was nearer my age . . . we grew up together. He was master at Chimère long before my father died. It was not until I had inherited Vilmorin, and Gabriel was in his grave, that Jean-Auguste and I became fast friends."

Lysette shivered. "Must we speak of such terrible things? If I am to be married tomorrow, I wish to be gay tonight!" She smiled brightly at them both, saving her tenderest glance for André. How she ached for him! Would this tedious supper never end? She scarcely took note of what she ate or drank, or what she said; her mind rehearsed again and again the scene in his bedchamber, the moment when she would be in his arms, and he unable to resist the lure of her passion. As the evening wore on, she made less and less of an effort to notice Marielle, or include her in her conversations, so rooted was she upon André and her fantasy.

"Mon Dieu!" André leaped to his feet, his face wreathed in smiles. "But what a surprise!" Lysette, still focused upon him alone, reluctantly dragged her eyes away and turned to the doorway that seemed to hold her attention.

Jean-Auguste stepped out of the dim corridor into the salon. The light of the chandelier shone full upon his open face; his countenance was pleasant enough, but his eyes glittered in a way that made Lysette fidget in her chair. Had he seen the way she looked at André—standing hidden there in the shadows of the doorway for who knew how long? She felt a hot flush creep up from her bosom and burn her cheeks. To cover her embarrassment, she rose quickly from her chair and hurried to greet Jean-Auguste at the door, noting as she did so that, while André gaped in surprise, Marielle seemed hardly ruffled by Narbaux's sudden appearance.

"But . . . what brings you to Vilmorin tonight?" Lysette stammered.

His mouth twitched in a crooked smile. "I thought, mayhap, my bride might be restless . . . or bored. Besides, Chimère is waiting and ready—there is no more to be done. I thought I might spend my last night as a bachelor with my comrade in arms, drinking to the future . . . and the past!"

"And welcome you are!" boomed André. "Did you ride over alone?"

"No. I took one of my grooms with me, and several horses. I shall send him back tomorrow with Lysette's maid and her baggage."

"Will you take supper?"

"Indeed, yes." He doffed his wide-brimmed hat and swept his mantle from his shoulders, laying them across a chair. "But I crave your pardon for a few moments."

Saying thus he took Lysette firmly by the elbow and steered her out into the corridor, leading her to a candlelit alcove and swinging her around to face him. He put one hand on her shoulder and tipped up her chin with a long forefinger; thinking he was about to kiss her, she closed her eyes and waited dutifully. When nothing happened she opened her eyes again to see him smiling down at her, one eyebrow raised quizzically.

"I assume, my love, that your sensitivity and shyness at seeing your bridegroom was what brought the roses to your cheeks a moment ago." While she yet gasped in fury, he crushed her in his arms and took the kiss she would have given grudgingly. She struggled in his embrace, angry that he had once again taken command, stung because his words made it clear that he had watched her with André. She felt like a thief caught red-handed, which only increased her wrath. At length he released her and stepped back, laughing gently at her discomfiture.

"*Mon Dieu*, Lysette, what a transparent child you are!"

Sulking, she would have turned away, but he gripped her

hands firmly and held her at arm's length while his glance took in her costume.

"Come, come," he said good-naturedly, "let me have a look at you. I scarcely need to ask how you have amused yourself these past days—the boxes and packets have been arriving from Vouvray all week!"

She thrust out her chin belligerently. "I could only suppose that you wished me to have all that I needed!"

"Of course. I hardly thought that you would deny yourself! Rest content," he added more kindly, as her lip began to tremble. "It was my pleasure to indulge your vanity, and truly, *ma petite,* it was worth the cost." His gray eyes swept her appreciatively. "If every gown you chose becomes you as well as this one, I shall consider my coins well spent."

"You have been more than generous," she said, "and I thank you." Why did she find the words so hard to speak? Was it her conscience that nagged at her—that she took his gifts and contrived to betray him with his friend? She smiled uneasily. "I vow it must have cost you dear to buy this bride!"

"Do you really wish to know?"

"No!" No, by *le bon Dieu!* It had cost her a dowry to get Guy as a husband; she was entitled now to marry for whatever Jean-Auguste could afford!

He laughed aloud at her intensity. *"Eh bien,* since I am to be prized as a husband only so long as my purse jingles, methinks I had better take pains to lavish you with gifts! Before we rejoin Marielle and André . . ." He reached into his pocket and drew forth a small oilskin packet that he unwrapped carefully. Within lay a necklace of pearls, two strands of large, luminous spheres joined by an intricate filigree clasp of fine gold. Lysette's eyes opened wide in surprise and pleasure; when he lifted it from its wrappings she turned quickly and offered her nape to him. But as he clasped it around her throat and she felt the soft coolness of the pearls against her skin, she was glad he could not see her face. She bit her lip in sudden consternation and dismay. If only he were not so kind!

"They are lovely," she murmured. "I can scarce find the words to thank you." No, she thought. I know the words, but cannot utter them. I hate him. For being good, and kind, and thoughtful. For treating her well . . . for marrying her, though he did not truly wish it. She felt a pang of guilt, half tempted to release him from his obligation. But . . . why should she? He had chosen to dishonor her, and then to offer marriage . . . it was hardly her concern if he had not expected her to accept! She turned about and smiled prettily, executing a slow circle before him as he beamed his approval. After all, only a fool would refuse marriage to such a generous cavalier!

It was a strange quartet that finished supper around the large table. André, boisterous, expansive, pleased with his life and the marriage of his friend, poured out the wine and laughed and joked. Marielle sat quietly, her lovely face radiating a serenity that had been absent all the week—until Lysette swore to herself that there must have been a message sent to Narbaux, to bring him to Vilmorin so unexpectedly. As for Jean-Auguste, he drank a great deal of wine, growing more and more morose as the evening wore on. He glanced repeatedly from Lysette to André and back again, and each glance deepened the lines of doubt and misery that creased his face.

Lysette smiled bitterly to herself, reflecting on the irony of her situation. She had trapped Guy with charm—but surely Jean-Auguste was equally trapped, betrayed by a momentary weakness and his own sense of honor, and only she held the key that might release him from his pledge. As for André . . . as much as he might secretly care for her, he would never openly declare himself because of Marielle; sooner or later she would have to trap him into an admission of his affection. Always traps. Always guile. She felt suddenly old, tired, unworthy.

It was clear that the men were content to sit and drink for half the night, and Marielle did not seem inclined to leave Lysette alone with them. With a weary sigh, Lysette arose and excused herself, motioning the men back to their chairs.

The corridor was dim and cool, lit by a large torch set high up in the wall. She had just crossed the vestibule toward the marble staircase when footsteps behind her made her turn around. Jean-Auguste hurried toward her. His face wore an odd expression in the flickering light, a look of indecision, unsettled, wrestling with some deep torment. Silently he stood before her, his gray eyes searching her face, and once or twice he opened his mouth as though he were about to speak, then he said nothing. Ah, *Dieu!* she thought, already he is filled with regret.

She waited for the words—half hoping, half dreading—that would tell her he had changed his mind. Instead he raised her hand to his lips and gently kissed her fingertips.

"Good night."

"Good night," she choked, and fled to her room, consumed by remorse.

Chapter Ten

LYSETTE SIPPED DAINTILY FROM THE SMALL CUP THAT JEAN-Auguste had handed up to her. She settled herself more comfortably in the saddle and returned the empty cup, feeling somehow that she ought to nod graciously or dismiss him with an airy wave of her hand. Was she not a queen today, adored and admired, entitled to his homage? She watched him kneel once again at the small stream and refill the cup; when he had drunk his fill, he stowed the goblet in his saddlebag and swung easily into the saddle. She smiled regally at him—noblesse oblige—enveloped still by the aura of happiness and well-being that had filled the whole day.

Her day. Queen Lysette. Madame la Vicomtesse de Narbaux.

She had slept late, waking at last to the sounds of Dominique bustling about the room, and had breakfasted leisurely on bread and cheese and a fine apple comfiture. While she downed a large goblet of honey-sweetened wine thinned with warm water, she had watched the maid pack all but her violet wedding gown and the handsome riding outfit in which she would travel to Chimère. By the time she arrived at Narbaux's chateau, all her beautiful things would be unpacked and waiting for her.

She had bathed and dressed with care, pleased with the image that smiled back at her from the mirror—the violet silk

107

that showed off her voluptuous figure, the pearls opalescent against her fair skin. Marielle had sent in two small nosegays of purple asters and pale pink rosebuds that she tucked above each ear, nestled among the black ringlets. When Marielle herself had appeared, looking almost plain in a deep green velvet, Lysette had felt positively beautiful.

And so it had gone all the day. Lysette the fair, Lysette the beautiful. She had seen admiration in every eye—André, Jean-Auguste, the wedding guests, all the young lieutenants from Vouvray whom Marielle had invited. They had praised her with their eyes and their words . . . and their lips. After the ceremony, Jean-Auguste had kissed her gently, and André as well—a sweet kiss that had set the ground to spinning beneath her feet. The lieutenants had been less gentle, while Jean-Auguste looked uncomfortable and André chided him good-naturedly. She had danced with them all in the long gallery, and held court, drinking in their flattery and approbation, gratified particularly by the obvious misery of the lieutenant who had been so attentive on their journey from Soligne. She had almost felt sorry for Marielle, so quiet, so unobtrusive, seeming incapable of catching any man's eye.

Now she and Jean-Auguste were on their way home to Chimère. Home. Her own home. Not to be dwelt in at the whim of her brother and his cheeseparing wife, but her very own! She smiled happily, content with her lot, the lovely day, the comfortable silence she shared with Jean-Auguste. They rode slowly along the narrow path strewn with the first reds and yellows of autumn, their horses' hooves crunching on pine needles and dried twigs and grasses. After the warmth of the last weeks, the weather had turned cool, the tang of fall sharp in the air.

The sun had already set, though the sky still glowed pink and pale green, when they left the path and crossed a wide highroad, entering a broad avenue overarched with ancient trees. Under this green canopy it was already night, dark and leafy; the luminous sky beyond shone like a distant light at the end of a deep cavern. When at length they emerged, Lysette blinked, as much for the sight that greeted her eyes as the sudden brightness after the gloom.

In the deepening twilight, Chimère glowed like a jewel. It had been built directly on the Loire, on a small inlet where the placid river bent toward the shore. Surrounded thus on three sides by water, it cast its graceful reflection on the gentle current; the pale golden stones, tinged still with pink from the sky, found echo in the rippling waters. The chateau was large and square, but at each corner was a round tower surmounted by a high, conical roof, the whole in such pleasing proportions that, in spite of the heavy stone, it seemed almost to float on the serene river. Through the trees Lysette caught a glimpse of a large park and gardens, as well as outbuildings and stables and servants' quarters, but Chimère had been designed to appear isolated, alone and perfect, carefully screened from the plainness of workaday living.

She had never seen anything so lovely in all her life.

When they rode up to the wide front door servants appeared, as if by magic, to bow low and welcome Monsieur and Madame, to help her from the saddle, to lead away the horses. Beyond the door was a corridor, tiled and stone-arched, that traversed the length of the chateau, a hall so wide and handsomely appointed that Lysette reckoned it had been used on many occasions for large fêtes and receptions. Jean-Auguste ushered her into a small room off the corridor, then excused himself to instruct the servants. It was a cheery room, with a warm fire blazing on the hearth to ward off the early autumn chill; Lysette strolled about for a moment, noting the leather wall coverings, gilded and tooled, the comfortable velvet armchairs, the fine Savonnerie carpet. She crossed to the large windows and stared out at the river below, royal blue now as the sky beyond, and reflecting back the first twinkling star. She was filled with peace and happiness and gratitude; her heart, overburdened with joy, betrayed her and she began to weep, large tears that welled up in her eyes and coursed down her soft cheeks. She had always taken what was given her—or what she could maneuver for—as her right, without question or hesitation; now she thought of the empty meanness of her life with Guy, the cold loneliness that would have been her lot at Chartres, and was overwhelmed by her indebtedness to Jean-Auguste. She would be a good wife to him! She swore it on her father's grave!

"I have arranged for a small supper to be served to us here." Jean-Auguste strode jauntily into the room. Startled, Lysette drew back into the shadow of the window draperies, surreptitiously wiping away her tears with the heel of her hand. "Does that please you?" She nodded, unsure of the steadiness of her voice, then turned and smiled brightly at him as though nothing were amiss. If he noticed the tears that still clung to her dark lashes, he chose not to acknowledge them. "Tomorrow, if you wish, I shall show you Chimère."

"Yes. Thank you," she said stiffly.

"The ride was not too tiring for you? After all the dancing?"

"Indeed, no. But I thank you for your concern."

"You dance well. It pleased me to watch you."

"Thank you." She almost whispered the words. While the servants brought in a small table and set out supper, she paced the room nervously, filled with a sense of unworthiness in the face of his solicitude.

She laughed suddenly, unexpectedly, as her eye was caught by a portrait hanging on the wall above a small marble console. It was a painting of a woman, fresh-scrubbed and buxom, the cool elegance of her old-fashioned gown and glittering jewels an odd contrast to the merry openness of her face. She was not beautiful, but her warm smile illuminated her plain features with a glow that made her appear so. Her hair, a riotous shade of scarlet, was piled formally atop her head and anchored with a small silken cap in a style heretofore popular in the Court, but several wayward tresses, like leaping tongues of orange flame, had sprung loose from the orderly coiffure to curl in charming anarchy about her forehead and ears. In truth, it seemed as though the artist had caught her likeness at a felicitous moment; at any second the whole mass would surely come cascading down and she would dissolve into helpless laughter.

"This can be none other but your mother!" exclaimed Lysette. "That perverse hair . . . that ungodly color . . . !"

Jean-Auguste smiled crookedly. "There are those who say her son's perversity is a matter of the spirit! Think you so?" He threw back his head and laughed when Lysette nodded emphatically. "As for the color—you made known your sentiments the day you tried to uproot it!" He shrugged. "However, there is nothing to be done for it . . . unless I wear a wig!"

"Ugh! Guy wore a wig. When he had spent the night in some hay rick with a trollop from Soligne, it was my task to air his wig and shake it free of whatever . . . creatures . . . had taken up residence therein!" She shuddered in disgust at the memory, then frowned at Jean-Auguste, her flashing violet eyes making it plain she would not welcome his pity.

"Very well, then. I shall not wear a wig! And you must reconcile yourself to the sight of this . . . ungodly color! For my part, I shall pray to *le bon Dieu* that our children favor their mother rather than their grandmother."

Lysette's mouth formed a thin uneasy smile and she turned quickly from the painting, whirling about to indicate the portrait hanging above the fireplace, a young man in hunting garb with dark brown hair and a large, bushy mustache. "And is that your father?"

"No. Gabriel."

"Your brother."

"Yes. There is a portrait of my father in the Great Hall. I shall show you in the morning."

"And they are all dead?"

"Yes. I scarcely knew my father. And Gabriel died when I was still just a young man."

"And your mother?"

"Soon after Gabriel. The loss . . . she had buried three children in infancy . . . it was too much. . . ."

"But you were fortunate. I never knew my mother at all."

Jean-Auguste smiled indulgently. "But your father spoiled you outrageously, that is plain enough! No, do not pout. Though your 'moue' is charming, it does not gainsay the truth. I have no doubt your brothers—as well as your father—indulged your whims!" He seated her at the small table, taking his place opposite; when the servants had laid out the last of the food and poured the wine he dismissed them. Raising his glass to his lips, he saluted her.

She sipped at her wine, her violet eyes soft over the rim of her goblet. "And will you spoil me, Monsieur?"

He frowned and started to shake his head, then thought better of it and laughed ruefully. "Not willingly." She noted how his steady gaze wavered, as though he doubted his own resistance to her charms.

"Then beware, my lord, for I mean to have my way!" She smiled warmly at him, her gentle teasing meant to hide the smug triumph that filled her heart.

They supped quietly, picking at their food, for neither was hungry after the large dinner that they had had at Vilmorin. At length Jean-Auguste arose and helped Lysette from her chair, leading her across the wide corridor to an enclosed stairwell on the opposite side of the chateau. The staircase, all carved marble tracery, spiraled upward to the second and third floors. Though one side of the enclosure was made up of large windows that looked out onto the river, it was now quite dark outside and the only light within came from a large *torchère* set on the first landing.

"Dominique should be waiting for you in the passageway upstairs," said Jean-Auguste. "She will show you to your bedchamber."

"Thank you," she said, feeling suddenly uncomfortable again, half tempted to yawn noticeably. She took several steps up the stairs, then stopped and turned, contriving to look weary, though her brain whirled with stratagems. Perhaps if she hurried, she could be in bed and feigning sleep before he came to her room.

"Will you sleep directly?" His eyes, deep gray in the torch-light, gazed steadily into hers, telling her nothing. Damn him, she thought. If the words had not been spoken, she might have managed to avoid his attentions this night; but his question hung in the air, forcing her to make a decision. And how, after all his kindness, could she refuse him to his face? Reluctantly, she shook her head.

"You are not too tired?" he persisted.

"No," she said, almost sharply.

"Then I shall come to your chamber in a little while." He left her to make her way up the staircase alone.

The hallway above was not nearly so wide as the one below it; as she stepped through the archway leading from the stairwell, Dominique hurried across the tiled floor to greet her. A polite smile. A discreet curtsy. "Madame la Vicomtesse!" But the expression on Dominique's pinched features made it clear she considered Lysette's elevated station an extraordinary stroke of fortune.

"Ah, Madame! Wait until you see your rooms! They are the best in the chateau. Not even Monsieur has such fine appointments!" She led Lysette to the end of the passage; the last door on the right led into a large corner room, its two window walls draped and swagged in soft rose velvet. Raised on a carpet-covered platform, an imposing bed was tucked into the inner corner of the room, its carved mahogany frame softened by hangings of the same velvet. There was a massive armoire and a small cabinet, and several comfortable chairs covered in pink and deep blue brocade. The walls of the room had been paneled in the same brocade, and hung with fine paintings and a large Venetian mirror. A small dressing table sat under one of the windows, and a *prie-dieu* was next to the bed; one or two small gilded tables completed the furnishings. A cozy fire burned on the hearth, and someone had taken the care to place a large vase of fresh flowers on the mantelpiece. Lysette exclaimed in delight at everything: it was a splendid room, far more beautiful than anything she had expected. Dominique smiled happily and picked up a candle, motioning Madame to follow her.

"There is more, Madame. Look! Ah, what joy it will be to serve you here at Chimère!" She led Lysette to an open archway at the juncture of the two window walls: this was the corner of the chateau and the small round room beyond the arch was one of the turrets that Lysette had seen from outside. It was a kind of sitting room, with comfortable upholstered settees and chairs; the small-paned windows, undraped save for sheer gauze curtains, traversed the curve of the wall, a fine vantage point for viewing the river in all directions. "Is it not lovely, Madame? Is it not grand?" Dominique danced excitedly about the room, while Lysette, overwhelmed again by gratitude and conscience, returned silently to the bedroom.

She stood quietly and frowned as Dominique peeled off the layers of her clothing: jacket and riding skirt, chemise and petticoats; she sat while Dominique removed her soft riding boots and stockings. With a heavy sigh, she stood up, now quite naked, and waited for the maid to fetch her nightdress and peignoir.

"It is almost too grand for me," she murmured, half to herself.

"Too grand? Nay, Madame! Wherefore too grand?"

"Monsieur le Vicomte is a great and kind gentleman, whilst I . . ."

"Madame, you are a lady of exceeding beauty!" exclaimed Dominique, suddenly defensive. "Monsieur is very fortunate! Is it not your right to take the gifts he offers?" She snorted in contempt. "He will take what *he* wishes, as all men do!" She slipped the nightdress over Lysette's head and helped her on with a flowing silk peignoir, nodding her approval. "They say that when Madame du Crillon married Monsieur le Comte she was but the daughter of a doctor, and now she reigns like a princess at Vilmorin! Why then should Chimère be too grand for you, my lady?"

Yes, thought Lysette. Why indeed should she feel beholden to Jean-Auguste? She was a nobleman's daughter, an asset to him in society, his equal, not his inferior! She was tired of thanking him for every kindness! As Dominique said, she was entitled to his gifts and his deference. He had not got a bad bargain in her! She would give him her favors—albeit grudgingly—she did not owe him humbleness! Seating herself at the dressing table, she allowed Dominique to unpin her chignon and comb out her hair.

There was a gentle knock at the door. At Lysette's response, Jean-Auguste entered, bearing a golden ewer and two embossed goblets. He was clad in a long brocaded dressing gown that served to accentuate his broad shoulders and rangy frame. Dominique turned as if to leave, but Lysette held fast to her hand, indicating she was to continue her combing.

"I thought you might care to try one of our Chimère wines. This is ten years old. It was a good harvest that year." He poured out a pale stream of wine, faintly tinged with pink, and handed the cup to Lysette.

"Ten years? And it is fit still to drink?"

He laughed softly. "It is the caves. All the Vouvray wines are long-lived . . . the coolness of the caves, the peculiar quality of the grapes in the region . . ." He shrugged. "Whatever the causes, you will not taste wine like this elsewhere!"

She sipped at the wine. Despite its pale color, it was rich and full-bodied, fruity and slightly sweet, with a pleasing effervescence that lingered on her tongue. She smiled in satisfaction. "And this is your own?"

"It is yours as well, now. If we sell enough casks and hogsheads, I have no doubt the silk merchants and jewelers of Vouvray will enjoy your trade!" He refilled her goblet and sat in a large armchair near her dressing table, watching with great interest as Dominique combed out the raven tresses and curled the ringlets over her fingers. Much to Lysette's surprise, he seemed in no hurry to see Dominique leave, but lolled in his chair enjoying the wine and the details of her toilette. She felt a sudden pang of annoyance—was he as reluctant to take her to bed as he had been about marrying her?

"You may leave now, Dominique," she said, a sharp edge in her voice. "I shall finish myself." She took the comb from the girl and continued to groom her hair, conscious of the silence in the room after Dominique had gone. She stole a look at Jean-Auguste in her mirror; there was not a clue in his calm expression. A few moments before she had wondered how she might evade her wifely duty; now she frowned to herself at his seeming lack of interest.

"You have lovely hair," he said suddenly.

She turned about to him, instantly the coquette. "Oh, think you so?" And smiled beguilingly, her eyes wide and innocent.

"Indeed I do." His mouth twitched, cool, amused, cynical. "As do you, else you would not seek out every opportunity to make a show of it." She gaped, then pressed her lips together in a hard line, annoyed at being caught once again in a game. The smile faded from his face, his gray eyes thoughtful. "Your vanity can be charming," he said, "but I dislike coyness . . . and deceit."

Sulking, her mouth set in a sullen pout, she turned her back to him. If she had hated him for his piercing eyes, she hated him even more now for the frankness that gave her no refuge. Her shoulders sagged unhappily; she did not like to be scolded.

Standing up without a word, he lifted the comb from her drooping fingers and began to pull it gently through her locks. There was something almost sensual in the softness of his touch, a delicacy in his wielding of the comb that touched a chord deep within her. She closed her eyes, enjoying the unexpected pleasure, the luxury of feeling pampered once again.

"It is beautiful hair," he said. "You have every right to flaunt it. I mark I was struck by its glory the first moment I saw you at Soligne."

Her eyes shot open in surprise. "In the midst of the battle and the turmoil?"

He grinned, his eyes twinkling at her reflection in the mirror. "Though he faces death upon the instant, a man always notices a comely woman!"

Disarmed, she touched her curls self-consciously. "But . . . the disarray . . ."

"No matter. Its beauty caught my eye at once."

She smiled in pleasure, basking in his compliments. He could be so agreeable . . . when he chose to be. "But you did not like it that day at the inn!" she said, petulant again. "You were quite insulting!"

"To the contrary . . ."

"You said I looked like a child!"

"And so you did. But a very lovely and charming child!"

"You did not say so!"

"I was more than a little angry at you, as I recall."

She frowned. Why did their conversations always drift into this—his unspoken disapproval of her behavior, her feeling that she was a naughty child and he the parent who expected better of her? Not even Guy had dared to chide her openly, though she had tormented him often enough. Until Jean-Auguste, she had never had a second thought, a single twinge of conscience, about what she said or did.

"If you please," she said hastily, raising her empty wine goblet. When he had refilled it, she moved quickly away from him, going to stand at the window, avoiding the condemnation she felt sure would be in his gray eyes. For had she not deliberately tried to tempt André, that evening at the inn— combing her hair, plaiting the black tresses seductively? She stared out at the night, the silver crescent of the moon rising over the river.

"It was a lovely day," she said softly.

"Yes. And you were a lovely bride."

A breeze rippled the river for an instant and the reflected moon shattered into glittering shards. "How plain Marielle looked! It must be sad, to grow older and know one is losing one's beauty!"

"She is not many years your senior," he said dryly. "Perhaps because it was your wedding day, she did not choose to . . . be a rival!"

"Pooh!" She turned from the window. "No woman pretends to plainness!"

He was about to respond, then thought better of it and shrugged. "As you wish."

"Were you pleased with my gown? I cautioned the seamstress to take special pains with it."

"I confess I scarcely noticed the gown, only your grace and loveliness in it. You looked like the goddess of the night, all purple silk and hair the color of midnight. You quite took my breath away." He stared at her for a long moment, a gentle smile playing about his lips, then moved easily and gracefully to the large bed, holding out his hand to her in invitation. "Come to bed," he said.

She crossed to a small table, meaning to put down her goblet, then changed her mind and picked up the gold ewer, refilling her cup yet again. As she slowly sipped the wine, she saw that he had draped himself across the bed and was waiting patiently, one eyebrow raised in quizzical amusement.

Welladay, she thought, and finished the last of her wine. With a shrug, she loosened her peignoir and released the string of her nightdress, allowing both garments to fall to the floor at her feet.

He sat up in surprise, taken aback by the unexpected sight of her nakedness, her lack of modesty. "But . . . wherefore . . . ?" he stammered.

She smiled, pleased to have shaken his composure for a change.

"And wherefore not? Firstly, you are my husband. And then . . . shall I pretend to innocence? Shall I be coy, when you dislike it? I am beautiful, *n'est-ce pas?* Then let me rejoice in that beauty!"

"*Mon Dieu!*" he laughed. "Were you thus with Guy?"

She snorted in derision. "He would scarcely have noticed! It was my dowry, not my person that Guy found alluring!"

"Then I must compensate for his neglect, and honor your beauty fully! Come!" He traced a circle in the air, indicating she was to turn about. She revolved slowly, feeling his admiring eyes upon her, his smoldering glance that ranged her body in silent praise.

"Come to bed," he repeated at last, his voice husky in his throat.

The wine had begun to make her head spin. She padded about the room extinguishing the candles, feeling the soft carpet under her feet, the cozy fire that touched her naked body with its gentle warmth. She felt mellow, lulled by the wine, his admiration, the remembrance of his caresses. The room was now quite dim save for the fireplace and one small candle near the bed. Stepping onto the carpeted platform, she saw that Jean-Auguste had removed his dressing gown. A wave of unease swept through her at the sight of his naked body, so virile, so potent. She almost fled his side, but he reached up and pulled her down to the bed.

Ah, *Dieu!* she thought. Why had she drunk so much wine? She could not think clearly, could not feel his kisses and caresses, could only close her eyes to him and the fear that clutched at her. Think of André. André! The fantasy had served once before: it was André's mouth, André's body, André's passion! To no avail. Her brain whirled, a red mist of confusion. What was the woman's name? The lawyer's wife in Chartres. Mademoiselle Lysette, he loves me, my husband loves me . . . and the children tugged at her skirts and her eyes were haunted and filled with despair. And the screaming! Monsieur Avocat, tell me of my father's will. What shall I have for a dowry? And his hand about her schoolgirl waist and his coarse fingers fondling her buttocks and all the while his wife upstairs screaming and screaming to bring forth another child!

She was aware that Jean-Auguste had withdrawn from her, that her fists were clenched tight and her face was screwed up in a grimace. With a start, she opened her eyes, thrust once again into the present. He seemed spent, limp; she could only assume that he had had his way and was finished with her, although she had no recollection of the moment.

"Perhaps you were too tired after all," he said quietly. His face was in shadow; she could not see his eyes. He arose from the bed and donned his dressing gown, passing quickly out of the door before she had a chance to collect her thoughts.

She breathed deeply, feeling the tenseness leave her body. The effects of the wine had begun to dissipate, and she lay quietly, aware of innumerable details that assailed her senses: the ceiling painted with roses and butterflies; the not unpleasant smell of his sweat that lingered still on the pillows; the tingling on her lips from kisses she could scarcely remember.

Disregarding her nightdress, she crawled under the downy

coverlet, pulling its warmth about her ears and smiling softly to herself.

All would be well. She could endure. Madame la Vicomtesse de Narbaux.

But she must remember to tell Dominique in the morning that she wished her bath to be very hot.

Chapter Eleven

ANDRÉ WAS STANDING IN THE MEADOW, BECKONING TO HER. The warmth and love that shone in his blue eyes filled her heart until she felt she must explode with longing. She tried to run toward him, through the cloud of butterflies that seemed suddenly to have invaded the meadow, that tickled at her nose and ears, insistent, intrusive. She grunted in annoyance and brushed them away. André! *Mon amour!* She could no longer see him for the brightness that filtered through her closed eyelids; impatiently she flopped over onto her stomach and pressed her pillow over her head, searching to recapture the vision of André in the welcoming darkness. The butterflies had returned and were tracing a gentle line between her bare shoulder blades, distracting her, keeping her from her love, waiting in the meadow beyond the shores of dreams.

"Go away!" she shrilled and sat up, eyes springing open, pillow clutched in both hands above her head, poised for assault.

Jean-Auguste stood over her, his face split in a wide grin. "Slug-a-bed! Would you sleep the whole day through, when Chimère awaits your inspection?" He laughed and took the pillow from her, tucking it behind her head, his fingers grazing her bare shoulders. She pouted in annoyance, pulling up the coverlet to shield her nakedness, and settled herself sulkily against the pillows. Devil take him! Even her dreams of André were not safe from his intrusion!

Ignoring her mood, he perched himself on the edge of the bed. She saw that he was dressed for riding: sturdy twill doublet and breeches, soft leather boots pulled well up above his knees so the heavy linen boot hose barely showed over the tops. On a chair nearby he had laid his mantle and wide-brimmed hat. He pulled off his leather gauntlets and chucked her coaxingly under the chin; he was filled with such good humor she smiled in spite of herself. "Forgive me," he said kindly, "I could not wait for you to get up. The grapes must be harvested in a few days and there is yet much to be done, but I wished you to ride with me this morning. Will you come?"

She smiled weakly at him, her thoughts elsewhere. Perhaps if she hurried, there might be time to take that hot bath. She beamed at him in sudden warmth. "Of course I shall ride with you! Now . . . begone! Out with you that I may dress and breakfast quickly."

"Nay! I have had no food myself today. Dominique is setting a table for us both in your sitting room." He motioned toward the round tower room from whence emanated the clatter of dishes and glassware. "I shall await you there. If you tarry too long"—he ran one slim finger along the line of the coverlet that just covered her bosom—"I shall be less chivalrous than I was that day at the lake, and most assuredly peek!"

She would have responded with a sharp retort, but Dominique bustled into the bedchamber and the moment passed. Lysette frowned in annoyance as Jean-Auguste ambled into the sitting room. There would be no bath this morning! She donned the shift and petticoats that Dominique held out to her, then tapped her foot impatiently as the maid filled a small washbasin with warm water. Dominique's sullen face seemed to echo her mood. She raised an eyebrow questioningly, inviting the girl's confidence; as she scrubbed her face over the basin, Dominique leaned close and hissed in her ear.

"I hope that Madame will feel welcome here at Chimère, but . . ."

"But . . . ?" Lysette straightened, drying herself with the linen cloth the maid proffered.

"But . . . I do not think that Bricole is glad for your coming!"

"Bricole?"

"The chief steward at Chimère. He has been here so long, you would think that he was the mistress!" She helped Lysette to slip into her soft high boots, then fetched a velvet jacket and riding skirt. Her voice rose in an aggrieved whine. "I tried to tell Bricole that I serve you, Madame, but he ordered me about this morning as though I were just a chambermaid!" She nodded her head for emphasis, then hooked up the front of Lysette's snug jacket and tied on a lace-trimmed linen collar. "Louise is the housekeeper at Vilmorin, but Madame la Comtesse du Crillon would never allow such a lack of respect . . . Madame du Crillon is the mistress of Vilmorin, there is no disputing that!"

Lysette frowned at her reflection in the mirror and adjusted her broad-brimmed plumed hat, deep red velvet to match her riding costume. What was the good of being mistress of such a fine chateau if she must tolerate insolence? Well, she would see to it that Bricole learned soon enough that she meant to rule here!

Jean-Auguste grinned broadly as she entered her sitting room, his eyes filled with pleasure and admiration; in one stride he was at her side and had swept her into his arms.

"Mon Dieu! Jean-Auguste! Mind my hat!"

"Damn your hat!" With a swift gesture he raked it from her head and tossed it down, crushing her more determinedly to him. She submitted to his lips, finding his kiss pleasant enough (and safe, since it would scarcely lead to more serious lovemaking at this hour of the day!), but her mind was busy cataloging her many grievances. The rude awakening, the thwarted bath, Bricole's effrontery. And now her hair would have to be recombed and the hat brushed! It was really too much!

"If you please, Monsieur le Vicomte. There is a . . . person . . . here who says he was instructed to come to you!"

Jean-Auguste released Lysette and smiled crookedly at her, his open face sending a message so explicit that she blushed and cast down her eyes; then he turned to Dominique waiting at the doorway. Her sour expression disapproved equally of the visitor and the behavior of Monsieur le Vicomte.

"Ah, yes! Simon! Show him in!"

While Dominique vanished into the bedchamber, Lysette retrieved her hat and tried to restore order to her tangled locks; Jean-Auguste commandeered a comfortable chair near the breakfast table and set to the food, busily dispatching a small partridge and a large flagon of ale. There was a sudden muffled yelp from the room beyond, then Dominique reappeared, her face blazing scarlet, and ushered in Simon, taking care to stay at some distance from him.

He swaggered into the room, his face wreathed in a cocky grin, and bobbed politely to Jean-Auguste, a movement that was both deferential and strangely far from humble. He was not a large man, though strongly built, but his good humor filled the room, his incorporeal presence far weightier than flesh and blood. He was all in brown, from the tip of his peaked cap to the dusty and well-worn boots that had shaped themselves to the contours of his feet through years of snowy days and rain-soaked nights. His skin was as brown and tough as the leather of his boots; indeed only his white teeth and sea-green eyes encroached upon the uniform color of his person.

"Simon Vacher," explained Jean-Auguste, "chief forester at Chimère," and Lysette nearly laughed aloud at that. For did not the man look like a tree, planted firmly in her sitting room, umber-breeched legs spread wide, acorn-hued arms sprouting from a dark brown leather jerkin? He grinned again and allowed his impudent gaze to sweep the still blushing Dominique before turning back to Jean-Auguste.

"What of the new lands, Vacher?" Jean-Auguste took a final swig of ale and wiped his fingers on a large linen handkerchief.

"Good forests, Monsieur. Oak and beech, and a small stand of pine."

"Enough to support more swine? Some of the new tenants have sued for grazing privileges, and are prepared to pay a goodly rent."

Vacher scratched a calloused finger against his chin. "There are acorns and chestnuts aplenty in the woods. It is good for the trees when the pigs root around them. Still, what is your will, Monsieur?"

"No, no. You must speak plain to me. I scarce need the added revenue—there are a score of tenants now who pay me for grazing rights. I will be guided by you in this matter."

Vacher pursed his lips and frowned, his head nodding slowly up and down as though the rhythmic movement aided his concentration. "The forests themselves can support more swine, sure enough. And there is a small orchard just off the path to Vouvray—I never saw a pig that did not like a rotten apple! But pigs are peculiar creatures, my lord. Even the few farmers who are allowed to graze their animals can not always keep them under control! If you should allow more, what is to prevent them from leaving the forests and rooting among the vineyards? That would be a pretty mess, it would!" And he nodded again for emphasis.

"Still, the farmers depend on their swine. What if I were to grant them the right to forage . . . to take from the ground those fruits and nuts that have fallen from the trees, in order to feed their pigs?"

"The forests would not suffer, Monsieur."

"Nor would the vineyards." Jean-Auguste stood up decisively and began to draw on his gloves. "That is what I shall do. And the other matter . . . ?"

"I think I have found the perfect spot, Monsieur. There is a large stand, mostly beech, with a clear stream flowing through it, and not too far from the path, if I understood your instructions aright."

Narbaux nodded in satisfaction. "Beech makes the best ash, I have been told. And the path can be widened, if it proves necessary. What about fuel for the furnace?"

"All to the good, Monsieur. The new lands have been sorely neglected for many years—there are fallen logs and rotted trees at every turn. It makes for bad hunting. I would have put my woodsmen to work clearing them, whatever your designs. Even the old forests of Chimère need clearing—broken branches and uprooted trees—a heavy storm we suffered this July past. Nay, my lord, it will be many years before we must touch a living tree, for all your hungry furnace!"

Jean-Auguste smiled in pleasure and dismissed Vacher, who walked to the door of the sitting room and then paused, waiting for Dominique to show him out. Reluctantly she led him through the bedchamber, her cheeks reddening at his brazen grin; again there was the sound of a scuffle and a muffled cry, followed this time by the sharp report of flesh striking flesh.

Lysette had been nibbling at her breakfast; at the sound she put down her partridge bone and looked up sourly into Jean-Auguste's twinkling eyes. "Do all the men at Chimère take what they wish?" She watched the smile fade from his face, then went on. "And what is all this about furnaces?"

"Glass. There is a goodly supply at Chimère of all that might be necessary to make glass. Sand from the river bed, lime from the caves, trees to burn for the furnaces and the ash . . ."

"And will my noble husband become an artisan?" she sneered.

"Not I! *Mon Dieu!* It takes more skill than I possess! But a master glassmaker might find conditions here to his liking, and be willing to pay a good fee—as well as supplying Chimère with bottles for our wine. It would save me the cost and the trouble of bringing in bottles from outside. But you need not concern yourself with these matters. Put a smile upon your pretty face and come and ride with me!"

They descended to the ground floor where the servants were waiting to be introduced to Madame la Vicomtesse. Gracious and dignified, Lysette greeted them all, though she scarcely bothered to listen to their names as they were presented. It sufficed to have servants aplenty; when they displeased her would be time enough to know their names. She took special note of Bricole, however; as Chimère had no housekeeper, Bricole, the chief steward, ran the household. Tall and thin and stately, his snowy hair clipped neatly to his ears, he greeted her with proper deference, but she could not forget Dominique's remark that he considered himself mistress of the chateau. And, truth to tell, was there not a certain superciliousness lurking just beneath his respectful manner? She acknowledged him brusquely, determined to keep a watchful eye lest his servility be merely sham.

They rode out at last into the sunny morning, past gardens and stables and wide lawns trimly manicured. At length the flatland—the riverbed in some prehistoric eon—rose sharply before them, becoming limestone cliffs riddled with openings that, here and there, had been sealed off with rough-hewn doors and gates. Jean-Auguste dismounted and helped Lysette from her horse. A young man, blond and pink-cheeked, ran to greet them, and Jean-Auguste introduced him as Pasquier, one of the *vignerons*. He was a good-looking fellow: Lysette turned her most dazzling smile to him, just for the pleasure of seeing him blush.

Pasquier lit a small lantern and led them through a door into one of the caves. It was cold and damp within, and the low ceiling, covered with a pale green mold, made their voices echo hollowly in the gloom. The small passageway opened up into a larger cavern with a high domed roof and a dozen niches and corridors carved into its walls. Each niche was piled high with casks and barrels, slime-covered like the walls, and when Lysette ventured a peek into one of the corridors, she saw that it led to another large chamber, filled with as many kegs again. Pasquier led them through the maze of caverns, occasionally stopping, at Jean-Auguste's request, to take down a barrel and pour out a small cup of wine for them to taste. At length, feeling chilled and bored, Lysette turned about and started back, meaning to retrace their steps; the corridor before her angled suddenly and sharply, and she found herself in total darkness, cut off from the gleam of the lantern. For a moment, panic clutched at her; then the light reappeared and Jean-Auguste hurried to her side.

"The caves are treacherous to a stranger," he said. "They cut in and out of the cliffs for many, many leagues—well beyond Orleans—no one has ever charted all their paths and byways. You must never come here alone."

"Pooh!" she said, annoyed at his tone. It was easy to feel brave once again with the lantern shining brightly and Pasquier close at hand to lead them out of the caves. "I should have found my way, even without your help!"

"I beg of you . . . give me your promise."

She tossed her curls at him in disdain. "I do as I please!" she said, more sharply than she had intended, and was dismayed to see him redden slightly, while Pasquier fidgeted in embarrassment that anyone should speak thus to his master. Without a word, Jean-Auguste turned on his heel and rapidly followed Pasquier from the cave. Skipping to keep up with them, Lysette was filled with remorse; when they were once again in the sunshine she put her gloved hand upon his sleeve and smiled sweetly up at him, her violet eyes soft and apologetic.

"Pray do not be angry with me. I am . . . used to doing as I please!"

Her contrite expression made his own stern glance waver, and he sighed resignedly as he helped her onto her horse. "Perhaps, someday," he said, regaining his own saddle, "it will please you to please others." He led her up to the top of the cliffs, where the land gave way to rolling plateaus that stretched into the distance, patchworked with rows of vines, broken occasionally by a small grove or a *vigneron*'s hut. They rode through the vineyards and past green meadows where sheep grazed in contentment; they skirted dense woodland, and fields of ripened wheat and corn that would feed all of Chimère during the long winter. At first Lysette was dazzled by the breadth and wealth of Chimère; but after she had mentally conjured up half a dozen gowns with the profit from this vineyard, that stand of oak , she began to tire of the game and, indeed, the whole tour of the estate. *Mon Dieu!* Was she expected to share Jean-Auguste's enthusiasm as he pointed out yet another field or stream? It was enough that there would be coins to spend when she wished, that every grove and meadow meant crowns and livres for her indulgence.

They had been lolling in the saddle, stopped near the edge of a leafy wood, while Jean-Auguste explained how Vacher and his men thinned out the forests and burned the excess wood for charcoal that could then be sold; with an impatient cry, Lysette spurred her horse and plunged headlong through the trees. She had had her fill of explanations and show; she needed the challenge of a difficult ride through the woods to keep from dying of boredom. Taken aback, Jean-Auguste hesitated for a moment; then he urged on his own mount and followed her. She led him on a merry chase through the dense underbrush, relying on her considerable skills as a horsewoman to keep her mare from stumbling or herself from crashing into an overhanging tree limb, and once a stray branch brushed against her and swept her hat from her head. But nothing could stop her, not the difficult way nor Jean-Auguste's shouts from behind; only a small pond, that loomed up suddenly before her, forced her to rein in sharply, mischievous eyes sparkling in pleasure. Laughing, Jean-Auguste drew up alongside her.

"By my faith, you are the devil's own spawn!" He leaped from his horse and held his arms up to her.

She smiled wickedly down at him. "Had you forgot so soon what you said that night at the crossroads? That you did not trust me?"

"I forget at my peril that you are as changeable as the phases of the moon! I shall be on my guard, Madame! But come, let us rest here for a while." He lifted her down from her horse, strong hands about her waist, and set her on her feet, but instead of releasing her, he pulled her closer and smiled warmly, his gray eyes glowing with desire.

Lysette was aware suddenly of the isolation of the woods, the strength of his arms about her, the way he towered above her. She cast down her eyes and moved uneasily within his embrace.

"Pray do not look at me thus," she murmured uncomfortably.

"Nay. It is one of the pleasures of marriage, methinks, that I may look at you thus and dream of further delights!" She glanced up at him sharply and received a crooked grin for answer. "A mistress is a chancy thing," he continued, "but a wife . . ."

She felt anger begin to boil within her breast. He had not truly wished to marry her, but now, the deed concluded, he was willing to solace himself with the pleasures of the bedchamber, whether she willed it or no! She thought again of her grievances of the morning. Even now she might be carrying his unwelcome seed because his intrusion into her room had precluded her bath. Petulantly, she wriggled free from his grasp and turned her back to him.

"A wife . . . even as a mistress . . . is not to be treated lightly! I do not enjoy being wakened so roughly in the morning. Kindly do not come to my room unannounced again! There is no pleasure for me to be disturbed thus!"

He turned and gathered up the reins of his horse. "As you wish." His voice was cool, distant. "We can ride back through the woods. Mayhap we will recover your hat. I must see to the vineyards this afternoon. Bricole will show you about the rooms of Chimère, if you but ask him."

They rode slowly and silently back toward the chateau, retracing their path through the woods and finding Lysette's hat still dangling from the branch; but the talk of Bricole had set Lysette's mind to whirling yet again.

"Is Bricole then in charge of Chimère?" she asked, an edge of belligerence in her voice.

Jean-Auguste turned in his saddle, his eyes searching and perceptive. "The household is yours, to run as you wish—

naturellement—but Bricole has been chief steward for many years. He can be of service to you, if you will but defer to his wisdom in some matters.''

"But has he been instructed to obey my wishes?" she snapped.

"Of course!"

"I will not be crossed, nor treated with disrespect!"

"Only you have the power to be less the mistress than you should be," he said gently, but his eyes bored into her as though he had searched her soul and found her wanting. "Chimère is large, and complex to manage . . . let Bricole be a friend as well as a trusted servant. You will not regret it."

The wisdom of his advice only increased her ire. "Do you think me a child?" she said defiantly. "I have been mistress of a household ere now! I have been a wife!" Wife. With a pang she recalled her indifference to him the night before—his wedding night—and turned away in consternation. That had scarcely been proper behavior for a wife, more especially one who had had a husband before. Curse Jean-Auguste! Why could he not be cruel and indifferent and thoughtless as Guy had been? She had always pleased herself and thought it right and natural; why, with those serious gray eyes bent to her, did her every action seem suddenly tinged with childlike selfishness?

They rode back to Chimère in silence. At the chateau Bricole appeared and handed Jean-Auguste a small packet of food; he murmured his thanks to the steward and, with a brief nod to Lysette, turned his horse about and made his way back toward the vineyards. Lysette dismounted and went indoors. Bricole's solicitude, urging Madame to take a bite of food, only exacerbated her mood and she refused him sharply. At her haughty command he showed her about the chateau, from the large stone kitchens below to the stately apartments and the small chapel glowing with stained glass, but she found no joy in any of it. He was too polite, too proper, too obsequious—surely his manner was pretense and he was laughing at her for presuming to think she could ever rule here! She longed for a reason to dominate, to take command, to prove her superiority.

At length they passed a door near the ground-floor staircase.

"Wait!" she said, pointing. "That room!"

"A small library, Madame."

"Show me."

Bricole shook his snowy head. "I cannot, Madame. It is locked."

"Then unlock it," she said, her voice rising shrilly.

His kind eyes did not waver. "Monsieur le Vicomte has forbidden it."

She stamped her small foot in annoyance. "Madame la Vicomtesse insists upon it! I shall explain it to Monsieur . . . open the door!"

"Monsieur de Narbaux has the key," he said gently.

There was no quarreling with him. "Have I seen all the rooms then? Save for this one?"

"Yes, Madame. Have I your leave to retire?"

"Yes. No! There is the matter of my maid Dominique."

"Given to idleness, my lady, when she is not serving you. But I shall find chores for her when she is not occupied, if you wish it, Madame."

"I do *not* wish it! She is answerable to my authority alone. I shall not have you ordering her about!"

"Forgive me, my lady, if I have presumed too much. It is my fervent wish to serve you as I have served the Narbaux all of my life. You must not hesitate to chide me if I overstep my bounds." He bowed low, his thin frame bent stiffly, his eyes filled with genuine humility that, nevertheless, did not rob him of his natural dignity and bearing. Lysette stirred uneasily. His courtesy only added to her sense of unworthiness. Bricole straightened up and went on smoothly. "Monsieur is in the habit of taking supper at six by the clock, in the small salon. Do you wish the cook to prepare a special dish?"

"No."

"And the arrangements suit you, Madame?"

"Yes."

Bricole bowed again and turned to leave. On an impulse, Lysette called him back.

"Wait! We shall dine at seven!"

"Seven, Madame?"

"Seven!" she said with some asperity.

Silently, he nodded and left the room, but she could almost hear the words echoing in the quiet corridor. As you wish. Jean-Auguste would have said it: as you wish. Well, by *le bon Dieu*, it was what she wished! To make them know that she was mistress here, that she expected to be treated like a grand lady, not a child!

She looked about her: the arched hallway, with its high-set windows and imposing tapestries seemed suddenly to dwarf her. With a heavy sigh that rose from a wellspring of discontent deep within her, she made for the cozy safety of her sitting room.

Chapter Twelve

JEAN-AUGUSTE SMILED GENTLY AT THE PORTRAIT OF HIS MOTHER in the small salon; she grinned back at him as though they were exchanging secrets. Seated within a window alcove, her fingers drumming nervously on the lute she had had Dominique search out for her, Lysette cursed her own foolishness.

Jean-Auguste had come in from the vineyards at six, expecting supper; when Lysette had explained in a small, cajoling voice that she preferred to dine at seven, he had not even bothered to say "as you wish," but had agreed with a good-natured nod and seated himself in a comfortable chair, passing the time in reading. It was she, Lysette, who suffered. Bored, restless, her poor stomach crying out for lack of food (what had ever possessed her to refuse lunch when Bricole had offered it?), she watched the hands of the clock on the mantel tick out the hour in agonizing slowness. Did he know? she wondered. Was he laughing at her, glancing up from his book to smile cheerfully at the picture of his mother?

Supper came at last; Lysette was so hungry she scarcely bothered with idle conversation, but fell to the food with gusto. At length, sated, she heaved a prodigious sigh and smiled across the table at Jean-Auguste. He returned her smile, his eyes filled with warmth and pleasure.

"You have a healthy appetite! One would think you had

worked in the vineyards all the afternoon! Did Bricole show you the chateau?"

"Yes. It is lovely. There are so many rooms. So much to see. Oh!" She frowned suddenly. "But one room . . ."

"One room?"

"The library."

"Ah . . . yes. The library. Do you know that your hair curls most charmingly about your ears?"

"Of course I know!" she said impatiently, too piqued by curiosity to be coy.

He laughed aloud at her frankness, then relented his teasing. "Ah, well, I suppose you must see the library. Come along." He picked up a small candelabra from the table and led her across the hall to the library door. Taking a key from his pocket, he turned it in the lock, then paused and turned to her. "You must not be disappointed. It is only a library, after all, and the few rare volumes in it are almost too dull to be read, but . . ."

"But . . . ?" Lysette thought she must surely scream at him in another moment.

He grinned in self-satisfaction. "But there is a gift for you. . . ."

So saying, he swung open the door. It was a small room, its walls lined with book-filled shelves, and a few comfortable chairs placed near the windows. But what caught Lysette's eye was a writing table, placed awkwardly in the center of the room, as though it scarcely belonged there. It was a handsome piece, a large closed cabinet resting on a beautifully inlaid table, intricately set with strips of gold and mother-of-pearl, and swirls of ivory and ebony. Still, it was hardly the kind of gift that thrilled Lysette to any great degree.

"Oh, how lovely," she said, trying to keep the regret out of her voice.

"Wait." He reached out and opened the cabinet doors, swinging them wide to reveal the interior. Lysette gasped in genuine pleasure. The inside of the cabinet was like the miniature facade of a two-storied building, with rounded arches and paneled doors, and tiny niches set with diminutive statues. There were ebony columns, finely fluted, their Roman capitals overlaid with gold, and delicate friezes of carved ivory, creamy white against the dark mahogany wood.

Lysette dropped to one knee in front of the cabinet, exclaiming in delight as her fingers traveled every pediment and archway. Her eyes sparkled as she smiled up at Jean-Auguste. It was like having a writing desk and a toy all at the same time!

"Now, watch carefully," he said. He grasped one of the tiny statues and gave it a sharp twist; to Lysette's surprise, it turned under his fingers until it was facing the rear of the niche. Next he reached out and pushed a column on the second story, sliding it gently to the right until it had moved a scant inch. Finally he pressed the inlaid pediment above the main archway; there was a soft click from somewhere within the cabinet. He pulled at the center archway and it glided out of the cabinet, proving to be a drawer already filled with quills and ink and writing paper.

Lysette clapped her hands in joy and jumped to her feet. "Show me! I must do it for myself!"

Jean-Auguste laughed and replaced the drawer, reversing the steps that had released the secret spring. He scarcely had to show Lysette how it was done; in a moment she was unlocking the drawer then closing it, locking and releasing, over and over again, and squealing in delight each time the small catch clicked.

"Oh, thank you!" she said at last, her eyes shining. "It is the finest gift I have ever had!"

"It was made in Florence," he said. "In Italy they seem to have a need to hide things. There are more drawers, you know. Perhaps you should see what they hold."

Lysette gasped in surprise and touched the statue, the column, the pediment; this time, when she removed the center archway, she examined the cabinet more carefully. Sure enough, surrounding the space where the drawer had been were the fronts of half a dozen more drawers, buried deep within the cabinet. She pulled at them excitedly; five of them were empty, but the sixth held two large ribbon shoe roses, each centered with a cluster of diamonds. Clutching them tightly, she threw her arms about Jean-Auguste's neck, bubbling with happiness.

He grinned in satisfaction, enjoying her pleasure as much as if the gift had been his. "But there is more inside," he said.

Dazzled, she bent once again to the cabinet, discovering, to her wonderment, that every door opened up and every tiny window swung wide to reveal a hidden space. At last, when she had found every secret hiding place, she sighed deeply and leaned happily against the cabinet, surveying her treasures laid out on the writing table.

Besides the shoe roses, there were two pearl tassels to grace the band strings of a lace collar, a jeweled clasp of rubies and diamonds, and a dozen buttons of gold filigree set with emeralds, as well as a pair of large pearl drop earrings.

"How kind you are to me," she said, choking back tears.

"What . . . weeping? I shall not have it! They were my mother's things. It pleases me that you should have them." He smiled warmly down at her and tweaked the tip of her nose. "Now put away your booty and lock up your cabinet—in the morning you can have it placed in your rooms where you wish it."

Reluctantly she stored the jewels and closed up the writing desk, looking uneasily over her shoulder as he shut the library door without locking it. "They will be safe, *n'est-ce pas?*"

He laughed gently. "Of course. Only you and I know the secret." He took a step toward her, his face suddenly serious, and laid his hand on her arm. "Shall you sleep directly tonight?"

"No," she said kindly, filled with warmth and gratitude.

"I shall come to you when you have dismissed Dominique."

Her eyes were still shining when he entered her bedchamber, and she danced merrily about the room. "By my faith, I cannot decide where I may put my lovely gift! Here?" She indicated a spot near a window. "In my sitting room? There? Beside that chair?"

"Enough!"

"Forgive my chatter tonight! It is such a splendid gift . . ." She smiled sheepishly at him, then pressed a finger to her lips in a promise of silence. Unself-consciously, she released her peignoir and nightgown and allowed them to fall to the floor at her feet, as she had done the night before, then waited for him to cross the room to her. He took her in his arms and kissed her tenderly, then lifted her and carried her to the bed. He really is a very agreeable man, she thought, as she lay passive, enjoying the sweetness of his gentle kisses and caresses. To have given her such fine gifts, then added to her pleasure by hiding them in that magical cabinet . . . those beautiful jewels . . . she paraded them before her mind's eye once again. The ruby clasp cried out for a velvet cape lined with fur, and the emerald buttons would need a dress with an overgown that buttoned on to either side of the bodice—not green, it did not suit her —perhaps white—would André admire her in white? Perhaps she would give a party—in the great hall of Chimère— and she, dazzling in white, dancing with André. . . .

In the one corner of her mind that was not lost in reverie, she was aware suddenly that Jean-Auguste had ceased his labors above her and had withdrawn. With a start, she opened her eyes and found him peering down at her, his penetrating gaze searching her face. Consumed with guilt, after all his kindness, she managed to smile coquettishly at him, then sighed meltingly, as though his lovemaking had left her breathless and satisfied. His eyebrow shot up in surprise, one bright red peak that angled into the smoothness of his forehead, and his lips twitched in a sardonic smile. Without a word he arose from the bed, shrugged into his dressing gown, and left her room.

She could scarcely apologize to him, of course. And, after all, what was there to apologize for? She had not meant for her thoughts to wander last night; it was habit, nothing more, because of Guy. Still, she resolved to be especially sweet to him today, if only to show her appreciation for his generosity. She dressed carefully in her most becoming gown, her skin still tingling from the scalding bath she had had Dominique pour.

Encountering Bricole in the passageway, she was dismayed to find that Monsieur le Vicomte had ridden out a good hour ago. It was a busy day at Chimère; he might be anywhere on the estate. She had her writing desk brought upstairs and placed in her small sitting room, spending the better part of an hour releasing the intricate catch and going through the drawers once again. But her joy was hollow; without Jean-Auguste to share her delight, the jewels lost a bit of their luster, the complex mechanism seemed less clever.

Seating herself at the desk, she drew out paper and ink, and penned a long letter to her brother in Chartres. It was filled with glowing descriptions of Chimère and the beautiful countryside, and detailed lists of the gowns she had bought and the gifts from Jean-Auguste, whom she set forth in the most flattering of terms: his handsomeness, his character, his noble bearing. *That* should give her sister-in-law the colic for a week! Her brother in

Rouen was a different matter—he was a priest as well as a brother—it did not seem right to indulge in as much effusive exaggeration. As simply as she could, she told him of her marriage, of Jean-Auguste's goodness, of the wisdom of her choice, of her wish to be worthy of him. She put down her quill and stared into the distance; idly pulling open a drawer in the cabinet, she fingered the jeweled button within. Sighing, she picked up her pen again.

". . . oh my dearest brother," she wrote. "Teach me what I must do to be a better person in God's sight. There is much wickedness in me that I had not seen before. I am assailed by black humors, and yet am powerless to change. Give me your guidance as I may call you friend, brother, Father.

"Chimère is large. I could wish I had attended more to our good aunt. I fear me the skills of husbandry and good management will never be mine! Welladay! I shall learn, or learn instead how I may charm my husband into blindness toward my failings!

"God keep you until we meet again.

Your dearest sister, Lysette."

She sealed the letters, then called for Dominique and changed into her riding clothes. Instructing the maid to see that her horse was saddled, she sought out Bricole.

"I shall go riding now. Where may I post these letters?"

"There is a postal office in Vouvray, Madame. But you would be better served taking the carriage, and Dominique. She knows the town and can be helpful."

"But I wish to ride!"

"Vouvray is a long way on horseback, Madame, and perhaps not so safe for a woman riding alone. Besides, the stagecoach will not come for the mail for another two days. If you will leave your letters on the marble table in the small salon, I will see that one of the grooms posts them in Vouvray in good time."

"Very well," she said sourly, knowing he had bested her once again.

He bowed politely. "Madame, forgive me, but . . . do you wish to dine at seven again tonight?"

She hesitated, feeling foolish and trapped. If she changed her mind so soon, surely Jean-Auguste (and Bricole even!) would mock her. "Yes!" she snapped.

She spent a good part of the afternoon riding through the fields and vineyards, hoping to meet Jean-Auguste, if only because she found his company amusing; but travel where she might she could not find him. She was too proud to stop and inquire after him; besides, the farmers and *vignerons* that she passed seemed unusually busy, though they took the time to bow and doff their caps to Madame la Vicomtesse as she rode by. She was in an ill humor by the time she returned to Chimère, half convinced that he had deliberately avoided her all the day. She was in the small salon pacing restlessly when at last he came bounding in, his face wreathed in smiles. How she hated him! Playing the gallant, he swept off his hat and bowed low, taking her hand and planting a kiss on her fingertips. Was that the only greeting she could expect from her bridegroom? she thought bitterly. Already he begins to tire of the charade!

"Are we to wait supper again tonight?" he asked.

"Yes," she said curtly. "It was my habit at Soligne."

"Indeed?"

Her chin jutted belligerently. "Guy always dined at seven!" she lied, then turned away so he might not read the lie in her eyes.

"As you wish." As before, he picked up his book and seated himself comfortably, this time facing the fireplace and the portrait of Gabriel. Lysette was too restive even to play the lute, and she prowled the room, crossing first in front of him and then behind, annoyed at his indifference. Ah, *Dieu!* The long ride had made her hungrier than she realized; in the silence of the room her stomach began to growl angrily and audibly. Startled, Jean-Auguste looked up from his book, then discreetly lowered his eyes. Lysette felt her face go red and she whirled quickly about, willing the offending organ to be still. It was no use. Her stomach meant to protest the long wait until the hour of seven—and protest it for all the world to hear. In defense she snatched up the lute, playing it steadily until the long hour had passed; but Jean-Auguste, his face still buried in his book, could hardly suppress the grin that twitched at the corners of his mouth.

At long last, supper was brought in and laid out in the center

of the room. Immediately Jean-Auguste arose and went to the
table, motioning Lysette to join him. The aroma of the food was
maddening, but she forced herself to finish the tune she had
been strumming before crossing the room nonchalantly to join
him. Hateful man! Always laughing at her! As she passed the
marble console beneath his mother's portrait, her eye was
caught by the two letters she had placed there earlier. She
stopped and fingered the missive to her brother in Rouen. What
moment of weakness had overtaken her—to write such a
sniveling letter? With an impatient movement, she snatched it
up and tore it in two before moving to the fireplace and tossing
it into the flames.

Jean-Auguste was warm and friendly throughout supper,
filled with stories of his busy day, explaining that the grapes
would be harvested upon the morrow and that there would be
a merry fête in celebration. He did not ask her how she had
spent her time; indeed, though his manner was far from cool,
there was a certain distance, an inclination to keep his conversation light and impersonal that she found maddening. Annoyed,
she even inveigled him into a compliment or two; he responded
willingly enough, but there was disinterest in his tone.

She found herself growing more and more angry with him as
the meal progressed—for his indifference, for laughing at her,
for his comfortable self-esteem. Just let him invite himself into
her bedchamber this evening! Just let him dare to ask! She
would blister him with her refusal; she would make a scene that
would scorch the very walls of Chimère! He had ignored her all
the day—now let him pay for his neglect!

Supper finished, she tarried at the table for a short time, then
bid him good night. Though she lingered overlong on the
staircase, he did not hurry to her side; when at length she
tiptoed across the hall and stole a peek into the small salon, she
saw that he had resumed reading, his chair drawn up to the
fireplace, his booted feet propped comfortably on a small stool
before the hearth, as though he intended to stay there all night.

How glad I am, she thought, to be relieved of a wife's burden,
if even for one night.

Then why did her chamber seem cold and lonely, and sleep,
when it finally overtook her, fitful and filled with uneasy
dreams?

Chapter Thirteen

THE FIRST THIN LIGHT OF DAY WAS STREAKING THROUGH THE casement windows when Dominique hurried in and woke her.

She sat up grumbling, yawning and wiping the sleep from her eyes. *"Nom de Dieu,* Dominique, it is still the middle of the night!"

"Monsieur has requested it, Madame!"

"Devil take Monsieur!" She eased herself back onto the pillows and pulled the coverlet more firmly about her shoulders. "Go away," she mumbled.

"But Madame!"

Annoyed, fully awake at last, she sat up in bed and glared at the girl. "I do not wish to rise so early," she said evenly, her violet eyes flashing.

Dominique glanced nervously at the closed door and began to whimper. "But Madame! Monsieur is waiting!"

"Out, out, out!" she shrilled, and hurled a pillow at the maid's departing form. She had just settled herself once again when the door burst open and Jean-Auguste entered, in high good humor. He strode across the room and whipped the coverlet from her bed. She scarcely had time to recover from that indignity before he grasped her about the waist, swung her out of bed, and set her firmly upon her bare feet.

"Come!" he boomed. "It is the harvest today! There is much

140

to be done and much to see! Save sleeping for a cold winter's morning! Put on your handsomest riding things and come with me!"

She frowned and pouted, suddenly remembering his indifference of the day before. "I am still tired," she sulked.

He put his hands on her shoulders. "Lysette, come," he cajoled. "There will be feasting and dancing when the grapes are in."

"Pooh! What care I?"

"As mistress of Chimère you should be there."

"Are you ordering me to go with you?"

"Nom de Dieu!" he said impatiently. "Will you ever cease to be a child?"

Stung, she shook her shoulders free of his grasp. "Why did you come to my room this morning, when I forbade it?"

"Forbade?" His gray eyes flickered with a hard light; she fidgeted nervously and softened her tone.

"I . . . asked you most kindly not to . . . invade my chamber in the morning," she said in an aggrieved voice. "Are my words of such little moment to you that you can have forgot so soon?"

"I could not wait on such a busy day. Now, will you come with me or no?"

With careful deliberation she turned her back to him and yawned extravagantly. "No."

He shrugged in disgust. "As you wish." At the door, however, he paused and turned. "Lysette," he said gently, "come later to the harvest then. When you have had your fill of sleep. I beg you. Do not spend a lonely day at Chimère merely for the sake of your pride—and your violated bedchamber!"

She hesitated, then jutted out her chin in defiance. "No!"

When he had gone, closing the door quietly behind him, she stood for a long time, shivering, in the center of the room, warring with her pride; at length, rousing herself, she crept back to the warmth and comfort of her bed. She found she could no longer sleep, but she stayed in bed all the morning, picking at the tray of food Dominique had brought, pretending to herself that she was too weary to rise. When at last even her bed had become vexatious, she rose and dressed carelessly, annoyed that Dominique seemed clumsy and distracted.

"By all that is holy, Dominique," she snapped at last, "what has beset you today? You have pulled at my hair, and torn my band string—in faith, I would be better served by a palsied half-wit!"

"Forgive me, Madame, but it is the harvest!" she burst out. "One of the *vignerons* has promised to let me tread the grapes."

"And you wish to leave now?"

"If he does not see me there, he will find another!"

"What nonsense!"

"Oh, Madame!" she wailed. "I never missed the harvest at Vilmorin! Not ever!"

Lysette sighed in resignation. In her present mood, the maid would be of no use to her anyhow. "And is he handsome, your *vigneron?*" Dominique smiled and blushed. "Then go. I shall have no more need of you." She shrugged off the girl's effusive thanks, and wandered to the casement window, leaning against the leaded panes and watching the serene river below. If Jean-Auguste does not see me at the harvest will he find another? she wondered. How foolish to have been so stubborn and proud! But he would surely think her a child if she changed her mind now. No! she thought. I said I would not come, and I shall not!

She had never spent such a long and tedious day in all her life. Even as Guy's wife, hated and ignored by half of Soligne, she had always managed to find someone to chat with, someone with whom to share the delicious gossip of a small town. But Chimère was almost empty save for the frenzied activity in the large kitchens, as food was prepared and shuttled out to the workers in the vineyards.

Pooh! she thought. What matter? Better to sup alone . . . when she wished, where she wished! Surely at the fête she would be expected to dine with the servants, smile at them, even (Mon Dieu!) dance with them!

She dined in the small salon at seven (still stubborn, though Bricole was out in the fields supervising the feast), then sat and played the lute until boredom and the lateness of the hour overtook her and she nodded over the strings. A draft from the door woke her; she opened her eyes to see Jean-Auguste smiling above her, his sparkling eyes belying the weariness in his face.

"It was a good harvest," he said. "I did not think we would

pick all the grapes before dark! The fermenting vats are full to bursting—I cannot remember them so full ere now! And sweet! Here!" He held out a cluster of grapes, pale green tinged with pink, and watched pridefully, like a mother with an exceptional child, as Lysette tasted the grapes and nodded her approval. "There is dancing still—will you come?"

She hesitated, torn by his humble persistence—hating him for his unfailing kindness, despising herself for the spitefulness that had blighted her whole day. "No," she said at last, very softly.

He smiled warmly, still enveloped by an aura of satisfaction. "Then come to my bed tonight."

"Alas," she murmured, her face suddenly sad and woebegone, "my head troubles me . . . a slight malaise. You will find no pleasure with me this night." She cast down her eyes meekly. "Will you forgive the weakness of this woman's body?"

He bowed stiffly, all the joy drained out of his face. "As you wish, Madame. I shall bid you good night. There is still dancing . . . and wine . . . at the fête to beguile away the evening." He turned on his heel and was gone.

In the morning, she was assailed anew by her conscience. She had not meant to hurt him, but how could she welcome his lovemaking with any great enthusiasm when her fear of conceiving a child was never far from her mind? She resolved at least to blunt her cruelty by prolonging the charade: despite her growing weariness with her chamber, she stayed in her bed and sent word through Dominique that she was still too ill to get up.

To amuse herself, she insisted that Dominique tell her all about the harvest and the fête, easing her envy by persuading herself that she would not have enjoyed a moment of it. The servant girl dwelt at length upon her handsome young *vigneron,* Etienne: how he had stolen a kiss or two, and would have danced with her all the night—holding her more tightly than he ought—but for that fool of a forester, Simon Vacher. Half drunk, he had capered about like a madman, dancing with all the women, snatching her from the arms of her *vigneron* each time it seemed that Etienne would pull her into the shadows beyond the glow of the bonfire. Despite Lysette's persistent questioning, she could not recall if Monsieur le Vicomte had danced with any one particular woman.

A gentle knock on the door announced Jean-Auguste, waiting to be received; Dominique ushered him into the room and then vanished. He bowed low, as though he were in the presence of a queen, but the coolness in his gray eyes put the lie to the pleasant smile on his face. He hoped she was feeling better, that her illness was not due to ennui; with the harvest in, there would be more time to dispel her languor in trips to Vouvray and visits to Paris and Vilmorin. There was work for him this morning, he said, but if she were so inclined, and her spirits somewhat revived by the afternoon, he would be pleased to ride with her.

She smiled weakly at him, contriving to look ill, regretting the healthy glow on her cheeks that still lingered from the long journey through Poitou and Touraine. She could not promise, she said, that she would be fit to ride but . . . she lowered her eyelids and turned her face into the pillows. The game was becoming too difficult with his piercing glance on her! Mercifully he chose to leave, whether because of his pressing duties, or out of pity for her discomfort, she could not say.

By mid-afternoon her lethargic body cried out for movement, activity; even to sit a horse seemed too sedentary. The day was sunny and pleasant, with that peculiar autumnal tang in the air—a sharpness, for all the warm sunshine—that promised a cool evening. On such a day, a long brisk walk was what she needed. She dressed in a soft woolen skirt and snug jacket, and two pairs of red silk stockings to keep her feet warm under her soft Moroccan leather shoes. She sent for Bricole to enquire as to the whereabouts of Monsieur de Narbaux.

"He is downriver, Madame, less than half a league. Vacher and his men are clearing a field near the bank. You will see the smoke as you go out of doors."

"Thank you, Bricole."

His eyes took in her costume, the fragile leather shoes. "Will Madame la Vicomtesse ride?"

"No. I prefer to walk today."

"Then you will need pattens, Madame, for it is muddy where they work." He smiled kindly. "Such fine shoes . . ."

"Thank you," she said, touched by his solicitude. Perhaps he could be a friend after all. She smiled winningly at him; his pleased response told her he would be an easy conquest. She hesitated for a moment, then lowered her voice as though she were sharing a secret. "Bricole," she said, "Monsieur is too kind to speak of it, but I do not think he is happy with the lateness of the dinner hour. When a man is hungry, it is difficult to wait. For his sake, I think we shall have supper at six—I shall contrive to change my habits to please him."

He nodded in deference, then waited politely as she slipped into the pattens that Dominique had fetched—red velvet scuffs with thick cork soles that fit over her shoes to keep them dry. "If I may be allowed," he said. "Monsieur is indeed fortunate to have found a Lady with such a kind and generous nature. How I should like to see his face when you tell him you have deferred to his wishes! Monsieur le Vicomte is an amiable man, with few demands—your graciousness does honor to him and to Chimère. Rest assured, Madame, I shall see that supper is waiting at six of the clock."

As she strode along the river bank toward the billowing clouds of pale gray smoke, Lysette reflected on her interview with Bricole. It had not gone exactly as she would have wished. For though it was pleasant to discover that Bricole viewed her as a paragon of all that was virtuous in women, she was not at all pleased that he had somehow maneuvered her into the distasteful position of being the messenger to Jean-Auguste.

The path along the bank dipped toward the Loire, and she picked her way carefully through the marsh grass; at this spot the river fell away steeply from the shore, and flowed swift and deep and dark. Ahead of her, she could see Jean-Auguste on a small rise just above the river, his doublet off, shirtsleeves rolled up to show his sinewy arms. Beyond him was a large open stretch of land, still smoldering from the fire that had been set to clear the underbrush. Vacher and some of his men were engaged in hauling from the earth the last few charred and blackened stumps, straining against the ropes looped about the remains of the trees; the rest of the men had formed a kind of chain, passing up large wooden buckets from the river to douse the remaining sparks. The embers hissed softly under the onslaught as the smoke turned from pale gray to silver, and then became steam.

Jean-Auguste, a smudge of soot upon his cheek, had been helping to pass the buckets along; at the sight of Lysette he put down his pail and smiled warmly at her.

"You are feeling better?"

"Yes." She went to stand beside him. "And this"—the sweep of her hand encompassing the open field—"will you plant grapes here?"

"No. Wheat and rye. Bricole tells me the cook has been complaining of late because of the maslin. Too much barley, she says—it spoils the flour mixture."

"But she is fortunate—I had to buy my maslin in the markets of Soligne. It was often old and filled with weevils, and I could never be sure that it contained only wheat and rye flour—by my faith I think there were milled acorns in the blend last summer when the crops were bad!"

"There are those who have nothing when the crops are bad," he chided gently. "Did you ride over from Chimère?"

"No. It seemed a pleasant day for a walk."

"Then perhaps we can return in a while to the chateau and ride out for an hour or two."

"But the time will be late!" she blurted.

"And wherefore late?"

There was no escaping it. "I . . . because . . ." She took a deep breath. "I have informed Bricole that we shall dine at six," she said, with as much dignity as she could muster.

"Hum. At six."

"Yes."

"For all time?"

"Yes! I told him it was for your sake!"

"Hum. For my sake."

"Must you echo my words?" she snapped. Damn him and his mocking eyes! She knew he must be laughing at her behind his bland expression, must be remembering (even as she was) how her noisy stomach had betrayed her hunger. "Go to the devil!" she shrilled. Whirling, she snatched up the bucket of water and hurled its contents full into his face. He sputtered with the unexpected shock of the dousing, then wiped his face with his hand, a small crease furrowing his brow.

There was a sudden stillness. The servants, aghast at the humiliation visited upon their master, had put down their burdens and waited now to see how Monsieur le Vicomte would deal with a wife who dared to treat him thus. For a second, seeing the look in his gray eyes, Lysette regretted her rashness. Then, abruptly, he began to laugh heartily, a warm guffaw that invited her to share the absurdity of the moment.

Relieved, the servants joined in the laughter, timidly at first, then merrily at sight of his dripping red curls and drenched shirt.

Lysette could not share their mirth; she burned with shame and anger. She had made a fool of herself—and Jean-Auguste had salvaged her pride by sacrificing his own. With a wail she sprang for him, her hand poised to strike his face. Still smiling, he parried the blow, pushing aside her upraised arm, then scooped her up in one swift movement and pitched her into the river. She shrieked as she hit the icy water, and flailed about with her arms; her skirts billowed wide on the surface of the river and left her bare hips and thighs unprotected from the cold current. She cursed him with every street oath she had heard in Soligne, then cursed him again in Spanish, using the words she had heard from soldiers newly returned from the front. Still laughing, he knelt by the bank.

"By my faith, Madame, you have blistered my ears! But I fancied you enjoyed swimming!"

"Villain!" she spat, struggling more violently as her skirts, soaking up the water, began to drag heavily against her movements.

"Will you swim until six? Or seven?"

"Oh!" she sputtered, then turned away from him, making small circles in the water with her hands. When she turned back again, he saw to his dismay that she had begun to weep. "It is very c-c-cold," she sobbed, "and you are hateful to treat me so unkindly!" She swam closer to the shore. "Please," she said in a small voice, "will you give me your hands?" She reached up one dainty hand and then the other, which he grasped in his own two. Captivated by her large violet eyes, so woeful behind their mist of tears, he did not realize she had braced her feet against the bank until a sudden jerk of her hands pulled him, head first, into the river. He plummeted into the depths, then righted himself and broke the surface of the water, coughing and choking and shaking his head from side to side, until the droplets flew out from his hair. As soon as he recovered his breath, he began to laugh again. Lysette, still glaring with righteous retribution, nevertheless could not deny the humor of the situation; relenting, she joined in the laughter, and soon the two of them were clinging to one another in helpless merriment. At last Jean-Auguste made for the shore and hauled himself up on the bank; he hesitated for a moment, still wary, before offering her his hands and pulling her up to stand beside him on dry land.

"I have lost my pattens!" she said.

"I shall buy you another pair."

Lifting her sopping skirts, she began to giggle again. "I fear me they did not keep my feet dry!"

"Useless things!" he laughed. "But you are cold," he said, as she began to shiver. He retrieved his cloak from the ground and wrapped it tightly about her, then pulled his doublet over his wet shirt and lifted Lysette in his arms, marching resolutely in the direction of the chateau. The steady squish of his boots sent them both into peals of laughter again; by the time they reached Chimère they were thoroughly chilled and positively giddy. Once inside the door, Jean-Auguste set her on her feet.

"There is a small antechamber next to my apartments," he said, "very warm and cozy. Come there when you have changed your clothes. We can have supper."

She grinned wickedly up at him. "But . . . is it six of the clock, my lord?"

"It is supper by my stomach, Madame!" His eyes glinted in amusement. "What says your stomach?"

"It speaks in a very loud voice!"

"Yes. So I have heard! And it says . . . ?"

"It says, be it six or seven or five, let us eat when we are hungry!"

"A wise stomach, Madame," he said, suddenly gentle. "Now, be off with you before you catch the ague!"

She changed quickly into dry chemise and petticoat, and covered it with a fur-trimmed dressing gown; toweling her wet hair, she pocketed a large comb and padded down the passageway to the antechamber he had indicated, her soft slippers whispering on the tiles. The room was indeed cozy: heavy draperies at the windows, walls hung with tapestries to keep out stray drafts, and a large rug of red fox on the floor before the blazing fireplace. Jean-Auguste was already there, a sleeveless leather jerkin thrown carelessly over fresh breeches and shirt; he had not even bothered to put on a falling band, but wore his shirt collarless and open at the neck. He was standing at a small table in the center of the room that was filled with platters of fruit and meats; when Lysette entered, he poured out a mug of hot cider from a large pitcher and handed it to her. She thanked him, then plunked herself down on the fur rug, kicking off her slippers and wriggling her bare toes gratefully in the direction of the fire. She gulped her cider quickly, enjoying the warmth that flowed through her body. Setting down her mug, she began to comb her hair, fluffing out the tresses to speed its drying; when she was satisfied, she plaited it into one long braid, pulling it over one shoulder as she worked. Slowly sipping his cider, Jean-Auguste watched in fascination, surprised as always by the contradiction of innocence and vanity in her behavior. She seemed so comfortable before the fire he was reluctant to disturb her for dinner; instead he took the platters from the table and put them upon the hearth, then sat down beside her on the rug. It was a fine meal the cook had prepared: roasted capon and a large bowl of sauce for dipping, redolent with apricots and ginger and saffron; thin strips of ham with a spicy mustard, braised carrots, and, for dessert, fresh grapes and milk curds with sugar. The cider that washed it all down was rich and spicy, heavy with the scent of cloves and cinnamon.

Lysette licked the last of the sauce from her fingers, then wiped her hands on her napkin and held out her empty mug to Jean-Auguste. He refilled her cup and his own, then sighed contentedly and pushed the platters out of their way.

Lysette began to laugh. They were really quite ridiculous, sitting cross-legged in front of the fire like a couple of children. "This is the strangest feast I have ever had!"

He chuckled. "No. I shall tell you of a stranger one! My mother—she was a droll creature—presided once at a most unusual feast."

"Were you there?"

"Oh, yes. I was almost grown, and Gabriel was already the master of Chimère. You must understand, firstly, that my mother had a very large fortune of her own. And then—and she herself was forthright about it—she was a plain woman."

"Nay! I have seen her portrait! Hardly plain!"

He laughed gently. "The artist caught her spirit—and her spirit was beautiful—but it is not a true likeness."

"*Eh bien.* She was plain and she was rich. Now you must tell me of the feast!"

"She had a suitor, a very important man at Court. He had pursued her for more than a year, and claimed to be burning with unrequited love. She was fond of him, I think, but something in his manner gave her pause. As for Gabriel, he was dazzled by the man's title and position."

"And you?"

"I am my mother's sprig! Never as somber as Gabriel, nor as sensible or conventional, I found it easy to dislike the man because"—he shrugged—"because his sword was rusty, because he smiled too much at my mother, because he patted me on the head!"

"Pah! What a fool!"

"Undoubtedly! I plead my youth. However . . . the time came when this gentleman announced to my mother that he wished to come to dine at Chimère. It was quite apparent that he meant to propose marriage. On the assumption that to invite him was tantamount to accepting his proposal, my mother was disinclined to bid him come. She had begun to suspect that her fortune was the allurement that drew him to her. Gabriel, with all the stiff-necked propriety of the young . . ."

"How old was he?" she said, suddenly belligerent.

He tweaked her nose, his mouth twitching. "Rest assured, *ma petite*, you are far older than he was in wisdom and experience." He poured out another cup of cider for her. "At any rate, Gabriel was horrified that she should refuse such a fine man. He had lands and holdings of his own—what need had he for her wealth? My mother was adamant. He hungered only for her gold, and would do anything, endure anything, to win her hand . . . and her fortune. She would prove it to Gabriel. She sent word to her suitor that she looked upon him with favor, and was happy to invite him to come to supper. However, for the sake of discretion, she told him, she thought it wise to invite other guests, some of whom were equally fond of her. He must not mind, she said, if she treated them with the same deference she showed to him; it was in her nature to be generous. The night of the feast came; the honored guest arrived, puffed with his own importance and the certainty of his victory. Gabriel and I were burning with curiosity; my mother had been secretive for days. She ushered us all into the salon—the large room next to the library—a long table had been set up, and at each place, save the spaces that had been reserved for us, was . . ." He laughed suddenly at the wide-eyed anticipation on Lysette's face, and popped a grape into her gaping mouth.

"Nom de Dieu!" she sputtered, swallowing as fast as she could. "What?"

"An animal! Cats, dogs, a rabbit, I think . . . and even a mummer's trained goat, brought from Vouvray, that stood upon its hind legs and tapped insistently on the table with one foreleg, as though it were impatient for dinner. My mother had even gone so far as to dress them gorgeously in silks and brocades, with stiff neck ruffs and lace cuffs; the goat was wearing upon its head an exact replica of the kind of melon-shaped hat favored by our nobleman. Very seriously, my mother introduced them all, giving them the most outlandish names, while she clutched at the rabbit to keep it from scampering the length of the table. Once recovered from our surprise, Gabriel and I joined most readily into the game, bowing politely and greeting each guest in turn. The nobleman did likewise, whether out of fear of her displeasure, or because he thought her mad, I cannot say. And the more he fawned upon her, the more outrageous became her behavior. She seated herself between him and the goat, and smiled equally at one as the other, feeding sweetmeats to them both, and then insisting he feed the goat himself. Her guest was most partial to lace cuffs, she said, would Monsieur be so kind as to oblige? I thought that Gabriel would fall under the table when the man actually untied his cuffs and fed them to the animal. But mother had not finished with him yet. He must sing the praises of all her guests, she said. Did not Monsieur le Chat have fine eyes? And the pink ears of Monsieur le Lapin—without equal! Monsieur praised them all lavishly, though his face had turned red with apoplexy, and at the end of the evening my mother insisted that he kiss each of the guests on both cheeks. I can still see him stooped down with the goat's forelegs on both his shoulders; as he leaned forward to deliver his kiss, the animal took an enormous bite out of his hat!"

"Stop!" said Lysette, who had begun to laugh so hard the tears were pouring down her cheeks. Jean-Auguste arose and put another log on the fire, then stood looking down at her as she wiped her eyes. Recovering her composure, she took another drink of cider. "But what happened to the suitor?"

"Before he left, my mother asked him if he still wished to marry her. He assured her that his feelings for her had not changed, and he would be honored to make her his bride. She demurred, saying she would have to search her soul for the answer; within a week, she wrote to him, refusing his kind offer on the grounds that she still clung to the memory of her dead husband. If, in consequence, he was wounded by her decision, she begged him not to speak ill of her in the Court circles; in return she promised to keep silent about her supper party and his extraordinary behavior therein."

They laughed together at that. Then Lysette began to tell him of some foolishness of Guy's, of how he had been drunk, and hunting for a missing band string. She was a good mimic; getting up on all fours, she crawled around the rug, pretending to search frantically, mumbling incoherently, poking at an imaginary wig that kept falling into her eyes. When they had both laughed until they could laugh no more, she rolled over onto her back, exhausted.

"Help me up," she said at last, lifting her arms to him.

He started to give her his hands, then thought better of it and shook his head. "Ah, no," he chuckled, dropping down beside her, "for surely I should find my nose crushed against the hearth! By my faith, those eyes of yours cozened me at the river . . . you are a veritable devil!"

She smirked with pleasure, then frowned in mock dismay. "But then I never dreamed that you would toss me into the water—so we are quits!"

"Agreed!" he said, and smiled warmly down at her, his eyes searching hers. He reached out a gentle hand and stroked her face, his slim fingers tracing the line of her cheek and jaw. *"Mon Dieu,"* he said softly, "my mother would have envied that face. If the angels themselves mixed the pigments, they could not match the color of your eyes." He bent over and covered her mouth with his own. Lysette wriggled comfortably on the fur rug, luxuriating in the softness of his kisses, the warm fire, the glow of the cider that lingered still within her. His lips caressed her face and neck, and his arms circled her body where she lay; with a languid sigh, she slipped her hands about his neck. Half drowsing, she was content to let him go on kissing her while she drifted in and out of sleep, delighting in the pleasures of her senses—the feel of his strong arms, the downy curls at the nape of his neck, so silky against her fingertips, the sweetness of his mouth. Would André's kiss be like this? she wondered idly. Ah, André! *Mon amour!* She opened her eyes and smiled hazily at Jean-Auguste. Odd. For a moment, nodding, she thought she had spoken André's name aloud. But how could that be so? Surely she would see it in Jean-Auguste's eyes, and even now he was smiling as he rose to his feet and helped her up.

"You are tired," he said. "Go to bed." He poured himself another cup of cider and passed a hand across his eyes. "I have letters to write this evening. I shall be leaving Chimère tomorrow for a few weeks."

"But I thought we would go to Paris," she said, crestfallen.

"Such pleasures must await my return. If I am to lease the woods to a master glassmaker, I must obtain the necessary papers and see that a license is issued. And then, there is a loan to be secured—there are few glassmakers who can afford to start up a glasshouse without an advance of capital. Now, off to bed with you and stop your pouting. When I return, there will be gowns and parties and fawning admirers enough to satisfy even your vain little soul! I shall leave a purse with Bricole—you may go to Vouvray and spend it to your heart's content."

Placated, she stood on tiptoe and kissed him on the cheek. She bid him good night and Godspeed on his journey, then made her way down the corridor to her own chambers, enveloped still in an aura of warmth and contentment. It had been a lovely evening—the companionship, the laughter, the flattery in his words and eyes, the pleasure of being petted and kissed (and nothing expected in return!).

From the doorway, he watched her progress toward her room; had she turned, she might have seen that his face, illuminated by a small candelabra in the hall, was as bleak as a winter's landscape.

Chapter Fourteen

WITH JEAN-AUGUSTE AWAY, THE WEEKS PASSED SLOWLY. Lysette rode almost every day, and played the lute, and spent countless hours before her mirror, admiring herself in all her new finery. It was far pleasanter than her life in Soligne had been: forever pinching pennies, riding seldom, and then only when she could afford to rent a horse. But Soligne had been a bustling town, filled with gossip and handsome young men; she missed the delicious wickedness of a scandal, the zest of an innocent flirtation. And she was still a stranger here. To amuse herself, she set about charming all the servants and tenants at Chimère, noting with satisfaction how easily each one was swept into her orbit. The *vigneron* Pasquier, the young man who had shown her and Jean-Auguste about the caves, was particularly vulnerable, and it pleased her to manage an encounter with him as often as she could, just to see him blush to the roots of his blond hair; only when she learned he had a wife and child did she cease her thoughtless beguilement.

Bricole was especially kind to her, tending to her every wish, treating her with a deference that almost made her uncomfortable. As the days dragged on, and her restlessness grew, a boredom that sprang from the aimless, indolent life she had always led, Bricole tried to draw her into the running of Chimère, now bustling with preparations for winter. He sought her approval on innumerable details; even as she smiled and nodded, assuring him that she trusted his judgment, she cursed herself for her irresponsible years under her aunt's tutelage. The details were all so complex, and she scarcely had any idea of how—or what—to approve! As for money, she could hardly handle it with any wisdom. Guy had always given a fixed sum to their servant to run the household, and Lysette had had whatever she could wheedle from him on an irregular basis; after Guy had died, she had continued to give the same fixed amount to her housekeeper, neither questioning nor wondering where it went. And now, here was Bricole, eager to discuss the household accounts with her; he might as well have been talking in Greek for all it meant to her, and she was too proud and ashamed to ask him to be her tutor. At length she convinced herself that such domestic details were beneath her, and told him, with some testiness, that she no longer wished to be bothered by such trivialities.

Accompanied by Dominique, she took several trips to Vouvray, directing her coachman through the narrow streets that meandered up and down from the valley to the limestone cliffs and caves, stopping at one shop and another to make small purchases with the coins that Jean-Auguste had left. She always spent more than she intended to, and she always journeyed back to Chimère filled with wretched remorse, while Dominique, oblivious to her mood, chattered on about her Etienne, or complained bitterly of Simon Vacher who seemed determined to bedevil the maid, snatching an insolent kiss or pinching her familiarly when she ventured out of doors.

The weather turned unexpectedly cold, with a sharp wind that blew through the trees like a sorcerer's spell, changing them overnight to glowing reds and golds. It was too windy for long rides; Lysette spent more and more time in the cozy antechamber, hunched up on the fur rug with her lute or a book of poetry. The room reminded her of Jean-Auguste. He had been gone for more than a month; the one brief note she had received indicated that he expected to return at the end of October. Not that she missed him, of course! Only that his company was amusing, and the days were long and tedious— that was why she looked forward to his homecoming.

But October is peculiar. Just when it seemed that the trees, shivering in their bright raiment, would shed their leaves and surrender to winter, there came a morning at the end of the month when the sun shone brightly and the air was as sweet and mild as midsummer. A beautiful day, thought Lysette, breathing deeply at her open casement window. Surely Jean-Auguste would return on such a glorious day! So convinced of it was she, that she decided not to ride—though the blue sky and warm breezes called to her—but spent her time dressing carefully in her most becoming gown and strolling about the manicured gardens. By nightfall, when it was clear he would not come, she felt angry and cheated.

The following morning, the weather was even more beautiful. This time—devil take Jean-Auguste!—she would ride for the whole day. Let him return and find her gone! It would do him good to cool his heels and wait on her pleasure! She had Dominique fetch her a small packet of food; there would be no reason now to return before evening. She would ride and ride, free, undirected, wherever her fancy took her.

Dominique handed her her riding gloves, a small frown creasing her pinched features. "But Madame, if Monsieur should return today."

She shrugged. "I shall not be here."

"But if he asks where you have gone . . . ?"

"Tell him I have gone to the moon!" How could he have left her alone for so many weeks? She smiled maliciously. "Tell him I have gone to the wine caves."

She told herself she had not planned it, of course—yet she found herself, after an hour or so of aimless riding, on the path that led toward Vilmorin. Well, perhaps it would be pleasant to see Marielle and André; it had been well over a month and a half since her wedding. And they were neighbors . . . and friends. She spurred her horse on through the golden forest glades, ignoring her heart that had begun to thump in anticipation. André! To see André again!

She drew up into the courtyard of Vilmorin and cast her eyes about her. On the wide lawn near the summerhouse, two men were dueling fiercely; only the sheathed tips of their rapiers indicated that it was all in sport. Even at this distance, there was no doubt that one of the men was André: the golden hair, the bronzed skin of his sword arm, shirtsleeve rolled up above his elbow, his extraordinarily broad shoulders. Lysette watched him for a moment, his lithe grace and strength, then rode down to the two figures and dismounted, waiting. Praise be to God! No children about! No Marielle!

André looked toward her and saluted with his sword, then attacked his opponent in a flurry of lightning thrusts and parries until the man shouted *"Touché!"* and, laughing, threw down his rapier. Stripping off his fencing glove, André handed them both to his servant along with his sword, and dismissed the man. Smiling broadly, he turned toward Lysette and embraced her with the easy familiarity of a brother, his blue eyes radiating a warmth that took her breath away.

"Has Jean-Auguste returned then?" he asked, looking beyond her toward the courtyard.

"No," she replied, then stopped, struck dumb by the sight of him, the spell of his sapphire eyes. "It . . . it is warm in the sun," she stammered at last. "Come." She led him into the shadowed coolness of the summerhouse. "How foolish of you," she scolded, "to run about playing with swords on such a warm day!" She withdrew a large handkerchief from her pocket, directing him to duck his head down that she might mop his brow. *"Mon Dieu!"* she said coquettishly, smiling up at him. "I had almost forgot what a handsome man you are!"

He laughed, taking it as a joke, and shook his head in reproach. "Am I to be compromised by a married woman?"

She pouted. "Was there ever a married woman so quickly abandoned by her bridegroom?"

"Will it cheer you to know that Jean-Auguste was filled with misgivings to leave you so soon? He rode through Vilmorin when he left Chimère; I had letters of introduction to several merchants and moneylenders in Paris. He was not happy to leave your side, but he was anxious to see the work begun before winter sets in. You may take his remorse as proof of his affection!"

"Pah! What need have I for his remorse? When I am neglected for all these many weeks. . . ." She turned away, frowning. "It is clear his glassmaking means more to him than I do!"

André laughed ruefully. *"Eh bien!* We all suffer from neglect! I must engage my servants in swordplay because . . ." He shrugged, then was silent.

"I quite forget my manners! How is Marielle?"

"Enjoying the pleasures of domesticity," he said, a sharp edge in his voice.

"On such a lovely day? When you might have gone riding

together? I marked how beautiful the trees were as I came from Chimère. They quite dispelled the loneliness of my ride."

"You should not have come alone! I shall be your companion on the journey back."

"How kind you are. How I have missed you!" She smiled disarmingly as his eyes widened in surprise. "Both of you."

"Come," he said. "Let us see if we can divert Marielle from her duties, if only for an hour or two!"

They found Marielle in the kitchen, Louise at her side. The place was a beehive of activity, with the last frantic preparations before winter set in. Once the snow was on the ground, there would be no fresh meat at Vilmorin save for the occasional stag or boar run to earth in the hunt. A dozen pigs had been slaughtered, and the carcasses were being cut up and prepared in every corner of the cavernous room. Large salting tubs, filled with coarse, dry crystals, were being stocked with the various cuts of pork; in a week or so, the large hams and the lean underbelly would be taken from the salt and hung in the small smokehouse behind the kitchen, to be smoked and cured. Used sparingly, the hams would grace many a winter's table; the savory bacon could flavor a fine stew, and its rendered fat, slathered on a slab of bread, would be a solid, warming breakfast on a cold morning. The fat-back, that layer of fat over the pig's spine, would come out of the salting tubs to be air dried and hung in the root cellar next to the sacks of dried peas. Cooked together, they would make a hearty meal, or enhance a savory soup. The tongues and the feet of the pigs had been washed and placed in a barrel of brine, and a red-faced and robust cook was busy chopping the pork scraps to be smoked in the smokehouse and forced into the scraped intestines for sausage. Two fattened cows had been similarly slaughtered, their parts apportioned out to the various salting tubs and brine baths.

Marielle, a large ledger book in her hands, had been making notations when Lysette entered with André. She kissed Lysette warmly on both cheeks, seeming delighted with her visit, but her green eyes flicked nervously to André. "A moment," she said. "You must forgive me. Louise"—she consulted her ledger —"we will need more grain sacks, I think. The mice . . . can we get another cat, do you suppose? And cook tells me the copper kettle is quite worn through. Send for a tinker from

Vouvray to mend it . . . but get another kettle as well. I gave you a hundred crowns Wednesday last—will that be sufficient?" Louise thought a moment and then nodded. Marielle turned, frowning distractedly at André. "I wonder if we have laid in enough beef? Last winter . . ."

"*Nom de Dieu*, Marielle!" André cut in testily. "Will you be here all the day?"

"No, of course not, my love! It is only that . . ." She hesitated then pushed the ledger into Louise's hands. "The beef was short last winter, Louise. Take a careful account. I should not like to think that someone . . ."—she cast an uneasy eye about the room at the score of servants—". . . still, we must be wary."

"Come, Madame!" said André, growing annoyed.

"Yes, yes!" Still reluctant, Marielle followed André and Lysette to the kitchen steps, then stopped and turned for one final caveat. "Louise, see that the apples and beans are stored carefully in the root cellar; there was far too much rot last winter."

Though she pretended casualness, Lysette was wonderstruck by Marielle's capability. To remember so much, to direct such a complex household with ease, to have time even to consider if there was pilfering among the servants—ah, *Dieu!* she would never begin to be able to manage Chimère with such skill. She laughed ruefully to herself. Her housekeeper in Soligne must have taken her for a perfect fool! How many times, though the housekeeping money was generous, had the maid announced that there was no meat in the house? And fed her own family well, no doubt, on Guy's money! She knew she could trust Bricole, of course, just as Marielle trusted Louise, but . . . she sighed, filled with discontent. A *proper* wife would run the household herself.

They lunched together, the three of them, on the open lawn before the summerhouse, a strange and diffident trio. Lysette flirted outrageously with André—she felt joyous, alive; her eyes sparkled with the pleasure of being near him again. André seemed pleased and flattered, yet there was more than simple enjoyment in his attitude—an undercurrent, an odd tension that hung in the air between him and Marielle; it seemed to Lysette that he was inviting her coquetry out of spite to his wife. As for Marielle, she feigned indifference to their playful exchanges, her forced smile almost hiding the pain in her eyes. She chattered on about her domestic duties, the heavy responsibility of Vilmorin, the difficulties with the children, while they listened in polite sympathy. Then Lysette told of her adventures with Jean-Auguste—the feast in front of the fire, the dunking in the river, the gift of the writing desk (editing the stories carefully to include only the pleasant or humorous aspects)—until Marielle's life seemed dull and pale in comparison.

At length Lysette announced that it was time to leave, lest darkness overtake her before she reached Chimère.

André turned to Marielle. "Will you return to the kitchens?"

About to nod her head in assent, Marielle thought better of it and smiled warmly at André. "No, *mon chér.* You have been wishing to show me for weeks how to play the guitar—and I have been a reluctant pupil for too long. Perhaps for an hour or two this afternoon . . . ? I vow you shall have all my attention."

André frowned. "I cannot. I promised Lysette I would see her safely home to Chimère."

Marielle's smile seemed suddenly frozen, her green eyes glittering with a hard light. "Of course. I had quite forgot your gallantry. *Naturellement,* you must see to Lysette. Could we forgive ourselves if anything should happen to her? And Louise may need me after all." With forced graciousness, she kissed Lysette on both cheeks and fled to the chateau.

For a moment André hesitated, filled with unease; then, with a shrug, he summoned a servant and sent for Lysette's horse and his own.

They rode slowly through the leafy woods, chatting amiably, Lysette bent on prolonging the afternoon as much as she could. When they came to an open meadow, she insisted they dismount and walk, to take advantage of the warm sunshine. As they strolled, André talked of the last time he had been to Court, the latest liaisons, the beautiful courtesans anxious for a wealthy patron. Lysette pretended surprise at such scandalous behavior, but André laughed at her innocence.

"But there is no denying they are attractive women!" They had reached the end of the meadow and he turned to help her into her saddle, grasping her firmly about the waist.

She melted into his arms, hands clasped about his neck, and smiled coyly up at him. "And do you find *me* attractive?"

His eyes scanned her face, not with the searching glance of Jean-Auguste, but with the uncritical look of an admirer. "I find you far too attractive. You disquiet a man!" He swung her up into the saddle. He had the easy charm of a man who is used to flattering women—the words rang hollowly in her ears. What was it Jean-Auguste had said once? That André had been a rakehell in his younger days? Well she could believe that—he was attentive, smooth, charming, effortlessly so—but did his words reflect his true feelings about her? He would be a more difficult conquest than she had at first supposed—but infinitely worth the effort!

They had come to the highroad just before Chimère's long avenue of trees. Lysette reined in her mare. It would not do for any of the servants to see her ride up with André—there might be awkwardness in explaining it later to Jean-Auguste. "André," she said, her voice warm with kindness, "it will soon be dark. I should not like to think of Marielle sitting alone at Vilmorin waiting for you. Do not trouble yourself to see me to the door, but turn your horse about now and speed to your lovely wife's side!" Despite his protests, she was adamant, and bid him adieu and waved him out of sight.

As she rode up to Chimère, she saw a groom holding a solitary horse in front of the door; with a start she recognized Jean-Auguste's animal. She reined in and slid from her saddle, beaming in pleasure at his return, just as Jean-Auguste himself came rushing out of the chateau. At sight of her he stopped in his tracks, his face drained of color. A few long strides and he stood before her, his eyes probing her so penetratingly that the smile faded from her face.

"You did not go to the wine caves!" It was almost a question.

"Certainly not!"

"But you told Dominique you were going?" This time it *was* a question.

She hesitated, filled with guilt. Had he seen her with André? "Yes, I told Dominique—but it was only a jest."

"*Merde!*" he cursed under his breath. "Did she know you were jesting?"

"*Nom de Dieu!* What is amiss that you must torment me so?"

"Did she know?" His voice rasped like the edge of a sword.

"Oh what nonsense! No!" she said waspishly, her eyes

narrowing in annoyance. "I told her so because I wanted her to tell you! That you should return and think me lost! You did not mind absenting yourself from me all these many weeks!"

He frowned in disgust and swung himself into the saddle. "Do you care that half the men of Chimère have been searching the caves for you all afternoon?"

She bristled defensively, her small chin jutting out. "You may ride out and and tell them that I have been found!"

"Well, Pasquier has not," he said tightly. "He was the first man into the caves, looking for you. He has not been seen since. Pray God he is alive and safe." He swung his horse about and made for the bluffs, his bright orange hair glowing in the late afternoon sun.

Pasquier. Lysette gasped, her hand flying to her mouth. Pasquier. So young and robust and bright-cheeked. So obviously devoted to her. Pasquier—lost. Consumed by remorse, she stumbled into the chateau. Bricole's delight at seeing her safe and well only added to her misery. She crept into the small chapel and sank to her knees, her fervent prayers as much for forgiveness for her thoughtlessness as for Pasquier's safe return.

The last rays of the sun were streaming through the stained-glass windows, vibrant reds and blues and greens shimmering against the pale stone walls, when she heard the sound of a horse outside and Jean-Auguste's voice shouting for a groom. She rose from her knees and hurried out to meet him in the great hall. How tired he looked, his face drawn and haggard.

"Well?"

He stripped off his gauntlets and rubbed his eyes wearily. "Pasquier has been found. He must have slipped. The barrels fell on him. . . ."

"Ah Dieu! But is he alive?"

"His foot was crushed. If it festers, we must send for a surgeon to . . . remove it. In any event, he will be crippled for all time."

Lysette began to weep softly. "I had not meant . . . I only wanted . . . what may I do to make amends?"

"You cannot give him back his limb. But you might go to him . . . to his wife . . . and beg forgiveness that your reckless words brought him to grief."

Stricken, her tears forgotten, Lysette began to shake her

head. "No! I cannot! To abase myself . . . and after all, it was his carelessness, not mine. . . . I should die of shame! I did not ask him to go into the caves!" she finished belligerently.

He sighed heavily. "As you wish."

" 'As you wish! As you wish!' " she mimicked, her voice rising shrilly. "Always 'as you wish'! Must the burden forever be mine? What do *you* wish?"

He turned his cool gray eyes to her. "I wish . . ." Then he shrugged and was still. The unspoken words, heavy with accusation, hung in the air. With a shriek, Lysette leaped forward and slapped him across the mouth. Without a word he turned about and strode into the deepening night, while Lysette, already regretting her words and actions, longed to have the courage to call him back.

She wept bitter tears into her pillow all the night, refusing supper or the comfort that a distressed Dominique begged to give. In the morning, though it hurt to admit it to herself, she knew that Jean-Auguste had been right—she could scarcely make amends to Pasquier, but she owed him at least the mortification of her humbled pride.

The day was cool and damp, and a heavy mist lay low upon the ground as she made her way to the cliffs and the small cavern in which Pasquier made his home. A rough-hewn door had been fitted into the cave opening, and though the lime-stone had been chipped away to accommodate it, it still hung at a peculiar angle. A small window had been carved out next to it, and covered with oil-soaked parchment that let in a maximum of light while keeping out the chill air. The door was opened by a thin young woman who bobbed politely at Lysette and ushered her in, shooing a cat off a long bench that was almost the only seating in the dim room. Lysette sat gingerly, her face frozen in a gracious smile, and looked about her. Despite the window, the cave was dim; an unlit candle sat on the table, meant only for nighttime use. The walls of the cave had been roughly squared away and covered with a thin coating of whitewash, and a small niche, badly vented, had been cut out as a fireplace; nevertheless, the single room was nearly as cold and damp as the wine caves. Besides the bench and table, there was a small cupboard and a large leather chest, studded with brass tacks; a cradle, a three-legged stool before the fire, and the straw pallet upon which Pasquier lay completed the meager furnishings.

The two women smiled shyly at one another, then Lysette arose and went to stand beside Pasquier. His handsome face was drawn, the once rosy cheeks as ashen as the stone walls; his closed eyes were sunken and tinged with blue. Carefully she lifted the bottom edge of the coverlet and gulped, the gorge rising in her throat. His left foot, a shapeless mass, was bound in soiled linen from which, here and there, fresh blood still seeped. She dropped the coverlet and turned quickly to the young girl.

"I shall light a candle for him every day whilst he lies here."

"Thank you, Madame de Narbaux. Surely *le bon Dieu* will heed the prayers of such a fine lady!"

Lysette hesitated, the words of apology still stuck in her throat. What a fool she was! Had she been less stubborn with Jean-Auguste, she might have been able to persuade him to accompany her and ease her painful embarrassment. Suddenly a baby's wail came from the cradle, hesitantly at first, then swelling to a loud cry that filled the small room and caused Pasquier to stir restlessly upon his pallet. Pasquier's wife knelt quickly and lifted the infant in her arms; with an apologetic smile to Lysette she seated herself upon the stool, loosed the drawstring of her chemise, and put the babe to her naked breast. The child sucked hungrily, seeming to drain the mother of every drop of strength. How thin she is, thought Lysette, noting the pinched face, the angular shoulders, the rawboned ankles bare above the wooden clogs. How could she nurse her child when it was plain she had scarce enough food to sustain herself? And now, with Pasquier crippled, there would be even less. An unfamiliar wave of compassion swept over Lysette.

"How old are you?"

"One and twenty, my lady."

One and twenty. Younger than Lysette. And already there were streaks of gray in the girl's hair, lines of care on her face.

"You must know," blurted Lysette, close to tears, "how sorry I am for what has happened to Pasquier. It grieves me to think that he has suffered because of me!"

"Yes. Monsieur le Vicomte has told me how troubled you were. But you must not grieve, Madame." She smiled timidly and indicated Pasquier with her chin. "He has told me much about you. He admires you greatly, Madame. And he does not give his allegiance without cause. He would give his life for you, I think."

Lysette choked back a sob, remembering the insouciance with which she had charmed Pasquier. "I must go," she said, jumping to her feet and making for the door.

"Madame. A moment, please."

Reluctantly, Lysette turned about. The young woman had put the infant back into his cradle and was straightening her chemise; without a word she crossed the room and took Lysette's hand in her own two, pressing it fervently to her lips, her soft eyes filled with gratitude. "We should be forced to go begging but for you, Madame. Monsieur de Narbaux has told me of your wish to provide Pasquier with a pension. May *le bon Dieu* bless you all the days of your life!"

Lysette pulled her hand away and fled into the misty morning.

Jean-Auguste was there, seated on his horse, just outside the cave. At sight of Lysette his eyebrows shot up in surprise, but a small smile of satisfaction twitched at the corners of his mouth. Silently he reached his hand down to her; she hesitated for a moment, then allowed him to swing her up in front of him on the saddle. She sat stiffly, biting her lip to keep it from trembling, while he guided his horse down from the cliffs and into the sheltered gardens of Chimère. He dismounted then, and lifted her down, but when she would have turned away to hide her agitation he held her firmly by the shoulders, his eyes searching her face. With a small cry she burst into tears and threw herself into his arms, sobbing out her grief and dismay.

"I . . . I had never known . . . the meanness . . . ah *Dieu!* They have nothing . . . I did not care until now. . . . she kissed my h-h-hand. . . . and I have brought them naught but m-m-misery."

Jean-Auguste held her tightly until her racking sobs subsided, then he wiped her tear-stained face and handed her his handerchief. She sniffled and blew her nose, gazing up at him with violet eyes that were filled with genuine contrition.

"I am so very sorry. It was foolish and cruel of me." She began to weep again. "And now he will be crippled."

"You must not blame yourself overmuch. It was an accident, after all. Pasquier works in the caves every day. It might have happened at any time. . . ."

"I thank you for speaking in my behalf—and for the pension in my name—did you promise them a great deal?"

"Enough so that they will not starve until Pasquier learns to get about on a crutch. There will still be work for him in the caves, but he may find it difficult to tend the vines in the field."

"How kind you are. I struck you yester eve . . . and still you went to them on my behalf."

He laughed wryly. "I have almost become used to your wayward hands—though they please me little! As for the pension—do not overburden yourself with reproach. I intended to sell your pearl necklace to pay for it!"

"Oh, no!" she gasped in shock and shook her head. "You cannot!"

He smiled sardonically. "For a moment I feared you had been transformed! But rest content, my vain little peahen. Since you went to Pasquier of your own accord, I have changed my mind. There will be gold enough from the harvest to manage a pension."

All was well. She smiled triumphantly at him. "And were you not proud of me?"

"It was your place to go." Then, seeing how her face fell, he went on more kindly. "I am pleased that you saw your duty. It bodes well that in the struggle for your soul, the woman may yet win out over the child!"

For a moment she bristled, then laughed at his frankness and drew herself up in mock disdain. "Then you owe the woman an apology, for you had no faith in her, else you would not have gone to Pasquier yourself!"

He ducked his head sheepishly. "If the woman will allow it, I shall apologize this evening at supper."

She giggled. "At six?"

"At six, Madame!" He turned to mount his horse, then thought better of it and swept Lysette into his arms, crushing her mouth in an exuberant kiss. Releasing her, he grinned broadly and swung himself into the saddle, galloping off in the direction of the woods.

She told herself it was absurd to stand there in the garden like a silly fool, smiling at the autumn flowers and the pale yellow leaves of the willow—simply because he was home, because he had let her know that he was proud of her, because he had kissed her like a rowdy schoolboy. Still, her step was jaunty as she entered the chateau. Meeting Bricole, she greeted him effusively, filled with a well-being she could scarcely fathom. She headed for the staircase then stopped and turned.

"Bricole, have we enough beef for the winter?"

"Beef, Madame?"

"I mind that when the pigs were slaughtered I saw no cows! Are we to subsist on pork and mutton alone?"

"No, Madame," stammered Bricole, surprised. "Last year Monsieur le Vicomte was away. . . . The Court, and then the fighting on the front, and before that, Lorraine, where he won his honors and was grievously wounded. Chimère has seen no fêtes or winter entertainments for some time now. There is still more than enough beef in the salting tubs to last through this winter."

"Oh," she said, deflated.

"Would Madame care to see the ledgers? It would be my pleasure to show them to you and explain how Chimère is run."

She bridled at that, suddenly defensive. "Manage it as you wish. It is scarcely worth my trouble!" And she sailed up the stairs, head held high.

Supper in the small salon was a jolly affair: Jean-Auguste was happy to be home, while Lysette, delighted to have company at last, teased and joked with him, oddly pleased when he saw through her games. She had never seen him so enthusiastic, describing for her his trips to Paris to secure a license and loans, then the chore of scouring the countryside for a master glassmaker who would be willing to enter into a contract with him. She could scarcely understand the details, following the complex business arrangements as best she could. Having lived with Guy's profligacy, however, she knew something of loans, and she frowned as Jean-Auguste told of the sums he had borrowed to finance the enterprise.

"But what did you use as collateral?" she asked, thinking of her jewels, safe in their cabinet.

"Next year's harvest."

"And what will you do for money next year when you must pay off the loan?"

"To begin with, if the harvest is good, our expenses will be considerably less than heretofore, since there will be no need to buy bottles for the wine we sell. And then, the money I have borrowed is simply a loan to Rondini—as he sells his glassware, he will repay the loan, with interest." He grinned wickedly. "And I am a usurious landlord! He has agreed to pay an exorbitant rent for the use of Chimère's woods and sand and water."

"And who is this Rondini?"

"A master glassmaker from Nevers. His family came from Venice centuries ago—they still pass the craft down from father to son. Rondini has promised to bring his son with him."

"Pooh!" she said. "How much is to be earned from making bottles? It is a foolish enterprise!"

He laughed, then rose from the table and took a large, irregular packet from the marble console, carrying it carefully and setting it down before her. When she would have reached for it with eager fingers, he cautioned her away.

"*Nom de Dieu!* It was trial enough to carry it safely from Nevers. Allow me. A present from Rondini." He stripped back the wrappings and pulled away an inner covering of straw to reveal a clear and delicate wine goblet, a transparent cone set upon three separate stems that intertwined and ended in a base of shining crystal in which one perfect bubble had been imprisoned. Lysette's sparkling eyes reflected the lustrous glass as she turned it this way and that, admiring its fragile artistry. "You see," continued Jean-Auguste, "Rondini is skilled at much more than bottles! And a gift from me"—he took a small packet from within his doublet—"in recompense for my neglect of you these past weeks." He unwrapped the packet and pulled out a string of the largest pearls Lysette had ever seen.

She gaped in astonishment. "*Mon Dieu!* They are as big as grapes! What creature of the sea spawned such things?"

"No creature of the sea. I bought them from Rondini."

"They are exquisite! But where did Rondini get them?"

He laughed and put the string of pearls into her hand. Lysette was surprised at their lack of weight, the feeling that she was holding a handful of empty eggshells. "Rondini made them. They are glass!" he explained.

She shook her head in amazement, examining them more closely. "What makes them shine so . . . like real pearls?"

"Fish scales, I think, blown into the interior of each tiny glass bead."

Lysette put the string about her neck and danced around the room. "How may I thank you?" she bubbled happily.

His eyes traveled her body, then came to rest on her face with a look of such unabashed desire that she felt herself go red. His mouth twitched at her discomfiture, but his voice, when he spoke, was gentle, not mocking. "You might give me a proper welcome."

She lowered her eyes and looked away. "Of course. Come to my chambers when you see Dominique leave."

A soft knock announced his arrival, but when he had entered her room he closed the door and leaned against the panels, laughing aloud at the sight before him. As was her wont, Lysette stood in the center of the room, her nightclothes about her ankles, but the large string of pearls still hung around her neck, incongruous against her naked bosom.

"If I must bed you with those beads between us," he chuckled, "I fear me we shall both suffer from glass shards!"

She pouted in dismay. "They are too beautiful to take off!"

He crossed swiftly to her, his face suddenly serious, and lifted the beads from about her neck. "You are too beautiful, *ma chère,* to need their glow." He kissed her almost roughly and lifted her in his arms, and when he made love to her it was with an urgency, a passionate intensity that was new to her. She felt herself swept along by his ardor as she had not been before; it was only when he lay still above her and she felt the fires slowly die within her breast, that she remembered the possible consequences of their encounter. In her mind's eye, she saw Pasquier's wife, old before her time, drained of joy and youth and beauty, robbed by the creature that sucked at her breast and stole her life from her. Terror welled up within her and she began to weep.

Alarmed, Jean-Auguste withdrew from her and sat up. *"Mon Dieu,* Lysette, what is it?"

She clutched at him, needing his arms around her, and sobbed out her fears. "Will you still bring me gifts when I am dry and old . . . when I have lost my beauty?"

He kissed the stricken look from her eyes, cradling her and murmuring soothing words until at last her trembling ceased and her eyelids grew heavy with sleep. She burrowed more closely into his embrace, sighing contentedly, lulled by his hand that still stroked her hair, the warmth of his body next to hers.

"Where did you ride yesterday?" he asked suddenly.

"Vilmorin," she murmured, half asleep.

For a moment, the rhythm of his stroking fingers was disturbed; then his gentle hand caressed her as before. "And Marielle and André . . . they are well?" he asked more softly.

She grunted in assent, too tired even to speak, and snuggled against his chest.

If, tomorrow, she must live with her fear of bearing children, and the responsibilities of life, and the thieving years that put a stranger into her mirror—tonight she was safe in his sheltering arms.

Chapter Fifteen

NOVEMBER BROUGHT WITH IT A COLD WIND, THE FIRST LIGHT dusting of snow, and Rondini. More properly, as Jean-Auguste introduced him with a flourish, Giacopo Rondini, master glass-maker, and his son Guglielmo. Darkly handsome, father and son, with crisp black hair and liquid eyes, their faces spoke of olive groves in the warm sun, of the hills of Tuscany and the lagoons of Venice, of the heritage their ancestors had left a century before. Rondini swept off his plumed hat and bowed elaborately to Lysette with a flamboyant panache all the more remarkable because there was not a shred of arrogance in his manner. A proud man, sure of his skills, aware of the special place his art reserved for him in society—not quite the equal of the lord of the manor, yet far above even the most exalted servant. A young man about Lysette's age, Guglielmo had the sparkle of his father but with the impetuosity of his own tender years; Jean-Auguste's presence scarcely dampened the enthusiasm with which he kissed Lysette's hand and appraised her with his dark brown eyes. Accustomed as she was to flattering glances and masculine admiration, she still found herself almost disconcerted by the openness of his regard; as though he deemed it perfectly proper to ravish her with his eyes as long as he respected her virtue as the wife of the seigneur.

By the time they sat down to supper in the small salon, however, Lysette had begun to relax and enjoy Guglielmo's approbation. He seemed to find her fascinating; he laughed delightedly at all her witticisms, and smiled dazzlingly only for her. Indeed, even the elder Rondini was more and more beguiled by her charm, telling her at great length about his ancestors who had been master glassmakers in Venice. In those days, he said, the glassmakers had lived as virtual prisoners on an island in the lagoon, enjoying great wealth and honors—the glassmakers of Murano being the only commoners allowed to intermarry with the nobility—but prevented from communicating with the outside world lest the secrets of their art be revealed. While Lysette sat spellbound he told her of one glassmaker who had managed to escape; members of the Guild had tracked him to the very gates of Paris, and there murdered him horribly. That was, of course, he said, in the old times, when the secrets were more carefully guarded; many men knew the formulas today, he said, though few possessed the fine skills of the past. That was why a man needed a son—to keep the art alive.

After supper, armed with a bright torch, he insisted that Lysette and Jean-Auguste come to the stables to see the supplies he had brought with him; besides two geese, an old brown cow, and half a dozen sheep with which he and his son would set up housekeeping, there was a large, ox-drawn wagon piled high with the trappings of his trade. Iron rods and pipes and pincers. Sacks of fire clay to make bricks for the furnace and the kiln. Powders and salts and metal oxides that, used with skill, would clarify the glass, purging it of unwanted colors or adding hues developed through centuries of the art. A strange chair—a blower's bench, Rondini called it—with disproportionately long arms extending out some fifteen to eighteen inches, at which the master sat and rested his blowpipe between prodigious puffs. A large barrel filled with cullet, bits and pieces of broken and discarded glass. Added to a fresh batch of sand and salt and lime, it would hasten the melting and aid the fusion of the ingredients.

Proudly, Rondini pointed out half a dozen large clay bowls, as big across as the distance from a man's shoulder to his fingertips; Lysette smiled in admiration, though she scarce could see what made them so extraordinary. Crucibles, he said, for melting the mixture in the furnace. It had taken many months to make them, he said, for if they were fashioned carelessly they might shatter in the heat of the furnace, spilling out their contents of molten glass. It was properly a potter's skill, he said, but a master glassmaker, trained in the old ways, knew how to mix the fire clay, curing it for several months until it was the proper consistency. Like his father before him, he had been taught to knead the clay with his bare feet; the resilience of it under the weight of his body gave a more accurate reading than that produced by his hands. When the clay had been rolled into a rope it was spiraled into a pot shape, and then pounded into its final form. After more months of drying, it was baked in a kiln. Even after such care, there was always the possibility, however slight, that some small flaw, a tiny air bubble perhaps, might still live in the heart of the crucible, waiting to explode in the depths of the furnace. It was the glassmaker's nightmare, he said with a shudder, making the sign of the Cross and glaring at Guglielmo until he too crossed himself to ward off the disaster.

The next few weeks saw Chimère bustling with activity. The forester, Simon Vacher, set to work with his men clearing a space in the stand of beechwood near a wide stream. Workmen had been hired from Vouvray, carpenters and brickmakers and plasterers; the first order of business was a small stone and timber house in which the Rondini would live. There was a narrow pen for their animals, and space left for a garden to be planted in the spring; a widow from Vouvray, a robust woman with a young son, was brought in to run the household for the two men.

A small kiln was fashioned of clay, protected from the elements by a shed; while the brickmakers baked their finished bricks within its heated interior, Vacher and his men used the roof of the shed to stack and dry the wood they had begun to clear from the forests.

When the bricks were baked and cool, Rondini directed the building of the furnace: a huge dome shape, like a giant beehive, with a vent at the top and a stokehole at the bottom for feeding the flames and raking out ashes. There were two openings in the sides of the thick walls, large enough for the crucibles, and two smaller holes ("glory holes," Rondini called them, for reheating the glass as they worked), placed to take advantage of the hottest portion of the fire. Attached to the side of the furnace was a large hollow space, like a bubble with an opening—the cooling oven, in which the finished glass could cool for the several days necessary to retain its strength. After the bricks of the furnace had been mortared into place, the whole was covered with a thick skin of plaster and smoothed over.

Now the carpenters set to work building the glasshouse around the furnace. It was a rough wooden structure, open at the top, with an adjustable roof that could be slid open or closed to regulate the heat and drafts. There were large, paneless windows in the walls, with heavy wooden shutters to be used only in the most inclement weather, for without an outside breeze the heat within the glasshouse could be intense.

Beyond the stream a wide but shallow pit had been dug; within it a large fire had been set, fueled by a steady supply of beechwood and oak and ferns. Even the children of the *vignerons* were put to work gathering ferns, and they danced merrily about the bonfire, throwing on armfuls of their gleanings, squealing in glee each time a burning log crackled and sputtered. After several days portions of the fire were allowed to die down; the ashes were raked out and placed in a wooden tub that was set over a large iron pot. Water from the stream was poured over the ashes until the solution leached from the tub into the pot. Finally the pot with its liquid was heated slowly over a small fire until the moisture evaporated and only a fine powder was left. "The salt," Rondini called it in the manner of the old glassmakers, and if the fire was kept burning steadily and the ashes leached and evaporated, a great deal of this potash could be produced in a short time.

Several workmen had been sent to the cliffs to gather chunks of the limestone and crush them with heavy sledges; poured into burlap sacks, the powdered lime had been trundled to the clearing and stacked in a sheltered corner of the shed. Rondini himself selected the site near the river from which the sand would be dug, running the grains through his fingers and examining them closely with a practiced eye before pointing to the very spot wherein the gravel pit was to be dug. Washed in the river, then sifted and crushed, the sand would be the essential ingredient in the making of the glass. It was not, in itself, of a fineness that would produce anything but common glass (though Rondini possessed the oxides and salts necessary to purify the mixture should he wish to mold a fine piece of crystal); still, if he selected his sand with care, even the ordinary wine bottles would be pleasing to look upon as well as useful.

Lysette was fascinated with all the activity; she rode often to the clearing or, heavy cloak bundled about her, trudged through the woods to watch the work in progress. The Rondini never failed to treat her with the dignity due her station, though Guglielmo could never quite hide his ardor, and even Giacopo's soft brown eyes had begun to appraise the woman as well as the Lady. They answered her questions patiently, pleased at her interest. And, truth to tell, though she had begun out of mere politeness, she found herself more and more absorbed by the details of their work. It was odd. There surely had been glassmakers in Soligne as well as Chartres, yet her preoccupation with her own small world had precluded even the tiniest spark of curiosity; indeed, she had shattered half a score of goblets and vessels in some childish rage or fit of pique, and never once had wondered about the magical glass she destroyed so wantonly.

She was surprised to find Dominique often at the glasshouse, bent on some errand or other; it was not like the maid to seek out extra chores (much as Lysette disliked admitting it to herself, Bricole had perhaps been right when he spoke of the girl's idleness). Then she discovered that the young *vigneron*, Etienne, had been put to work helping the carpenters; as if by magic Dominique would appear at the glasshouse, bearing food and drink from the kitchens, and linger in the clearing long after the men had been fed.

One day, just as Dominique was enjoying a coy flirtation with Etienne, he was sent up to the roof to fasten the crossbeams. The maid, fearful for his safety, and proud and shy all at once, moved back from the clearing until she stood on the path leading from the woods, from whence she could watch him at her pleasure, mouth agape, one hand clutched to her bosom, while he made his precarious way from one beam to another, calling down occasionally to his fellows on the ground below. So engrossed was Dominique that she did not see Simon Vacher and his men, laden with heavy branches and rotted tree trunks, coming down the path from the woods; when they stopped before her so that she might step aside and let them pass, she clucked her tongue in annoyance and moved reluctantly out of their way. But her interest in Etienne was not to be dampened; within a few minutes she had quite forgotten Vacher and had drifted back onto that spot on the path that gave her the clearest view of him, perched on the roof. When Vacher and his men returned from the wood shed, empty-handed, she glared defiantly at the forester and held her ground. Without a word, he picked her up, sunbrowned hands circling her narrow waist, and planted her in a patch of dried leaves beside the path. She squealed in surprise and anger; when he had passed, she lost no time in recapturing her place, hurling venomous curses at his retreating back. This time, when he and his men returned burdened with a fresh load of wood, the knots on Vacher's brown arms swollen with the exertion until there seemed scarce any difference between his limbs and the gnarled tree limbs he bore, Dominique crossed her arms stubbornly and refused to budge, her narrow face pinched in belligerence. Vacher put down his log and sighed deeply, wiping the sweat from his brow with the back of his arm, but his eyes twinkled merrily. Then he smiled, his white teeth startling against the mahogany of his face, and took a step toward Dominique. She hesitated, wavered, stamped her foot as though she would halt his progress by the very movement, then scampered out of his way, fearful of the determination that lay behind his impudent grin.

Watching the scene from her horse, Lysette frowned at Vacher's behavior. It was scarcely fair to Dominique. While she herself found Etienne little to her liking—singularly handsome, with the arrogance of one who knows he is well-favored—the maid clearly was smitten by him and had no need to be humiliated so by Vacher in Etienne's presence. Lysette determined to speak to Jean-Auguste; Simon Vacher should be made to understand that he must stop tormenting the girl.

A new problem arose. While the work went on—the gathering of the materials, the finishing of the glasshouse—Giacopo Rondini and his son had begun to mix up sample batches to be melted in the kiln. So much sand and potash, lime for stability and strength, a handful of cullet—that store of glass shards—ground to a powder and added to the mixture. But they were hot-tempered and volatile, father and son, and each day the glasshouse shook with the arguments that raged back and forth; Guglielmo, young, imaginative, filled with new ideas and proposals, Giacopo just as firmly convinced that the old ways were best. In vain Jean-Auguste was sent for, and spent long hours closeted with the two; he emerged exasperated and haggard, convinced there would be no rapprochement, that the glassworks would fail before a single bottle had been molded.

Lysette had observed the proceedings with a certain sense of annoyance: what impossible children men could be when they put their minds to it! After two days of listening to Jean-Auguste complain of the hopelessness of the situation, she marched resolutely to the glasshouse to beard the lions in their den.

The Rondini, cowed by her flashing violet eyes, listened humbly as she chastened them for the turmoil they had caused; then she smiled sweetly at them both until they melted into malleable clay. How could Guglielmo play the ingrate, she chided gently? Was his father not wise and good, his teacher, his mentor? And as for Giacopo—did not he, when a young man, chafe with impatience to try new ways? Was not Guglielmo son to the father, touched by his wisdom and molded in his image? Surely there was a compromise to be striven for by two such fine men! She found them both so charming, she said—what a disappointment when they behaved thus, with such intransigence! When she left, having shaken the father's hand warmly and patted the son on the cheek, the Rondini, all smiles and cooperation, had already begun again to mix their batches of glass, deferring one to the other—an extra grain of sand for Guglielmo, a pinch of oxide for Giacopo.

For her part, Lysette was pleased at the reaffirmation of her power to charm and entrance. She was fond of the Rondini, of course, and truly had wanted peace between them; still, it was gratifying to see the influence she had over them. Gratifying, too, that Jean-Auguste seemed equally dazzled by her bewitchment of the glassmakers. Had he thought about it, she reflected wryly, he might have realized that, since his return, she had used that same charm to keep him at a distance and out of her bed as often as she could.

It had become too cold for constant baths—her skin chafed and itched under the onslaught of the northern winds—and long wild rides left her shivering and numb. Dominique had discovered another preventive from a friend in Vouvray— something to do with drawing a cross on her belly with the ashes from the fire; but by and large, though Lysette was careful to make for the hearth as soon as Jean-Auguste had left her room at night, she was inclined to doubt the efficacy of the method.

Of course, she could always prevail upon Jean-Auguste to withdraw at the precise moment when his seed was dispatched (what was the line from the play she had seen once—the heroine cautioning her paramour: "Ye may romp with reckless joy upon the shores of love, but not one drop shall ye spill!"), but while that might do for a mistress with an accommodating lover, she was scarcely sure that a husband would find it to his liking. Not even a husband as agreeable as Jean-Auguste!

No. She did best to rely on her wits and her charm. It had become easy to read Jean-Auguste's mood, to know when he would stop her on the staircase with his gentle question—"Shall you sleep directly tonight?"—and to compose her face into a mask of dolor long before she had crossed the hallway to the stairwell. Alas. A headache. A slight chill. A touch of dyspepsia. She begged his indulgence, her large eyes soft and helpless. As you wish, he would murmur, and turn away.

And sometimes, when he seemed to be studying her over the supper table, his open face creased in a frown as though he would brook no excuse that night, she would pout and find some small reason—genuine or invented—to quarrel with him and flounce angrily to her room.

There were times, however, when they had laughed together at supper, or spent the afternoon riding in warm companionship, that he caught her unawares, his amiable request couched in such genial good humor that she could not refuse him. It always annoyed her, to be rendered helpless by his affability, to find she had lost the battle without a skirmish. Aggrieved, she would submit to him sulkily, so that he found no satisfaction in her, despite his ardor.

But during the day she was charming and sweet to him, taking his hand, kissing him on the cheek, playing the helpless maiden victimized by her own feminine weaknesses, until—seemingly puzzled, confused—he almost forgave her her nighttime capriciousness. She was never completely sure, of course (the devil take those piercing gray eyes!), that he was not aware of her games and manipulations, but what did it matter? As long as he was willing to defer to her, let him think what he wished!

Toward the end of November, word came that Corbie had

been recaptured. It seemed the perfect opportunity to plan a
soirée in celebration, as well as to introduce Lysette to some of
the local gentry. She was delighted to leave the details to
Bricole (once she had seen to it that André's name headed the
list of invited guests!), and concentrate on her gown, her jewels,
her coiffure. My vain little wife, Jean-Auguste called her, though
not with the same indulgence and lightheartedness he had
shown heretofore. Indeed there was a growing coolness in his
manner which disturbed her greatly, inasmuch as she found it
more and more difficult to wring a compliment from him, a kind
word, a flattering glance—the vital elixir that fed her spirit.

She was surprised at how bored she was at her own party.
Except for André, splendid in rich brocade, there was not a
single noble or magistrate or government functionary in the
whole district who was worth a second glance. She might have
been amused had her young lieutenant appeared, but he had
eased his disappointment at losing her to Narbaux by marrying
some merchant's daughter from Vouvray who guarded her
prize jealously and kept him away from the society of other
women.

The company buzzed with political talk: the war with Spain,
the glorious recapture of Corbie, the unrest in much of France.

"Thirty thousand men!" exclaimed one red-faced Marquis,
hobbling about on gout-gnarled limbs. "I should like to have
been there! To see His Majesty at the head of his army. *Mon
Dieu!* What a sight it must have been!"

"Ah, no," exclaimed another, whom Jean-Auguste had
introduced as the Lieutenant Governor of Touraine. "There is
not a man in all of France, of course, who would not die for
Louis, but I would put myself beside Cardinal Richelieu in
battle. *There* is a sight to stop the heart and freeze the marrow
in every enemy soldier! I mind him at La Rochelle, black armor
over his red robes, skirts tucked up to free his boots and
spurs—proud and fierce and angry! There was no cleric in him
that day!"

"I knew him at the academy," said an old man. "He would
have had a brilliant military career had there been another
brother to take the bishopric at Luçon."

The Marquis laughed sardonically, "And then he might have
counted among his enemies only those who bowed to a foreign
flag!"

Lysette found it all terribly dull, even when the talk turned to the fresh uprisings in Angoumois; Soligne seemed a lifetime away, and scarcely worth her concern anymore. Jean-Auguste and André were debating the finer points of some campaign or other; in desperation Lysette sought out Marielle and some of the other women—domestic trifles could hardly be more tedious than another battle!

"We shall go to Paris in a few weeks," Marielle was saying. "The Court will be gay, what with the victory of Corbie."

"And half the army disbanded until the spring campaigns!" exclaimed a pretty young thing, the wife of the red-faced Marquis. "I intend to break the heart of every handsome courtier at the Louvre!"

"And what of your husband?"

The Marquise shrugged. "So long as his gout gives him pain, he needs must sleep alone!"

"And you?" asked another, archly, to a chorus of giggles.

The Marquise smiled like a cat. "There is no place in all the world more filled with wicked delights than Paris!"

A heavy-set woman in green silk sat down in a froth of petticoats and began to fan herself angrily. "Aye! But what is one to tell one's husband? By my faith, Monsieur my husband seems to have more spies than Cardinal Richelieu himself! How tiresome it is to have to lie to him at every moment!"

"But why lie?" said the Marquise. "My dears, have you not heard of the charming Madame de . . ." and here she named a woman whose husband held a high position in the government.

The woman in green opened her eyes wide. "But she is a scandal! They say she has more lovers than the Seine has fish!"

"Riddle me this," said Lysette to the Marquise. "How may a woman *lie*, and yet not *lie?*"

"Oh, bravo!" cried the woman in green, clapping her hands at Lysette's wit.

"I shall tell you," said the Marquise. "The lady is an equestrienne! She mounts and rides all her lovers. When Monsieur her husband questions her fidelity, she swears on the Blessed Sacrament that she has lain beneath no man save him!"

The women laughed uproariously at that, but Marielle only smiled her gentle smile. "But *le bon Dieu* alone knows what she tells her confessor," she said softly.

"Ah, you are too virtuous by half, Madame du Crillon! I wonder that you and Monsieur le Comte bother to come to Paris at all!"

Marielle smiled stiffly. "There are friends to see, and we enjoy the theatre. Monsieur le Comte is particularly anxious to see Monsieur Corneille's new play."

"And the women of the Court are as anxious to see Monsieur le Comte!" said the lady in green wickedly. "I vow he is as handsome as ever he was in the days when he broke hearts—and crossed swords with half the outraged husbands of Paris!"

Marielle bit her lip, and even Lysette frowned in annoyance. It was one thing to have designs on a woman's husband—it was quite another to mock her to her face! She put her hand gently on Marielle's arm. "Come, *ma chère*. Will you take a turn about the hall with me? I am longing to know more of this Monsieur Corneille. Will there be other entertainments in Paris this season?"

"I do not see why we cannot go to Paris, Jean-Auguste!" cried Lysette, her voice rising in an aggrieved whine, her mouth a stubborn pout across the supper table. It was the third time in a week she had broached the subject, growing more petulant each time.

He sighed deeply and put down his knife. "But the glass-works, Lysette," he said patiently. "Must I tell you yet again? I should be here."

"Pooh! The Rondini said it would be weeks, while the furnace and crucibles were heated up! And the teams of men must be trained. And in the meantime I am dying of misery and boredom!"

"Are you so unhappy then?" he asked, an edge of concern in his voice.

Caught off guard by the warmth and sympathy in the depths of his soft eyes, she arose from the table and went to stand by the window, shielding her face from his all-seeing gaze. Unhappy? Searching her mind for the first time, she nearly laughed aloud, surprised at her own feelings. Unhappy? So far from it was she that, though her heart ached constantly for André, her life was filled with a contentment that was closer to happiness than anything she had ever known before. Still, it would hardly do for him to know!

"Are you?" he repeated, coming up behind her and turning her into his embrace.

She could not lie with those eyes upon her! With a heartbroken wail, she burst into tears and pushed him away. "You promised! Before you went away! You promised! And now I shall be old and ugly before ever I see Paris again! Even Guy was not so cruel!"

He threw up his hands in exasperation. "In a few weeks then. Please, Lysette. Be patient!"

"No!" She stamped her dainty foot in fury. "Hateful! Hateful! Hateful!"

"*Nom de Dieu,* Lysette! Stop! I shall not be hectored in my own home! We shall go to Paris when I choose it, and not a moment before!"

"Then go to Paris! Go to the devil, for all I care!" Whirling to the table, she snatched up the wine jug and smashed it at his feet, her jaw outthrust belligerently.

For a moment he stood immobile, his eyes filled with cold anger and disgust, then he knelt and fingered the shards of fine porcelain, shattered now beyond all hope of repair. His eyes were almost sad when he straightened again and looked at her. "It was from Limoges," he said quietly. "Gabriel brought it. You might have chosen something less dear to me."

"Oh-h-h!" she moaned, her tears starting afresh. "I hate you!" she cried, and fled the room so he might not see that her misery arose from shame, rather than her failure to change his mind.

By morning, however, the pain had faded, and she was able to view her Paris campaign with the dispassionate eye of a general. She should have remembered from all their clashes on the journey from Soligne: her fury was powerless against his calm determination. She always ended up the fool, or consumed by remorse. So resolved had she become to have her way in this matter, however, that she was prepared to fulfill her wifely duty, if need be (and in good humor, to please him!), if the victor's baton would be hers.

She found him in the library, writing letters at a small desk. At sight of her, he put down the sealing wax he had begun to heat at a small candle, and waited for her to make the first move, his gray eyes cool and distant.

She fell on her knees before him, gazing up at him contritely.

"I am truly sorry," she said, soft-voiced, her eyes misty with tears, "for my wickedness and vile temper, and for badgering you so! And for Gabriel's wine pitcher." (*That*, at least, she genuinely regretted!) "You are very patient with me, and kind, and I bring you naught but grief. Will you forgive me?"

He grunted gruffly and nodded in assent, then started to turn back to his desk. "Now leave me to my correspondence."

She jumped to her feet and plunked herself determinedly on his lap. "No! Not until you tell me you forgive me! You must say the words, or I shall not rest content!" She smiled pleadingly at him. "Please." The voice soft and melting.

He fidgeted in his chair. "Very well. I forgive you."

She kissed him fervently on the mouth so he looked at her in wonder (though not without pleasure at her unexpected warmth); then she ruffled his hair with playful fingers, shaking her head in mock dismay. "It is still an ungodly color, but I have grown quite fond of it!" She stroked the naked spot above his lip, so recently adorned. "More especially since it no longer rives your face in two! Did you shave it for me?" she asked softly, and was delighted to see his face turn as scarlet as his hair.

"I . . . I know not!" he said uncomfortably. "I simply wished to do it!"

"Eh, bien. I care not! I am glad it is gone!" She kissed him tenderly, then scanned his face, her violet eyes filled with pride and pleasure. "How handsome you are! How the women of the Court will envy me!" One red eyebrow shot up in surprise. "When you decide we are to go—*naturellement!"* she amended quickly.

"Are you really so anxious to go?" he asked, wavering.

She smiled beguilingly and took his hand in hers, placing it over her full round breast. "I defer to you in *everything*," she said softly. "You are my husband. But, yes, I should like very much to go to Paris."

His mouth twitched, but he allowed himself to fondle her bosom for a moment before removing his hand. "Indeed, you must be impatient for the journey, that you are willing to barter so for it!" She frowned at him, mystified, missing the tone of sarcasm in his voice. "Very well, then. I see I shall have no peace until I am agreed to your wishes. We shall leave on Tuesday next."

Eyes shining, she flew from his lap and pirouetted happily about the room, chattering away, filled with questions that tripped one upon the other, without waiting for answers. "Oh! And how long shall we stay? Will the Court be at the Louvre . . . or Fontainebleau? I have never been to the Louvre! They say it is beautiful! Is it? And may I have a gown made to go with my emerald buttons? Do you fancy me in white brocade? We must go to the theatre! May we go to see Monsieur Corneille's new work? Marielle says that is the only reason she and André will be in Paris this season. Marielle says there are mulberry bushes in the Tuileries Gardens, for the silkworms! I have never seen a silkworm! Will you take me to the Tuileries? André knows the old gardener there . . ." Her voice trailed off as she danced out of the library, pausing at the door to throw him a kiss.

He had smiled in amusement at her enthusiasm, but after she had gone the smile lingered for a moment, frozen upon his face, then slowly faded away. Carefully he folded his letter and reheated the sealing wax, allowing a large dollop of wax to drip onto the overlap. He made a fist with his left hand, contemplating for a moment the signet ring on his finger, then pressed its incised surface into the warm wax. His unseeing eyes stared vacantly at the letter; his fist tightened, the fingers so firmly clenched the knuckles gleamed white. The signet ring rose and fell, again and again and again. Like a man in a stupor he pounded absently at the letter, a tight muscle working in his jaw, until the wax had been reduced to crumbs.

Chapter Sixteen

PARIS IN DECEMBER OF 1636 WAS A BUSTLING, COMPLACENT city of half a million souls, busily preparing for the Feast Days and Holidays to come. Forgotten for the moment was the war with Spain, the disastrous campaigns of the last year, the terror that had gripped the city when Corbie had fallen and left open to invasion the road to the capital. Was it only a few months ago that Cardinal Richelieu had been the most hated man in all of Paris, his name appearing in curses scrawled upon the walls, his carriage hissed and reviled as it passed through the city? But the threat of invasion had aroused the population; full of patriotic fervor, they had banded together and risen to the challenge of the enemy, mobilizing into volunteer brigades, raising funds to pay those mercenaries commissioned by the Crown, prepared to defend their city with the pride and unity that had characterized embattled Parisians from the time of the Romans. And Corbie had been retaken, and the Spaniards had retreated to their holdings in the Netherlands to await the spring campaign. From Notre Dame to the Place Royale, from the Sorbonne to the Luxembourg Gardens, Paris was enjoying the respite.

At the Louvre Palace, however, the Court buzzed with matters more mundane but ultimately more vital to the future of the realm: the King's latest liaison. Mademoiselle de La Fayette was a young girl, chaste and pure, with a sweetness that appealed to the melancholy Louis. She had not as yet submitted to him (and there were those who insisted he would never make her his mistress, whether due to his piety or his well-known antipathy toward carnal love), but while she reigned as his favorite she was the center of much speculation and partisanship. She numbered among her friends those who were opposed to the war—and by extension, to Richelieu—who urged her to cement her relationship with Louis at the earliest possible moment. But there were those who viewed her as a threat. So long as Louis moped about the palace, sighing of his tender sentiments and composing sonnets to Mademoiselle's charm and grace, the Queen, Anne of Austria, slept alone. And there was as yet no heir to the throne. Not since the birth of Louis himself in 1601 had the cry of "Noel! Noel!" been heard in the streets to herald the birth of a prince.

Lysette found it all exciting and wicked, far more titillating than the small-town gossip of Soligne. Would the King importune? Would Mademoiselle de La Fayette weaken? The talk sparkled in the salons, witty, droll, filled with plays on words and clever puns, but always, at bottom, basic and bawdy. Men and women. In bed. Out of bed. Betraying spouses. Afflicted with the pox, (that disease that walked hand in hand with loose morality), which the Court, in patriotic self-defense, had begun to refer to as the "Neapolitan Malady." The regularity with which high-born ladies, finding themselves with an unwanted dividend in their wombs, sought out surgeons and doctors to rid them of the burden, despite the civil laws against the practice and the disapproval of the Church. Lysette found this particularly revelatory, and determined to add it to her growing store of knowledge.

The whole licentious air of Paris gave her a new sense of freedom. Each day, when she and Jean-Auguste had left their suite in the Louvre to go to the theatre, or a fashionable salon, or a ball, she managed to distance herself from him as much as possible so that she could flirt, engage in ribald conversation, allow herself to be captured for an innocent kiss from some panting admirer—without his critical and disapproving glance. She had seen Marielle and André seldom since their arrival at Court, but she knew that in this atmosphere, and freed from the constraints of home and household, André would be an easier and more willing prey.

Alas. There were others who sighed for André as much as she did. For the first time, seeing him constantly surrounded by fawning women, she wished that he were less attractive, less the object of every feminine heart. And what was the matter with that fool Marielle, that she did not lay claim to him once and for all, or at the very least make some attempt to compete with the women who would steal her husband from her? Lysette said as much to Jean-Auguste one day—she could not tell if her pique stemmed from her own inability to get André for herself, or her pity at Marielle's helplessness.

"I can scarce understand it! One would almost think that Marielle goes out of her way to be plain and uninteresting! She is handsome enough—and with a little assistance, Nature might serve her passably well!"

Jean-Auguste laughed shortly. "Marielle is a beautiful woman—when she chooses to be!"

"Pooh! Why should she choose not to be?"

"There was a time," he said, his face suddenly dark with remembrance, "when André burned with jealousy—he would have liked, I think, to kill every man in Paris who looked at her!"

Lysette felt an unexpected pang of jealousy. "Even you?"

His mouth twitched at the note in her voice. "Would it disturb you, my vain little coquette, to think I spend less than every waking moment dreaming of your charms?" He laughed as her lip jutted out in an angry pout, then went on more seriously. *"Eh bien!* I fancied myself in love with her for a time. But for Marielle there is only André, always André. That is why she chooses to dress plainly, to let diffidence be her rule. She does not wish to provoke him by encouraging other attentions."

"Then she is a fool! Will a man notice the ground beneath his feet when there is a rainbow in the heavens?" She frowned in irritation at Marielle's folly, but in her heart she felt a certain tranquility. When at last she had won André away, she would revel in his love with nary a twinge of remorse, knowing his blind wife had relinquished him without a struggle.

But in the meantime, André seemed to belong to no one—and everyone. Even Marielle had begun to grow testy, her sweet serenity shattered by the women who paid court to him, and by his acceptance, if not encouragement, of their flattery and admiration.

Unable to get close to him herself, Lysette was beginning to feel positively neglected. She stood one night in the Grand

Salon of the Louvre, watching him dance with one beauty and then another, aching with jealousy and longing. Feeling peevish and miserable, she had refused Jean-Auguste's repeated invitations to dance until, with a shrug, he had gone off to the card room to try his luck with piquet.

"But it is Madame la Marquise de Ferrand, is it not?"

She whirled to see one pale blue eye—and a large black patch. "Monsieur le Comte d'Ussé! What a surprise to see you in Paris!"

He took her hand in his and brought it to his lips. "Madame de Ferrand. You are much changed since last we met!" His eye raked her body with such obvious desire and approval that she shivered with pleasure, glad she had put on her violet dress this evening.

"Madame de Ferrand no longer. Madame la Vicomtesse de Narbaux!"

He laughed conspiratorially. "Ah! Our red-haired friend! I would have thought that Crillon had caught your eye! But perhaps, on such a long journey . . . both . . . ? You can hardly blame me for wishing to"—he gave a small shrug—"join the game?"

"I am pleased to see you do not reproach my behavior that night, Monsieur," she smirked.

"Ah, Madame. I was very drunk—and most ungallant. Shall I then chide you for spurning my attentions?"

"How gracious you are."

"How tempting you are!" And he slipped his arm about her waist, smiling ruefully down at her. "However, it was but a kiss—albeit taken without your leave. You used me ill in return!"

Her eyes widened in feigned innocence. "Oh, Monsieur! And would you not have used me?"

"Aye! As a woman is used . . . for pleasure!"

"But then I would have been sore tried!"

"Had I used you well, then surely you would have been sore!" He grinned at his own lewd humor.

She pouted at his bawdiness, but made no move to dislodge his encircling arm. "Then you would bring me to grief."

"Only to bed, Madame, only to bed."

She dimpled prettily at him, enjoying their banter, and shook her head. "Then grief would follow—in a nine-month!"

He allowed his hand to slip down a bit from her waistline to the first rounded curve of her buttocks. "Why assault the front portal of the fortress and bring grief, when one may enter harmlessly from the back entrance?"

She gasped and pushed him away, too surprised to hide the look of shock on her face. He laughed at her discomfiture and she flamed scarlet, feeling like an innocent fool.

"You have lived too long in the Provinces, Madame. It is a practice favored by many women of the Court!"

Indeed. She recalled a bit of gossip she had heard only the day before, that had mystified her. The women had been speaking of a lady of the Court.

"She has so many lovers, she sleeps with her rump facing heavenwards," a fat Duchesse had simpered.

"A fine way to pray, if one wishes no 'complications'!" said another.

"But do her prayers bring her lovers?"

The Duchesse cackled in malicious delight. "They say her great moons outshine the orb of heaven itself!" Perplexed, Lysette had turned away.

Now, with Ussé's single eye watching her closely, she felt the blush still staining her cheeks and bosom. She was relieved to see Jean-Auguste coming across the parquet floor toward them; then she saw the scornful smile upon his face and blushed again, knowing he had seen her flirting with Ussé.

"Ah, Ussé!" said Jean-Auguste with an elaborate bow. "I heard that you were in Paris—the brothels and gambling halls of the Quartier du Marais have found a steady patron, if one is to believe the rumors in Court!"

"Monsieur de Narbaux," responded Ussé, equally polite. "And you have found a charming wife!" Deliberately, he lifted Lysette's hand to his lips and kissed it fervently, while his eye glittered in malice. "I regret that I was not more insistent that evening in the woods! This lovely creature might now be mine!"

Jean-Auguste smiled benignly. "It was your folly. However . . ." He shrugged with indifference. "They say you gamble heavily. Trefontaine must be thriving! How fortunate you are in these troubled times!"

"I have found new sources of income. I could no longer depend upon the meager pensions of the Crown!"

"Then you should take a wife, while you have the riches to keep her in petticoats!"

Ussé laughed shortly. "I have taken more than a few wives here at Court—without petticoats—and it has cost me nothing!" He smiled goatishly at Lysette. "Mayhap my good fortune will continue!"

"I wish you well, Monsieur," said Jean-Auguste pleasantly.

Lysette seethed at his nonchalance—it was lovely to have Ussé lusting after her, but only half a victory if that lust did not touch a spark of jealousy within her husband's breast. Damn him! "Monsieur Ussé!" she said brightly, placing a hand on his velvet sleeve, "I am longing to dance a pavane with you! Will you forgive my presumption and oblige me?" She moved off to the dance floor with Ussé, her head held high. To her utter frustration, she saw that Jean-Auguste, smiling cheerfully, had already crossed the floor to return to the card room.

On the Rue Saint-Honoré, near the Louvre, was the Palais Cardinal, built by Richelieu but a few years before. An elegant and imposing structure, it was the object of much curiosity and gossip, centered largely on the source of the riches that had gone into its building. But even wagging tongues could not prevent it from becoming the focal point of all the elegant society of Paris: a portion of the palace grounds consisted of a large sheltered garden surrounded by more than a hundred public shops, tiny stalls filled with the latest books and trinkets. It was fashionable to shop, to stroll about the garden, to meet and gossip with half the Court. Lysette loved to come to the Palais—it was not unusual to find an unescorted woman in these surroundings—and Jean-Auguste, bored with trifles and gewgaws, was only too glad to give her a purse of coins and arrange to meet her later in the garden when her whims had been satisfied.

She was delighted one day to come upon André, leaning against the counter of a small book shop, riffling the pages of a leather-bound volume. At the sight of her, he swept off his large beaver hat and bowed, his sapphire eyes crinkling in pleasure, his teeth dazzling against the bronzed skin. How her pulse raced, the blood coursing through her veins like rivers of fire! How she ached to tell him of her longings, the fantasies that put her in his arms, lips pressed to lips in a fervent kiss!

"Are you alone, then?" he asked. "Has Jean-Auguste abandoned you?"

She nodded her head, contriving to look forlorn. "And you?"

"I thought I might get a small volume of verses for Marielle. She is partial to Voiture's poems."

"They say that reading is harmful to the eyes!"

"Indeed?"

"Can you doubt it?" She smiled beguilingly. "I read as little as possible. And do not my eyes sparkle?"

He laughed at that, his blue eyes sweeping her face appreciatively. "They are beautiful eyes. I think they will always shine . . . when you smile just so!"

She sighed. "Ah. Alas. But will they speak for me? Come." And she held out her hand to him. Intrigued, he let her lead him to a mercer's stall, quite forgetting Marielle's book. "You must help me choose a fan," she said, "so my eyes may speak as eloquently as ever did Voiture's verses!" She motioned to the shopkeeper to hand her down a delicate fan fashioned of carved ivory and painted with a charming country scene. "Now," she said, unfurling it before her face so that only her violet eyes peeped above its lace edge, "will the man I love know—from my eyes alone—that I adore him?" She gazed at him ardently, her voice soft with longing, her very soul peering out from beneath her black-fringed lids.

He cleared his throat gruffly, uncomfortable at the depth of her feelings, too personal, too private to share with a friend. "He would be a blind fool not to know—if you look at him thus," he said gently.

No! She wanted to cry out. It is you! It is only you! "André," she breathed, putting down the fan and laying her hand on his sleeve. And looked up to see that Marielle watched from just beyond André's shoulder, her green eyes as icy as the wintry sea. "La!" she said brightly. "Here is your wife, André!" She smiled tightly at Marielle, barely managing to hide her pique at the untimely interruption. "André was helping me to choose a fan!"

"How gallant of him! But I wonder you need his advice. One would have guessed you know exactly what you want!" There was unexpected steel in Marielle's voice.

"André!" cried Lysette, in sudden surprise. "You have forgot

Marielle's book! He wished to buy you a book of poems, my dear, though I should find it a rather tedious gift myself. So plain and uninteresting. A lace falling band . . . a pair of ear drops would be so much more flattering to a woman, *n'est-ce pas?*"

"My father used to say a woman is but an empty mask without books to fill her. He would have me study whatever my brother did. And so I have always heeded the words of Saint Augustine: *'Tolle lege, tolle lege.'* Do you not agree?" The green eyes held a hostile challenge.

Lysette squirmed uncomfortably, recalling her indifference to her lessons, wishing suddenly that her attentions to her Latin master had been concerned with his words, rather than the peculiar way his nose wrinkled each time he uttered a sibilant sound. Then she brightened as a sudden thought struck her. What was it Dominique had said—that Marielle's father had been only a doctor? "Ah, Madame du Crillon," she said helplessly, "when one has been raised an aristocrat, there is so little time for books!"

"I had no time for luxury—nor patience for indolence! I helped my father as he moved among the poor and infirm—mayhap a nobler calling than courting a Venetian glass all the day."

"André, how fortunate you are!" cooed Lysette. "They say that the sight of too much suffering ages a person, brings ugly lines to the face, and yet behold your beautiful wife!"

Oblivious of the battle that had been raging between the two women, André smiled warmly at Marielle. "Indeed. She is beautiful. Still," he turned to the mercer's stall, fingering a delicate cambric falling band, "there is wisdom in Lysette's words, *ma chère*. A pretty trifle to brighten your eyes would not be amiss!"

"You find me plain, then?" she demanded, all pretense stripped away.

"No! Of course not!" he stammered, surprised by her sudden anger, "I only thought . . ."

"Make my excuses to Madame de Rambouillet this afternoon, if you will. I can scarce keep my eyes open from weariness!" She stalked away, her frozen smile barely disguising the fury that raged in her heart.

Triumphant, Lysette turned to André, meaning to claim her prize, then stopped at the sight of Jean-Auguste's approach.

Nom de Dieu! Was she never to have a moment alone with André? Her angry frown turned to embarrassment, however, at the look of accusation in Jean-Auguste's cool gray eyes, and she averted her gaze.

"André! *Mon ami!* What good fortune to find you!" said Jean-Auguste jovially. "I have not had one good fencing match since we came to Paris! Is your rapier as skillful as ever?"

"Better! I am prepared to lay a small wager on the outcome!"

"Ha! Did I not best you when last we met?"

"And before that? You ate the dust at *my* feet!"

"I do not choose to remember!" said Jean-Auguste grandly, then motioned for André to follow.

"A moment!" pouted Lysette. "Will you abandon me yet again?"

Jean-Auguste turned to her, one eyebrow raised in mockery. "I am sure you can find fresh amusements to keep yourself occupied." His arm swept the stalls, then the gardens where men and women strolled in warm intimacy. "If you 'shop' long enough, you will find something—or someone—to please you." And clapped his hand on André's shoulder and led him away, leaving Lysette gaping in stunned anger.

Across the garden she spied Ussé and almost called out to him, then thought better of it and turned away. The gardens were not a good place to be alone with him. Too many high hedges, too many secluded nooks wherein she might be trapped. As charming as it was to flirt with him, as flattering to her vanity as were his attentions, she was not entirely sure she was as worldly-wise as she thought. There was a wantonness, a sense of hidden evil in him that made her uneasy. She would play at love with him, because it pleased her—and in the hope she might arouse a flicker of jealousy in Jean-Auguste—but only in the salons, surrounded by the Court, where he could ravish her with words and glances, and nothing more! Hurrying past the stalls, she fled to the safety of her own apartments.

"Ah, *Dieu*, André, you must hold me very tightly until the room ceases to spin!" Lysette leaned against André's chest and closed her eyes, hearing the pounding of his heart a few inches from her ear. To her delight, she had found him alone this evening—Marielle had not appeared since the afternoon, and somehow the women in the Grand Salon had missed their opportunity. She had commandeered him for every dance (having long since deserted Jean-Auguste), and now clung tightly to him, breathless from the lively galliard they had just danced. Let Marielle sulk forever, locked away in her room! She was glad she had worn her new white brocade dress; it made her look soft and young, helpless and fragile. Small wonder André had stayed at her side, as though he were answerable for her well-being!

They had just begun a stately saraband, pacing majestically about the floor, when there was a commotion at one of the large doorways to the salon. Women twittered excitedly and men hurried forward. Absently following the steps of the dance, Lysette craned her neck to see what was amiss.

It was Marielle. But a Marielle she scarcely recognized. The plain velvet had been replaced by a gorgeous taffeta gown the color of ripe apricots, clinging silk accenting the fineness of her figure, the stateliness of her carriage; the bodice, cut shamelessly low, was edged with snowy lace that failed to conceal the beguiling curve of her bosom. Her chestnut hair was piled high atop her head, save for one tantalizing curl that hung over her shoulder, and her cheeks glowed with a rosiness that owed its luster as much to her rouge pot as her own fresh complexion. She was the most magnificent woman Lysette had ever seen, and the murmurs that accompanied her progress through the salon made it clear that half the Court shared that opinion. André had stopped dancing, frozen to the spot at sight of her, but as she smiled and sparkled to each man she passed, he turned back to Lysette and resumed the dance, bending more attentively to her, though a small pulse had begun to beat in his temple.

Marielle nodded carelessly to André, barely acknowledging his presence, and took the arm of a thin young man, beaming at him with such warmth that he blushed and almost tripped over his own booted feet. By the time they went in to supper, she was surrounded by half a score of breathless courtiers, each anxious to prove his devotion—to toast her in his wine, to help her to a sweetmeat, to bring a smile to her rosy lips. Lysette sat André next to her, but at each trill of laughter from Marielle his head snapped up indignantly and his nostrils flared in anger.

Mon Dieu! It was enough to make Lysette scream—from frustration at André's divided attention; from discomfort be-

cause Jean-Auguste watched coolly from across the room,
mocking her helplessness with his gray eyes; from jealousy in
the presence of a woman so much more beautiful—and witty
and capable and admired—than she could ever hope to be.
When the dancing began again and Marielle was besieged
afresh by supplicants, Lysette dragged André to a small drawing
room where half a dozen courtiers and their ladies were
engaged in a lively game of charades. Though he entered into
the game with seeming enthusiasm, the distracted look in
André's eyes made it clear to Lysette that his thoughts were still
in the Grand Salon, seeing Marielle with her admirers. She was
glad when the game was over and someone suggested Blind
Man's Buff. With a kiss for a prize, it might prove an amusing ·
divertissement.

A young Marquise was chosen to begin, and a silk handkerchief was tied over her eyes. The women of the company
stepped back while the men made a circle about the girl.
Sightless, she turned about, groping in the air—to the accompa-
niment of many giggles and innuendos from the women—until
her hands touched a fat Duke and she laughed, naming him at
once, his girth the unmistakable clue. She whipped off the
blindfold and he collected his kiss; then the handkerchief was
tied about his eyes and the men stepped out of the circle while
the women took their place. Lysette smiled to herself: a
delicious thought had just struck her. As the Duke passed close
to her, his hands sawing the air, she contrived to suppress a
sneeze, managing a small squeak that stopped him in his tracks.
He grinned beneath the blindfold and turned back to her,
inching forward until his fingers touched her shoulder. She
smiled stiffly as his hands roamed her body—breasts and hips
and thighs—while he pretended not to know who she was; at
length, unable to bear another minute of his pawing, she
laughed gaily and pulled off his blindfold.

"Come, Monsieur! Collect your kiss! If I allow you to
continue, you shall soon know me better than my own
husband!"

For all his immodest hands, his kiss was surprisingly gentle
and timid (or perhaps her words had shamed him), and in a
moment he was tying the handkerchief about her face. She
thanked le bon Dieu once again for her small stature: it was a
simple matter to duck her head a fraction of an inch, without

anyone being the wiser, until she could just see below the silk folds. She had taken the care to notice the precise color and cut of André's shoes—fawn-colored leather with gold shoe ribbons —and she sought them out while she simpered helplessly and waved the air. To be sure, she did not overreach herself, lest she touch some other man before she had found André. At last she spied his shoes; she touched him, allowed herself the pleasure of stroking his face, putting her hands on his wide shoulders before announcing to the company that this could be no other save Monsieur du Crillon. She would have removed the blindfold, but his arms went about her and caught her in a fierce embrace, his mouth finding hers in a kiss so passionate it took her breath away. She swayed against him, trembling at the fervor in his kiss, and when he released her, her hand shook as she slowly pulled the handkerchief from her eyes.

"André," she whispered, near tears, and looked up to see he was glaring at something over her shoulder, his eyes filled with malevolent fury. She turned to follow his glance. Marielle, her green eyes throwing sparks, was glaring back at him from the doorway. Lysette tried to laugh lightly, found she could not, was saved from humiliation by Jean-Auguste's jovial voice, dispelling the tension in the room, bringing a sense of normalcy back to the company.

"By my faith, it is time I had a dance with my wife! Come, *ma chère,* you have begged me for a dance all the night, and I have been a neglectful husband. Let me prove the constancy of my devotion!" He took Lysette by the arm and led her gently away; she was still so agitated by André's kiss that it was not until they were alone in a long corridor that she realized he was leading her not to the Salon for dancing but in the direction of their apartments. She murmured a word of protest and would have broken away, but he held tight to her arm, and his voice, when he spoke, was edged with steel. "You have done enough mischief this night." He did not speak again, but when they had reached their sitting room she turned upon him in cold fury, demanding to know what he had meant, why she was to be denied the evening's pleasures.

"Must I tell you yet again?" he said wearily. "Leave Marielle and André alone!"

"Pooh! What have I to do with them?"

"Did you see the way she dressed tonight? Her behavior? That was because of you!"

She tossed her head. "What nonsense!"

"She did it to make André jealous. To hurt him."

"Why should André be jealous?" she said sarcastically. "*You* are not jealous! *Mon Dieu!* I could kiss every man in this Court and you would not forbid it!"

His mouth twitched in a sardonic smile, but his eyes—cool, accusing—bored into her. "Why should I treat you as a child? Shall I prohibit that behavior which your own conscience should forbid? And your own willfulness would direct, whether I will it or no?"

She stamped her tiny foot, stung by his indifference. "And what if I take Ussé as a lover? He does not seem to find me a child!"

He threw back his head and laughed heartily. "Poor Ussé! How soon would he weary of headaches and dyspepsia, and all the little ills that keep you safely alone in your bed!"

She gasped at that, humiliated in the knowledge that all her weeks of games had not been lost on him, furious at being found out, a simple child that he merely tolerated. She raised her hand to slap him, but he caught her wrist and pulled her toward him.

"I have endured the tyranny of your hands long enough," he said softly. "You shall not strike me again." The coldness in his gray eyes propelled her, trembling, to the safety of her bedchamber and a securely locked door.

Marielle moved slowly down the passageway to her apartments, her restless fingers worrying the pale apricot silk skirt. She paused absently at a large mirror in the corridor, dismayed to see that her eyelids were still puffy from weeping, though she had sat for hours, it seemed, in the darkness of a small chamber, seeking to regain her composure before venturing out. Oh, André! she thought, feeling again the sharp pain in her heart that sprung as much from bewilderment as unhappiness. What has happened to us? We tear at each other like angry dogs—wounding, hurting, even when no hurt is intended. Where is the love, the joy that we shared? Is it so very long ago, that we have lost it forever? Is such a love meant to flame and burn—and then die, remembered only by poets and dreamers? She sighed deeply, willing herself to think of more mundane matters. The note from Louise, handed her only this evening by a footman. A simple note, printed painstakingly and laboriously; one of many she had received since coming to Paris. Louise had just learned to read and write, and took advantage of her newly acquired skills by keeping Marielle apprised of each small happening at Vilmorin. This time it was young François, who had fallen from a tree and split his lip and wrenched his knee; he would recover soon enough, but in the meantime he was sulking in his bed, filled with self-pity. Dear François. How like André he was. Not only the blond hair. But the little boy who needed comforting and love. She felt the tears begin to prickle behind her eyes again. Ah, *Dieu!* It had been a long time since André had needed her comfort! The King's General, she thought bitterly. There was always another battle to be fought, another helpless maiden to be rescued! And always adoring women to praise him when the battles were through!

Heavy-hearted, she opened the door to their sitting room. He was there, leaning against the mantel, the scowl on his face scarcely hiding the pain in his eyes.

"Have you danced your fill, then?" he asked, a ragged edge in his voice. "I fancied the young magistrate was quite taken by you!" And managed a melancholy smile.

She swept past him, too spent for a quarrel, and headed for her bedchamber, but he crossed the room in two long strides and spun her around, his hands pulling at the pins in her hair until the chestnut curls tumbled down about her shoulders. He tangled his fingers in her locks and pinioned her in a savage embrace, his mouth hard and bruising upon hers. Then—proud, vulnerable—he turned away and made for his own chamber. She stood for a minute, hand clasped to her mouth, crystal tears sparkling in her lashes; a whisper of silk and she was at his side, smiling shyly up at him, her fingers reaching for his hand. With an answering smile, filled with love and need and longing, he led her into the shadowy darkness of his room.

Marielle stirred uneasily in André's arms, uncomfortable with the silence that hung between them. Locked in passionate embrace they felt as one, thought as one—one heartbeat, one soul, one love. But when the passion died, the silence returned to cleave them in two, the hurts and misunderstandings building a barrier that seemed insurmountable. She sighed. Best to talk of trifles, to fill the emptiness.

"I had another letter from Louise tonight."

"All is well at Vilmorin?"

"Yes. Well . . ." She hesitated. "François has hurt his leg. He will be abed for a week or so."

André sat up beside her, his fine features silhouetted in the light from the fireplace. "But surely it is not serious!"

"Oh, no. Still, I thought perhaps I should like to return sooner than we had intended."

"*Mon Dieu*, Marielle! The lad is only five! The scrapes and bruises are just beginning! If you run to him for every wound, you shall never leave Vilmorin!"

Bristling, she sat up in her turn. "I shall always be there when my children need me!"

"Marielle," he said gently, putting a conciliatory hand on her arm. But she pulled away and flounced out of bed, sweeping his discarded cloak off the floor and wrapping it about her nakedness. "Have you forgot we came to Paris to see Monsieur Corneille's play?" he added.

"Then stay in Paris without me, and see the play. Try to understand, André," she said, her voice soft and pleading. "I truly think I should see to poor François."

"By all means!" he said, his tone of a sudden sarcastic and filled with bitterness. "One would think you were married to Vilmorin!"

"Far better than pretending one is not married at all!" she snapped. "Will you enjoy yourself in Paris, without your wife as chaperon?"

"Indeed, Madame, I will!" he growled.

She stormed to the door, then turned, seeing her clothing strewn about the floor. "I shall send my maid for my things in the morning. I expect to be in Vilmorin by tomorrow evening!"

His eyes glowed with anger, and swept the cloud of apricot silk on the floor. "Have your seamstress raise the bodice of that gown, or by my faith, Madame . . ." He glared at her, the threat unspoken.

Chin held high, she sailed out of the room, slamming the

door loudly behind her. When she had gone, he got out of bed, pulling the coverlet about his shoulders, and paced the floor, a deep frown creasing his brow. He picked up her silk dress and rubbed its softness against his cheek; then, with an angry grunt, he tossed it to the floor again, and sank onto a small bench near the fire, dropping his head in his hands.

Chapter Seventeen

THE SMALL CARRIAGE CREAKED ITS WAY LABORIOUSLY UP THE cobbled street to the top of the hill. In the frosty air the breath from the pair of horses hung suspended for a moment before swirling away on a passing gust. Within the drafty coach, Lysette shivered and pulled her fur-lined cloak more tightly about her body; Dominique, huddled in a corner, smiled in reassurance, tucking the woolen lap robe about her mistress's knees.

Mon Dieu, thought Lysette. She had never known a January so cold. Even here in Vouvray, where the cliffs and gabled houses managed to block off a portion of the wintry wind. Paris had been no better. The Louvre was chilly, for all its many fireplaces, and she had suffered unhappily. Besides, after Marielle had returned to Vilmorin (*le bon Dieu* knew her reasons!), André had become sullen and distracted. She had dutifully seen Monsieur Corneille's play *Le Cid*, but found herself bored with it and the storm it had aroused: Madame de Rambouillet's Salon had questioned its form and structure, and there was talk that Richelieu wished the Académie Francais to censure the playwright for violating the prescribed rules of the Theatre—the Three Unities. *Nom de Dieu!* What did it matter to her that time and place and action were not unified in some foolish play, when André was distant and Jean-Auguste was cool! And when she knew—as she had known as early as Paris, in that corner of her brain that could not deny it—that she carried a child in her womb.

The coach reached the top of the hill and stopped. They were in a small plaza ringed by tiny shops and centered with a fountain and trough long since frozen over. The coachman leaped from his box and held the door for Lysette.

"Go and warm yourself with a mug of cider," she said, pressing a coin into his wind-raw hands. "But be sure to have the coach waiting for me here in an hour. If I am delayed too long, I shall send Dominique to tell you."

The coachman hopped back onto his seat and directed the horses toward a side street and the boisterous sounds that attested to a nearby tavern. Lysette watched him out of sight, then nodded to Dominique, who indicated a narrow lane, bumpy with cobbles. As they made their way down the lane Lysette could feel the sweat oozing from her pores, running down the center of her back and between her breasts in tiny rivulets, despite the chill of the day. She could not bear a child. Babies meant pain and blood and death. Always before there had been someone to look after her, to care for her, to shield her from harm—but no surrogate could save her from the inevitability of the creature in her womb. The pain would be hers alone, and the burden, and the loss of her youth and beauty. And who would save her from his neglect, when the child supplanted the mother—to be petted and spoiled and indulged in her stead?

Dominique stopped at an iron gate centered in a high stone fence, and turned sympathetic eyes to Lysette.

"This is the place, Dominique?"

"Yes, Madame de Narbaux."

"And he is very discreet?"

"Yes, Madame."

Lysette tugged at a brass bell that hung beside the gate, and walked through to a small garden fronting an ancient brick house. The sound of the bell hung in the frosty silence, loud as a tocsin, and Lysette stirred nervously, fearful she would have to ring it again to get a response. At length the door to the house opened, and a coarse woman, her face red and puffy, beckoned to Lysette.

"Wait here," Lysette said to Dominique, motioning her to a small bench in the frozen garden. "If it becomes too cold, ask them to let you into the kitchen. Here"—handing her fur cloak to the maid—"I shall not need this for a while."

The frowsy housekeeper led her through a dim corridor to a small, wood-paneled room, damp and cold despite the fire that roared on the hearth, then bobbed politely and left her alone. She removed her gloves, rubbing her hands nervously together while her eyes swept the chamber. There was a long table covered with a patterned tapestry, two or three chairs and small stands, and a much used oaken cabinet, its drawer fronts curved and worn from years of service.

The door opened and a cheery little man bustled into the room, his balding pate ringed with a crown of snowy hair, his face wreathed in a benign smile. His doublet strained against his paunch as though the buttons would give way at any moment.

"Madame," he said, then put a pudgy finger to his lips. "I do not wish to know more." He smiled again and indicated a chair for Lysette, then seated himself beside her and took her hand. "How cold your fingers are! Well, we shall put you to rights soon enough!" And patted her hand reassuringly.

"And I may . . . depend upon your . . . discretion?"

"But certainly, Madame!" He cleared his throat delicately. "Discretion—alas—is expensive. You have brought the fee?"

She nodded and drew a small pouch of coins from the silk purse that hung at her waist. What a deal of trouble it had been to wheedle it out of Jean-Auguste, livre by livre! He had scolded her for her profligacy and suggested once again that she learn, with Bricole's help, to keep the household accounts. *Mon Dieu!* As though she did not have enough troubles already!

The little man took the pouch from her and carried it to the oak cabinet, depositing it in a small drawer, then walked to the long table and motioned for Lysette to come to him. "Shall we begin?"

She hesitated, chewing on her knuckles. "But . . . Dr. Landelle . . . how can I be sure it will not happen again? It must be unhealthy and unnatural . . . to take as many baths as I did, and still . . . !" She wrung her hands in anguish.

He laughed gently. "My dear Madame, once the stone begins to roll down the hill, it is not so easy to stop it! Not with baths, nor purges, nor physics of any kind. No, nor by eating the pip of an apple by the first rays of the sun, nor casting a magic amulet into the Loire! There are ways, of course, but it is far simpler to keep the stone from beginning its journey! A lovely lady such as yourself . . . surely a gallant gentleman can be persuaded to . . ." He smiled in cherubic innocence, but his eyes twinkled knowingly.

She frowned at that, his assumption that she had a lover, then thought better of her anger and turned away with a pang of guilt. Surely to take a lover was far less shameful than to deceive a husband, more especially one so kind as Jean-Auguste. Foolish Lysette! This was no time for high principles! With a winning smile, she turned again to Dr. Landelle. "But Monsieur, there are times when one does not . . . wish the gentleman to know! You understand." She dimpled prettily at him. "Is there nothing to be done?"

"Well, there are women in Vouvray and Tours"—he harrumphed uncomfortably—"who are . . . generous with their favors. For them, a 'complication' is . . . ahem! . . . a matter of poor business. But a noblewoman such as yourself . . ." He shook his head. "No. It would be a dishonor to you, Madame, for me even to consider . . ."

"Of course. How kind you are. How sensible of my repute." But she looked so crestfallen that he hurried to the cabinet and returned with a small velvet pouch.

"Ah, Madame, you move me in spite of myself!" He dropped the sack delicately into Lysette's lap; opening it quickly, she saw that it contained three or four sponges each about the size of a large plum. "Should you be so inclined, Madame . . . the matter is entirely at your discretion, of course! But a sponge, placed deep enough to go unnoticed, n'est-ce pas? It is important that it remain in place for several hours . . . afterwards." Lysette nodded in understanding and put the pouch into her purse. "Now," he said cheerily, and began to bustle about the room, carrying several candle stands to one end of the long table. "I would suggest you remove your skirt. The room is chilly, however . . . the skirt should be sufficient."

She turned her back to him and unhooked the heavy woolen skirt, stepping out of it and placing it on the chair along with her gloves. An edge of fear had begun to gnaw at her insides. When she turned about again, she saw that he had draped several linen cloths over the tapestry on the table; the cloths seemed washed and clean enough, but they were spotted with large ugly stains that made her stomach churn. Ah, *Dieu!* What am I doing here? she thought.

"If you please." He helped her onto the table and settled her comfortably on her back, slipping a small pillow beneath her head. She could feel the blood drain out of her face, and her breath catch in her throat, but he did not seem to notice as he went from cabinet to table and back again, fetching basins and rags and instruments, moving the candle stands closer in, all the while chattering away about the weather, the war with Spain, the possibility of the King taking Louise de La Fayette as his mistress. He paused for a moment to call in his housekeeper, and she came and stood above Lysette, grinning down at her with a wide smile that wanted several teeth. At a nod from Dr. Landelle, she unceremoniously reached down and stripped back Lysette's petticoats. With a gasp, Lysette clamped shut her eyes, feeling the shame burn her cheeks. I must be mad! she thought. She could feel him manipulating her legs into position—poking, probing—the panic rising in her breast. Her eyes flew open, but she could see only the shiny top of his head beyond the barrier of her petticoats. She felt a sudden sharp twinge and tried to sit up.

"No! You cannot!" The start of a scream—stifled by a fat hand clamped across her mouth, an angry curse, a strong arm pushing her shoulders back against the table. She struggled fiercely against the hands that held her down, her eyes wide with terror. But it was too late. There was another sharp twinge, a searing pain that seemed to tear her very insides, and then a warm flow. She sagged back against the table, her strength gone, aware suddenly that the rough hands that still muffled her mouth reeked of onions.

The doctor looked up in annoyance. "Why did you move, Madame?" Then, seeing the look on her face, he relented and fetched her a small glass of wine, raising her up by the shoulders and holding the glass to her trembling lips.

"Curse you!" she cried, fighting back tears. "Why does it hurt so?"

"You have brought it on yourself," he chided. "There was no child."

"But there must have been!"

"No, Madame. No child. I felt only a cyst—a sac of fluid

pressing on your womb. I should have merely sent you home to rest and you would soon be well. But your foolish struggles caused it to rupture; now there will be much bleeding and distress." He patted her cheek and lowered her back onto the pillow. "Well," he said kindly, "it cannot be helped."

She closed her eyes against the sharp pain within her body, the sharper pain in her soul. Had it been a child, it would be gone now—and she the cause of its destruction.

Landelle examined her once more; then, the bleeding having subsided, he inserted a wad of rags and helped her from the table. "A word of warning, Madame," he said. "You must change your linens more frequently than you are accustomed to for your monthly flux. Keep to your bed until your strength returns. You will feel pain for several days—it will pass. Do you wish to rest for a while?"

She shook her head, hating him, loathing this awful room, sick from the smell of onions that still assaulted her nostrils. "I wish to go home," she said. "At once!" The housekeeper helped her on with her skirt, then led her to the garden where Dominique waited to throw the fur cloak about her shoulders and guide her, still tottering, down the lane to her coach. She sat dry-eyed in the carriage, but when they passed the old church in Vouvray, perched on a hill, its golden stones beginning to crumble from the centuries it had stood there, she called out to the coachman and made him stop.

Despite Dominique's protests, she entered the church alone, seeking comfort from its solid arches and shadowy nave. A young priest hurried toward her.

"Madame la Vicomtesse! We are honored by your presence."

Father! she thought, filled with shame at what she had wanted to do. Will you hear my confession? But the walls had begun to ripple before her eyes, the floor to spin—and the words remained unspoken. Alarmed at her pallor, he helped her out the door and into her coach, cautioning the coachman to speed with all haste to Chimère, for surely Madame de Narbaux was grievously ill.

The tears burst then, and she sobbed in Dominique's arms for the whole of the journey home. She was too wicked. Le bon Dieu would never forgive her, however much she repented her sins. Only an evil woman would wish to destroy a child!

She was glad at least that Jean-Auguste was still at the glasshouse when she returned. When he found her in bed, it would be soon enough to invent a reason, and her ashen face would attest to the genuineness of her illness. For how could she ever tell him of her visit to Dr. Landelle? He would know—his gray eyes probing her soul—that she did not want to bear his children.

Dominique helped her on with her nightdress and would have urged her into bed, but she shook her head. "Bring me a basin of warm water. And the strongest soap you can find!" And stood there, swaying, in the center of her bedchamber, until Dominique returned. She picked up the soap and moistened it in the basin, scrubbing it across her mouth and cheeks until the skin was sore and red.

But, scrub as she might, she could not expunge the ugly smell of onions.

"Oranges! *Mon Dieu,* Jean-Auguste! Where did you get oranges in the middle of February?" Lysette sat up in bed, wriggling contentedly against her pillows. She smiled at him in genuine warmth. What a treasure he had been these past weeks, bringing her presents, spending long hours beside her bed, regaling her with amusing and ridiculous stories until she laughed with delight, enjoying his company, the lack of pretense between them. She did not, of course, allow herself to dwell on the fundamental lie: the dishonesty that had brought her to her bed, the falsehood—a feminine weakness, a winter fever, her inherent fragility—that explained away her condition. He had accepted it without question, concerned only with her health, almost ready to call in a doctor from Tours if her color did not improve. And now here he was, on this sunny afternoon, offering her a basket of oranges and grinning triumphantly as though he had summoned them out of thin air. He perched on the edge of her bed and watched in pleasure as she greedily peeled back the orange flesh and popped each juicy segment into her mouth.

"My Aunt Marguerite arrived today," he explained. "You remember I told you she had written from her chateau near Luçon asking if she might come and visit for a few weeks. She has an orangerie on the estate that is kept warm all the year through. I took the opportunity of writing her to ask if she would be so kind as to bring something along for you. 'Tis a pity. Another few weeks and there might have been strawberries as well."

"No matter," she said, smacking her lips. "The oranges are delicious!" He laughed and took out his handkerchief, dabbing at a stray drop of juice on her chin. "May I meet your aunt soon?" she asked.

"She is resting now. It was a tiring journey for a woman her age. I shall bring her to your room after supper, if she is so disposed."

"And is she as droll as your mother was?"

He shook his head. "She was sister to my father, but . . . alas . . . without his powers of mind—or tact, as you shall soon discover. I have already endured a searching catechism on the loss of my mustache! Eh, bien! She is, however, exceedingly kind and warm-hearted, and her late husband, Monsieur le Marquis de Mersenne, was a great soldier, much honored by the King. She will be pleased to know you are enjoying her oranges."

About to eat another piece, Lysette stopped, a sudden thought striking her. "Oh! I have not even asked if you should like a morsel or two! How thoughtless of me!"

He smiled. "On the contrary. There was a time when it would not have crossed your mind at all! However"—he slipped his hand behind her neck, cradling her head in his fingers and leaning close to her—"I should prefer the taste of the oranges on your lips, ma chère." His gentle kiss roused such a confusion of emotions within her, stirring guilt and tenderness in equal measure, that she smiled thinly and turned away, anxious to change the subject.

"How are the Rondini managing at the glasshouse?"

"All goes well. It is slow work, training a team of men, but the bottles they have begun to produce are consistent and will hold a uniform measure of wine. I could not ask for better than that. Ah! And do you remember the young widow from Vouvray who was hired to be housekeeper to the Rondini? She has a lad—ten or eleven, I think—Honoré by name. He was to mind the Rondini's sheep and milk their cow, but I fancy the glasshouse was more inviting. He took to hanging about so often that Guglielmo Rondini has taken him under his wing, and is teaching him how to blow and work the glass; though I suspect that Giacopo, as the master glassmaker, feels it is *his* place to train apprentices. I fear me we will need your peace-making again, ere long!"

"And do I do it well?" she asked coyly, her eyes wide and innocent.

He shook his head, frowning at her guile. "You do it exquisitely, as well you know. But it never ceases to amaze me," he added more kindly, as she began to pout, "that you always seem to know how vulnerable a man is to those beautiful eyes of yours! By my faith, I cannot fathom if you learned the art, or were born with it!"

She guessed that he meant it as a compliment and smiled happily, glad to have pleased him. He penetrated her deceptions so often that a word of flattery or praise from him represented genuine approbation, not mere puffery nor the blind—and ultimately hollow—devotion she was used to receiving from her admirers.

By evening, Aunt Marguerite had recovered from her journey and announced herself ready to meet Jean-Auguste's bride. A stout, big-boned woman, she strode into Lysette's bedchamber with such zest, her voice booming genially, that it was almost impossible to accept that she had needed a moment's rest. Indeed, Lysette was quite prepared to believe that this robust female, who would never see her fiftieth summer again, had come from Poitou on foot, slaying dragons in her path! She stood at the foot of the bed, hands on hips, surveying Lysette with a thoroughness that made her squirm; then she smiled broadly and slapped Jean-Auguste on the back.

"*Mon Dieu,* Jean-Auguste! What a little thing she is! You must pray that the sons she gives to you have the stature of the Narbaux! It is a fine thing to have tall sons," she said warmly to Lysette, seating herself in a small chair next to the bed. "But it would scarcely be amiss if they had their mother's features. You are a very beautiful woman, *ma petite,*" she said, patting Lysette's hand. "Unless my nephew is a fool, there should be a child for every year of your union!" Lysette bit her lip in consternation, feeling a hot flush stain her cheek; she dared not look at Jean-Auguste, grinning sardonically at her, lest he see beyond her embarrassment and humiliation to the shame that gnawed at her heart. But Marguerite de Mersenne, oblivious to the effect of her words, was blithely chattering away. "It is fine to have sons. I had three, you know. Ah, well"—a deep sigh—"*le bon Dieu* loved them as much as I, and gathered them in for his own. I have a grandson, now—in New France—he fought with Champlaine at Quebec—a fine lad. But Jean-Auguste has been as a son to me, and more! *Mon Dieu!* Many are the times I have boxed his ears when he tried my patience! Have you found him so?"

Now it was Lysette's turn to grin as Jean-Auguste blushed and winced. She opened her eyes wide, her rosebud mouth a circle of woe. "Ah, me!" she sighed, "he is a trial! I have prayed to *le bon Dieu* to stay my hand that I might not strike him in unseemly anger!" Her violet eyes glittered wickedly. "And still I find him peevish and surly when I wish to have my way."

Marguerite clicked her tongue in sympathy. "You are fortunate, at least, that he is good and kind. For the rest, you may pay no mind to his perversity—he ofttimes has done things that others would not, because it seemed fitting to him."

The smile faded from Lysette's face. Fitting to him. Like offering marriage when he did not wish it, because it seemed fitting and proper. And she had mocked him but a moment before, enjoying his discomfiture.

Madame de Mersenne, seeing the cloud that had passed over her face, lifted her chin in one strong hand. "Jean-Auguste tells me you have not been well. In truth, I like not your color. Did you enjoy your oranges?" Lysette nodded gratefully. "Good. You must eat every single one. And I shall cook you a strong broth tomorrow—you are too thin! Send that lazy maid of yours to me in the morning—I shall give her instructions as to your food!"

Lysette bristled. "Dominique is not lazy!"

"Indeed she is, as well you must know if you have your wits about you! And what is more, you should see to it that that handsome young farmer keeps well away from the chateau!"

Lysette gasped. "Etienne?"

"If that is his name. He skulked about all the afternoon, waiting to catch a kiss. And she was content to take every opportunity to neglect her duties. I could hardly close my eyes for all the comings and goings in the courtyard beneath my window! You mark my words—he will find his way under her petticoats soon enough, and there will be the devil to pay!" That line of thought led her to a bit of gossip about some nobleman's latest bastard, and from thence to a searching inquiry of Lysette's background and heritage, her parents, her brothers, her marriage to Guy—each frank question followed by equally frank, and sometimes outrageous, commentary on Lysette's answers. There was no time for subterfuge, or coyness, or guile—Lysette found her more exhausting to deal with than Jean-Auguste's penetrating eyes. At last, seeing her drooping, he came to her defense, forestalling any more questions and leading his aunt to the door.

As the weeks passed, however, Lysette found herself not merely tolerating, but beginning to like this hearty, open woman. She submitted to special diets and long hours of sitting in the sunshine at her open window, bundled in her furs against the cold. She found her strength growing daily, but she contrived to languish a bit whenever Jean-Auguste appeared, lest he take her good health as a sign to resume his conjugal visits.

There came a day, however, when she could not bear the sight of her rooms for another moment; when Aunt Marguerite suggested that she might wish to come down to supper, she leaped at the chance. Simply to dress, to walk down the stairs, to enjoy the companionship of Jean-Auguste and Marguerite in the small salon—she had almost forgotten she was supposed to be convalescing until, with supper over, Jean-Auguste insisted on carrying her back to her room. Despite her protests, he swept her up and made for the staircase. Rendered captive, she settled into his arms, enjoying the comfort of his strong embrace, the ease with which he held her.

"And why are you grinning, my lord?"

He chuckled down at her. "Do you remember when I carried you from the river? And all your skirts heavy from the water? I like to have near broke my back that day!"

She giggled in her turn, then frowned. "I am minded of the way you carried me in Angoumois! As though I were an old cloak to toss over your shoulder!"

He snorted. "You deserved no better! Tormenting André as you did! When a man has been celibate for many weeks . . ." He stopped on the landing and looked at her, his eyes suddenly burning with desire. "For too many weeks!" He bent low and kissed her hungrily; she clung to his neck and returned his kiss, her heart pounding wildly despite herself. Reluctantly he pulled his lips away and continued on up the stairs, but his step seemed jauntier now. "I think I must send for a doctor from Tours!"

Her heart stopped. Did he suspect, had he guessed her guilty secret? "But . . . wherefore?"

"I must see if there is a cure for me—to still my impatience until you are well!"

She smiled uneasily. But, after all, now that she had the sponges, carefully stowed in a secret compartment of her writing desk, what had she to fear? "Mayhap I am well now," she offered, and watched the grin of pleasure spread across his face.

He set her down outside her door and kissed her hand. "I shall return in a little," he said, then stopped, his lips still on her fingertips, as the sound of weeping came from her chamber. He pushed open the door. Dominique crouched on the hearth, clutching at the tattered remnants of her chemise about her arms and shoulders. There were red marks and scratches on her bare flesh, the obvious result of rough hands. At sight of Lysette she began to weep all the louder.

Jean-Auguste knelt beside her. "Dominique! Who has done this?"

"He said . . . S-S-Simon . . . such terrible things." She sobbed.

Lysette stamped her foot in annoyance. "Vacher! Have I not asked you a thousand times, Jean-Auguste, to speak to that man? And it has come to this—that he would have the effrontery to attack my personal maid?"

Dominique struggled to her feet, shaking her head. "Oh, no, my lady! It was not Simon! It was Etienne! I . . . we . . . had gone to one of the old barns. I thought he only wanted a kiss or two, and then he . . ." She gulped and could not go on.

"Are you yet intact?" asked Jean-Auguste.

"Oh yes, Monsieur! Indeed yes! But I should not have been without Simon! He came and gave Etienne a sound drubbing, and I was glad! And then . . . and then . . ." she began to wail again. "He said such terrible things to me—that I am a foolish girl, and he is vexed with me. And I am never to come to the glasshouse so long as Etienne is there, and I am not to flirt with anyone again or else he will . . . oh, I cannot tell you the hateful things he said!"

Jean-Auguste comforted her and sent her off to her room, then he kissed Lysette gently and promised to return in a few minutes. She changed quickly into her nightclothes, then released the secret catch on her desk and removed one of the sponges that Dr. Landelle had given her. God forgive my wickedness, she thought.

When Jean-Auguste knocked softly at her door, she was combing out her raven tresses. He sat and watched her for a few moments, but made no move to go to her. At last she rose from her dressing table and slipped off her peignoir; her hand was on the drawstring of her nightgown when she remembered one piece of unfinished business.

"What do you intend to do about Etienne? Or Vacher, for his cruel words to poor Dominique?"

"There is nothing to be done about Etienne. She *has* been a fool, encouraging his attentions. All Vouvray knows he has ruined many a lass. But I think he will leave her in peace now. As for Simon Vacher . . . I expect he will marry the girl in good time."

"What?"

"He has been smitten by her from the first. Did you not know?" He stood up and moved easily to her, his fingers tugging at the string of her gown until it loosened and fell to the floor at her feet. "But what care I tonight for Dominique or Vacher or Etienne?" His hands caressed her rounded hips and full breasts so she trembled at his touch. He laughed softly, his voice deep in his throat. "Aunt Marguerite has served you well—Love's pillows are firmer than I remember them! You must be sure to have her receipt before she leaves!" He kissed her hungrily, impatiently—and when he made love to her it was with a haste she found disconcerting, as though he were more concerned with his own pleasure than hers. To be sure, she responded stiffly to his ardor, conscious of the presence of that pernicious barrier, fearful that he might be aware of it. Still, she did enjoy being caressed and kissed, passively accepting the praise of his hands and lips; she felt positively cheated by his selfish haste, almost sorry she had voluntarily put an end to her confinement.

In the morning, however, she was glad. The day was fine and sunny; freed of the necessity for pretense, she strolled in the garden and rode her horse about the courtyard, under Jean-

Auguste's watchful eye. He beamed in pleasure at her rapid recovery, and, at her urging, agreed to let her ride down to the glasshouse with him in a day or two. It was so good to see her up and about again; he could not offer enough. Perhaps she would like to go to Paris in a month or so, if the spring rains did not flood the roads? And in the summer, if she wished to invite her brothers to visit—he would be pleased to receive them.

On the following morning, having dutifully eaten the large breakfast Marguerite pressed upon her, and bundled up against the chill day, Lysette at last set out for the glasshouse with Jean-Auguste. She was astonished at the changes in the clearing since last she had been there: the path had been widened to allow for small carts and wheelbarrows, the clearing itself had been broadened and extended to include the site beyond the stream where the potash was made, and a dozen small hovels for the workers had sprung up between the Rondini's house and the glasshouse. There were far more men than she remembered, and a great deal more bustle, but without the chaotic activity she remembered from the fall. What was it Giacopo Rondini had said—that a well-run glasshouse depended upon the closest cooperation and precision between every man and his fellows? Well she could believe that. Each man seemed to have a purpose, and few took the time to do more than nod quickly in her direction before continuing with his chore. She saw Simon Vacher directing his woodcutters as they gathered fuel; remembering Jean-Auguste's words, she looked at him more closely, seeing for the first time beyond his brash and craggy exterior to the lovesick swain too proud and shy to declare his feelings openly.

They entered the glasshouse and Lysette gasped and blinked her eyes, struck by the fierce heat, the blinding glare of the fires that burst forth from the openings in the large furnace. Jean-Auguste held her back, but in truth she could not advance had she wanted to, so intense was the heat. The men within seemed hardly to notice it; save for an occasional worker stripped to the waist, or a head bound up in a damp cloth, or an extra pair of hose and a protective cape or tunic, no one seemed to mind. Jean-Auguste explained that Guglielmo Rondini, the son, was a gaffer, or chief blower; Giacopo, as the master glassmaker, was expected only to supervise. But since the furnace had been fashioned with room for two crucibles of melted glass, two teams were at work, father and son both acting as gaffers.

Each team worked with a rhythm that was as formalized as a dance, their movements quick without being overhasty; while Lysette watched, Giacopo's chief assistant, his gatherer, thrust a heated iron pipe, some five feet in length, into a crucible of molten glass and withdrew a large gob that glowed a brilliant orange. He rolled it for a second on a slab of marble to retain its roundness, while it cooled to a bright red, then returned it to the crucible for another coating. Taking a prodigious breath, he blew into the pipe once, twice, until a pear-shaped bubble was formed; when he stopped to catch his breath, he thrust the rod into one of the "glory holes," those small openings in the side of the furnace designed for rapid reheating. In the meantime, Giacopo had seated himself at his blower's bench with its disproportionately long arms and was marshaling his strength for the most difficult part of the work. Working rapidly, so that the piece of glass barely had time to cool from a brilliant red to a deep ruby, he took the blowpipe from his assistant and began to blow, stopping to rest the pipe on the arms of his chair and roll it back and forth to keep its symmetry. A deep breath, a mighty puff, a twirl of the rod—Lysette looked on in amazement as a bottle was formed before her eyes. A small paddle to flatten the bottom of the bottle, pincers to form the neck—and at the precise moment his job was completed his assistant took a small gather of glass on an iron rod, called a pontil, and touched it to the bottom of the bottle where it attached at once. While his helper held the bottle thus, Rondini deftly cracked off the blowing pipe from the top; the bottle being once more thrust into the glory hole to reheat, Rondini took a shears and cut and smoothed the neck, then added a small lip of hot glass to finish it. The bottle was then taken on a fresh rod thrust into it, and the pontil was tapped lightly to release the finished bottle. The whole process had taken no more than two or three minutes; the finished bottle was placed in the large annealing oven next to the furnace where it would temper and cool for several days. It seemed so simple that Lysette was surprised when Rondini exhaled heavily and wiped his brow with one sinewy arm, seeming to droop before her eyes. He stopped a moment and splashed his face and arms with water from a nearby bucket, then nodded to his gatherer, who, blowpipe in hand, was preparing to collect another gob of molten glass.

Jean-Auguste laughed at the look of awe on Lysette's face. "Rondini says it is a simple task, and monotonous, but I suspect his experience renders it so! For, look you, he must shape his bottle to hold the exact measure each time, and teach his gatherer to take only the correct amount of 'metal'—that is what they call the hot glass. Guglielmo, on the other hand"—he indicated Rondini's son—"is more modern in his ways. The bottles he is making are smaller, but he prefers to use a mold for accuracy."

Lysette turned her attention to Guglielmo Rondini, who was busily instructing the young boy Honoré to gather the glass. The lad lifted the heavy pipe to his mouth and attempted to blow the initial bubble, but the weight of the rod was too much for him; he balanced it precariously, his thin muscles straining, while the glass cooled from bright orange to deep red and lost its glow. At length the pipe sagged to the floor and the cooled glass shattered, sending shards in every direction. Giacopo growled angrily and Honoré handed back the pipe to Guglielmo's gatherer, and scurried to retrieve his stoker's rake. Ignoring his father's scowl, Guglielmo patted the boy on the head.

"There will come a time when you can heft it, my lad!" Honoré smiled in gratitude and poked up the fires at the bottom of the furnace, while another apprentice swept up the broken bits and put them into the barrel of cullet.

In the meantime, Guglielmo's gatherer had prepared the gob of glass much as before, but this time when the gaffer took the blowpipe with its bubble he lowered it into a hinged applewood mold; the mold was closed and Guglielmo continued blowing for a moment or two, while the glass expanded within and filled every crevice. When the mold was opened, the bottle was attached to a pontil and the neck was finished much as Giacopo's bottles had been. Honoré put down his rake and ladled a bit of water over the mold to cool it for the next bottle.

Lysette was fascinated by it all. The colors were dazzling, reverberating before her eyes until she must blink and turn away: the brilliant orange of the fire in the stokehole, the whitehot openings of the glory holes, the vibrant red balls of glass, and, beyond the windows, the blue of the sky that seemed to shimmer with the same intensity.

The heat had begun to bother her; she turned to leave with Jean-Auguste, noticing as she did so several shelves of fine goblets and beakers, a commission no doubt from some wealthy bourgeois in Tours or Vouvray.

Outside the glasshouse she was both pleased and dismayed to find Pasquier, the young *vigneron* who had been crippled His damaged foot still seemed a shapeless mass beneath its bindings, and his leg was drawn up, with a small wooden peg strapped to his knee, so that he might hobble about without the aid of crutches, and without putting his weight on what remained of his foot. But his spirits were bright and he greeted Lysette with such warmth that she smiled uneasily, wishing she possessed the same kind of courage. Pasquier was busy sorting the finished and cooled bottles, supervising their loading into large wheelbarrows lined with straw that would be trundled up to the caves and filled with wine. The bottles were a pale gray-green, and clouded with tiny air bubbles, the result of imperfections in the sand, but more than adequate, as Jean-Auguste explained, for the shipping of wine.

The Rondini, having taken a moment to rest from their labors, came out to greet her more properly, their soft eyes almost black against faces still flushed from the heat. But their pleasant conversation soon drifted into a near quarrel over Honoré—whether he was worth training, and if so who was to train him. A fine thing, Lysette chided them, to welcome her back to health with a foolish quarrel—it was plain they could not behave like grown men when she was not around!

Chastened, they returned to the glasshouse. Lysette allowed Jean-Auguste to help her into her saddle, ignoring the wide grin on his face. They rode slowly back to the chateau, while he explained that the filled bottles of wine would be put into boats and shipped down river to Tours. He was very pleased with himself; because of the glassworks, the vineyards would return a far greater profit.

"Gabriel would have found it to his liking," he said, an edge of regret in his voice. "He always wished that Chimère might grow and thrive." He sighed heavily. "I would give a king's ransom to have him here to see what we have accomplished."

The sadness of that thought seemed to cast a pall on his pleasure and pride for the rest of the day; when he stopped Lysette on the staircase that night with his gentle question ("Do you wish to sleep tonight?"), she had not the heart to refuse him.

He was a solicitous and tender lover this evening, not nearly as impatient as the night before—she found herself swept along on a tide of feeling and sensation that suffused her body with a warm glow. But still—why did her thoughts always turn to André? Even as Jean-Auguste took her mouth she recalled André's kiss in Paris, half convincing herself that he meant more by it than just making Marielle jealous. And when Jean-Auguste possessed her body and she found herself responding to his ardor, her hands clasped about him, her whole being opening to receive him, it was André in her thoughts, André who owned her heart and her mind.

Afterward, feeling mellow, contented, she burrowed into his arms, enjoying his warmth, the pleasure of being held, the sweetness of his kisses, devoid now of passion. But her conscience, that foreign part within her that no longer gave her any peace, had begun its gnawing. What a wicked person she was—to think of another man in her husband's arms. And the sponge—that he did not even suspect. And that frightful day in Dr. Landelle's house. Ah, *Dieu!* Surely she would burn in hell for all eternity!

Jean-Auguste, kissing her, put his hands on either side of her face and gave a start, his fingers touching the tears that had begun to flow. Confused, miserable, she pulled away, curling up in a corner of the large bed, feeling suddenly unworthy of his kindness. For a long time they were silent, she weeping quiet tears into the pillow, he staring into the darkness above his head. At last, with a heavy sigh, he arose from the bed and left her room.

Chapter Eighteen

"I SCARCE CAN FATHOM WHAT AILS YOU, JEAN-AUGUSTE!" AUNT Marguerite's hearty voice boomed across the supper table in the salon until the wineglasses seemed to shake. Lysette, busy rinsing her fingers in the small basin held by the footman, looked up in alarm at Marguerite's words. That tone of voice was always a prelude to something outrageous. She dried her hands on the snowy linen towel and hastily dismissed the servant. Sure enough, Marguerite pressed forward like a great cannon primed for battle. "You have a perfectly charming wife, and you have been married for more than a six-month—and still her belly is flat!" Lysette gasped; she had almost become used to Madame de Mersenne's frankness by now, but this was touching a nerve too raw for comfort. Marguerite went on cheerily, ignoring the look on Jean-Auguste's face. "It can hardly be a lack on your part, my dear nephew! Did you not beget a bastard or two in your time?"

Jean-Auguste threw down his napkin and jumped up from the table; behind him, his chair teetered precariously, seemed about to topple, then righted itself at the last moment. He snatched up his wineglass and strode to the window, left open to the mild evening, and gazed sightlessly at the river below, a small muscle working in his jaw. But Marguerite's battle wagon, once set in motion, could not be stopped. She turned blithely to Lysette. "Do you suppose, *ma chère*, it would be wise for you to see a doctor in Tours or Paris?"

Lysette turned scarlet, but managed to keep her composure. "Would that not be—mayhap—premature, Aunt Marguerite?" she said softly. Then, unwilling to endure Marguerite's stare, unable to bear the sight of Jean-Auguste's back, stiff with hurt pride, she too rose from the table, and began to pace the small room, her thoughts in a turmoil. They had almost reached an impasse these past weeks since her recovery. More and more she had been consumed with guilt at her use of the sponges, torn with fears that they might not prove effective, unable to rid her mind of thoughts of André whenever Jean-Auguste touched her. She found herself sliding back into the old pattern ("Will you take it amiss? I am feeling poorly this evening"), her violet eyes helpless and begging his indulgence. He still stopped her on the stair from time to time, but she had refused him so often that he almost never asked anymore.

Even Marguerite could no longer fail to see their distress. "Ah well," she said, "there is a time for everything. You must forgive my thoughtless chatter—I should not wish to die without knowing that there are sons and grandsons to carry on the proud name of Narbaux." She stopped Lysette in her pacing and took her gently by the arm. "Have you seen what a fine figure of a man was my brother?" She led Lysette into the great hall and pointed proudly at the painting of Jean-Auguste's father, noble in his gleaming armor.

Lysette nodded in acknowledgment. "But I wonder that Jean-Auguste does not keep the portrait in the small salon, with his mother's picture!"

"Because Gabriel was as much father as brother to Jean-Auguste. The lad was barely five when his father died. Gabriel was near sixteen."

"He seems a gentle sort," mused Lysette, drifting back into the salon to stare thoughtfully up at the painting of Gabriel—warm dark eyes, fine mouth curved in a sweet smile beneath his large mustache.

"Indeed he was. Is it not so, Jean-Auguste?" asked Marguerite.

Still at the window, Jean-Auguste nodded his head, and when he turned back to the table to refill his wine cup, his face was again composed. Lysette had already swung around to contemplate the picture of Jean-Auguste's mother. She fingered the pearls at her ears, a legacy from the woman in the portrait, then peered more closely, examining the painted jewels, recognizing some of the treasures that were cached in her writing cabinet. Her eye was caught by a delicate gold chain that she had scarce noticed before: hanging from it was a tiny golden cross, no more than an inch or so, she judged, and centered with a finely carved lily in remarkably high relief for its diminutive size.

"Oh! What a lovely necklace! I have passed this painting a score of times and never seen it!" She turned, smiling, to Jean-Auguste, attempting to keep the eagerness out of her voice. "And was it as beautiful as the artist has painted it—when your mother wore it?"

Her guile was wasted. His mouth twitched at her words, as though her covetousness had been spoken aloud. "It was. Alas, it is lost now. She was very devout, my mother, and always wore it. I thought she would be buried with it. But on her deathbed she . . . placed it about my neck." He sighed, his voice heavy with regret. "I lost it fighting in Italy, in the attack on Casale. *Eh bien*"—he shook off his somber mood—"many a good man lost more than a gold necklace in the Piedmont!"

There was a solid knock on the door. At Jean-Auguste's command the door was opened and Simon Vacher strode in, his face still as brown and weather-beaten at winter's end as it had been in the fall. Dominique, passive, compliant, trailed humbly in his wake. Lysette nearly laughed aloud, remembering the maid's words that first day at Vilmorin—the smug pride that would bend to no man, the belligerent avowal of her independence. Lysette had learned the lesson, but Dominique —*Mon Dieu!* There was no rebellion in the cow-eyes she turned upon Vacher; indeed, she hung on his words with more attention than she gave to her mistress.

"My lord," began Vacher, bobbing briskly to Jean-Auguste, "I should like to have your permission to marry this girl. I fear me she will be a trial, but it is fitting that a man should take a wife, and I have been single far too long. I have some money put aside, and Monsieur Rondini has offered me a small stipend to see that the furnace is kept burning—we shall not be a burden upon you or Chimère unless there is some great calamity."

"But your cottage is deep in the woods—how can you tend the glasshouse at such a distance?"

"Ah, Monsieur. It would be a hardship for Dominique so far away from the chateau. With your permission, I shall build a small house near to the Rondini."

Jean-Auguste smiled. "I see no reason then for me to withhold my approval!"

Lysette pursed her lips in annoyance. No one had asked *her* approval, and Dominique was her maid! "Is this agreeable to you, Dominique?" she asked sharply.

A shy glance at Vacher, a soft sigh. "Oh, yes, Madame!"

"You are not . . . forced to marry?"

"Oh no, Madame! Simon has shown me naught save respect! I am untouched, and shall remain so until the day we marry!"

There was a loud guffaw from Aunt Marguerite. "But if one may judge by the look in a man's face," she said, indicating Vacher, "you will do well to speed the day, else you will not be a virgin bride!"

Dominique smiled shyly and turned away, while Vacher blushed so deeply that the rosy suffusion could be seen even beneath his browned skin. Lysette flinched at the warm glance that passed between them; it was obvious they were deeply in love, she thought with a pang. How different from her own marriage. She loved André. And Jean-Auguste merely tolerated her, that was apparent. Trapped into the marriage, he only wished the delights of the bedchamber, and—God forgive her—she denied him even that. She could scarcely join in the merriment when Jean-Auguste called for more wine and toasted the health and happiness of the young couple.

The weeks drifted by while spring peeped forth in the first crocuses, the meadows clothed in fresh green, the pink haze of trees swelling with new buds. Simon and Dominique had exchanged their marriage vows in a lively ceremony held in the gardens of Chimère on the first balmy Sunday in March. As a wedding present, Jean-Auguste had contributed much of the food, and all of the wine—by mid-afternoon, most of the farmers and *vignerons* of Chimère were happily drunk, and dancing to the tunes of a skirling bagpipe, all cares put aside for the day. Even Pasquier managed to hobble about on his peg leg, stomping out the rhythms, and Etienne, long reconciled to the loss of Dominique, was attempting to seduce the daughter of one of the tenant farmers.

Lysette was surprised at Dominique's behavior in the weeks that followed—cheerful, contented, her belligerence subdued, a new note of responsibility in the carrying out of her duties, as though her marriage had been an invisible threshold between the child and the woman. Lysette felt a certain envy at the ease of the transition—and the girl's acceptance of the burdens of maturity. Not for me, she thought. By *le bon Dieu*, never for me! She would never accept the loss of her freedom to do exactly as she wished, to please no one save herself!

In the beginning of April, she was to celebrate her birthday. Jean-Auguste had mentioned it to André one day when they rode together, and the next afternoon brought a note from Marielle begging that she might be allowed to give a small party at Vilmorin in honor of the occasion. Lysette was delighted, of course, at the opportunity to see André again, for though Marielle had visited her once or twice during her illness, she had not seen André since Paris. They were to stay for three days; Marielle had invited many guests and was planning a number of gay entertainments.

It had rained for several days before the party; the path through the woods to Vilmorin was muddy and uneven. Aunt Marguerite, bundled into the bow of a small boat and crowded in by boxes and chests of clothing and jewels (as well as two strong oarsmen), was sent ahead on the river; Lysette and Jean-Auguste would follow on horseback, threading their way over the bumpy path.

Marielle had planned well. There were jugglers and acrobats, and a company of actors brought in from Tours who entertained the guests with lively comedies and farces. By day the men rode, or fished on the river, while the women tried their skill with bow and arrow, or passed the time at backgammon and gossip. But despite the merry times, Lysette could not help but notice the estrangement between Marielle and André: Marielle played the perfect hostess, preoccupied with every small detail; André, unhappy, restless, tried to hide his pain behind a hearty laugh.

For the last evening, there was a sumptuous supper—five different meats and fowl, half a dozen sweets, fish and soup and pudding, and, to celebrate Lysette's birthday, a large cake in the shape of a lily, sculpted of crisp pastry and spun sugar. Radiant in her purple gown, her hair caught up with the first tender violets of spring, Lysette accepted the good wishes and toasts of the assembled company, then took her place with Jean-Auguste in the center of the long gallery, there to lead the guests in the dancing that followed. She gloried in the admiration of all, graciously dancing with one nobleman and then another, bestowing her smiles like tender favors upon all who came within her orbit. But André held back from the merriment—distracted, preoccupied. At length, when the music had stopped for a bit, and Jean-Auguste had gone to fetch a glass of wine for an elderly and out-of-breath Duchesse, Lysette approached André and slipped her hand through his arm.

"It is such a pleasant night, and the gallery is warm. Will you walk with me in the garden for a spell?"

He smiled gallantly. "Since it is your anniversary, I must do your bidding, lovely lady!"

She let him lead her through the gallery door onto the wide lawn; then, seeming to drift aimlessly, she turned toward the small secluded garden sheltered from the chateau by a curve of trees. She hesitated for a moment, recalling that it was here that Jean-Auguste had proposed marriage—and she was quite prepared tonight to break every vow she had ever sworn. It was not as dark as she might have wished; all the gardens and parks of Vilmorin had been lit in festive manner, and several bright torches adorned the fountain in the center of the bower. But the line of trees screened them from the chateau, and the sounds of the music drifted through the soft air to cloak the words of love she meant to speak this night.

"I fear me you are not yourself tonight, André. It grieves me to see you out of sorts."

He shrugged off her concern. "I am nagged by trifles, nothing more."

"Trifles? Nay, it is not so. For surely something has blighted your cheer. Where is my joyful companion of the journey?"

He frowned, musing. "Yes. I was joyful, was I not? Dreaming of Vilmorin and . . ." His words drifted off.

"And now?"

He laughed raggedly. "Can the dream be sweeter than the reality? A serpent came into the garden, and I cannot find it—nor name it even!—to cast it out! We are strangers, Marielle and I, and I know not why!" He shook his head impatiently. "But this is not your burden."

"And wherefore not?" She pulled him over to the stone bench to sit beside her, and held his strong hand in her own two. "Was it not in this very spot that you kissed me and called me sister? Oh André. My heart is so filled with"—she hesitated—"tenderness . . . for you that your pain is mine. Can I be of no comfort to you?" She gazed up at him, her eyes dark as the night sky, her lips parted in warm invitation.

He cupped her chin in his hand, his eyes searching her face as though he were seeing her for the first time, the soft eyes, the tempting mouth. Leaning forward, he pressed his lips to hers in a tentative kiss, hesitant, exploring. She trembled, feeling her head spin—the sweetness, the perfection, the culmination of all her dreams. She had always known it would be like this.

She reached up to encircle his neck and found herself suddenly thrust away with rough hands. With an angry growl, André jumped to his feet and turned away from her, his shoulders rigid with the effort at self-control.

"*Mon Dieu!* I must be mad. To betray your kindness . . . to hurt Jean-Auguste. Forgive me, Madame de Narbaux!"

"No, André! You must not reproach yourself!"

He spun around, shaking with fury at his own weakness. "Who, then? You? Who offered solace and comfort as a sister? *Dieu!* I would have dishonored you, visited my unhappiness upon you, and brought grief to Jean-Auguste!" His shoulders sagged, the fury replaced by self-loathing. "What a fool. And still Marielle and I would be strangers." Wearily, he passed a hand over his eyes, his voice low and tormented. "If ever I am to root out the canker, and regain my wife, it shall not be by seducing the wife of my dearest comrade. Forgive me." Then he was gone, slipping through the line of trees and vanishing into the night.

Lysette's hand went to her breast and she stood up, meaning to call him back, then thought better of it. To do so would be to humiliate herself. He had spurned her, but at least he thought only that he was denying himself. If she called him back, he might refuse her openly, thereby shaming them both.

Through bitter tears, she looked up to see Jean-Auguste at the edge of the garden. Weeping, she threw herself into his arms, wanting the comfort of his embrace, the warm assurance that would tell her he had seen nothing. His arms held her fast, but his voice above her was quiet, filled with a weariness she had not heard before.

"I wonder, *ma chère,* if those are tears of contrition, or merely disappointment!"

Shocked, she pulled away, struck dumb with shame. He had seen the kiss—that was plain enough; and if he had not heard André's words of rejection, he could not have misread the anger and haste with which André had fled her side. She was glad at least that it was too dim to see the contempt that would be in Jean-Auguste's eyes.

"I came seeking you to give you your birthday gift," he went on, as though nothing had happened. "I found a clever goldsmith in Vouvray." From his pocket he drew a small gold chain and cross, a perfect replica of the necklace worn by his mother in the portrait.

Touched, Lysette began to weep again. "I shall wear it always, as she did."

He shrugged, and dropped it carelessly into her palm. "As you wish. It matters little to me. I should like to return early to Chimère on the morrow. You will doubtless be still abed. I will take your horse with me. You can travel with Aunt Marguerite in the boat." He turned back to the chateau.

"Jean-Auguste!" He swung about to face her. Ah, *Dieu!* Why were the words so hard to utter with those accusing gray eyes bent to her? "Thank you," she whispered, unable to say more.

Lysette hurried up the stairs to her chambers, thankful that she was alone. Since they had returned from Vilmorin, she found herself increasingly uneasy in Jean-Auguste's presence. He had become cold and distant, with a tenseness that was disconcerting; she had laughed a great deal, and played the coquette, hoping to jolly him into a better mood, but his eyes had snapped with impatience at her obvious guile, and she found it easier to avoid him. Besides, he had begun to look at her in a different way when he thought she was unaware of his glance—a kind of smoldering (anger? desire?) that was new and surprising in such a forebearing nature. She did her best to evade his question on the stair—slipping her arm through Marguerite's so that they ascended together, or skipping off in a hurry after supper while he was yet sipping the last of his wine. And once, when she had started up the staircase, and he emerged unexpectedly from the library to stand staring silently up at her, she had contrived to droop and yawn and smile sheepishly. Motionless, he had watched her until she had disappeared on the landing above, his eyes never leaving her.

Now, she was glad he was nowhere about. He had vanished to his rooms shortly after supper; she had stayed to play cards with Marguerite, then lingered after the elder woman had gone to bed, watching the soft spring rain patter on the river beyond the salon windows. She was tired. It was late. Chimère was still; with a pang she realized that Dominique must still be waiting for her in the passageway, unable to go to her own bed (or her husband's! *Mon Dieu!* Would her conscience never give her any peace?), until her mistress was abed. Sure enough, she found Dominique fast asleep in the corridor; she shook her gently and the maid roused herself and picked up a candelabra from a small table, leading the way to Lysette's bedchamber.

The room was dim, lit only by a candle on the dressing table; when Dominique would have lit more, she shook her off. It was hardly necessary—she would be asleep ere long. There was no fire; despite the rain, it was a warm evening. She glanced at the shadowy bed, its curtains parted slightly. There would be no need to close them against the night and the mild air. She breathed deeply, the scent of spring and warm rain sweet in her nostrils. It was lovely.

"Dominique, when you turn back the coverlet, open the bed hangings fully. The air is so fresh tonight!"

She stood motionless in the center of the room while Dominique stripped off her garments, then preened, naked, in front of her mirror, admiring her body, the firm breasts unwizened by a suckling babe, the thin belly and flawless skin. At last she allowed the maid to slip a nightdress over her head and comb out her chignon, twisting her ebony curls into a soft braid. While Dominique went to prepare her bed, she took the single candle and her jewels and entered her turret sitting room, releasing the magical catch on her writing table and tucking away her earrings and gold necklace in their drawers. She never tired of her desk; even now, weary as she was, she lingered to stroke the delicate pediments and finger the tiny columns.

When she returned to her bedchamber, she clicked her tongue in annoyance. Devil take the maid! She was nowhere about—and the draperies of the bed were still half closed! Impatiently she grasped the edges of the curtains and whipped them open, then gasped and stepped back, almost slipping on the edge of the carpeted platform. Jean-Auguste was there, lolling on the bed, a crooked smile on his face. As she watched, he sat up and swung his long legs over the side of the bed.

"*Mon Dieu!*" she exclaimed, her hand clutched to her still pounding chest. "What a start you gave me! Is this some sort of jest? Are you drunk?"

"Must I be drunk to find your games wearying?"

She frowned in anger, but an edge of unease had begun to gnaw at her. "What do you here?"

"Simply this—I do not intend to be denied tonight."

She swirled away from him and began to pace the center of the chamber, her lip curled scornfully. "And so you come creeping in here like a thief! How long have you been there?"

He laughed mirthlessly. "I watched you admire yourself. You still have a beautiful body, though I had almost forgot what you look like!"

She cursed her own vanity, a hot blush staining her face. "And Dominique? Did you frighten her as you did me just now?"

"Poor Dominique! She could scarcely decide whether her fealty lay with the mistress—or the master who bid her go! Though I'll wager she understands the duty of a wife far more than you do."

"You will forgive this wife tonight," she said sarcastically, indicating the door. "I am extremely tired." She drew herself up proudly. There would be time for tears if her indifference did not drive him away.

"No." The voice cold and determined. "I have been more than patient, Lysette. Henceforth I shall come to you when *I* wish it! You will oblige me by loosing your gown."

"Oh-h-h!" She began to weep, her voice rising in an unhappy wail. "Am I a strumpet? Am I no better than a whore in Paris to be ordered about so?" She sobbed bitterly, covering her face with her hands. There was no response from Jean-Auguste. She sniffled loudly and looked up at him. His face was frozen, one eyebrow raised skeptically. She stamped her foot in fury at the look in his eyes, and turned her back to him, bosom heaving in anger.

"Mark me well, Lysette," he said, the voice so low and menacing that she turned back to him uneasily, in spite of herself. "If I lay aught but loving hands on you tonight, you will have cause to rue your willfulness! By my faith, I cannot judge what would please me more—to bed you, or to pull you across my knee and mete out the whipping you have more than earned half a score of times! Now, loose your gown!" he barked.

Her eyes widened in fear, terrified suddenly of this stranger who had invaded her sanctuary. She managed at length to pull herself together, but when she responded to him she was dismayed to discover that while her words were icy and scornful, her voice was unsteady, the soft lips trembling. "You will find no joy tonight, Monsieur, I promise you that!" Quickly she dropped her nightdress, then wrapped her arms about her naked breasts and shoulders, as though she would deny him even the right to look at her. Sullenly she waited, tapping her foot in annoyance, while he rose from the bed and began to remove his own clothing, all the while circling about her, his eyes raking her body until she felt almost degraded. Damn him! she thought, her blood boiling.

He lifted her chin and kissed her firmly on the mouth. Hands still folded across her chest, she held herself stiffly, her lips tight-clamped and unyielding. He stepped back for a second, his eyes narrowing, then, suddenly, unexpectedly, he grabbed her wrists and unwrapped her protective arms, pinning them behind her back. Pulling her close, he kissed her fiercely, his mouth rough and insistent, forcing her lips apart, compelling a response. It was impossible to be cold or indifferent; she found herself shaking (from fury? fear? passion?) at his brutal assault. She struggled in his embrace, trying to loose his cruel grip, conscious all the while of his body pressing hard against hers; when he released her wrists to scoop her up in his arms, she flailed at his chest and shoulders, aware suddenly of the strong sinews beneath her pummeling fists. He tossed her onto the bed and pinioned her body with his own, his burning mouth finding her breast. Gone was the gentle lover—his hands were strong upon her, touching, fondling, exploring with passionate intensity, until her violent spasms were as much response as resistance. She could not think of André—she was enveloped by Jean-Auguste, overwhelmed by his presence, the throbbing that had begun deep within her.

For a moment she opened her eyes to see his red hair flaming in the light of the candles, then closed them again as his hot mouth took hers and he possessed her body. He was the fire, the crucible, the furnace—she the vessel, consumed by a white hot flame, burning and burning and burning. An unbearable tension rose within her and she clung to him, returning his kisses. He was the glassmaker, molding her to his will. The fire burned ever fiercer within her; behind her closed eyelids the glass shattered into myriad shards—glowing, luminous—and she was transported in wondrous iridescence to radiant bliss.

Chapter Nineteen

"FORGIVE ME, MADAME! I DID NOT KNOW WHAT TO DO WHEN Monsieur le Vicomte sent me away last night." Dominique's eyes were wide with innocence, but she could scarce prevent her lips from curving into a knowing smirk.

Lysette cursed softly and burrowed deeper under her coverlet. "Leave me!" she snapped. "And do not return until I send for you!" She closed her eyes against the bright morning sun, hearing the soft click of the door as Dominique left the room. *Mon Dieu!* By now half of Chimère must know that Monsieur le Vicomte had forced himself on his wife! She opened her eyes again, staring sightlessly at her bed hangings, wide awake despite the fact that she had hardly slept all night. She burned with anger and humiliation. How she hated him! How she despised herself!

Her thoughts churned within her poor brain, recalling again and again the events of the night. When at last Jean-Auguste, exhausted, had rolled away from her, she had curled up in her small corner of the bed, shaking violently, panting to recover her breath, frightened of the passionate frenzy he had awakened within her. She had lain thus for a long time, while her racing pulse slowed and her head ceased its spinning—an hour, perhaps two. The rain had stopped. The last of the candles had sputtered and gone out, plunging the room into darkness. She guessed that he slept, but peaceful slumber had eluded her. Then he had stirred, and his hand had slid around her waist and reached up to her breast. His touch had burned her, and she had begun to quiver again, twitching helplessly under his searching fingers. He must have taken her trembling for a rebuff; with rough hands, he had turned her to him and kissed her fervently, his mouth draining her of the last shred of will and pride. Then, with no further overtures, he had entered her abruptly, fiercely. She had cried out, a passionate moan that had escaped her lips as she felt herself yielding—helpless, enervated—to his ardor. Thinking she had cried in pain, he had begun to withdraw; with a piteous whimper ("No! Please!") she had clutched at him, holding fast to him that they might not be parted.

She cringed now, remembering, filled with self-loathing. She had never wanted to let him go. Ah, *Dieu!* She would have begged him on her knees to stay if he had left at that moment! He had reduced her to helplessness—for one terrible night she had been his pawn, his plaything. She shivered, an unfamiliar edge of fear working at her. She had never thought of him as particularly strong before—surely not beyond her controlling and manipulation; she had always equated his gentle agree-ableness with a kind of weakness. Though he had sometimes won a small skirmish or two, she had never doubted her ultimate mastery of him—through her guile and his own reluctance to make her unhappy. She fidgeted nervously in her bed, biting her lip in consternation. Up till now, she had felt sorry for him, because it was clear the marriage had been a mistake he regretted; now she was overwhelmed with self-pity. What was she to do, yoked to this brute of a man? She scanned her bare arms, beginning already to discolor into ugly bruises because of his cruel grasp, and nearly wept aloud.

Still, to be practical, she was glad at least that there was little chance of her conceiving a child from this encounter. She had learned enough from questioning of Aunt Marguerite to guess that she was in the infertile portion of her cycle. And if Jean-Auguste should invade her bechamber again, she would keep her wits about her, distracting and charming him long enough so that she could use one of Dr. Landelle's miracle devices. She laughed softly. After all, she *had* gulled him on that account! How often had she used the sponges, and he never the wiser! Perhaps he was not so strong or all-seeing, despite last night! She had been very sleepy, too tired to use her wiles, to be on her guard against him. That was why he had frightened her, overpowered her—no reason other than that! Smiling confidently to herself, she picked up the bell on her bedside table and rang for Dominique.

Jean-Auguste's behavior all that day seemed to bear her out. Very quiet, he hardly looked at her, a cloud of embarrassment, almost shyness, seeming to envelop him. Lysette, on the other hand, made good use of her advantage, playing the gracious lady, all-forgiving, as though she understood his momentary lapse.

In the late afternoon she invited him to stroll with her in the gardens. It was a beautiful day, did he not agree? Would he take the spring air with her? As they walked, she chattered gaily, pretending not to notice his unease, absently twisting a ring on her finger—a ring she had taken great care to put on before inviting him for their walk. As they passed a small pond, afloat with lilies, she contrived to let the ring slip off her finger and sink into the water. With an unhappy "Oh!" she sank to her knees to retrieve it, rolling up her sleeves before plunging her arms into the pond. When she stood up, triumphant, the rescued ring in her hand, she was delighted to see that his unhappy eyes were drawn to the purple welts on her forearms and wrists. She smiled gently at him, all soft forgiveness, but she allowed her chin to tremble bravely as she dabbed at her arms with a handkerchief and rolled down her sleeves.

For the next few days she gloried in his contrition, taking every opportunity to make it apparent that his abasement of her was a humiliation she did not intend to allow again. She lingered on the stairs, almost defying him to intrude upon her modesty, then sailed to her room in a sanctimonious aura. She managed even to wheedle a new saddle from him, though he had refused her request several times in the past, calling it a needless extravagance.

She was glad, however, when Aunt Marguerite announced one day over lunch that she intended to return to her home in Poitou in a few days. Madame de Mersenne had shrewd eyes; surely she had noticed Jean-Auguste's new humility, and was already priming herself with a barrage of probing and unwelcome questions. But with April almost over, there was much to be done on her estate, and, besides, she did not wish to feel she had overstayed her welcome.

"Will you come to see me, Jean-Auguste?" she asked. "And bring this charming thing with you! I must confess I have grown quite fond of your wife! Though the day will come, *ma chère,*" she said, not unkindly, to Lysette, "when you will regret that you have not troubled to become the true mistress of Chimère. In my day, a woman raised her children and ran the estate while her husband was at war, and if she was slow at learning her lessons, her husband taught her with a switch cut from a birch tree!" She shrugged to Jean-Auguste. *"Eh bien!* Bricole does well enough. And Lysette is too fragile and tender to treat roughly."

Jean-Auguste smiled stiffly, a muscle working in his jaw; he almost seemed to blush as he rose from the table and went to stand at the window, as though he regretted afresh his rough assault.

Lysette scarcely noticed, so stung was she by Marguerite's implied criticism of her as wife. She turned a bright smile to the elder woman. "But how perceptive you are, Aunt Marguerite! How I have longed for Bricole to instruct me in the management of Chimère—long before my illness even!—but he has been reluctant to relinquish what has been his for so many years. I have not the heart to bring him pain! And I cannot do it without his help. My dear aunt was like a mother to me—in all save those instructions that would help me to be a better wife!" She sighed deeply. "But I shall learn. Jean-Auguste has been the soul of patience—I would crave your sympathy a little longer as well! As for children"—she crossed herself quickly, her face shining with perfect piety—"may *le bon Dieu . . .*"

"Merde!" At the window, Jean-Auguste's face had turned white. He raced for the door and flung it open; they heard his boots clicking rapidly on the stone floor of the Great Hall, the sound of the main door crashing wide, and then silence.

"Jean-Auguste! *Nom de Dieu!*" cried Lysette. She hurried to the casement where he had stood and peered out at the bright day. The river was calm, the sky a pure and limpid blue, and far off, over the edge of the trees that hugged the shore, was a pillar of thick black smoke. She frowned for a moment, then gasped in comprehension. "Ah, *Dieu!* The glasshouse!" She hurried into the Hall, calling for Bricole to send for her horse, and paced restlessly, ignoring Marguerite, until one of the grooms brought her mare around.

Jean-Auguste had not bothered even to wait for his horse, but had gone on foot; nevertheless, by the time Lysette arrived in the clearing he was already there, doublet off, sleeves rolled up, barking commands to the men. The glasshouse was a mass of flames, crackling and roaring, and the air was acrid with thick smoke. Lysette dismounted and stood helpless, as men shouted and ran back and forth, seeking in vain to douse the flames with hastily fetched pails of water, beating out the sparks that threatened to catch the kiln shed and the drying stacks of wood.

Lysette caught sight of the boy Honoré, barefoot, watching in wide-eyed terror, and went to kneel beside him, her heart unexpectedly softened at his distress. "Are you hurt, lad?" His face crumpled and he began to sob; she folded him into her embrace, unfamiliar words of comfort issuing from her lips.

He sobbed afresh, tried to speak and could not.

"But how did it happen?"

He wiped his nose with the back of his sleeve. "We . . . Monsieur Guglielmo . . . the men . . . were s-s-setting a new crucible in the furnace. It did not spill, I think—it must have burst. There was a snap, a loud crack . . . I know not . . . and then the sparks were shooting up through the vent at the top, and the roof, and the roof . . . !" He stared at Lysette, gaping in horror. "It was all on fire and I looked at the stoke hole and the hot glass was pouring out and the bench was burning, and Monsieur Guglielmo grabbed me round and pushed me out the door, and I lost my shoes and my mother will whip me and . . ." He stopped to catch his breath, a great gasping intake.

Lysette looked up. Giacopo Rondini, wild-eyed, stood before them. He snatched Honoré from Lysette's arms, taking him roughly by the shoulders and shaking him until the boy wailed in terror.

"Where is Guglielmo? Where is my son? You were inside with him . . . where is he?"

A high squeak. "Please, Monsieur! He pushed all of us out—Charles and Michel and the rest—I have not seen him since!"

Rondini blanched, his eyes darting to the flaming glasshouse. "My son!" he screamed. "My son!" Like a madman, he hurtled toward the burning building, and the large doorway that was now a wall of fire. Some of the men caught him and held him back, while he struggled and fought and cursed them, his strength the strength of desperation. Simon Vacher, busily directing the human chain of water buckets, paused for a moment and came nearer to the doorway, holding up an arm to shield himself from the intense heat. Beyond the flaming entrance, there still seemed a portion of the interior that had not caught fire. Vacher turned to one of the glassworkers and snatched off the man's protective leather cape, draping it about his own head and shoulders. Then he picked up a bucket of water and poured it over his face and arms. Taking a deep breath—and before a horrified Jean-Auguste could reach his side and stop him—he plunged into the inferno.

Lysette rose to her feet, her hand clutched to her mouth. Poor Dominique! It seemed an eternity of waiting. Honoré's mother, the widow, who had run from the Rondini house, fell to her knees, hands clasped, lips moving in silent prayer. Someone coughed and retched as a fresh puff of thick smoke rolled over the clearing. There was a shout of relief that turned to a groan as Vacher appeared in the doorway, carrying the charred and lifeless body of Guglielmo. He stumbled into the clearing; his face went white and pasty, a pallor that tinged his bronzed skin a ghastly shade of green. Dropping his grisly burden, he pitched over onto his face. Jean-Auguste and several of the men leapt to him and turned him over, pounding on his chest to force out the smoke and let in the healing air. In a little, his color returned and his eyelids fluttered weakly. Sighing in relief, Jean-Auguste gave orders that he should be taken to his cottage; it was Lysette who thought to commandeer one of the men and send him to the chateau to fetch Dominique to tend her husband.

It was clear that nothing could save the glasshouse; the men worked frantically to keep the fire from spreading to the other buildings or the surrounding woods. And for all the hours they toiled, Rondini sat like a dead man; the moment he had seen Guglielmo's body he had sunk to the ground, all the life draining out of him, his dark eyes tearless and unseeing. At last, the widow came to him, and raised him up, and forced a jug of strong wine into his hands, leading him to his house and the blessed forgetfulness that wine would bring.

The sun hung low in the sky, glowing in brilliant counterpoint to the last smoldering embers. Most of the glasshouse was gone; the furnace itself had cracked and caved in—only the cooling oven remained, filled with bottles fused together now by the intense heat.

Lysette rubbed her eyes tiredly, feeling a certain pride that eased her grief at Guglielmo's death. When it had become apparent that she could do nothing at the clearing, neither to ease Giacopo's pain nor to be of any help, she had ridden back to Chimère and called for Bricole. They would need food and drink at the glasshouse, a steady supply while they worked, and all the night, if need be. She did not care if it would leave the larders short-stocked; there would be time enough to deal with that problem. For now it was important that the workers be fed—and why had Bricole not thought of it? Must every burden be hers? She grew positively righteous while Aunt Marguerite gaped in wonder, and Bricole, filled with new respect, invited her into the kitchens to supervise the work firsthand. Now she sighed as she surveyed the devastation in the clearing. The workers at least were fed, and she had instructed Bricole at the last to send down several hogsheads of wine. Jean-Auguste was nowhere about—someone told her that Monsieur le Vicomte had returned to the chateau.

She found him in the small salon. His shirt was torn and smudged; his orange hair speckled with soot and ashes. He sat sprawled in his chair, facing the cold fireplace—and the portrait of Gabriel. Her heart sank at the haunted look he turned to her. She had come seeking his strength for her grief, his praise for what she had done; he could not ease his own pain, let alone give her comfort.

"Gabriel would have succeeded," he said, the words hardly meant for her, his eyes looking past her to some dark recess in his own soul.

"Jean-Auguste," she said softly. "Come and sup with me in my sitting room."

"Leave me!" he growled, shaking her off. "I cannot eat!"

Sighing, she went to her rooms, to be greeted by a young

maid who curtsied and begged Madame to accept her service
this evening while Dominique nursed her husband. Lysette
nodded. *Mon Dieu!* She did not even know the girl's name. She
had been mistress here for eight months—and she did not even
know her name, though she had seen the girl every day at
Chimère!

"What is your name?" she asked, shame-faced.

"Claude, my lady."

"Well then, Claude. Please go and tell Bricole that I shall sup
in my room. And ask Madame de Mersenne if she will do me
the honor of joining me. But first, you may help me into my
dressing gown—I cannot bear the smell of smoke another
moment!" With Claude's help, she stripped down quickly,
putting on fresh chemise and petticoat which she covered with
a blue velvet peignoir, and splashing her arms and bosom
lavishly with perfume to drive out the last traces of smokiness.

She and Marguerite dined together, but the tragedy had
drained them both, and they found they had little to say to one
another. At last Madame de Mersenne, begging weariness,
went to her own rooms. About to change into her nightclothes,
Lysette hesitated. It was very quiet. Surely if Jean-Auguste had
retired to his apartments she would have heard the sound of
servants moving about in the passageway. She went out into
the corridor. It was still lit, as was the staircase. Descending, she
found one or two footmen nodding in the Great Hall, waiting
for Monsieur to go to bed that they might extinguish the torches
and candles and seek rest themselves. Crossing to the small
salon, she peered in and saw that Jean-Auguste was still where
she had left him hours before, staring morosely up at Gabriel's
picture.

She put a soft hand on his sleeve. "Jean-Auguste. For the
love of God. Have something to eat and go to bed. Please."

"I cannot. Leave me be." But his voice was more gentle than
it had been earlier. He breathed deeply, catching a whiff of her
perfume, and uttered a sad laugh. "I did not think my nostrils
would ever again smell anything save smoke!" He sighed. "Go
to bed."

"Good night, then," she said. "May *le bon Dieu* be with
you." With heavy heart, she crossed to the staircase.

"Wait!" He called to her and strode quickly to where she

stood, hand poised on the balustrade. "Send your maid away tonight." His face was haggard, the gray eyes almost pleading.

"*Mon Dieu*, Jean-Auguste! It has been such a terrible day! Do not importune me tonight, when I desire only the solace of my bed—and my solitude!"

His eyes narrowed as though he had not heard her aright; grabbing her fiercely by the elbow he steered her up the stairs to her chambers, ignoring her protesting squeals. Brushing past the maid Claude, waiting outside her door, he stormed into the room and flung Lysette away, slamming the door on the gaping servant. He glared at Lysette, his eyes filled with cold fury.

"Did I not make it clear to you that I would bed you when *I* wish it? I much regretted my brutishness of last week, but that does not gainsay the fact that I meant my words to be heeded!"

This time she had her wits about her. "And will you force me . . . against my wishes?" Her lip curled in scorn. "Will you threaten to beat me if I do not please you?" And was glad to see him flinch at her words.

His eyes scanned her face with a look that was almost hatred. "No, my dear wife," he said at last, his voice thick with sarcasm. "Mayhap there should be a contract, that your conjugal duties should wait upon my predilections! Would you care to amend it with particulars of your own choosing? A new brooch for your favors? A lace handkerchief for a smile or kiss?"

"How crass you are! How disgusting!"

"To the contrary! I think it a capital idea. If it is writ down on paper, I may tally the ledger from time to time to see if you are worth the expense!" He moved toward her sitting room. "Let me fetch pen and ink—it would be amusing to learn how high you value yourself!"

She seethed in fury at his tone, tapping a petulant foot on the tiles as she waited for him to reemerge. She could hear him rummaging at her writing desk, seeking paper and ink, and cast about in her brain for ugly words of scorn that would put an end to this ridiculous charade. By *le bon Dieu*, he would not have his way tonight! His voice called out to her from her sitting room.

"Mayhap I shall title it 'Permission to Share My Wife's Bed.' Think you that . . ." His voice broke off abruptly. After a long moment, he moved unsteadily into her bedchamber, his face as ashen as his shirt. He held out his hand to her, uncurling his long fingers to reveal her sponges on his broad palm.

She felt her mouth go dry, but managed to open her eyes wide in feigned innocence. "Whatever is that?"

"God save me from your games tonight!" he choked. "You know well what these are—and so do I! Every harlot in Paris has a box of sponges next to her rouge pot! Have I married a harlot then? Did you earn your living in the streets of Soligne after Guy died?"

"How dare you!" she raged. "That you could imagine that I . . . Oh!" Her eyes blazed, deep amethyst fires throwing off sparks.

"For André, then," he said, his voice soft and deadly.

She laughed contemptuously. "Pah! What nonsense!" But her pulse had begun to throb with the beginnings of fear.

"Think you I did not guess that André was the attraction and the reason for Paris?" He looked at the sponges in his hand, and closed his fist tightly about them. "Have you lain with André?" he asked, not looking at her.

"No," she said icily. "I have known no man save Guy and you!"

A hollow laugh. "And one may hope that Guy was rewarded more often than I!" His eyes bored into her, a sudden sharpness in his voice. "Did you use the sponges when you lay with me?" She hesitated, suddenly afraid to reply. "Answer me!" he barked. "I would not regret wringing your neck tonight if you keep silent! By le bon Dieu, I am sick unto death of your lies and deceptions!" With an angry growl, he threw down the sponges. "Did you use them?"

She started to cry, genuinely upset at her own perfidy. "Only a few times, Jean-Auguste. Truly."

"And you swear it, no doubt, by the reality of those tears that do your bidding, and spring to your eyes when you stand in need of them!"

Lashed by his words, her body began to shake with sobs. "Stop, Jean-Auguste. No m-m-more. I beg you."

His shoulders sagged with weariness and disgust. "How well you do it. How often I find myself believing your words. And where did you get the sponges?"

A frightened whisper. "In Vouvray."

"Where?"

"She swallowed hard, fear driving out her tears. "Dr. Land-elle." Barely audible.

He reeled back as though she had struck him. "Landelle? But he is the doctor all the women attend when they wish . . . did you? *Mon Dieu!* When you were ill . . . was that the reason? Was it?!" His voice had risen to a roar, his face purpling in fury. She had never known he could grow so angry. She backed away, terrified. *"Was it?"*

"No . . . No . . . Jean-Auguste . . . I only . . ."

"Curse you!" he said, and strode to her, his gray eyes black in his face; he raised up his hand and struck her down to the floor, so violently that the hairpins were dislodged from her coif and flew clattering onto the tiles. Her face stinging from the force of his blow, she sobbed in pain and grief as he stormed to the door. About to quit her room, he stopped and turned, seeming to reconsider, then marched back to where she still lay huddled on the floor.

She looked up at him through the curtain of her hair. "What would you?" And raised a shaking arm to ward off another blow.

"I would have a son!" His hand closed about her upraised arm and he jerked her roughly to her feet.

"No!" She shook off his grasp and turned to flee.

He grabbed at her, his fingers tangling in her raven hair, pulling her back by the tight-clasped curls until she cried out in pain. Swinging her around, he bent her back over his arm and glowered down at her face, his eyes like burning coals. His free hand tore at her bodice, rending the blue velvet and the chemise beneath. Paralyzed with fear, she could not even struggle, could only beg him with piteous eyes and soft voice. "Please, Jean-Auguste, please . . . please . . ."

He seemed not to notice or care. "By God," he said through clenched teeth, "if I must tie you to your bed—I shall plant my seed this night! Once for all, there will be a child of this union!" He lifted her in his arms and flung her onto the large bed as though she were a toy discarded in disgust. There was a sickening thud, the hollow wooden thunk of the carved head-board.

"Lysette!"

He rushed to her side. She lay very still, her hair across her face; when he parted the silken tresses he saw that her eyes were closed, her face (save for the glowing red mark of his fingers across her cheek) deathly white. "Lysette!" He ran gentle fingers over her skull, feeling the lump that was already beginning to swell behind one ear, grateful at least that when he took his hand away there was no sign of blood. He wrung his handkerchief in a small pitcher of water near her bed, and dabbed at her face until she began to moan softly and her skin regained a bit of its normal color. Shaking, he rubbed a hand across his eyes, then hurried to the door and summoned the waiting Claude.

"Attend your mistress," he said, his voice unsteady, and strode away down the passage.

The moon, rising late in the sky, illuminated the last wisps of smoke lingering in the ruined glasshouse, swirling like ghostly fingers around the man who staggered through the debris, a pitcher of wine clutched in one hand. The boy Honoré crouched behind an upturned wheelbarrow, his eyes never leaving the stumbling man, his small hands clutched together as if in supplication. At length Giacopo Rondini (for it was he in the ruins) drained the last of the wine and flung the pitcher from him. Drunkenly he stooped and picked up a pontil, fingering it aimlessly and poking at the crumbling remains of the furnace. He turned to the cooling oven, still intact, his eye caught by the bottles within. While Honoré watched, trembling in his hiding place, Rondini shook the pontil skyward, as though cursing the gods, then swung it violently against the bottles, smashing and destroying in a shower of glass, seeking out every fragment and shard that could be pulverized. And all the while, from his wide-gaping mouth, came forth feral howls of pain and rage.

The persistent moon crept through the stained-glass windows and into the tiny chapel of Chimère. It touched the small votive candle on the altar and caressed the white shirt and orange hair of the figure who knelt in prayer, bespotting all with the night-muted colors of the patterned glass. Jean-Auguste rose to his feet and paced the floor, wringing his hands in anguish, his steps carrying him in and out of the impersonal moonbeam.

Suddenly he fell to his knees again, his hand clawing at the carved stone upon the floor that marked the entrance to the burial crypt below; feeling no movement, he groaned, and his fist pounded rhythmically against the unyielding stone.

"Gabriel!" A haunted, hollow whisper.

With a tormented cry, he threw himself face down upon the floor, his shoulders shaking violently, and gave himself over to his grief.

Chapter Twenty

"SHALL I BRING YOU YOUR BREAKFAST NOW, MADAME?"

Lysette looked up from the chaise in her sitting room, where she had lain for the last half hour after dragging herself painfully from her bed, and absently watched Dominique bustling about, parting curtains, opening windows to the bright day. Her head throbbed, and there was a numbness where her heart should have been. She could not think of food when Jean-Auguste's stricken look haunted her, filled every corner of her brain. She sighed and peered more closely at the maid.

"How pale you are, Dominique. Pale and dark-eyed! I'll wager you have not slept all the night!"

"It matters not, Madame. I am so grateful to *le bon Dieu* that Simon will be well. They said his throat was seared and he will not talk for a week or two, but with a bit of rest he will be himself again in no time!"

"And you must rest! Go to your bed for a little."

"Nay, Madame. I would not leave you. You do not seem well today!"

"Nonsense! It is merely weariness and grief from the fire. I shall lie here until my spirits revive—if I am in need, I shall send for Claude. She does not please me near as well as you, of course"—a proud smile fleeted across Dominique's tired features—"but I shall be happier knowing you are resting. Now, off with you, and not a word of protest!"

She was grateful to be alone; she could not bear to talk to

244

anyone. Trembling, she rubbed her hand against her cheek where he had struck her, seeing again the hatred in his eyes. Ah, *Dieu!* Where was her heart, that day at Dr. Landelle's, that she had not thought for a moment of Jean-Auguste, of the grief she might be visiting upon him? Had she been so fearful, so selfish—to think only of herself? She had meant to be a good wife to him, despite her abiding love for André, if only to repay him for his kindness. And what a mess she had made of it all! It had never occurred to her—until last night—that the life she had wished to destroy so wantonly belonged as much to Jean-Auguste as to her. Or that it was her husband's pride, not merely his loyalty to a friend, that suffered from her courting of André. She leaned back on her pillows and closed her dry eyes, wishing she could weep, knowing herself too wicked for the simple relief that tears would bring.

There was a soft rustle in the doorway; opening her eyes she saw that Jean-Auguste had entered unannounced and stood looking down at her, his usually open countenance dark and unfathomable.

"Aunt Marguerite is leaving tomorrow," he said—cool, detached. "Her coachman arrived this morning at her summons. When the horses are rested and she can pack her things, she will return to her estate. There have been reports of brigands in the Poitou region. I shall send several of my men to accompany the coach—you shall be safe enough."

"I?"

"You will accompany her."

"But—" Lysette struggled to sit upright.

"A few weeks . . . months . . . the separation would be wise." Without another word, he turned about to leave her.

Dismayed, she called out to him. "Wait! Please!" She could hardly bear to look into his eyes, so filled with remorse was she. "Jean-Auguste . . . I . . . can you forgive . . . I was foolish, and fearful. But there was no child, I swear to you! Go and see Dr. Landelle. There was no child. . . ."

His eyes were cold. "And what of the child that might have been—but for the sponges?"

"Please, forgive me. I cannot bear . . ." She stumbled over the words and could not go on.

His face twitched, a cynical smile twisting his mouth. He scanned her face, shaking his head in disbelief. "And without

tears? Remarkable!" A hard edge of bitterness in his tone.
"Monsieur Corneille should invite you to be the leading player
in his theatre!" He rubbed his hand across his face, suddenly
tired and played out, and when he looked at her, his gray eyes
were dark with weariness, not anger. "I might have killed you
last night," he said raggedly. "It is best that you go."

"Yes!" she burst out, stung by the finality of his rebuff. "I shall
be glad to be quit of you for a little—I scarce can bear the
torment of your accusing eyes for another day! I shall not take
Dominique with me—Simon needs her; but I shall be far too
busy packing to give you one small measure of my time or
company until my departure!"

He nodded brusquely and strode from her chambers. She
hated him! She was not sorry to be going—she would be free to
indulge her fantasies of André without Jean-Auguste's intrusion!

But the tears, the healing tears that had eluded her for so
long, burst suddenly forth—scalding, burning—a great river of
grief that flowed from her heartbroken sobs—yet brought no
relief for her pain.

The days that followed were like a dark dream, a mist-
shrouded nightmare through which she moved, wraith-like,
numb with unhappiness. All unknowing, she had come to
depend on his praise, his warmth, the joy he brought to her
days. Without them, she felt starved, empty, useless. She tried
to see Giacopo Rondini, to comfort him for the loss of his
son—and perhaps to return to herself a measure of worth—but
the glassmaker sat in a drunken stupor, unreachable, fortifying
himself with fresh wine each time reality threatened to intrude.
She had Dominique put away all her lovely gowns in the
armoire, packing only one or two simple outfits and her riding
clothes, and keeping out the sturdy jacket and skirt and heavy
shoes she would travel in. Except for the tiny gold cross and
chain that she now wore constantly, all her jewels would be left
behind for safety's sake. And, after all, why would she need
beautiful things in Poitou? In exile? For the last time she released
the secret catch of her wondrous cabinet and put away her
pearls and gems. Ah, Dieu! How she would miss her little
writing table! Jean-Auguste sent her a small purse of coins
through Bricole, but made no attempt to see her, and her pride
would not allow her to go to him.

The journey was interminable: although it was only a few days with stops overnight at pleasant country inns in Touraine and Saumurois, Madame de Mersenne's cheerful chatter soon made it unbearable. Lysette breathed a sigh of relief when the coachman, having stopped in a high meadow to let the women stretch their legs, and to bid adieu to Narbaux's men who had accompanied them, pointed out the city of Luçon in the distance. Just beyond this town, where Cardinal Richelieu had started his career as a Bishop, lay Marguerite de Mersenne's estate.

It was a small chateau, nestled in the midst of lush and verdant farmland, but the Marquise governed it like an admiral piloting a great ship of war. All her overseers and farmers and *vignerons* paraded before her in the days that followed, reporting on the fields and crops, the disposition of the estate, the condition of the grounds and livestock and workers. Madame de Mersenne nodded her approval or snapped out sharp commands—a change of crops here, a reshuffling of men there—with the precision and confidence of an officer in battle.

Filled with envy, and bored with riding and gossip and playing the lute (how could she ever have found such empty foolishness satisfying?), Lysette ached to return to Chimère. She had wasted her opportunities, spurned the help that Bricole offered, fled from her responsibilities as mistress of the chateau. And all because of her stupid pride. But Bricole would have proven a friend, and Jean-Auguste would have praised and encouraged every attempt, no matter how often she stumbled. Was it too late now? Would he ever send for her—or was she meant to spend the rest of her days in unhappy idleness, dreaming of the might have been?

April drifted into May; May blossomed prettily and gave way to June, warm and sunny and charged with sudden showers that darkened the sky for a moment and then rolled away, leaving the sky fresh-washed and bluer than ever. Lysette seldom noticed, her heart was so heavy with confusion and pain. She ached for André with a sharpness that cut her like a knife, but her dreams were filled with Chimère. And every time a gurgling brook sang to her, or a stand of trees silhouetted against the twilight held her in unexpected awe, she longed to have Jean-Auguste by her side to share her wonder, to laugh with her in simple delight at being alive. She had never laughed so freely and genuinely as she had with him; now her days were long and cheerless.

Aunt Marguerite must have seen her unhappiness, for the older woman was surprisingly gentle and full of tact, accosting Lysette seldom with her blunt questions or advice. But one evening, when the rain had persisted all day, a cold gray drizzle that had kept the two women indoors, spending the hours in glum silence, Marguerite could hold her tongue no longer.

"*Nom de Dieu*, child, go home to Chimère!"

Swallowing her surprise, Lysette smiled stiffly, willing her chin to cease its trembling. "I do not wish to, Aunt Marguerite. I am quite content here, if you will have me for a little longer."

"Nonsense! I may be a meddlesome old woman, but I am not a fool! It has been plain from the moment we arrived that you are filled with misery. The cure for your distress lies not here, but at Chimère, I'll wager. Go home!"

Lysette rose from her chair and went to stand at the window, gazing out of the rain-streaked panes at the black night. "I . . . I cannot," she said at last.

"Ah, *Dieu*. He has sent you away?" An answering nod from the desolate figure at the window. Marguerite sighed. "I saw, even at Chimère, that there was a discontent, though I knew not why. But mayhap time will soften his heart, and you shall once again take your rightful place at his side. 'Tis a pity you have not borne him a child. It would do much to bring him peace—to have a son . . . Gabriel."

Surprised, Lysette turned from the window. "Gabriel?"

"Aye. He will name his son Gabriel, I think."

"But wherefore Gabriel?"

"For his brother, *naturellement*. He has spoken of it often through the years. It is the dream most dear to him."

Lysette frowned, mystified. "The naming of a child? Why?"

"My dear, did you not know? Has he never told you? Gabriel died because of Jean-Auguste!"

Lysette gasped. "But Gabriel died of the smallpox!"

"Yes. Jean-Auguste had been ill of it. Their mother was not well. Gabriel insisted on nursing Jean-Auguste himself. Jean-Auguste recovered without a scar, but Gabriel, sweet, gentle Gabriel . . ." She sighed heavily, remembering. "I think that Jean-Auguste has never forgiven himself—for being master of

Chimère, and inheriting the title—though he has brought more honor and glory to the name than ever Gabriel did."

Lysette closed her eyes, feeling the hot tears begin to burn behind her lids. "A son named Gabriel."

"And Chimère will return someday to its rightful owner. It is a foolish conceit, this wish of Jean-Auguste's, but . . ." The older woman shrugged.

No. No, not foolish, thought Lysette. Good, and kind, and noble. And it explained so much. His grief and fury the night of the fire. His loyalty to André, who had been Gabriel's friend, and was become the elder brother he had lost. And Lysette had thought it was his long-ago love for Marielle that made him so protective of them. There was something more, an odd thought that nagged at her brain. In her mind's eye, she saw the portrait of Gabriel in the small salon at Chimère. "Tell me, Aunt Marguerite, when did Jean-Auguste grow his mustache?"

"Let me see. Gabriel died in the summer of '24, and my sister-in-law soon after. Was it that fall? Yes!" She nodded her head with assurance. "That fall. When Jean-Auguste became master of Chimère. I remember with what merriment we greeted his changed looks. That innocent face, as though he wished to appear older. It did not suit him! I scarce could fathom why he did it!"

With a sob, Lysette buried her face in her hands. "It was his penance," she whispered. Ah, *Dieu*, she thought, what will be mine?

By the end of June she was almost beside herself. It had been two long months—and no word from Jean-Auguste. In desperation, she wrote a humble letter, begging to be forgiven, to be welcomed back to Chimère—then destroyed it, too proud to send it, too fearful he would refuse her plea. She had exchanged several letters with her two brothers, telling them something of her unhappiness, but not the reason for it, nor the truth of her exile, and was dismayed to discover that they still viewed her as their pampered little sister. She had always pouted when she did not get her way, and made a great to-do over trifles that displeased her—was it not so? Surely her distress now was hardly worth the fuss and bother; it would pass like a gentle spring rain.

She went at last to a church in Luçon and sought out a priest with kindly eyes, soft with forgiveness and an understanding of human frailty. In the darkened confessional, she poured out her soul to him, sparing herself nothing in her condemnation and self-loathing, more honest than she had ever been before. Afterward, emerging into the bright sunshine, she felt as though a heavy burden had been lifted from her heart, wishing only for Jean-Auguste's forgiveness to make her absolution complete.

As part of her penance, the priest had insisted that she give some of her time to helping the Sisters in the parish hospital, caring for the old and needy, tending the orphans and foundlings that appeared from nowhere—left on the church steps, wailing and mewling, the surplus from a family too destitute to feed another mouth, or the unhappy mistake of some desperate peasant girl. Lysette was surprised at her own patience and competence: all her charm and bewitching ways that, heretofore, had been employed in her own service became instruments of comfort and joy to the sick and helpless. The frail old crones, bent with age, their painful joints swollen from disease, brightened at her approach, a ray of sunshine in the gloom of their last years; the infants gurgled at the sound of her voice when she cradled them in gentle arms, until she began to seek out the most colicky and difficult one each day just for the pleasure of working her magic.

But July turned hot, the air close and suffocating. Even the dogs in the streets of Luçon had ceased their barking and lay, panting, in whatever shadowy corner they could find. The infants in the hospital became cranky with the heat, and no amount of comforting could still their cries; and Sisters and patients alike grew testy, snapping at one another, until Lysette thought she could not bear another moment. She was tired of the heat, of the stench of sickness and poverty, and the danger of plague and diseases that hung in the hot and crowded town. It did not take much urging from Marguerite for her to return to the safety of the estate, although it was hardly cooler at the chateau, despite the green countryside. She found herself growing more and more angry. It was cooler at Chimère, of that she had no doubt! And here she was forced to suffer in Poitou, because of Jean-Auguste's stubbornness and unforgiving nature! She had been wicked, but not so wicked that God would not forgive her! She had done penance; she had been truly sorry—what more did her husband want of her? Did he not need her? The comfort of the bedchamber? But *Guy* had been unfaithful! Mayhap Jean-Auguste? Ah, *Dieu!* That was why he had not sent for her! How she hated him, lying with some other woman, cursing his wife (no doubt!) to his paramour! Her blood boiled, thinking of the months she had curdled with remorse. And he in some brothel, enjoying his pleasures! Well, she would spite him! She would go to Paris and flirt with every courtier until the gossip reached even the walls of Vouvray! Or . . . home to Chimère, defying him, daring him to send her away again. And then . . . André. Once and for all, she would win his love. She would stalk him, pursue him, until the spark she had seen more than once in his eyes flamed into love. He had kissed her. He had meant to kiss her, and seduce her. It was no accident, no attempt to make Marielle jealous; he was attracted to her for her own sake, and she would turn that attraction to passion and then to love. How Jean-Auguste would suffer then, curse him! He would regret his abandonment of her!

By the end of July the weather had cooled, with pleasant breezes that rolled in from the coast, but Lysette's anger was still as hot as ever. Another week—no more—and then she would return home. She told herself it was her new-found patience, not cowardice, that delayed her going.

It was a pleasant summer evening, the sky still glowing with a pale green luminosity, when she and Aunt Marguerite, strolling in the garden, looked up to see a handsome coach approaching down the long avenue. It was a rarity to have company, and the two women stood, impatient, at the front portal of the chateau until the coach had drawn up to the door and the coachman had leapt down from his box. With a flourish he saluted them, then swept open the door of the carriage.

"*Mon Dieu!* Madame du Crillon!"

"Marielle!" Lysette smiled brightly, though her heart sank, thinking—praying—it had been Jean-Auguste.

"Good evening!" Marielle kissed them warmly on both cheeks. "Have you a bed for a weary traveler?" Aunt Marguerite led them into the chateau, giving orders for Marielle's bags to be carried in, exclaiming at the single small packet that Madame la Comtesse had brought. "I can only stay a day or two. There was no need to bring more," explained Marielle. While she supped on the food that Marguerite had ordered, Marielle conveyed the latest gossip and news from Paris. Louise de La Fayette had chosen not to become the Royal mistress, but had entered a convent with the King's blessing. He had obtained permission to visit her whenever he chose, and their love, unspoiled, pure, would remain so. Richelieu was delighted —Madame de La Fayette had far too many friends who had been opposed to the war with Spain; her retirement from society eliminated an unwanted influence. There had been more peasant uprisings in Perigord, and the town of Bergerac had been subdued; fresh operations had begun in Alsace against the enemy, and the Duc de la Valette had occupied Landrecies in the Spanish Netherlands. The weather was fine in Touraine—with God's help, the harvest would be good. Marielle paused, smiling diplomatically, until Marguerite de Mersenne became aware that her presence had become superfluous, and excused herself to go to bed.

Marielle smiled stiffly at Lysette, her green eyes recalling their rivalry, but her words were those of a friend. "I came to fetch you home again. You have been away far too long."

Lysette shrugged, trying to appear uninterested. "If Jean-Auguste wishes me to come to him at Chimère, he will send for me, of that I have no doubt."

"Jean-Auguste is not at Chimère! I thought you knew!" exclaimed Marielle as Lysette gaped in astonishment. "Following swift upon your departure, he was summoned by the King to take his men into the field. He and André have been fighting in the Netherlands with the Duc de la Valette!"

"Ah, *Dieu!* They were not hurt, either of them . . . ?"

Marielle's eyes flickered at the word "they." "No," she said softly, "your husband is well . . . as is mine. I saw André in Paris less than a month ago. He had come with dispaches for the Cardinal and wrote to me asking me to meet him there. He and Jean-Auguste expect to be released from their obligation within the week. Would it not be a delightful surprise for Jean-Auguste to return to Chimère and find you waiting?"

Lysette jutted out her chin in belligerence. "And wherefore? He has not written to me all these long months, not even from the front. He does not need me!"

"Chimère needs you."

"Chimère has endured without me ere now!"

"André says because of the fire and the loss of the glassworks there will be hard times ahead for Jean-Auguste. Chimère is rich in land and income, but there will not be a spare livre or crown until the debts are paid. The estate must be managed thriftily; who is to do it, save you, while Jean-Auguste serves his King or negotiates small loans?"

Lysette shook her head, panic clutching at her throat. "Not I! *Mon Dieu,* not I!"

"Bricole is getting old. He has become forgetful and careless these past months. And Giacopo Rondini cannot begin to repay even a small portion of the loan from Jean-Auguste—he has not been sober a single day since he lost his son! I have been heartsick each time I visited your chateau, seeing its decline."

"Why should you care? To come all this way to plead for Chimère?"

Marielle smiled gently. "I have known Jean-Auguste almost as long as I have known André. Each time they have gone off to war, I have charged Jean-Auguste with my husband's safekeeping. He has been a loyal caretaker. Can I do less for him? I know not what quarrel sent you, in anger, from his side—he has not confided in André—but I beg you to forgive him and return."

How like Jean-Auguste, thought Lysette, to spare her the humiliation—despite his own hurt and bitterness—and to bear the blame upon his own shoulders. "I shall pack my things tonight," she said humbly. "If Marguerite can supply us with fresh horses, would you be agreeable to returning upon the morrow?"

Marielle's coach was large and well-appointed: comfortable red velvet cushions and embroidered draperies, large windows that let in the sweet smells of midsummer. By the second day of their journey, as they traveled into Saumurois, some of the stiffness had eased between the two women. Despite herself, and her feelings for André, Lysette found her affection and admiration for Marielle growing. If I did not want her husband, she thought ruefully, I should be pleased to call this woman friend, for she has been a friend to me all these months, however much I betrayed her kindness. She turned from the window and the shadowy woods the coach had entered, and smiled warmly at Marielle. "Your eyes are far away, Madame," she said.

"I am thinking of my boys. I do not like to be parted from them."

"They are very handsome children."

"I see André in their faces—and all his past devotion." She sighed. "'Tis a pity the very permanence that comes with marriage quenches the thirst that brought it about!"

"Pooh! Surely you cannot believe that!"

"Indeed I do," said Marielle sadly.

Lysette frowned impatiently. "You should have spent less time with your Latin, and applied yourself to the study of men! Even a fool can see that André does not like to share you with Vilmorin!"

Marielle gaped, eyes wide, one hand going to her astonished mouth. "Then I have been more than a fool," she said at last, "hiding behind the children while I dwelt on his . . . weakness . . . for charming ladies."

"But surely he has not been unfaithful!" Lysette felt a pang of unexpected jealousy. If she had not yet captured André, she could not bear to think of him with another woman.

"No . . . I think not, and yet . . . there were so many women before I met him. You are fortunate in Jean-Auguste."

Lysette shrugged. "I hardly think he cares enough one way or the other."

Marielle's eyebrows raised in surprise. "But Jean-Auguste is far more likely than André to be constant and dependable."

"It is his nature . . . or merely habit . . . no more."

A soft laugh, full of doubt. But before Marielle could say a word, a sudden loud report from the road made the horses whinny in fear.

"Nom de Dieu!" cried Lysette, peering out through the window to the road ahead. "What is amiss?" And gasped at the sight of the half dozen men who now surrounded the carriage and were ordering the coachman to stop. They were a scruffy lot, rough-clothed, rougher of tongue, with a desperate look in their eyes that did not need the lethal pistols they brandished to make them fearsome.

"Brigands!" hissed Marielle. "What a fool I was not to travel with swordsmen! André will have a fit when he finds out! Be of good cheer, my dear," she said, seeing the stricken look on Lysette's face, "they mean to have our purses and nothing more. Paris was buzzing with gossip about the number of highwaymen in these troubled times. It will be a nuisance but . . ." She shrugged in nonconcern.

"But what shall we do for food and lodging for the rest of the journey?" Lysette found it difficult to be calm.

"There are many towns nearby and petty officials who would be delighted to show their hospitality. We are not so far from Touraine that the names of Crillon and Narbaux are unknown." Marielle smiled reassuringly.

"Mesdames, if you please." The door of the coach was thrown open; a burly fellow with grizzled hair and a square jaw covered with gray stubble ushered the women into the dappled sunlight at the side of the road. He held his pistol casually in one hand, almost apologetic, but his manner made it clear he would not hesitate to use it. Several of his fellows gathered around. "Your purses, ladies," he said, indicating the small pouches hanging from the two women's waistbands. When they were handed to him, he shook them appreciatively, feeling the weight of the coins. He smiled at them both, revealing large and yellowed teeth, then pointed his pistol at Marielle. "Begging your pardon, my lady, but your earbobs . . ."

Marielle drew herself up proudly, her lip curled with contempt, as she unfastened her gold eardrops and handed them to the man. Lysette was astonished at Marielle's composure; she herself could barely keep her body from trembling, grateful at least that she had taken no earrings on her journey, and fearful lest the robbers search her person and discover the gold cross hidden beneath her jacket.

"'Tis slim enough pickings, Dandin," grumbled one of the men to grizzle-face. "Have they no more jewels on them?"

The man called Dandin jerked his head in the direction of the carriage, where the coachman still sat in angry silence, kept to obedience by the pistol pointed at his breast. "Search the ladies' luggage, and look behind the cushions as well. Whoever has kept these lovelies in silks must have bought a favor or two with trinkets and trifles."

"You will find nothing there," said Marielle haughtily. "You would do well to allow us to continue our journey!"

"But mayhap a ring or two? Please, Mesdames, your gloves."

The women removed their embroidered gauntlets. Lysette's fingers were bare; Marielle's hand held a small gold circlet, old and worn. Silently, the man called Dandin held out his hand for it.

"No!" exclaimed Marielle, her green eyes flashing. "You shall not have this ring! If you wish it, you must cut it off my dead hand!"

Dandin scratched his head and eyed the ring, wondering whether it would be worth the trouble of a struggle. He was saved by a long low whistle that came from the nearby woods. Directing his men to repack the women's things, he disappeared into the leafy gloom. Marielle and Lysette watched in annoyance as their gowns were piled carelessly into their baggage. Dandin now reappeared, his face wreathed in a triumphant smile, and bowed low before the two women.

"Madame la Comtesse du Crillon. Madame de Narbaux. How fortunate we are that you chose this very day to travel through these woods! We shall have the pleasure of your company for a little! Such distinguished—and wealthy— gentlemen as your noble husbands should be delighted to pay for the return of their charming wives!" He called to his companions. "The ladies are to be taken to the old farmhouse. See that there is food and supplies sufficient to their comfort!"

"No!" The coachman, his loyalty to André aroused by the thought of his mistress in captivity, stood up on his box and waved his arms in wild protest. Dandin whirled, his pistol held in outstretched arm; a sharp crack, and the coachman cried out and pitched into the dust of the road, his body twitching for a second or two before it collapsed into awful stillness. Lysette gasped and clapped her hand to her mouth; Marielle crossed herself, a soft prayer on her lips. Quickly the women were bundled into the coach, accompanied by a foul-smelling oaf who closed the draperies against the day, then sat opposite them, grinning like a jackal, while stray beams of light glinted off the barrel of his pistol. Lysette was frozen with fear; Marielle, lips pressed tightly together, glared at the man in fury, her eyes dark with anger and scorn. They rode thus for an hour or so, jostling and bumping as the carriage careened wildly, seeming to take innumerable twists and turns in the road. At last it slowed to a stop, and they stepped out into a small clearing hemmed in by large and leafy trees. A small house stood before them, its pale amber stones and stucco beginning to crumble. They entered and passed through a large room, bare save for a rough table and chairs pulled close to the hearth; beyond was a smaller chamber, completely empty, that gave over to the loft above. Prodded by the deadly pistol, Lysette and Marielle climbed to the loft, then watched in dismay as the ladder, their only avenue of escape, was removed from its place and laid flat on the earthen floor of the small room.

The brigands leered up at them and laughed. "It is not the Louvre, Mesdames, but 'twill serve!" The men turned to leave.

"Wait!" cried Marielle. "What are we to do for light when the daylight goes?"

"Wherefore do you need light?"

"Fool!" spat Marielle. "What shall you tell Dandin if one of us should fall from the loft in the darkness?" She glared down at them.

There was muttering and some consultation among the men; at last one of them looked up at the women. "I shall leave a candle here below. It will be enough for you to see by." Then they were gone.

Lysette could contain her fear no longer. With a mournful wail she burst into tears and fell into Marielle's arms, grateful for the other woman's strength.

"Come, come," said Marielle soothingly. "All shall be well. A few days . . . no more. They will send a ransom note to André and Jean-Auguste, the money will be paid. We shall be safely home within the week!" She laughed ruefully. "And I to face the wrath of a husband for traveling unescorted!" The two women clung to one another while Lysette's trembling subsided. Over her head, Marielle's eyes swept their dreary prison: a broad-planked floor covered with straw, rough-hewn walls, and a small window high up in the gable. There was a heavy bucket in one corner to serve their sanitary needs, and a rickety table that held a pitcher of water and a large crust of bread. The loft was dim, airless, cheerless. Behind Marielle's calm words and placid exterior, an edge of fear had begun to flicker in the depths of her eyes.

"Nom de Dieu, André, will you cease your pacing?" Jean-Auguste refilled his wine cup and helped himself to another piece of cheese. "I came from Chimère to keep you company, and with the dust of the campaign still on my boots, but if I must watch you marching back and forth, I shall soon wish myself at home—or with the troops in the field!"

André strode to the window, watching the twilight shadows

stretch over the lawns of Vilmorin. "But Marielle should have been here by now! If she meant to stay only a day or two with your aunt, as Louise has said, where is she? She knew I was returning home! Why did she choose this very time to visit with Lysette? And you, *mon ami*," he growled at Jean-Auguste, "what ever possessed you to allow your wife to go wandering over half of France?"

"Yes," said Jean-Auguste thoughtfully, more to himself than André, "It is time Lysette came home again."

There was a soft knock at the door. At André's barked command, a footman entered, bobbing politely to his master. "There is a peasant here, Monsieur, who says he must speak only to you! He is very stubborn, my lord, though I threatened to box his ears for his insolence. But still he says his message is for you alone!"

André frowned. "Show him in, then."

A young man entered, casting his eyes warily about him. At André's scowl, he scraped his hat off his head and gave a half-hearted bow. "Monsieur le Comte du Crillon?" André nodded. The young man glanced at Jean-Auguste. "I must speak to Monsieur le Comte alone, if it please you."

"I have no secrets from Monsieur de Narbaux," said André coldly.

"Ah! Monsieur le Vicomte de Narbaux?"

"Yes. Certainly!"

"Then I have a message for him as well!" The young man handed them each a letter. André broke the seal and opened his at once; Jean-Auguste took the time to note that the seal bore no crest, but was plain and unadorned.

"Mon Dieu!" André, his hands shaking, had dropped his letter to the floor.

Jean-Auguste motioned to the footman to take the young man to one side of the room, then, heart pounding, he opened his own letter and read aloud: " 'Monsieur. Be advised that I hold your wife prisoner. She is safe and unharmed, and will remain so, so long as my commands are obeyed. You are to give this courier twenty thousand livres. As soon as the money is secured, your wife shall be returned to you. Go to Loudun. On the first market day, Madame de Narbaux will appear.' " Jean-Auguste looked at André. "And your letter is the same?"

André nodded dumbly. Then, with a cry of anger, he rushed to the peasant and clutched him by the throat. "What proof have I of the truth of your letter?"

Shaking, the man drew a small packet from beneath his doublet. "I was to give you this, Monsieur!"

Stricken, André gazed at the contents of the packet: a single gold earring. "Marielle's," he groaned. With a sudden roar, he swung at the man and knocked him to the floor, sending him sprawling. Placing one booted foot upon the man's chest, he drew his sword and held its point close to the man's groin. "Unless you wish to see your manhood on the end of my rapier, you will speak truth to me! How came you here?"

The man began to babble in terror. "I . . . I was sent, Monsieur! A man in Loudun. I know nothing! I was to give you and Monsieur le Vicomte these letters and the packet. He gave me money . . . a horse to ride. I know nothing!"

Jean-Auguste came to stand beside André. "And where are you to take the money?"

"To Moncontour. It is a village near Loudun. There is a tavern. I am to wait there. I know not how long. The man who gave me the letters will approach me when there is no one about! Please, my lords, I know no more!"

Reluctantly, André sheathed his sword and turned away, allowing the man to scramble to the safety of the doorway. Jean-Auguste, thoughtful, pulled André to one side, and spoke in a low, worried tone.

"Can we do aught but pay this ransom, *mon ami?*"

André clenched his fists in helpless fury. "God knows we have no choice. I can raise the money quickly enough, but what of you? After the fire, is there a financier who would advance you more capital?"

"The tax collector in Tours owes me a favor. I discovered once that he was sending underweight coins to Paris as his due. He claims he has not done it since, but it would be a scandal for him if I brought it to Richelieu's attention. He will loan me the gold I need—at a usurious rate, I have no doubt—but my credit, at least, is good."

"And then what? Are we to wait, helpless, in Loudun?"

Jean-Auguste sighed. "What else? And we cannot even be sure that the women will be returned!" He rubbed his forehead thoughtfully. "A moment. We can track this fellow"—he jerked his head in the direction of the young peasant—"and the man he is to meet in Moncontour. But will that lead us to the women? If the money is to be collected in Moncontour, and the women returned in Loudun, it is possible that Lysette and Marielle are being held in neither town."

André's eyes lit up, catching the drift of Jean-Auguste's words. "And if we were to arrive in Loudun *before* the money is delivered to Moncontour . . . !"

"Precisely! We could station troops around Loudun to see who goes out and in."

"Including the women? And the messenger from Moncontour?"

"Mayhap! And if not, what is lost? We must in any event be in Loudun come market day!"

"And once the women are returned, we may still capture the brigands as they attempt to leave the town!" André smiled in satisfaction, then frowned as a sudden thought struck him. "But so many unfamiliar troops—surely if we ride into Loudun with a large force, all men of Vouvray and strangers to Saumurois, they will arouse suspicion. I would not put at risk the lives of Marielle and Lysette!"

"What of the local nobility near Loudun? I know you do not like Monsieur le Comte d'Ussé, but his estate of Trefontaine is close by. If he would put his men at arms at our command, it could be done with no outward show. What say you?"

"Ussé!" sneered André. "That one-eyed jackal! And if we succeed in capturing the band of cutthroats, Ussé will petition the King for a pension as a reward, of that I have no doubt."

"*Nom de Dieu*, André! But are you agreed to the plan?" André nodded. "Then how are we to delay the courier?" went on Jean-Auguste.

"I shall have Grisaille take charge of the man, keep him under lock and key. He can be told that we are trying to raise the money, but these are cash-poor times and it is difficult. You and I will away to Ussé and Trefontaine with a half dozen men or so."

"And can Grisaille see that the man's horse goes lame, for good measure? I would not want him to return before we have set the trap."

"Grisaille will delay him, and then see that he is followed to Moncontour. If all goes well, my man can get word to us outside of Loudun." André turned to the footman. "Have that man put under guard, and send Grisaille to me."

Jean-Auguste threw his cloak over his shoulders and strode to the door. "I'm for Tours and a certain tax collector. When I have secured the loan, I shall join you here with three of my best swordsmen. Look not so gloomy, *mon ami*. It is a good plan, and we shall have our wives home before the next full moon."

André rubbed his chin, his face creased in a worried scowl. "If only we did not have to depend on Ussé!"

It was a soft scuffling noise that had awakened her. Lysette opened her eyes and grunted, her body stiff from the bare floor cushioned little by the mound of straw. By the dim light of the candle that shone from the room below, she saw Marielle standing in a corner, her head bowed, hands clasped tightly before her. Lysette sat up and rubbed her neck, feeling the tense muscles beneath her fingers.

"Marielle! What is it?"

Marielle turned and indicated the small table, covered with crumbs from the last of their bread. "The rats woke me."

Lysette shuddered. It was their third night in this awful place, and she still was not used to the rats, the fetid air, the dismal gloom. From the unseen room below she could hear the sounds of voices. Dandin and his men were always there, to guard the only door of escape, to stand below and mock them, to pass up a meager meal. Tonight it had been a thin soup, foul and rancid: Marielle had almost gagged, unable to eat. Disheartened, the two women had gone to sleep early, praying for a new day and a swift release. Lysette sighed. Surely she would have died without Marielle to keep up her spirits and fill her with hope. They had spent their days talking of their childhoods, discovering a common link: Marielle had had an older brother, now dead, to whom she had been devoted; she envied Lysette her two brothers, both living. As for Lysette, she listened to Marielle's stories of helping her father with his doctoring, and wished that someone had prodded her into such usefulness. Now she saw the edge of despair in Marielle's posture, and fear clutched at her heart. What would she do if Marielle's strength failed them both?

"Marielle, what is amiss?"

Marielle turned, her face wet with tears. "I think, ah, *Dieu!* I think I am with child! I cannot sleep . . . the food, the unyielding floor. Had I dreamed it was so, I should not have left Vilmorin! What am I to do?"

Lysette jumped to her feet. "You must have better food, a pallet to sleep on. Can we not demand such care?" She paused, surprised by her own boldness. "I shall call our jailers! Surely they can provide better for you!" She hurried to the edge of the loft, then stopped surprised. "Marielle!" she whispered urgently. "Look! They have grown careless!" She pointed to where the ladder still leaned against the rim of the loft.

"Can we escape, do you suppose?"

Lysette's shoulders sagged. "No. There is no way out save through the door of the large room, and it is never left empty." She frowned, listening as the voices below rose and fell. "Come!" she said with determination. "At least you shall have a bed to sleep on—if I must threaten Dandin with God's wrath and the King's vengeance, if you are not cared for as befits your station!" She started down the ladder, motioning for Marielle to follow. Below, the light from the larger room cut a path across the earthen floor; Lysette followed it to the noise of laughter beyond. As she stepped over the threshold, she could hear Marielle gasp behind her, but she ignored the sound, her eye caught by the figure who sat at the table, talking animatedly to Dandin.

"Ah! Monsieur d'Ussé!" she exclaimed delightedly. "How glad I am that . . . ah, *Dieu!*" Her hand went to her mouth, suddenly comprehending. What was it Ussé had said in Paris . . . his "new source of income"? Her heart began to pound as Ussé rose, his pale blue eye glittering, and bowed formally to her.

"Madame de Narbaux!" A nod to Marielle, hanging back in the doorway. "Madame la Comtesse! I trust you have not been too uncomfortable here!"

Lysette rallied. She had dealt with Ussé before, and she knew he viewed her with favor. What had she to fear? "Monsieur d'Ussé!" she said, drawing herself up regally. "Madame du Crillon is not well! I can only guess that we are near to Trefontaine—you would not be far from home at this hour of the night. If we are to be your prisoners . . ."

"Ah, Madame!" he exclaimed with mock concern, "you must consider yourselves guests!" He smiled benignly and rubbed his forehead above his black patch.

"Guests. Pah! You would not treat a dog as we have been treated! If we must be detained until the ransom arrives . . ."

"For shame, Madame! Tribute! Tribute to your worth!"

"Tribute . . . ransom . . . it is all the same! But Madame du Crillon is a great lady, and she is ill. I must insist that we be taken to Trefontaine, to wait there until our release!" Lysette was surprised by her fearlessness, angered only that Ussé seemed to find it amusing.

"Of course, Madame. How tantalizing you are when your eyes flash! Can I refuse you aught?"

"Tonight! Now! And we shall require our luggage that these . . . minions of yours have taken away!"

"Alas. Your gowns and furbelows have long since vanished! You must make do with what you are wearing"—his good eye raked Lysette's form—"or nothing!"

Dandin and his men laughed uproariously at that, while Lysette turned away, feeling her cheeks burning, remembering with what careless abandon she had encouraged him in Paris. Ussé crossed to her and slipped his arm about her waist. He bent low, his lips close to her ear. "You are as desirable as ever, *ma chère*," he whispered. "Mayhap we may beguile away the next few days with simple pleasures, until your husband redeems you from my keeping."

Lysette's heart sank, recalling his lecherous talk in Paris, the import of his words "simple pleasures." On the other hand, if she could gain favors for herself, and Marielle, and still keep him at bay until Jean-Auguste arrived, it might be worth her while.

She allowed herself to soften perceptibly, as though his words had touched a chord within her, and smiled tentatively.

"Indeed, you were amusing in Paris, Monsieur le Comte. And I am dying of boredom!"

"As well you might be, my lady, with Monsieur de Narbaux in the Netherlands, as I have heard! I am minded of your journey through Angoumois, when first we met—and you the lone woman among all those men. There was not a gallant whose head you did not turn, including my own! And some, perhaps, who were rewarded with more than a kiss . . . ?"

Lysette smiled uneasily, silently cursing Ussé. With dismay she saw that Marielle had turned to her—pale, stricken—her green eyes dark with accusation.

Chapter Twenty-one

LYSETTE OPENED HER EYES TO THE ROSY DAWN, AND STARED AT the velvet bed canopy above her. She had never felt so alone and abandoned in all her life; even when Guy died there had been one or two friends in Soligne, or, at the very least, acquaintances, to be charmed and beguiled into looking after her. But Marielle was useless. From the moment the door of the chamber in Trefontaine had locked behind them, Marielle had seemed to shrink into herself, her usual serenity replaced by a helpless fear that lurked behind her eyes. For two days now she had wandered about the room, distant, silent, spending long hours staring out of the leaded windowpanes at the woods beyond the chateau. Even now, and it barely daylight, she stood at the window, silhouetted against the pink sky. Ah, *Dieu!* Lysette wanted to cry aloud at that disconsolate form, to reassure her that nothing had happened on the journey from Soligne, to ease the despair that surely arose from Marielle's fear of André's infidelity.

"Marielle!" Lysette got up from the bed, wrapping the coverlet about her shoulders, and went to the window. "Have you slept at all?" she asked kindly.

Marielle turned, her face haggard. "Did you know that long ago, when the Huguenots rose up against the King, and there was fighting and civil war, that I was . . . held captive? I thought I would die of despair, and then André . . ."

"When he was injured . . . the scars he bears?"

Marielle nodded. "It was a terrible time. I lost my father, my brother. Until he rescued me, I thought that André was dead." She smiled almost apologetically at Lysette. "I had not thought the past could haunt me so, yet each time I hear the key turn in yonder door my blood runs to ice. It is a fearful thing to be imprisoned and helpless."

"But that was long ago, and there is no civil war now. Only a greedy man who will be content so soon as he holds our ransom in his hands! And until then, you must not think of that locked door."

Marielle sighed, her voice low and dispirited. "I wonder when Ussé will realize he cannot let us live."

Lysette gasped. "What? What are you saying?"

"What would he do should the King discover he maintains an army of brigands? He must kill us, to keep his secret."

Lysette felt the panic rise in her throat. "What are we to do?" But Marielle's hopeless eyes, filled already with the certainty of death, gave her no comfort—nor answers. It was as though, in some mystical way, she was waiting for André to save her again. But Lysette could not wait for Jean-Auguste, could not depend on Marielle; salvation, if it came, must be through her own devices.

She hurried to the door and knocked briskly upon it. In a moment she heard the key turn and the door was opened warily by a guard who peered in at them both, his brow wrinkled with suspicion. She smiled beguilingly at him, letting the coverlet droop low enough to reveal her creamy flesh and slender neck above the line of her chemise.

"What?" he grunted, but his eyes strayed to her bosom.

"It is such a lovely morning! I can smell the roses from the window. How fortunate you are to be out and around! Do you suppose"—the voilet eyes grew soft and misty—"I could walk in the gardens for a bit? With you by my side, of course!"

His stern glance wavered; he hesitated, face glowing red at the open invitation in her eyes. "I cannot!" he burst out at length, in an agony of disappointment. "I am to keep you ladies in this room. I know not why. But Monsieur d'Ussé has charged me with your care!"

Lysette sighed, allowing her full lips to tremble. "I am perishing of boredom!"

He shook his head back and forth, as though he would convince himself. "No. No! Monsieur le Comte has forbidden it!"

"But, perhaps if you were to ask Monsieur d'Ussé to accompany me . . . I do not wish to appear presumptuous . . . if you were to tell him I am in tears . . ." She gazed soulfully at the guard. "You do see tears in my eyes . . . n'est-ce pas?"

He gulped, totally ensnared. "Madame, I shall plead with him on your behalf. It is cruel that such a fine lady should be locked away from the world, whatever you have done!"

She smiled in satisfaction as the door closed behind him, mouthing a silent prayer that Ussé would be as susceptible to her charms. Still, she did not wish to arouse his suspicions by seeming to capitulate too readily. When afternoon came, and the guard appeared at the door to announce that Monsieur d'Ussé wished her to join him in the gardens, she dressed carefully, her jacket buttoned up in modesty. She nodded coolly at Ussé, ever the gracious lady, but declined his proffered arm and strolled casually toward a high terrace that overlooked much of the countryside. Below, in front of Trefontaine, was the main road, leading to Nantes and the sea in one direction, and Loudun in the other. To one side of the chateau was a large orchard of fruit trees and, beyond, half a dozen outbuildings: stables, servants' quarters, a smithy. There seemed to be a small path farther on, that twisted its way on into the woods, barely discernible except for a neat line that cut its way through the treetops. Northeasterly, Lysette judged, if the main road ran true—and the path that would lead them to Touraine. She felt her heart swell with hope. The guard had led her out through a rear door of Trefontaine, with no soldiers stationed along the corridor or on the staircase they had descended; and the key to her chamber was kept outside the door. With a little luck—and the darkness of night, she and Marielle could make their way, undetected, down the stairs and into the safety of the sheltering orchard and the woods beyond.

She dimpled charmingly at Ussé, and flounced about the terrace; all the while her eyes memorized every detail of the landscape. How beautiful the gardens were, she said, how sweet the perfumed air, how kind of Ussé to let her enjoy the lovely day.

"Mon Dieu," he growled impatiently, "I did not invite you here to admire the flowers!" His good eye glittered with annoyance.

She pouted at him, all bruised innocence. "Would you steal from me the joy of a pleasant summer day? For shame!" She turned her back on him, hurt, waiting for him to make the next move, then steeled herself as his arms went about her waist and his hands slid upward to cup her breasts. He leaned to her bare nape beneath the curls piled high atop her head, and kissed the vulnerable flesh. She pulled away, pretending modesty, and wrapped her arms protectively about her bosom.

"Monsieur! Please! I beg you—not here!" She glanced nervously around, as though she feared the prying eyes of the world.

"Mayhap . . . tonight?"

"Alone?"

"With no eyes to see, Madame!"

"And will you . . . steal a kiss or two?" she asked, suddenly coy.

"I shall . . . take more, if it pleases you. You wounded my heart—as well as my manhood—that night in the woods. I would be avenged!"

"Will I be . . . imperiled, then, if I come to you?"

A wicked leer. "Indeed, yes!" He ran his tongue across his lips. "For how am I to cool the heat of my passion, save by plunging myself into that pool, that wellspring, source of all delight that waits in the grotto of your soft thighs? Again, and yet again, until you needs must beg for respite!"

She gasped, her eyes wide with mock fear, and turned away from him. "Then I would be wise to abstain from your company! On the other hand"—she glanced back over her shoulder, her violet eyes twinkling—"Madame du Crillon is a very tiresome companion. Who knows? By this evening, I may be languishing with despair and ennui! I shall consider your . . . proposal!"

He laughed, but there was an ugly edge to his voice. "Take care, my charming dove, lest I usurp what you would not give willingly!"

She smiled, her cheeks tight with the effort at agreeableness. "But you must promise to give me supper! I am far more . . . amusing . . . with good food and wine!"

For the rest of the afternoon she avoided Marielle's questioning glances, willing herself to think of other things, playing endless games of patience with the cards she had wheedled from the guard. At last, when the sky grew dark outside the window, she rose from her chair and motioned to Marielle.

"I am to take supper with Ussé. If all goes well, we shall escape tonight. Hold yourself in readiness until my return." She unfastened her jacket and stripped it off, then pulled down the line of her chemise until her shoulders were seductively bare. For a moment her hand clutched the golden cross and chain about her neck, as though it would protect her from harm, from Ussé's evil.

"Alas, Lysette, what will you do?"

"Whatever I must!"

"Surely you cannot . . ." Marielle looked stricken.

Lysette gulped, feeling the edge of nausea in her mouth, then thrust her chin out resolutely. "I was married to Guy de Ferrand for two years. He was old and disgusting, and my flesh crawled each time he touched me. But I endured because it was my duty, and I had no choice! What can I not endure to gain our freedom?"

Marielle's eyes were dark with sympathy. "Is there no other way?"

"*Nom de Dieu!*" Lysette snapped. "Do not pity me! I need every bit of strength I can muster!"

The two women embraced, then waited in silence until the guard came to take Lysette to the Comte. He led her down the passageway and into a well-lit corridor, stopping at last at a paneled door. A polite knock, a command to enter, and Lysette found herself within the room, facing a grinning Ussé, while the door closed firmly behind her. Ah, *Dieu!* He intended no subtlety nor coyness. Beyond a large table set with a snowy cloth and cutlery and platters of fruit and meats, was a massive bed, its hangings pulled well back—waiting, ominous. Lysette forced her eyes to turn away from the bed, to smile at Ussé as though she were as eager as he. How powerful he was, for all his short stature: the strong arms, the barrel chest! He would not be caught off guard as he had been that night on the journey. She felt her blood run cold, aware suddenly of the full extent of her peril. If she attempted to hurt him this time—and failed—*le bon Dieu* knew what obscenities he would force upon her in revenge! She dared not assail him unless she were sure of success, and how could she be sure? Perhaps, afterward (she shuddered inwardly) his guard would be down. She prayed to God to give her the strength to endure until that moment.

He reached out and pulled her to him, but she twisted from his grasp and danced away. Laughing, he caught her and bent her back over his arm, his lips burning on her neck, the coarse hairs of his small beard scratching against her bare flesh. She giggled coyly and pulled away again, darting to a corner of the room. She waited, bosom heaving, all playful dimples, while he advanced upon her; then, or ever he could crush her in his strong embrace, she ducked under his arm and skipped away again.

"Will you trifle with me?" he growled, suddenly angry. There was something frightening, and evil, in his pale blue eye.

Lysette smiled and came forward, anxious to mollify him, to cool the anger that could only bring her to grief. "It is only that you go too fast, Monsieur! There is no pleasure in being . . . pounced upon!" She batted her black-fringed eyes, contriving to look fragile. "And your beard scratches me when you are too rough!" She rubbed dainty fingers against her neck, then gasped, genuinely upset. "Oh! I have lost my necklace!" Her eyes ransacked the room, looking for her gold cross; she would have searched in the corners, but Ussé slipped his arm about her waist and peered suggestively at her cleavage.

"Mayhap, it fell!"

The necklace would have to wait. It was more important to play Ussé's game. A tantalizing laugh. "Will you . . . search for it, Monsieur?" She felt the gorge rise in her throat as he plunged his hand down the front of her bodice, coarse fingers fondling her bare breasts and tweaking playfully at her nipples. "For shame! You shall not find it that way!" she chided.

He removed his hand from her chemise and encircled her waist with his powerful arms, holding her firmly with one hand while the other rubbed against her buttocks, all the while trying to lift her skirts. He went to kiss her, but she turned her head, and his lips caught the side of her cheek. Laughing, he whispered in her ear, his hand poking suggestively at her rump. "Shall I initiate you into the ways of the Court?" Then laughed again as she looked shocked and tried to hide it.

She pouted, her mouth set in a woebegone line. "How can I

be . . . adventuresome . . . when I am dying of thirst and hunger? Can we not eat first? Then you shall find me as bold as the ladies at Court!"

Reluctantly he released her and poured out wine for them both, while she picked up a knife and cut herself a small slab of meat from a platter piled high with mutton. She nibbled daintily, wandering about the room as she ate, afraid to sit down lest she be trapped in one spot. He had not touched any food, but stood drinking his wine, his one good eye watching her with an intensity that made her nervous. She saw to her dismay that his chest had begun to heave with deep breaths and the front of his breeches bulged tellingly.

"Will you not take supper?" she said gaily

"To the devil!" he said, his voice harsh in his throat, and flung his wineglass into the cold fireplace. One powerful arm swept across the table, pushing the plates and silver to one side. "You shall be my supper!" He picked her up, so swiftly that the food and drink fell from her hands, and flung her backward across the table, then leaned over her, his chest pressing against her bosom.

She wriggled helplessly, her feet off the floor, trapped by his insistent body upon hers. Her heart began to pound in fear. "But my supper . . ." she said.

He laughed, and reached across her to the wine pitcher. "Here," he said, "we shall share the wine!" He poured a small stream of the liquid into her mouth; she gulped, almost choking, feeling the overflow run out of her mouth and down the sides of her cheeks. Now he covered her lips with his own, sucking off the wine, his tongue searching her mouth obscenely until she thought she would gag with the wine—and the disgust she felt. Her hands, thrown up above her head to keep from touching him, clutched helplessly at the tablecloth. Ah, *Dieu*, she thought, I shall die. I cannot bear another moment.

And then, quite by accident, her fingers touched the knife on the table. There would never be a better moment, his body and mouth pressed against hers, his whole being focused on his burning loins. She groped with her hands until she had the knife firmly in her grasp, then she drove it into his back with all the strength that was in her. He gasped and straightened, his one eye wide with surprise, his hands trying vainly to reach the knife. With a moan he collapsed against her; she shuddered and pushed his body away, so he fell to the floor, twisting free of the knife still clenched in her fist. She struggled to her feet and stared down at him. He looked up at her, his mouth wide as though he would cry out, his face twisted in agony.

"Pig!" she hissed, and placed her foot over his open mouth. He twitched for a moment, then his eye closed and he lay still.

She began to shake, feeling hysteria about to overtake her, longing for someone—anyone!—to end this nightmare for her. Pah! Lysette! she thought suddenly. You have only yourself! She breathed deeply, willing the panic to go, her brain to clear; she wiped her face, still wet with the wine, on the edge of her sleeve, and patted and smoothed her hair into place. She saw that she still held the bloody knife, and almost dropped it, then thought better of it. They might need it on their journey. She swallowed hard and scrubbed the blade on the edge of the tablecloth, trying not to see the crimson smears that spread on the snowy linen. She wrapped the knife in a napkin and put it into her waistband. About to quit the room (carefully avoiding Ussé sprawled on the floor, a pool of blood beneath his body), she returned to the table and took up another napkin, filling it with fruit and bread and chunks of meat. She wrapped and tied it carefully, folding in the knife she had removed from her waistband, then returned to the door and peered out into the corridor. There was no one about. She tiptoed down the passageway; when she turned the corner she saw that the guard at her room was leaning against the doorframe, his back to her, seeming almost to nod. Carefully she put down the bundle of food and picked up a heavy *torchère*, empty of candles, that stood in the corridor.

God forgive me, she thought, for he has been kind to me, and bashed the guard over the head. He crumpled at her feet. Fetching the packet of food, she unlocked the door and hurried in to find a worried Marielle, her body stiff with tension, waiting for her.

"Quickly!" said Lysette, shrugging into her jacket.

"Where is Ussé?"

"I have killed him. *Nom de Dieu*, Marielle," she said, feeling the tears begin to choke her, "look not so tender-hearted upon me or I shall give way to weeping! Come!"

As they flew down the stairs, Lysette remembered, with a pang, that she had never searched for her necklace. And now, of course, it was too late. They sped past the orchard, grateful for the moonless night, then slowed their steps as they reached the outbuildings and stables. Most of the servants' cottages were lit, bright with the candles within; and more than a few of them, their doors open to the pleasant evening, cast long golden ribbons across the gravel paths. From one of the hovels came the melodious whistle of a reed pipe, soft and mournful in the still air, seeming to intensify the silence of the night. Lysette cursed to herself as the gravel crunched under their feet; motioning for Marielle to follow, she made her way slowly to the rear of one of the cottages, where the light was cut off by strings of laundry hanging on a line, and the noisy gravel gave way to packed earth and bumpy kitchen gardens.

Suddenly the night exploded with sound: shouts, and men's footsteps, and the loud whinnying of horses from the stables. Dozens of brightly lit torches seemed to pour from the chateau, swarming like fireflies through the gardens and grounds of Trefontaine until the night was turned to day. Lysette and Marielle, hidden deep within the hanging laundry, listened and trembled as the search went on, holding their breaths when a torch seemed to come too close, exhaling when the curses and shouts receded into the distance. A voice called out in alarm, begging to know what was amiss. Another voice replied that someone had tried to kill Monsieur le Comte. (Ah, *Dieu*, thought Lysette in gratitude, he lives! She had not wished his death on her conscience, no matter his wickedness.) Le Comte d'Ussé had offered a reward, the voice went on. One thousand crowns! Two women had escaped—they were the guilty ones. Thieves. Harlots, probably, though they pretended to be noblewomen. All of Loudun would be alerted, and half of Saumurois. They must be brought to trial before Ussé as the local magistrate. Twenty lashes, and prison afterward if they were found. And one thousand crowns to the fellow who brought them to justice!

At last the hubbub on the estate died down a bit, the search centered now on the roads. Tapping Marielle on the shoulder, Lysette indicated the direction of the path through the woods; struck with a sudden thought, Marielle pulled some of the clothing from the line, tucking it under her arm before following where Lysette led. Struggling through the underbrush beyond the outbuildings, they could scarcely miss the path in the woods: every few minutes men and horses raced by, marking for the women the direction of their freedom.

All night long they followed the line of the path, staying just within the trees, stopping sometimes to take turns napping, or to hide from the searchers who still traveled the road. Just before dawn they came to a fork in the path. By the rosy glow on the horizon they chose the more easterly way, reckoning it would take them nearer to Touraine. But after nearly an hour of walking, during which they saw no one, the dirt road petered out to a grassy path, then vanished.

"*Dieu!* We have come the wrong way!" cried Marielle.

"Did you not see, when we passed that linden tree awhile back, another path?" asked Lysette. "Mayhap if we retrace our steps and follow it, it will lead to the highroad!"

"Can we not rest a little first, and eat some food? And if we reach the highroad, shall we still be perilously close to Trefontaine? I am filled with misgivings!" Marielle indicated the bundle of clothing she still held. "We would be safer in disguise. I tried to gather in men's clothing. Yes, see! A doublet, breeches! Alas!" Holding up a second pair of breeches meant obviously for a small child. "I could not see in the dark!"

Lysette frowned. "Then only one of us can dress as a lad." She sighed, eying Marielle's voluptuous figure and exquisite features. "I have always found your beauty scarcely to my advantage—it is your misfortune as well now!" She took the doublet from Marielle and held it up to her lovely face, shaking her head doubtfully. "I fear me you shall never pass as a boy, but . . . there is safety in false colors. Wear the foolish things!"

"Nay! The sleeves are too short, and the breeches as well. 'Twere better if you wore them!" Marielle laughed. "You shall be my little brother!"

Lysette stripped off her jacket and skirt, then stepped out of her petticoat and tried on the men's garments. The breeches fit well, hanging loose about her calves; she eased her garters until her stockings drooped carelessly about her ankles, hiding the dainty curves of her legs. The doublet was another matter. It was scarcely snug, yet it draped over her bosom in a most unmasculine way. She tore a wide band from her petticoat and wrapped it round her breasts under her chemise, while Marielle giggled in amusement. But when she donned the doublet again, her chest was as flat as a lad's.

"I do not find it amusing!" she said with mock asperity. "It is very uncomfortable! And you shall not go unscathed, big sister!" She ripped a large square from her petticoat and handed it to Marielle. "We can hardly transform you into a boy, but you might at least try to look a little plain! Wrap your hair up in this, so you seem a farm girl, and smudge your face with dirt." She grinned wickedly. "Shall I help you?" Marielle shook her head and backed away, tying the scarf tightly and tucking up her hair until not a single chestnut curl showed. "But what am I to do with *my* hair?" said Lysette suddenly serious. "Ah, *Dieu!* I wish I had a hat!"

Marielle scanned her petite form. "Yes. 'Tis a pity. Save for your hair, you really *do* look like a lad!"

Lysette pulled the pins from her hair. The raven tresses tumbled down about her shoulders and she stroked the glossy curls, her fingers reluctant to let them go. Then, with a heavy sigh, she rummaged in the packet of food until she found the knife. Closing her eyes, she clutched at a hank of hair and began to hack away, trying to keep her chin from trembling while her beautiful hair, her pride, fell in pathetic ringlets at her feet.

They ate in silence, accompanied only by the songs of the birds, then gathered up the rest of the food. Lysette tied her skirt and jacket in the remains of her petticoat and slung the packet over her shoulder. Retracing their steps to the linden tree they saw that there was indeed another path, that wound through a meadow and led at length to a fair-sized road, its dirt surface incised with the tracks of many wheels. Using the sun as their guide, and guessing it to be mid-morning, they turned their steps eastward, praying that, sooner or later, they would reach a signpost that would tell them the way.

"Listen!" cried Marielle suddenly. From somewhere behind them on the road they could hear the creak of wheels, the squeaking of harness. They stopped and waited, as a small cart hove into view, pulled by a sway-backed mare. Perched on the seat of the cart was a handsome young farmer, a bright red handkerchief about his neck. "Quickly!" hissed Marielle. "Into the woods, lest we be near to Trefontaine and he in d'Ussé's service!"

"Pooh! Can a young lad not ask for a ride for himself and his sister? Come!" Lysette stepped boldly into the middle of the road. "But he is a lusty fellow. I would not want him to . . . dally with you! Keep your eyes cast down, and hang back from me. I shall contrive to sit next to him, that you may be spared any advances." She grumbled deep in her throat as the wagon approached them. "Ho! You there!" she called, pitching her voice as low as she could. The cart slowed to a stop. "Wouldst give a ride to my sister and me?"

The young farmer grinned, showing white teeth, and held out a hand to them. Lysette ignored it (a boy did not need help!), and scrambled nimbly up to the seat beside the farmer, then pulled Marielle up next to her, handing her the packet of clothing. Marielle sat thus, with the napkin-wrapped food as well as Lysette's gown clutched tightly to her, the large bundles serving to hide the sweet curves of her body. The farmer clicked to his horse and they continued down the road.

"Where are you going, lad?"

Lysette cleared her throat. "Hem! A few leagues on—to the next signpost!"

"Where are you from?"

"We have come from Nantes. My sister and I . . . are newly orphaned. Uncle . . . Charles has sent for us to help him on his farm. She"—jerking a finger to Marielle—"is not much use, but I will soon show him how a farm is run!" Lysette patted herself proudly on her chest, warming to the game.

"Where is his farm?"

"I do not know! We are to wait at the signpost—he will come for us."

"Have you heard aught of the excitement?"

Lysette shrugged. "What excitement? We are newly here in Saumurois!"

"Two fugitives—women—there is a reward!"

"Reward?"

"A thousand crowns! The women pretend to royalty, though I have heard they killed five men in Paris before attacking Monsieur le Comte d'Ussé!"

"A thousand crowns!" Lysette whistled, grateful to her brothers for having taught her that most unladylike skill. "What I could not do with a thousand crowns! And you, sister— passage to New France and that sailor of yours, eh?" She elbowed Marielle in the ribs, enjoying every moment of her deception.

They rode for a distance in silence, Lysette grinning at her own cleverness. In a while, however, she began to realize that the young farmer was staring at her, and she fidgeted nervously, aware that his eyes strayed repeatedly to her face and body. She plucked uneasily at her chopped curls.

"How old are you?" he said at last.

She gulped, feeling panic for a moment, then persuaded herself that he had not penetrated her disguise. (Had not Marielle sworn she looked like a young boy?) "Thirteen," she said at length, wishing her voice was deeper.

He smiled, looking pleased. Lysette allowed herself to relax a little; there was nothing suspicious in his eyes.

And then he put his hand on her knee.

Startled, she looked at him. Ah *Dieu!* she thought, seeing the expression on his handsome face. He *does* think I am a boy! And watched in terrified fascination as the farmer's hand crept slowly upward toward her thigh. If he does not find what he is seeking, she thought in panic, we are undone! She tried to pull away, before his fingers should reach the telltale juncture, then breathed a silent prayer of thanksgiving as her eye caught the signpost in the road ahead. "There!" she cried, jumping up. "There is where we are to meet Uncle Charles!"

The farmer reined in his horse, clearly disappointed. "Shall I see you here again?"

Lysette leaped down from the wagon and caught the bundles that Marielle threw to her. "But certainly!" she said, her cockiness returning.

"Monday next? In the morning?"

Lysette's eyes narrowed. "Will you give me two crowns?"

"One."

Lysette helped Marielle down, then shrugged indifferently at the farmer. "I do not know if I shall be here."

"Two crowns, then!"

"Done! *Au revoir*, then. Until Monday!" And watched the farmer, pleased with his bargain, continue down the road.

Marielle began to laugh. "What a liar you are, Lysette! I almost believed you myself!" She giggled. "And you wished to sit next to him to preserve *my* virtue!"

Lysette smirked. "Mayhap I should remain a boy! When I was a lady, no man ever offered me two crowns!" Her brow wrinkled, suddenly seeing the signpost. "Saint-Justine," it said, and "Dinet," neither of which meant a thing to the two women. They chose the path to "Dinet," since the young farmer had taken the other, and trudged off down the road. But the noonday sun beat down upon them and they began to flag, aware that they had scarcely slept since leaving Trefontaine the night before. When a large hay wagon appeared over a distant hill, they sought the safety of the trees, unwilling to risk a repetition of the morning. The wagon creaked slowly past, the old farmer fast asleep and snoring on his box. It was a simple matter to toss the bundles onto the back of the wagon and hop aboard as it made its slow progress through the gentle afternoon, then burrow under the hay so they would not be seen. But the hay was sweet-smelling and soft, and they were exhausted. Lulled by the rhythmic swaying of the wagon, the soothing creak of the wheels, Lysette and Marielle were soon fast asleep.

She was on a ship, sailing across the sea to Chimère. But it was hot and stifling in the hold—and why did the ship smell of hay? The rocking had stopped, leaving her stranded in the middle of the ocean; she would never get home! She awoke with a start, feeling the scalding tears on her face.

In the dimness of the hay she saw that the sudden stillness had awakened Marielle as well. Carefully, they peeped out of the mound of straw. It was twilight. The haywagon seemed to be in the middle of a farm, on a narrow, rutted path flanked by fields of wheat and corn; up ahead, and at some distance, was a barn and a small farmhouse. Just in front of the wagon was a large wooden fence; it was this that had brought them to a halt. Grumbling, the old farmer clambered down from his perch and unlatched the gate. While his back was turned, Lysette and Marielle, clutching their bundles, dropped to the ground and rolled into a grassy ditch that ran along the edge of the road, crouching there in the deepening light until the rattling sound of the wagon was heard no more. Then they turned about and followed the path through the fields, regaining the road as the last pink wisps of day vanished from the sky.

They stopped to eat, rationing their dwindling food as best they could, then set off down the road by the thin light of the new moon. They walked for several hours, speaking little, unwilling to voice the fear that had begun to gnaw at them both, the awful thought that filled them with dread. They were lost. The haywagon had carried them for half the day, they knew not where, while they slept. Even now their weary steps could be leading them back to Ussé and prison—and worse.

"I cannot—not another step!" said Marielle at last. "Please. Let us rest again until morning!"

Lysette sighed. "Yes. And, God willing, the new day will show us where we are. Not that I am afraid," she said brightly. "I feel sure that we are very near to Touraine!"

"Of course! We shall laugh about this journey when we are safe at home again!"

Reassuring one another with carefree words, they found a sheltering tree on the side of the road, embraced each other warmly, and quickly fell asleep.

The morning brought with it a chill mist that seemed to sap Marielle's strength. She shivered with cold and weariness, her face drawn and tired-looking despite the night's sleep. She refused the dry crust of bread that was breakfast, wishing instead they could find a stream, for her throat was parched. She grew more and more melancholy as the day progressed, stopping often to rest, complaining bitterly of the cold, the lack of water, the unmarked road that was surely leading them to their doom. Nothing Lysette said could shake her black mood. In the late afternoon, however, the sun struggled out from behind the clouds, warming the air, and Marielle's spirits began to revive.

"Forgive me," she said, smiling sheepishly at Lysette. "I am poor company today. But, the cold. And I am so very weary. I scarcely can imagine why it should be so!" She passed a hand across her eyes and Lysette was shocked to see how pale she was.

Let her not be ill, she thought. "Come!" she said aloud, her smile bright and reassuring. "Rest you here for a bit. I shall go back into the woods—if *le bon Dieu* smiles upon us, there may be a stream nearby!" She pushed through the sparse underbrush, coarse grasses and patches of moss, and passed a great tree that lay uprooted, its base forming a kind of natural cavern with the soft earth as its floor. Here and there the grasses gave way to ferns and reeds, and she pressed on with renewed hope, confident that there must be a stream. A soft gurgling made her look down: the rivulet flowed just in front of her, almost hidden by the high marsh grass. She knelt and scooped a handful of sweet water to her mouth, then straightened and turned back to the road. How pleased Marielle would be!

Marielle was standing bent over, where Lysette had left her, but her body was twisted oddly, her face buried in her hands. Sobbing, she rocked back and forth, an agonized whisper— "No. No. No!"—coming from her quivering form.

"Marielle! *Mon Dieu!* What is it?"

For answer, Marielle lifted suffering eyes to Lysette and took a step backwards. Lysette gasped in horror. There on the ground was a great gout of blood.

"Ah, *Dieu!* The child?"

Marielle nodded, then cringed as another sharp pain tore through her body.

"What shall we do?" cried Lysette, her eyes wide with fear.

"I should . . . lie down," gasped Marielle, "lest I swoon!"

"In the woods . . . a tree . . . like a cavern . . . think you, with my help, you can reach it?"

Shaking, Marielle leaned against Lysette and allowed her to guide them slowly to the uprooted tree. Only once did Lysette look back to see the trail of blood behind them: after that she kept her eyes firmly locked on the forest floor in front of her. When Marielle had settled herself well back under the tree, sheltered by the overhanging roots, she lifted her skirts with trembling fingers, tugging helplessly at her petticoat, too weak to tear a piece from the fabric. Instead, she pulled the scarf from her head, wadding it up and placing it between her thighs, then smoothed down her skirts and lay back, closing her eyes with exhaustion.

"I shall fetch our things," said Lysette, trying to sound brave for Marielle's sake. She jumped up and retraced their steps, covering the splashes of blood with dirt and leaves; the trail must not lead unwelcome beasts—or men—to their refuge. When she returned with their bundles, she was appalled to see the gory stain had already spread on Marielle's skirt. Ripping open the bundle of her clothing, she tore fresh pieces from her petticoat, replacing them again and again as they crimsoned— too soon. Marielle had begun to shiver violently, her face ashen; even with Lysette's skirt wrapped around her like a cloak, her fingers and face were ice cold, and the spasms had not ceased.

By nightfall, though Marielle had begun to mutter incoherently and her eyes were sunken and ringed with black, Lysette breathed a little more easily. The bleeding, at least, had almost stopped. Surely the worst was over. She ate a few mouthfuls of bread, forcing herself to save the rest (though her stomach growled in hunger) lest Marielle need food in the morning. She drank greedily at the small stream to fill her empty belly, then dug a hole in the soft earth and buried the bloody rags. Ah *Dieu!* she thought. If she had a flint she would light a fire, however risky it might be, for Marielle's shivering near broke her heart.

Marielle began to weep, her mumbling words filled with grief for the loss of the child. Lysette wept too, remembering her own selfishness—and Dr. Landelle, and her wickedness in seeking to destroy the child she had thought she carried. Creeping close to Marielle, she cradled her in her arms, willing the trembling to cease and the strength to flow from her own body to this piteous creature.

"I shall die," said Marielle, suddenly lucid. "I shall die!"

"Nonsense! What would André do without you?"

All night long she held Marielle tightly, rocking, comforting, soothing the frightened murmurs and stroking the clammy brow, aware that she had never before been responsible for a person's life, never been needed and depended upon so. And never before so capable of doing what she must. It was an odd and strangely gratifying feeling.

But a tiny voice cried out within her, louder and more insistent as the night wore on, opening the terrifying abyss at the bottom of her soul, the ultimate fear, the darkest secret. Let her not die! Let her not die! Death—that was what babies did. They killed you. *"Maman!"* she cried aloud to the black night. And the voices grew louder—her father, her aunt and uncle, her nursemaid—all of them filled with accusation. "Your mother," they whispered. "Your mother," they shouted. "But for you, she would have lived."

Chapter Twenty-two

LOUDUN. THE SIGNPOST READ "LOUDUN." LIFTING A GAUNT-leted finger, André pointed it out to Jean-Auguste, then signaled the half dozen riders behind them and spurred on his horse a little faster. Jean-Auguste nodded, his thoughts elsewhere. Ever since they had passed the crossroads the day before—his crossroads, Gabriel's crossroads, with its shrine to the Virgin—he had been filled with melancholy, burdened with regrets for the past, forebodings of the future. Unlike André, who chafed with impatience, he wished he might hold back time, fearful of what the morrow might bring.

But perhaps André was goaded by an uneasy conscience, for he had spoken of nothing but Marielle since they had begun their journey.

"I have been offhanded to her of late," he said morosely. "Before we left for the Netherlands . . . If I have lost her . . ." He sank again into silence, brooding. "Ah, my friend . . . marriage is a labyrinth—so many twists and turns, so many hurts and grievances until you find, one day, that you are far from where you started, and without Ariadne's thread to lead you out!"

Jean-Auguste clicked his tongue impatiently. "Unlike Theseus at Minos, you have built your own labyrinth—surely it is up to you to break it down again, stone by stone!"

André laughed ruefully, accepting the rebuke, then fell again to musing. "I had forgot—until Paris—how beautiful she is." He sighed.

"Only a husband, after years of marriage, would cease to notice!"

"What a witless fool I was! When she was plain, I ignored her. When she was beautiful, I could not see her for the jealousy that consumed me!"

"You *are* a fool! You have but to look in her eyes to see 'André' writ large. Her beauty is only for you! But . . . when you allow . . . other women . . . to tempt you . . ." He smiled gently at André, the words unspoken between them, the scene in the gardens of Vilmorin recalled, and acknowledged, and forgiven in the silent understanding that passed between the two friends.

They reached Trefontaine late that evening; despite the hour they knocked on the gate and asked to speak at once to Monsieur d'Ussé. It was out of the question, they were told. Monsieur d'Ussé was just now recovering from a grievous attack that had near killed him. A poxy harlot from Saumur. A madwoman!

"Cheated out of her earnings, no doubt," muttered André under his breath. He turned again to the gatekeeper. "Tell Monsieur d'Ussé that André, Comte du Crillon, General to the King, waits upon him on a matter of great urgency! I regret to disturb him, but I should not like to go to the Governor General of Saumur because Monsieur d'Ussé did not see his duty. Tell him that!"

As the gatekeeper scurried away, Jean-Auguste gave a small laugh. "Such words may win us an audience with Ussé. But will they win his support?"

André lifted a small pouch from his pocket and shook it so it clanked metallically. "From the first I have been of a mind that Ussé's support would be won by bribery alone. I shall use this if I must, though it does not sit well with me!"

After an eternity of waiting, the gatekeeper appeared with two armed guards. "You are to dismount and come with me," he said to André. "The rest are to wait here."

"No. Monsieur le Vicomte de Narbaux will accompany me. The matter concerns him as well."

The gatekeeper shrugged and unlocked the iron gate, fastening it again when they had passed through, and handing them over to the guards. It was a short walk to the chateau itself, and they strode briskly forward, their heavy boots crunching on the gravel. The guards led them to Ussé's chamber and followed them in, standing at the alert as they approached the figure in the large bed.

Ussé leaned up against the pillows, his face so pale the black patch stood out upon it like a blot of ink on snowy paper. He took in shallow breaths, his chest fluttering lightly, as though he were fearful that a deep breath would kill him. His one good eye, glittering still with the fever of his injury, darted uneasily about the room as they entered, relieved to see there were only two of them, but narrowing suspiciously when he saw that it was Narbaux with André.

"What is it," he said, aggrieved, "that you would threaten and harry a man who has so lately looked at Death?"

"It is our wives, Madame du Crillon and Madame de Narbaux. They have been captured by brigands in this district!"

A look of mistrust. "What has this to do with me?"

"They are being held for ransom. If you would put some of your men at our disposal . . . there has been entirely too much thievery and lawlessness in this district. With your help, we might be able to put a stop to it."

"And what is the matter with your own men?" grumbled Ussé, though he seemed to breathe more easily.

"If we are to set a trap for these blackguards, it will not be sprung so long as unfamiliar faces dominate this region. But if your men help us surround Loudun . . ." Quickly André explained the plan they had in mind.

Ussé sighed heavily, then winced as the movement caused him pain. "I have few enough men . . . and it costs money." He looked distressed, then managed a thin smile as André patted the purse at his waist. "I wish to be alone with the gentlemen," he said to the two guardsmen who still waited attentively at the door. "I shall be safe—return to your posts." He settled more firmly against the pillows, grunting with the effort. "Now," he said, when the guards had left, "you wish to negotiate?"

"I have a purse of one thousand crowns."

"That is all?" whined Ussé.

"Nom de Dieu! If we catch them, the King will no doubt be grateful!"

"Gratitude does not pay debts," Ussé said sourly. "And

Richelieu does not treat me as friend or loyal servant to the Crown!"

André gnashed his teeth in fury. "Narbaux and I," he said evenly, "have sent a ransom of twenty thousand livres each—that is nearly seven thousand crowns apiece! If the plan works, and we recover the ransom, one fourth of it will be yours!"

"And where is my guarantee? I cannot send out my men to aid you armed only with promises—and nothing more."

"Damn you, Ussé!" André, exasperated, strode angrily about the room. "Did that whore try to kill you over a sou or two? It would not astonish me in the least!"

"Please, André." Ever the conciliator, Jean-Auguste had stepped forward to Ussé, to smooth the ruffled feelings on both sides. "There must be a way to win Monsieur Ussé's cheerful cooperation! Perhaps a compromise. One thousand crowns now, ten thousand livres when the women are found, whether the ransom is recovered or no!"

Ussé smiled secretively. "Ten thousand—even if the women are not found!"

"Come, come, man!" cried Jean-Auguste. "That is the very purpose of our journey—not to refill your empty coffers!"

André had been prowling the chamber, impatient, keeping his temper in check by the strongest effort of will; now he snorted sarcastically and, stooping, swooped up something from the corner of the room. "You cry poor, *mon ami*," he sneered, "but you are careless with your gold!"

Jean-Auguste glanced at André, then started, leaping for the bed and Ussé. He clapped a hand over Ussé's mouth and drew his dagger, which he placed at the man's throat. "One sound and I shall kill you," he hissed. "André, lock the door!" Crillon moved swiftly, turning the key in the lock, but his eyes held a question. "It is Lysette's necklace that you found!" explained Jean-Auguste. He looked down at Ussé, his eyes murderous. "I want answers. But if you raise your voice I will surely slit your throat! Do you understand?" A helpless Ussé nodded, then inhaled slowly as Jean-Auguste removed his muffling hand. "The women were here, *n'est-ce pas?*"

Ussé glowered, his eye glittering in anger and impotence. "She is a madwoman, your wife! She nearly killed me!"

"Then she *was* mad! Had I been here, you would not still be drawing breath! But where are the women now?"

"I know not!"

"Have a care, Ussé," said Jean-Auguste, raising his dagger from the man's throat to his one good eye. "If you lie to me, I shall take out your other eye!"

"They escaped—after she stabbed me! As God is my witness, I know not where they are!"

"When?"

"Two days ago."

"And the brigands—they are your men?" Ussé nodded. "How many?"

"Half a hundred."

"They are people of Trefontaine?"

"No. My people here know nothing."

André leaned forward, his eyes burning. "Then why have the women not found succor among your people?"

"I gave it out that . . ."

"That they are harlots?"

"And thieves who tried to rob and kill me, and I promised a reward."

"And you have heard nothing? Neither from your tenants nor your henchmen?"

"Not a word. I swear it!"

"Small wonder you were frightened to receive us," muttered André darkly. He turned to Jean-Auguste. "We must hunt for Marielle and Lysette. They must be somewhere on the road to Touraine! We will take Ussé with us to guarantee us safe passage out of here."

"Very well then," said Jean-Auguste, putting a hand on Ussé's shoulder. "Get up!"

Ussé's face turned a shade paler than it had been. "Nom de Dieu! That knife almost pierced my heart! If I get up, I shall die!"

"It would be a small loss," sneered André. "But I would not have your blood on my hands unless I run you through someday with my own sword! Tie him up instead!" This to Jean-Auguste. While Narbaux busied himself with binding Ussé's hands and feet with a silk cord torn from the bed hangings, and gagging him with a handkerchief, André sat at Ussé's writing desk and scribbled a hasty message. As casually as they could, the two men left the room, cautioning the guard outside the door that Monsieur was very tired from his wound and did not wish to be disturbed before morning, adding a threat of retaliation that seemed characteristic of Ussé. Nonchalant, they crossed the gravel to the gate, informing the gatekeeper that they would spend the night in Loudun and return at dawn. As soon as they and their men had ridden out of sight of Trefontaine, André called a halt and motioned to one of his lieutenants.

"Take this letter to Saumur," he said. "It tells of Ussé's treachery. Charge the Governor General, in my name, to put Ussé under arrest. Then ride at once for Paris, that a Royal Commissioner may be sent with troops to purge the district of Ussé's brigands. See that Cardinal Richelieu himself gets my letter! And make haste, trusting no one along the way!" He thought for a moment, then laughed shortly. "There is no reason, *mon ami*," he said to Jean-Auguste, "that we must lose the ransom money as well! Henri!" He signaled to another of his men. "Do you remember the courier that Grisaille was to delay until our departure?" Henri nodded. "He should reach Moncontour in a day or so. Apprehend him before he enters the town, and . . . relieve him of his packet. Then let him go free—he is of no further use. There should be a man from Vilmorin who is following him—find him and return home together." Henri nodded again in understanding. André and Jean-Auguste watched as the two men rode off into the night, but when Crillon would have spurred his own horse, Narbaux stopped him.

"Let us not be too hasty to roam far from Trefontaine until morning. There are many smaller roads here. Who can tell . . . in the darkness . . . if we pass that path that may lead us to the women?"

"But I would find Marielle!" exclaimed André in impatience.

Jean-Auguste sighed heavily. "I suffer even as you do, my friend. But let us wait until daylight. And then . . . it is possible . . . that we may miss them entirely. Come, come," he said, as André looked stricken, "I feel sure that, though we journey all the way to Vilmorin without finding them, our wives will contrive to get home unaided. Marielle is strong and resourceful, and Lysette"—he chuckled in surprise—"to think that she near killed Ussé!" He shook his head in disbelief. "And I yet think of her as a child!"

* * *

The thin rays of the afternoon sun, straining to peek out from between heavy clouds, touched Marielle's pale face and the lavender crescents beneath her eyes. She shivered in the small puffs of wind that swept under the roots of the tree, as each gust penetrated her sweat-soaked jacket and chemise. All night, and all the morning as well, the fever had raged in her body; she had slept fitfully and awakened to find the sun low in the sky, her clothing drenched with perspiration, and Lysette bending over her, all smiles to find her free of delirium. She drank greedily of the water that Lysette put to her lips, then laughed softly, her voice an odd croak in her throat, to see that the cup Lysette held was her own heavy shoe, filled to the brim. At Lysette's insistence, she swallowed a few crumbs of bread. How good it felt to eat—to want to eat! "But what of you?" she whispered, seeing that Lysette took no food for herself.

"I have eaten my fill long since," said Lysette brightly. "And there are berries aplenty in the woods!" She gulped and turned away. How could she tell Marielle that there was but one crust remaining? In the morning she would give it to Marielle, pretending that there was more, and pray she could find more berries near the stream. But how long could they go on like this? Marielle was too weak to move, and without food how could she regain her strength? She must do something—or Marielle would die. "Listen," she said. "There are several hours of daylight left. If I walk down the road for a while, and return before nightfall—mayhap there will be a town, even a farm or orchard. People. Food." She bent down and tucked her skirt tightly about Marielle's shoulders. "Will you forebear whilst I am gone?"

Marielle looked doubtful, then nodded her head. "I shall think of my children," she said softly.

Lysette snorted and rose to her feet. "I shall think of food! That should hasten my steps!" She made her way to the road and turned eastward, away from the watery sun, trying to gauge the hour, to measure out her time so that she would not be caught away from Marielle in darkness, and unable to find her way back. But despite her blithe words, she could not think of food, could only think of Marielle and the look of death in her eyes. She did not wish Marielle to die, of course, but the thought no longer held the terror for her that it had only a few hours before. It was odd. Like everyone else, she lived comfort-ably with the thought of death; it was everywhere—in wars and plagues and all manner of disasters. People died of starvation when a crop failed, and whole towns burned to the ground, their crumbling walls trapping hundreds within. If a man lived to be forty-five or fifty he was held to be an ancient, wise in years and experience. But for Lysette, childbirth was something else. Because of her mother, that sweet unknown creature who had been torn asunder giving her life, she had always seen a dark and frightening angel hovering over the very moment of creation. She had come to believe, in some secret recess of her mind, that she would die if ever she bore a child, gasping out her life as her mother surely had done. And last night she had known—or thought she knew—that if Marielle died it would confirm her fears. Now she was no longer so sure. It seemed suddenly a foolish notion, a child's nightmare. Marielle would live, if she could find some food. As for herself, she thought of the babes she had cradled in the hospital at Luçon—how sweet they had been, how sweeter still had they come from her own womb. She was strong and young—why should she fear death? She felt suddenly steadfast and self-reliant—what a revelation was this journey!

She had been walking more than an hour, she judged by the angle of the pallid sun, and was about to turn around and go back to Marielle, disappointed that she had seen no sign of civilization. Then she sniffed, the scent of sun-warmed berries assailing her nostrils; before her, the road rose to a small hill, covered on each side by blackberry bushes. She hardly noticed the sharp thorns as she plunged her hands among the thick bushes, plucking the fragrant morsels and popping them into her mouth; only after she had satisfied her belly did she allow herself the pleasure of savoring their sweetness on her tongue. She glanced up. Her search for the berries had taken her to the very crest of the hill; below was an open stretch of road that led to a crossroad. At its juncture was an old wagon, overturned and abandoned, tilted against a rock, one wheel hanging crazily. But the crossroad was deserted, and the wagon looked as though it had lain thus for months. Discouraged, Lysette started to turn around and retrace her steps, meaning to pick a few berries for Marielle. Something about the crossroad jogged her memory, however, and she came closer. Ah, *Dieu!* There beyond the ruined wagon was a small shrine with a statue of the Virgin. Of course! The crossroads they had stopped at on their way from Angoumois! See! To her right was the road that had brought them from Soligne, and to the left . . . home! What was it Jean-Auguste had said—half a day's ride to Chimère! Weeping in gratitude, she sank to her knees before the altar, sobbing out prayers of thanksgiving. This was Touraine—her own province. And the crossroads were well-traveled, busy with the traffic to and from Paris, Orleans, Normandy. She almost flew back down the road to Marielle, bursting with the glad news, her plans for the morrow. She would come again, very early, and stay all day at the crossroads. People would pass—if she could not beg food or help for Marielle, she could at least prevail upon some kindly stranger to take a message to Chimère or Vilmorin. Marielle smiled wanly, too ill to share Lysette's enthusiasm, glad only that Lysette had returned before dark. Lying beside her, Lysette could hardly sleep, so heartened was she at the prospect of rescue. She scarcely noticed that her belly had begun to grumble again, and her feet were raw and sore.

An owl hooted in the distance, the sound hanging heavy in the damp night air.

"It will rain by morning," sighed André tiredly.

Jean-Auguste grunted, his eyes straining into the blackness ahead. "Look!" he cried suddenly. "A light! Could that be Vilmorin?"

"Yes! Indeed yes!" The gladness in André's voice died almost at once. "But to have come all this way . . . and no sign of Marielle or Lysette. I have never been sorry to see my home before, but now . . . damnation, man! How came we to miss our wives?"

"Come, *mon ami!* They may already be at Vilmorin!"

A sigh of pessimism. "And if not?"

"We shall rest for a day, gather fresh troops to comb the countryside, to seek out each hidden road."

"No! Tomorrow!" snapped André.

"But tomorrow is Sunday! Men will be at prayer, with their families. They will need time to prepare, to provide for their fields to be tended whilst they are away. We can leave Monday, at dawn."

"Perhaps you are right," said André, running a gauntleted hand across his eyes. "I think I could sleep till Monday next! Look"—he pointed at Vilmorin's dark turrets silhouetted against an even darker sky—"home! All will be well."

"Yes," agreed Jean-Auguste in reassurance. "The women are free of Ussé's clutches—of that we can be certain. I feel sure that they are safe and well. And, after all, what difference can one day make?"

The cold rain woke them both, bouncing off the stones at their feet and splashing back at them as they lay. Only by leaning well back against the uprooted tree trunk could they escape the downpour, and even then the earth was damp and uncomfortable, and the mossy carpet beneath them spongy and sopping. Lysette sighed heavily, reluctant to venture forth. Welladay! As nearly as she could reckon it must be Sunday; if she vowed to say an extra prayer at the shrine, mayhap le bon Dieu would let the sun shine on her! She gave the last crust of bread to Marielle, who smiled gently and broke the piece in two, handing half to Lysette.

"No, Marielle. It is for you! I have eaten already!"

"When?"

"At dawn. I could not sleep."

"You are a very skillful liar, Lysette, but I saw the size of the piece that remained yesterday! You could not have taken one single crumb!"

"Berries." It was almost a question, begging Marielle to believe it.

Marielle shook her head. "Your jacket is dry! Come, sister, let us share as equals."

"But you need your strength!" protested Lysette.

"And you must walk all that way in the rain. Please!" There was a sadness, a resignation in Marielle's voice that Lysette had not heard before.

Lysette took the proffered bread, downing it in three gulps. "But you must not worry. I shall be gone all the day." She stood up, pulling her jacket more closely about her, wishing its collar were wide enough to keep out the seeping rain. "Will you be all right?"

"Yes. I feel stronger already! I shall see you at nightfall."

Lysette nodded, but her heart sank within her breast. In

truth, Marielle looked ghastly. Without food, warmth, shelter, she would be dead long before nightfall.

The same thought must have been in Marielle's mind. Eyes dark with despair, she clutched at Lysette's hand and pressed it to her lips. "If . . . if . . . you do not return, you shall have everything you ever wanted!"

Lysette gaped and pulled her hand away, fleeing to the road as fast as she might, her brain whirling. Everything she ever wanted? André? That was what Marielle meant. She saw him again in her mind's eye: strong, noble, gloriously handsome. His beauty would always make her heart catch. But did she want him? Had she ever truly wanted him—the man, the person—beyond what her eyes could hold? No! He was perfection, the echo of her father, the child's dream—but she scarcely knew him! She thought of him with Marielle, with his children—*that* was reality! And they belonged together. Jean-Auguste had tried to tell her, warn her, protect her—from the very first. Jean-Auguste! She felt a sudden surge in her breast, an aching loneliness, a desperate longing. She wanted him. Ah, *Dieu!* She loved him! What a fool . . . what a blind child. It was not André whose kisses made her head spin, it was not André who made her laugh. It was not André whose praise warmed her heart and fed her self-esteem! And these last days of horror and despair—she had thought only of Jean-Auguste and how pleased he would be at her new-found strength.

Strength. There were so many ways to be strong. Jean-Auguste had shown her that. His tolerance of her, his under-standing of her child's ways was a noble strength she had not appreciated before, preferring to see it as weakness. He had waited, patiently, kindly, for her to grow up.

I love him! Dear Mother of God, she thought, how I love him!

The rain began to fall harder, soaking her through, until even the torn rag that bound her chest felt damp against her skin. She could feel her chopped hair plastered against her forehead and cheeks, and her vanity reasserted itself. How ugly she must look! Even if she came home safe to Chimère, would Jean-Auguste want her? He had admired her beautiful hair—he had told her so on their wedding night. She flinched, remembering their wedding night—and all the times he had made love to her. Even when he pleased her, set her aflame, she had denied him the satisfaction of knowing it, pretending indifference, coldness, dreaming of André. O childish spite! Would he ever forgive her? And Dr. Landelle's sponges, her deliberate subterfuge to keep from conceiving his child. How could he forgive that? She had suffered for her wickedness, would suffer in torment for the rest of her life, but what would take the hatred from Jean-Auguste's eyes? She would carry a score of sons in her womb, if only he would forgive her. Surely without his absolution her heart would break from its heavy burden.

Plodding along the road, the chill rain beating down upon her bare head, she began to cry, the scalding tears blending on her cheeks with the cold raindrops.

Thanks be to God it had finally stopped raining. Perhaps in a while he would come out from beneath the shelter of the wagon and stretch his legs. They were beginning to cramp from all the hours he had sat hunched up, protected against the driving storm. He wondered if his horse was still comfortably grazing in the leafy dimness of the nearby woods.

Perhaps, as André said, he was a fool. It was he who had given all the arguments in favor of waiting until Monday; yet he had turned about at the very gates of Vilmorin and ridden back to this spot, stopping only long enough to get a fresh supply of food and wine from Louise.

But mayhap Lysette would remember the story of Gabriel that he had told her so long ago—how he and Gabriel chose this crossroads for their rendezvous. It was a fanciful thought, but it had nagged him so he could not be content unless he returned to this very place. André could join him tomorrow with the men.

He yawned. Over the top of the hill, and at some distance, he could see a young lad, limping along. The poor chap must have been caught in the rain; his black hair, short-cropped, was still matted down about his face. But the lad might have seen Lysette and Marielle. In a moment he would come out from under the wagon and ask the boy.

Lysette winced in pain, unable to walk another step. Her shoe had worn through, she was sure of it. Seating herself on a large rock just over the crest of the hill, she took her shoe off and examined it closely. Yes. There it was. A large spot that had rubbed as thin as a piece of gossamer, then worn away entirely.

She pulled off her stocking, torn in the same spot. If she reversed the stocking, then patched the shoe with a piece of tree bark when she got to the crossroads, she might make it back to Marielle tonight without further damage to her foot. Still, the sole of her foot was red and sore. A piece of thistledown. Wasn't that what Jean-Auguste had used to protect her blister? She looked up, scanning the fields for a thistle. Someone was standing at the crossroads—a tall man. She had not seen him there as she came over the hill, but perhaps he had been sitting behind the wagon. As she watched, he pulled his large-brimmed hat from his head. The bright orange hair was like a beacon on the rain-swept road, drawing her to him. She gasped and jumped to her feet, quite forgetting shoe, stocking, sore foot, and ran hopping, and crying, and shouting, in his direction. He hesitated for a moment, then, as recognition came, he began to run to her. She stumbled once, stubbing her bare toe, then flung herself into his outstretched arms and clung to his neck, unwilling even to push him away enough so she could kiss him. It sufficed to hold him, and be held, to feel herself safe at last, with no more to fear.

Selfish Lysette! To think only of herself; and Marielle—dying perhaps—alone, with no one to comfort her, far from those she loved. Lysette tore herself from Jean-Auguste's arms and cast her eyes wildly about the deserted crossroads, her brow furrowed in distress.

"But . . . where is André?" she cried at last.

Chapter Twenty-three

THE WAGON CREAKED ALONG THE ROAD, ITS RUSTY WHEELS complaining of the weeks of neglect. Nestled among the pine boughs, a sleeping Marielle in her arms, Lysette stared, heartbroken, at Jean-Auguste's implacable back. He rode his horse stiffly, turning seldom except to inquire after Marielle.

He has not forgiven me, she thought. For a brief moment, when he held her, it had seemed as though he were glad to see her, but when she had pulled back to receive a welcoming kiss, she had seen that his gray eyes were cold and distant. They had ridden back to Marielle in near silence, she perched before him on his horse; the body she leaned against had been made of granite, and his arms were held away from her as he grasped the reins.

The food and wine had revived the women somewhat. All three had returned to the crossroads crowded awkwardly on Jean-Auguste's horse, Marielle in front of Jean-Auguste, lying weakly in his arms, Lysette behind, her breeched legs astride the horse's rump, her hands clutching Jean-Auguste's wide sash. The wagon had been righted, the wheel replaced; while Jean-Auguste hitched it to his stallion Lysette had fetched boughs from the stand of pine trees to cushion Marielle. Now they rode through the humid afternoon, still gray and overcast though the sun struggled mightily to appear. It would be warmer on the morrow, more typical of August than the past few chilly days. August. It had been August when she met him at Soligne. One whole year. She might have won his love in a year—instead of earning his hatred.

It was twilight, the sky a pale silver where the sun should have been, when they sighted the caves and bluffs along the river, then the high roofs and peaked towers of Vilmorin. The wagon pulled into the wide courtyard amid the shouts and cries of the servants; summoned by the noise, André rushed from the chateau. He was in shirtsleeves, his face haggard from worry and sleeplessness, but at the sight of Marielle, smiling wanly at him, his eyes lit up with joy. He did not see Lysette in the wagon, nor Jean-Auguste, nor the happy faces around him; he saw only her love. Tenderly he picked up Marielle, cradling her in his strong arms; her trembling fingers stroked his chin, the side of his jaw, his smiling mouth. Still on her knees in the wagon, Lysette began to weep. How perfect they looked together! How deep the love shining in their eyes! Her heart near burst with misery and longing. Would Jean-Auguste ever look at her like that? She turned her tear-stained face to him, seeking a spark of warmth; with a look of disgust he wheeled around and led his horse to the stable.

Someone helped her from the wagon and brought her into the chateau. There was a welcoming bedchamber, food, a hot bath—voices and hands to comfort and assist. She reveled in each sensation as though she were newborn—the taste of the food, the scented warmth of the bath, the feel of clean clothing against her skin. Drowsy, contented, she sat at last, clad in nightdress and peignoir, before her dressing table, and surveyed herself in the mirror. Ah Dieu! How awful her hair looked—chopped and hacked—she looked like a page boy in some ancient court painting! She nearly wept at the sight, not so much for the loss of her raven curls as for the loss of her beauty. How was she ever to win his love now? He would find her plain, ugly. But the maid Suzanne, with murmured words of comfort, fetched a pair of scissors and began skillfully to trim the uneven locks and curl them about her fingers, until Lysette's face was framed by soft ringlets, and she looked sweeter and more elfin than ever. She was admiring herself in the mirror, much heartened by the transformation, when there came a knock at the door. At André's entrance, Suzanne bobbed politely and disappeared.

He smiled warmly at Lysette, his eyes filled with approval. "How charming your hair looks!"

She dimpled prettily and returned his smile, surprised to discover that, though he was as handsome as ever, nothing stirred within her. Her pleasure at his admiration meant only that Jean-Auguste would see her with the same masculine eyes, and like what he saw. "How is Marielle?" she asked.

"Resting. Louise has not stopped clucking about her all the evening, but she seems to think that, with weeks of care, Marielle will recover fully. Pray God it be so!" he added fervently.

"Well you may say that now!" she scolded. "But you have brought her much grief of late. Many times she cried your name as she slept."

"Ah, *Dieu*," he said with remorse. "I should die if I lost her."

"I wonder it took such a calamity as this for you to appreciate her worth! I have brought her back to you alive. Now you must repay me by reaffirming your love for her."

"How good you are. How much we owe to you, Marielle and I. She has told me of how you cared for her. Whilst I"—he turned away, unwilling to meet her eyes—"I have been unworthy of your goodness."

She hesitated for only a second, knowing the words must be spoken. "Nonsense! That night in the garden, I was equally to blame. More so, perhaps. I wanted you to kiss me. I contrived to have it so!" She laughed softly as his eyebrow shot up in surprise. "It was a childish fancy, a whim of the moment—no more." She stood close to him and bent his head down to her, kissing him tenderly on the cheek. "You called me sister once. Let it be so again . . . and always!"

He took her hand in his and brought it to his lips. "I wonder if Jean-Auguste knows how fortunate he is?"

Jean-Auguste made his way reluctantly down the long corridor, his steps heavy. He was a fool even to seek her out tonight. Nothing had changed between them. He had been nearly mad with worry, then rejoiced to find her at the crossroads, thinking she must be as glad to see him. And her first words had been for André. She no longer bothered to hide her feelings—had she not wept unashamedly and openly at sight of André, her eyes dark with envy for Marielle? He had never felt such pain as he had at that moment when André had lifted Marielle from the wagon and Lysette had wept with love and longing. Not even when he had found the sponges, had learned the truth of her affliction from Dr. Landelle. Even then, he had told himself there could still be children. She would return from Poitou chastened, submissive. He might not have the wife he had dreamed about, but at least there would be sons, there would be Gabriel de Narbaux to inherit the lands once again.

But it was useless. He had lived for a whole year with her longing for André, convincing himself it was a fleeting passion; now he saw that André would haunt them forever. And he could not even hate his friend, for André had been unwittingly drawn by her enchantment until the kiss in the garden had broken the spell. No. Because of Marielle, the friendship of the two men, Lysette could never betray him in André's bed. But how could he keep from seeing betrayal in her eyes, knowing she dreamed of André?

He sighed heavily. He might perhaps write to Rome and seek an annulment—*le bon Dieu* knew there were grounds enough! He gnashed his teeth, thinking of the sponges he had found in her writing table. Deceitful little baggage! He should have sent her packing to her brothers in Chartres the moment he saw her casting moon-eyes at André in Soligne!

Well, mayhap he would wait a few weeks before deciding what to do. They had both been away from Chimère for many months; there might still be a chance for a rapprochement. He turned down the corridor leading to Lysette's room, then stopped as her door opened and a sudden stream of light flowed across the passageway. Lysette came to the door, her cropped hair curled beguilingly about her face, her silken peignoir barely hiding the tempting curves beneath. He shrank back into the shadows as André appeared beside her, stooped to kiss her softly on the forehead, then headed for his own room at the opposite end of the chateau. For long moments Jean-Auguste stood there; even after Lysette had returned to her room and closed the door he did not move. At last he turned about and retraced his steps to his own chamber, brushing aside the servant who waited upon him.

"Leave me!" he growled. He flung himself down upon a chair and snatched up a jug of wine from a nearby table, ignoring the goblet beside it and taking a long pull from the lip of the pitcher. "And if Madame Narbaux should inquire after me this evening, tell her I have gone to bed and cannot be disturbed!"

"You must only spend a few minutes this morning," admonished Louise, pushing the two little boys into Marielle's room. Watching the scene, Lysette smiled as François and Alain tiptoed close to Marielle's bed, their eyes wide with wonder; then their mother held out her arms to them and they tripped over one another in their haste to pile onto the big bed with her. There was a great deal of giggling and whispered secrets, and hugs and kisses. Of a sudden Lysette could not see for the mist that blurred her eyes; but for the sponges, she might be carrying Jean-Auguste's child by now. No matter what the future held, she could never still the remorse that tore at her heart. She went to the window and gazed with unseeing eyes at the sunny lawns of Vilmorin and the placid Loire beyond; she dared not trust herself to turn back into the room until Louise had led the children away.

"I shall be forever in your debt, Lysette," said Marielle softly. "You have given me back my life, my children. Ussé would have killed us but for you—I could have done nothing. And then, in the woods . . ."

"I have given you back André as well," said Lysette sharply. More than you know, perhaps, she thought to herself. "Do not let your children blind you to your fine husband!"

"I shall not forget. And while we speak of husbands"—she turned to the serving girl who was throwing open the windows to the bright morning—"has Monsieur le Vicomte de Narbaux awakened yet?"

The girl curtsied. "But yes, Madame! At dawn!"

"And where is he now?"

"He rode away, to Chimère I think, so soon as he had finished his morning meal."

Lysette gasped, her hand flying to her bosom, her violet eyes wide and stricken with dismay.

Marielle dismissed the girl with a wave of the hand, then turned to Lysette, her eyes filled with compassion. "Mon Dieu! You love him! But, I thought . . ." she laughed softly, relief flooding her face. "Go to him at once! I shall send André with you for company."

"No. His place is here. A groom will suffice." Lysette surveyed the nightdress and peignoir she still wore. *"Dommage!* I have not even riding clothes! Have you an old skirt, boots—anything! Just to see me to Chimère as soon as possible!"

"I shall send you to Chimère with the best I have, and my wish that your happiness with Jean-Auguste be even as mine with André!"

The ride through the leafy woods seemed interminable to Lysette, her heart pounding to the rhythm of the horses' hooves, while the groom struggled to keep pace with her. At last the path gave way to the broad avenue that led to Chimère, and Lysette slowed her horse, wanting to savor that first heart-stopping sight of the chateau. How beautiful it was, seeming to float upon the river, its pale golden stones beckoning to her in welcome, the river whispering its soft greeting. Home. My home, she thought. Our home. To raise our children. She spurred her horse forward, almost choking with emotion.

It was Dominique who first saw her as she rode into the courtyard, and rushed out to greet her, crying and laughing with happiness. Bricole came next, his thin back more stooped than she remembered it, his step less sure. Ah *Dieu,* he is getting old, she thought, and I have scarcely lifted the burdens from his shoulders! She slid from her horse and greeted each servant in turn, but her eyes sought the one figure that was missing, the one beloved face. At last Jean-Auguste came out of the chateau—reluctantly, she thought with a pang—and went to mount his horse that the stableboy had brought. Her heart stopped. Had he always been so handsome—the lean strength of him, the square jaw and wide forehead, the steady gray eyes, the mouth that she longed to kiss? How blind she had been! Even the color of his hair was beautiful, glowing copper in the sunlight! She smiled shyly at him as the servants fell back to give them privacy, and waited, timid, fearful, for him to speak. His eyes appraised her coolly, taking in the ill-fitting garments she wore. Louise had found clothing of good quality, but Lysette's petiteness had made a good fit impossible, and she fidgeted uncomfortably, aware of how foolish she must look.

"Have you missed all your pretty things, my vain little wife?" he sneered. "Is that what has brought you home?"

Stung, she answered him with sarcasm, trading insult for insult as she had in the past. "How gallant you were, ever the gentleman, to leave without a word! You might at least have told me you were returning to Chimère!"

"I assumed, with Marielle ill, you would want to take it upon yourself to keep André amused!"

She bit her lip, struggling against her tears. He would surely think them false. She took a deep breath, forcing her voice to be light, her words unthreatening. "Are you riding out now?"

"Yes. There are things to attend in the fields."

"Will you return in time for supper?" He nodded. She dimpled mischievously—perhaps she could recall the happy times. "At six? Or seven?"

He swung himself into the saddle and stared coldly down at her. "It has always been my habit to dine at six." Then he was gone, riding off into the sunny afternoon, and her heart with him. The joy was gone from her homecoming; she dragged wearily to her chambers, instructing Dominique to help her into her riding things and send for her own horse. She barely listened as the maid chattered gaily of her husband Simon Vacher, of their continued happiness after all these months, of her joy at submitting to his will as her lord and master. Lysette sighed at her own folly, contrasting her behavior toward Jean-Auguste with Dominique and her husband. There had not been a moment of their lives together that she had not struggled against submission, that she had not harried him and badgered him and played him false. Even when his ardor had stripped away her defenses, she had seen her response as humiliation and defeat. *Mon Dieu!* As though giving herself fully was an abasement, not an act of love!

Dressed in her own riding habit and seated upon her own horse, she rode out to survey Chimère, grateful to be home, drinking in the sights and sounds of it with a deeper thirst and hunger than the one she had slaked with good Vilmorin wine and food. She passed rolling fields of grapes soon to be ripe, mowed stretches where the wheat had already been gathered, streams, stands of oak and birch, orchards heavy with mellowing fruit. She guided her horse up to the cliffs and caves, waving amicably to the tenant farmers and *vignerons*, stopping to chat with a still hobbling Pasquier, smiling in pleasure (Ridiculous! Why should it matter to her?) to see his cheerful wife large with child.

She rode down at last to the ruins of the glasshouse, overgrown now with high weeds, the crumbling dome of the furnace soft-edged and worn from the summer rains. Dismounting, she wandered about the clearing, her horse following. Rondini's house was still intact, but the chimney was cracked and one window frame, missing a corbel, sagged woefully. The whole house had an air of neglect, save the kitchen garden, in which the widow now toiled while she hummed softly to herself. At sight of Lysette she put down her hoe and curtsied, calling to her son Honoré to fetch a jug of cool water for Madame de Narbaux. At Lysette's inquiry, she indicated a shady spot beneath a tree where Giacopo Rondini lay sprawled fast asleep, a pouch of wine beside him, his clothing begrimed, his face filthy and unshaven. What a pang it gave Lysette to see him reduced to this! He was seldom sober, the widow explained, but sometimes, between bouts of drinking, he would hire himself out as a day laborer to toil in the fields, putting aside the few sous he earned to pay back his debt to Monsieur le Vicomte. The widow sighed, her eyes filling with tears of sympathy and affection. Poor man! At that rate, it would take him a hundred years to repay the loan! She herself had stopped taking a housekeeping wage from him; the garden was small but it fed them, and she had slaughtered one of his sheep, selling the mutton she could not put aside to buy a length of warm fabric with which she would sew him a winter doublet.

She sighed again. "Poor man!"

Poor man indeed! It was nearly four months since Guglielmo had died in the fire—was Giacopo content to mourn forever? It made Lysette's blood boil, to think of the waste! Day laborer . . . pah! Lifting the jug of water she still held, she hurled its contents into his face. With a choking sputter, Rondini awoke and struggled upright, dragging himself to his feet at sight of her and swaying unsteadily, his fists scrubbing the water from his eyes. "Madame," he croaked, the voice a helpless whine.

She drew herself up, her violet eyes flashing. "Monsieur Rondini, please be so good as to come to the chateau tomorrow. Sober, if it please you! When I returned today, I found that the chain on my glass beads had snapped—they will have to be restrung!"

He began to shake his head, the deep brown eyes weak and watery. "I cannot, Madame!"

"And wherefore 'cannot'?"

"Look you!" He held out his hands to her. The fingers, once so sure and skillful, trembled violently. "It is hopeless."

She frowned and pointed an imperious finger at Honoré. "Then tell the boy how it is done, and let him be your hands! I mark that Guglielmo thought him clever and apt—he will make a fine apprentice!"

"Guglielmo," he said softly, and bent to retrieve his flask from the foot of the tree.

Lifting her riding crop in fury, she struck the wine pouch from his hands. "No! Tomorrow, Monsieur! And sober!" She wheeled about and remounted her horse, glaring down at him as he stood, mouth agape in amazement. "I would have my beads again!" Unexpectedly she softened, her eyes filled with warmth. "And my dear Rondini," she said with a gentle smile. "And my dear Rondini."

She returned to the chateau in the late afternoon and closeted herself in the library with Bricole, explaining that she meant to take over the running of Chimère herself. He was not to take it amiss, nor as a reflection of any dissatisfaction; it was only that the burden was too great for one person alone. She would need his help and advice, though she might sometimes ignore it. He must not mind that either—she had always been willful, and found it hard to change. By the end of half an hour, he was eating out of her hand, flattered at her trust in him, anxious to begin as soon as possible with books and ledgers and accountings.

She went at last to her chambers, pleased with herself, with the afternoon's work. And she had done it all with honesty, without games and tricks and guile. But Rondini, Bricole—they were easy. They did not have cold gray eyes that tore at her heart. It was easy to put her seal on them, to ask and request and insist that they do what she wished, because it was right for them. How was she to put her seal on a man who had married her reluctantly, whose indifference had turned to hatred, whose trust she had destroyed with lies and deception?

Heavy-hearted, she forced herself to think of more mundane affairs. The matter of the glass beads, for instance. She had told Rondini they were broken; despite her reluctance to damage such lovely things, it were better for Rondini if it were so. She seated herself at her writing desk, forgetting for a moment the secret combination. What was it? Ah yes! Turn the tiny statue, slide the column, press the pediment. She smiled in delight as the catch was released, opening each secret drawer and admiring anew her beautiful jewels. It took a second to snap the links of the glass pearls. She replaced them and withdrew the double strand of real pearls that Jean-Auguste had given her as a wedding present. She would wear these tonight with her violet gown—she wanted to look especially beautiful for him. Devil take Dominique—what was keeping her? Lysette had dismissed her for the afternoon, while she went riding, but it must be after five, and there was no sign of the girl. It would scarcely do to be late for supper—she meant for the evening with Jean-Auguste to start on a pleasant note. She heard the door of her bedchamber click. There was the maid now. "Dominique," she called, "I shall wear the violet silk tonight."

"Yes, Madame." The voice strangely muffled.

Lysette stepped from her sitting room into the bedchamber. Dominique was busy at the armoire, pulling out a cambric petticoat and a white satin underskirt—but she kept her face carefully turned away from Lysette. "Why, Dominique," she said, "what is it? Have you been crying?"

"It is nothing, Madame. Truly."

"But you *have* been crying! Come and sit by me and tell me what is troubling you!" Lysette pulled the maid by the hand, leading her to a small bench.

"No!" Dominique pulled away and held her hand gingerly to her rump. "I should not like to . . . sit . . . down!"

"*Mon Dieu!* Does he beat you then? That villain?"

Dominique looked surprised at the anger in Lysette's voice.

"Only when I deserve it, Madame! He has the right! The duty to teach me my place! I was a disobedient wife—he forbade me to speak to Etienne, but I . . . wanted to make him jealous . . . just a little, you understand. I thought it would be a game . . . but Simon was very angry. 'You do not play games with a man's heart,' he said. And he is right!"

"And so he beat you?"

"It will help me to remember how angry he was. Madame is fortunate that Monsieur le Vicomte is so mild-tempered—Simon is not such a man of patience!"

Yes, she thought ruefully. Mild-tempered indeed. She had done far worse than merely talk to André; yet Jean-Auguste, though he might threaten her, was far too kind and gentle to take a switch to her. The only time he had struck her was the night of the fire, and then he had been half mad with grief, imagining what had happened with Dr. Landelle, and suffering because of the loss of Guglielmo and the glasshouse.

Jean-Auguste was already seated at table in the small salon when she arrived for supper. He nodded stiffly, but his eyes flickered over her in admiration, almost in spite of himself. A good beginning, she thought, glad for the purple silk that reflected her eyes. She chattered gaily, telling him of her delight at seeing Chimère again, her pleasure at the well-run fields and vineyards. He responded coldly and as little as possible, until she swore he had never been so vexatious as he was this night. It would take all her forebearance to keep from striking him, as she had in the past, or bursting into unhappy tears. But if she struck him, he would grow colder still; and he did not believe her tears, even when they were genuine. She gulped back her unhappiness and smiled brightly.

"Do you realize it is more than a year since the uprising in Soligne? I wonder what has become of Madame Gossault?" She reached across the table and put a hand softly on his arm. "So much has happened in a year." Her eyes were almost pleading for his understanding.

He shrugged in indifference, his eyes raking her jewels and gown, then he laughed bitterly. "It has cost me dear, of that I am certain! Oh! I near forgot"—his long fingers groped in a small pocket of his doublet—"we found this at Ussé's chateau." He held out Lysette's golden cross and chain; with a pleased cry she took it from him and put it about her neck.

"How glad I am! I lost it when Ussé . . ." She turned away, her eyes dark with remembrance, and a shudder ran through her tiny frame. "I had to . . . pretend . . . Ugh!" She closed her eyes and said no more.

"That should have been easy for you," he said, in a voice so ugly her eyes flew open. "You were always good at pretense!"

She bit her lip and took another drink of wine. "Will you

open the glasshouse again?" she asked, changing the subject quickly.

"Why should I?"

"Because it was worthwhile before the fire—and is worthwhile still!"

"Are you a fool? Or yet a foolish child? Even if the ransom money is returned—and we cannot be sure it will be—I shall be cash-poor for a long time. There are loans to be repaid—this year's harvest is already mortgaged—and I would not burden my tenants with further taxes! Where am I to get the money to rebuild the furnace and glasshouse?"

"Sell my jewels."

He gaped in astonishment, his piercing eyes searching her face for a sign of deceit. "You cannot mean that!" he said, still skeptical. "Your vanity would not allow it!"

"If I may keep my gold cross and Rondini's glass beads, I should be content."

He laughed mirthlessly. "What will you do for admirers without all your frills and fancies?"

Mon Dieu, how he tried her patience! "I scarcely need jewels to win admirers!" she snapped, removing her pearls and tossing them across the table at him. "Sell them, and whatever else you must, to rebuild the glasshouse!"

He frowned, contemplating the idea for the first time, then shook his head. "No. Without Rondini, how is it to be done? Even if he were sober . . . with his son gone, he has not the heart for it."

"Pooh! He has the boy Honoré! The lad is willing and skillful—and he is devoted to Rondini! Not quite a son, but still . . ."

"And who is to persuade Rondini to begin again?"

"I shall! I have spoken to him already. He has promised to mend my glass beads on the morrow. He will do this for me."

Jean-Auguste's mouth twitched. "Of course! I had almost forgot how clever you are at twisting men to your will! All those months with Aunt Marguerite—and not a single man to fall under your spell! How boring it must have been—how you must have loved toying with Ussé! How far did the game go before you stabbed him?" The question was almost too nonchalant.

"Do you really care?"

He shrugged, bending again to his food.

Her patience was at an end. "Damn you!" she burst out. "I need neither guile nor jewels to tempt a man, or have you forgot? I did not need them . . . the night . . ."

His eyebrow shot up sardonically. "Yes? The night in the garden . . . with André?"

She stared at him, her violet eyes frosty as a winter's twilight. "The night you raped me." And watched him flinch and turn away.

They passed the rest of the meal in silence, Lysette cursing herself for her outburst. She had meant to be kind, to reach out to him—she had succeeded only in angering him further. At last they rose from the table. Jean-Auguste took a book and sat near the window to catch the last light of day. Lysette picked up her lute and strummed a few chords.

"Shall I play?" she ventured softly.

"As you wish. It matters not to me."

Sick at heart, she put down the lute. "I do not wish. I shall say good night now. It has been a long and tiring day." He barely looked up as she left the room, and though she paused on the stairs, he did not come to her. She fled to her chamber, hurrying Dominique through her bedtime ritual, choosing her most flattering nightdress and peignoir, still half believing he would knock softly on her door. Alone at last, knowing herself abandoned, she flung herself on the wide bed and poured out her grief in heartbroken sobs.

She must have slept. When she awoke, she found the chamber in darkness save for a small candle that Dominique had left. She sat on the edge of the bed and thought about Jean-Auguste. It was clear he would not bend, whether from hurt pride or anger—all her attempts at civility at supper had been wasted. There was nothing for it but to beard him in his den, demand his forgiveness, threaten to leave if he could not give it. She could not spend the rest of her life like this, with the pain, the hollowness that clutched at her insides, pretending that she did not want him and love him. She opened her door and peered out into the dim corridor. A string of light showed beneath his chamber door. She would go to him and pour out her feelings; about to quit her room, she recalled her conversation with Dominique. She turned back and picked up her riding crop. Jean-Auguste *was* kind and good, and he would not use it, of course, but it would be a nice gesture, a proof of her sincerity and contrition, if she were to offer it to him. Heart pounding, she knocked at his door, the riding crop held behind her in the folds of her dressing gown.

He was sitting at a small writing table when she entered, closing the door behind her and leaning against the paneling. He had taken off his boots and his doublet, and was clad only in wide breeches and slippers, his linen shirt buttoned high, the lace falling band and cuffs long since removed and put away. Before him on the table was a large ledger, and his brow was still furrowed from poring over the figures.

"Well?" he said, rising to his feet.

She trembled, suddenly frightened. What if he should refuse her, tell her to leave Chimère? She could not bear the thought! She squared her shoulders and took a deep breath, wishing her voice were steadier. "We cannot continue in this way," she said. "It is time to start anew! You desire sons. As your wife, I am obliged to bear your children—whatever our feelings for one another. You married me out of chivalry, guilt for your rape of me. No, let me finish!" she said, as he opened his mouth to speak. "I married you to be near André. All that is past. I behaved shamelessly with your best friend—I was not unfaithful, but . . . I am sorry for wishing it, and for . . . my secret visit to Dr. Landelle. I know I hurt your pride because of André, because I used the sponges and denied you the child you wished. But I want to start afresh . . . and . . ."—she gulped, her eyes soft with love and longing—". . . I would die if you sent me away again, for all my wickedness!" She held out the riding crop to him. "Punish me as you will; I am ready to be an obedient wife."

His face dark, he strode to her and snatched the riding crop from her trembling hand, flinging it aside. He grabbed her roughly by the shoulders; when he spoke his voice was a low growl in his throat. "I married you because I loved you! I thought in time you could come to care for me as well, that you would bear my children out of joy—not obligation! But I shall not bully you, nor force you, nor beat you into submission! It is André and Marielle you have hurt—not I!" He released her and turned away, struggling to regain his composure.

"Oh-h-h!" she almost shrieked in fury. "You insufferable man! All these months—when my heart ached for just one word . . . one word! And now, when I come to you, offering peace, and a new beginning, and all my love, you turn your back to me, and tell me—as though it were of small moment— that you have always loved me! Devil take you!" She grabbed at his arm, attempting to turn him about; failing this she stormed around to face him, her lip jutting in angry defiance. In one swift movement, she stripped off her peignoir and nightdress, flaunting her nakedness before him; he turned his head aside, but a small muscle had begun to throb in his jaw. She stood on tiptoe, the better to reach the buttons of his shirt, and angrily began to work each one in turn, her fingers shaking. When one of the buttons refused to give way, she cursed and tore it from the shirt, flinging it down to the floor. The last stubborn button caught in the fabric, resisting all her efforts to loose it or rip it off. She began then to weep, the brave show collapsing, feeling humiliated by his passiveness.

Of a sudden, his hands, cool and slim-fingered, were there to close over her trembling ones. She lifted her tear-stained face to him; his smiling mouth took hers in a kiss so sweet it left her breathless. He grinned and released the last button; she could hardly wait for him to pull off his shirt before her arms were about his neck, her bosom pressed against the hardness of his broad chest.

"Lysette," he breathed, and swept her into his arms, carrying her to his bed. Her hands tore at his breeches, in a frenzy to have him near her, to feel him inside her, to release the pent up hunger that had torn at her vitals for months. Her impatience was matched by his; their bodies fused, merged, moving in a dizzying rhythm until she exploded into ecstasy and he shuddered against her, inhaling sharply through his teeth.

With a contented groan he moved away from her, propping himself on one elbow and smiling down on her where she lay. He had barely kissed her before, so eager had they both been; now he explored her mouth with his own, his tongue finding the inner edge of her lips, tracing the contours of her mouth with a tantalizing gentleness that sent shivers down her spine. She had always enjoyed his kisses; how much sweeter now, knowing they were kisses of love, not merely desire. He ruffled her chopped hair and laughed softly.

"Mock me not," she pouted. "I have no doubt I look ugly."

"You look adorable."

"Pooh! I look like a boy!"

He kissed her hungrily, his mouth hot and demanding. "How glad I am that you are not!" he said, his voice suddenly hoarse in his throat. He sat up, surprised, as she began to giggle.

"On the journey, a young farmer . . ." She sat up beside him, hugging her knees to her chest, and told of her adventures with the young man who had found her more attractive than Marielle. Jean-Auguste roared with laughter.

"Two crowns," he said, placing his hand on her bare thigh, and sliding his fingers up toward the soft juncture in imitation of the farmer in her story. "Hum! Are you worth it?"

"Are you offering me two crowns?" The violet eyes twinkled.

"Only if you earn it," he said airily.

"Oh!" She pushed him down upon his back and pounced on him. "And you speak to me of vanity! Very well, Monsieur, I accept your challenge! But when I have finished with you, you will beg me to accept a hundred times two crowns!" She straddled his body, pushing his hands away when he would have held her. "You must not touch me!" Her fingertips were soft as they roamed his body, stroking his firm shoulders, the smooth expanse of his broad chest, his flat belly ridged with hard muscles. She laughed throatily as he twitched beneath her, his eyes dark with desire, his mouth curved in a smile that was half pleasure, half agony. She bent her lips to his chest, then moved upward to blow softly in his ear, nibbling at his ear lobe, allowing the firm points of her breasts to scrape against his body. He was enraptured, murmuring her name over and over again; she was surprised to discover that, although he never touched her, the blood had begun to race in her own veins, burning like liquid flame, as though she took fire from his ardor. At last, beneath her hips she could feel him growing hard again, and she grinned in triumph.

"Two crowns, Monsieur," she laughed breathlessly, and rolled over onto her back, trembling in anticipation. When he kissed her, she felt her body go limp and the smile fade from her face. She closed her eyes and let her knees fall wide, waiting, quivering. Nothing. What the devil was he waiting for? Half annoyed, her eyes flew open to see him above her, shaking his head.

"No, ma chère, not yet!" he chuckled. "You have more than earned your two hundred crowns—but I shall win them back again!" He began to caress her, his hands and mouth teasing, arousing, until she thought she must go mad; he made love to her slowly, enjoying her pleasure as much as his own. And each time she felt her senses raised to a peak beyond which she could not endure, he would touch, kiss, in some secret place, waking her body to ever more wondrous delights.

"No more!" she gasped at last, and gave a cry of ecstasy as he possessed her, her frenzy dissipating in one brief moment of exquisite joy.

And truly she was possessed—body, heart, soul—his forever.

She snuggled in the circle of his arms, her head pressed against his chest, listening to the pounding of his heart as it slowed to a normal beat. His skin was warm and slightly damp, and when she lifted her head and kissed his chest, she tasted the tang of sweat on her lips; but it was the dearest pillow in the world to her. She sighed in contentment.

"And did you really always love me?" she asked timidly.

"Yes."

"Truly?" Oh the wonder of it!

"Yes, truly. When I carried you up the stairs after the riot at Soligne, I wanted to spirit you away to Chimère on the spot!"

"You loved me! I did not know my own heart until the loneliness of being in Poitou without you." She shook her head in amazement. "Yet you loved me always!" She sat up suddenly, her eyes wide with dismay. "Despite my wickedness?"

"You were not wicked," he said in reassurance. "A child, perhaps, in many ways . . ."

"And you married the child who tried your patience!" She bit her lip, suddenly contrite.

He pulled her back down into his arms. "I married the child, but loved the woman who lurked in the shadows of your beautiful eyes!"

"Why did you never tell me? So many times I was lost, lonely, needing . . . who knows? Words of love?"

"I thought they would be wasted, because of your feelings for André!"

"Pooh!" she said. "I never *really* loved André!"

"But at the crossroads it was André you asked for!"

"I feared Marielle would die without seeing him again."

"And your jealous tears at Vilmorin when André appeared?"

"I *was* jealous! I thought that you would never love me as André loves Marielle. And all that time . . ." She clucked her tongue in annoyance. "You *should* have told me!"

They fell silent, thinking. At last Jean-Auguste grunted. "I'll wager I made many mistakes," he said. "I should have made a practice of chastising you from the first, as Aunt Marguerite suggested, to keep you from folly!" His hand caressed her bare bottom in a gesture that was more loving than reproachful. "Mayhap it would have saved a lot of grief!"

She giggled and cuddled closer to him. "But of course you could not have!"

"And wherefore not?"

"You are too gentle-natured. I always knew it. Mayhap it is why I tried you so!"

"Then why did you offer the riding crop to me tonight?"

"I wished you to know how sorry I was. It seemed a fine gesture!"

"Especially as you knew I would not use it!"

She smiled coyly. "Of course!"

His face darkened and he sat up suddenly, pushing her away from him. "Now upon my faith I grow tired of your deceit!"

"What? What do you mean?"

"You came tonight to tell me you love me—but you came as a child, still playing a game!"

"It was not intended . . . !"

"No. It was only a small dishonesty—you have long since become blind to the habits of a lifetime. But if you want my love—and my trust—there must be no more games, no more tricks, no more lies!"

Burning with shame, she reached out to touch him. Ah *Dieu!* Even Vacher and Dominique had more wisdom than she! What was it Simon had said about playing games with a man's heart?

Jean-Auguste turned to her, his eyes like cold steel. "Fetch me the riding crop!"

She laughed nervously. "Jean-Auguste. My love. You are jesting, of course—only to frighten me—*n'est-ce pas?*"

"Fetch it!"

Her eyes opened wide, panic clutching her insides. "No!" He glared fiercely at her. "N-n-no," she said more timidly, her courage deserting her. She was near tears now. "Please, Jean-Auguste! No one has ever beaten me! Ever! I should die."

He folded his arms across his chest, his eyes cold and implacable. With a sob, she stumbled out of bed, groping in the corner of the room until she had found her riding crop, frighteningly aware of her nakedness, the fragile unprotected flesh that awaited his anger. She returned to the bed, one hand holding the whip, the other attempting to cover her buttocks, as though she would protect herself until the last moment. He held out his hand; shaking, she handed him the riding crop, knowing, even as she did so, that to disobey him now would be to destroy their love. And he would beat her anyway, his anger at her willfulness adding strength to his arm. For a long moment he stared at her; then he grasped the riding crop in both his hands and snapped it easily in two, handing the pieces back to her.

"Keep it," he said, "as a reminder henceforth that trust is as fragile, easily broken—and difficult to mend."

She clutched the pieces to her bosom, feeling pain more sharp than if he had struck her. Weeping, she turned away and crossed to the window, looking through the leaded panes at the soft night, the quiet river below. The air was sweet and filled with the placid sounds of midsummer—the rhythmic croaking of frogs along the banks, the splashing of an occasional fish in the dark waters. Home, she thought. Home at last. Safe and secure. And loved. Her heart swelled within her breast, praying to be worthy of his love. God willing, a seed had been planted tonight. It was suddenly important to give him his son . . . his Gabriel.

"Dry your tears," he said softly behind her, "and come back to bed." She turned. He was smiling gently, lovingly, his hand outstretched to her.

She sniffled, her violet eyes sparkling behind their crystal drops, and smiled shyly. At the look in his eyes—welcoming, forgiving, adoring—she took a deep breath and squared her shoulders. For the first time in her life, she felt tall. She was his lover, his wife.

His woman.

"As you wish," she said softly.

Tapestry

HISTORICAL ROMANCES

Breathtaking New Tales

of love and adventure set against
history's most exciting time and
places. Featuring two novels by the
finest authors in the field of romantic fiction—every month.

Next Month From
Tapestry Romances

LIBERTINE LADY
by Janet Joyce

LOVE CHASE
by Theresa Conway

Here's your opportunity to have these romantic historical novels delivered directly to your door!

Tapestry

433

Enjoy your own special time with Silhouette Romances

Take 4 books __FREE!__

Silhouette Romances take you into a special world of thrilling drama, tender passion, and romantic love. These are enthralling stories from your favorite romance authors—tales of fascinating men and women, set in exotic locations.

We think you'll want to receive Silhouette Romances regularly. We'll send you six new romances every month to look over for 15 days. If not delighted, return only five and owe nothing. **One book is always yours free.** There's never a charge for postage or handling, and no obligation to buy anything at any time. **Start with your free books.** Mail the coupon today.

Silhouette Romances